# REBEL SWORN

## WINGS OF REBELLION BOOK 4

### BREE MOORE

PREQUEL NOVELLA

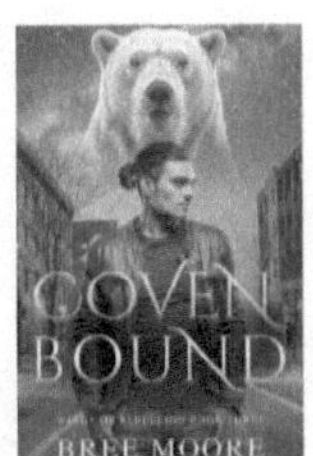

BOOK ONE

BOOK TWO

BOOK THREE

BONUS NOVELLA
BECCA + AVAAN

BONUS NOVELLA
IAN + KAMRI

BOOK FOUR

REBEL SWORN

Published by Innate Ink Publishing

www.AuthorBreeMoore.com

First Edition © 2023
Second Edition © 2025

This is a work of fiction. Names, characters, places, and incidents either are the products of the author's imagination or are used fictitiously.

Any resemblance to actual persons, living or dead, businesses, companies, events, or locales is entirely coincidental.

All rights reserved.



Ebook ISBN: 978-1-956668-44-5

Paperback ISBN: 978-1-956668-43-8

# PROLOGUE
## Reya

IT WAS JUST A matter of time before they were discovered.

Of course, an eleven-year-old would never see it coming. At eleven, Reya was more concerned with making friends, school-work, riding bikes, and the fascinating nature trails behind her house than whether or not her family would be betrayed by her best friend.

Until, one day, they arrived—men and women in tactical gear carrying heavy duty tranquilizers meant to knock out creatures with magic-enhanced strength.

Reya didn't know that's what the black gun-like objects were when she saw them. She eyed them nervously, standing at the door and wishing she hadn't answered it.

"Are your parents home?" A woman in a suit asked. Reya turned her wide gaze to this woman with her very tan skin and shiny brown hair.

"Who's at the door, Rey?" Reya's older brother, Jake, came up behind her, then pushed her away from the door.

Reya stumbled back. "Hey!" She couldn't help it. He'd *pushed* her.

"What do you want?" His voice seemed too harsh to belong to her kind brother. Had she done something wrong by opening the door?

"We just want to speak with your parents, son." A man in a suit stood beside the woman. How had Reya missed him before? She had been looking at the black and yellow guns, the probes on the front reminding her of stingers. The man's face was calm, his tone pleasant. Surely, he meant them no harm, but who were these people?

Jake gripped the doorknob, his knuckles white and his jaw tensed. He glanced at Reya, gave her a brief smile, then slammed the door in the man's face.

"Run!" Jake urged, giving her a shove. He locked the door just as someone on the other side jiggled the handle.

"But why? Shouldn't we get mom and dad?" Reya insisted.

"These are not friendly people, Reya. Whatever you do, don't shift until you reach the woods. Keep them guessing about what you truly are as long as possible." Jake's golden-eyed gaze was so intense, Reya could only nod dumbly. The door beside them thudded and shuddered. Had someone kicked it? Jake touched Reya's shoulder. "I have to warn the others. You grab anyone in the backyard and run to the den. No looking back. Okay?"

Reya nodded and took off running. She had a mission, but she didn't feel any less afraid as she left her brother blocking the door those people were trying to kick down. She leapt out the back door, heart pounding in her chest.

She saw her younger twin brothers playing first, and then, from the corner of her vision, two armed men came from the front, using a pathway beside the house.

"Halt!" One of them called.

Reya grabbed her nearest brother, Derek, by the arm and started hauling him to his feet. "Run!" she cried. Derek resisted, starting to cry. He'd always been the more sensitive one. Even at five, he cried too much. Reya pulled him frantically as the men jogged towards them.

David caught Reya's urgency and took Derek's other arm. "Come on!" he shouted.

Seeing and hearing his twin did the trick. Derek got his legs under him and bolted for the woods ahead. Reya ran behind them, glancing over her shoulder. The men were getting closer.

"Keep going!" Reya shrieked at her brothers, then pivoted back to face the men and ran straight at them.

They pulled up in surprise, one holding out a hand to catch her. She twisted out of the way at the last second, helped by her fox agility. She was limited in her human form, but retained some ability and some enhanced smelling and hearing. She headed back for the house. Something crashed inside, and glass broke.

A hand clamped down on her shirt from behind, jerking her off her feet. Reya shifted without thinking, hands morphing into paws, vision muting, eliminating the colors she could see with her human eyes.

Reya snapped with her powerful jaw, catching the man's gloved hand and biting it. He yelped and dropped her. She wriggled out of the jeans and t-shirt tangling her limbs and took off like a red-furred bullet around the side of the house to the front yard. Her father struggled against two men holding him, talking rapidly and saying things Reya was too panicked to hear properly. She headed straight for him, jumping at the two men nearby.

Her father's face contorted in anguish. "No!" he shouted.

One of the men raised his gun, and a crackling filled the air, sending pulsing electricity through Reya's slight fox frame. She collapsed to the ground, whimpering, the smell of singed fur filling the air. Her vision blurred, then went black.

Reya woke in an empty room. She shifted on the cot and sat up, tugging at the hospital gown hanging off her human frame. Steel gray cement walls met her searching eyes. There was a toilet, a tiny sink, the cot she sat on, and nothing else.

They'd caught her. The people in suits and the men and women in the gear with their guns, they'd been prepared to meet resistance. Worse, they'd seemed to be prepared for her family's abilities. Reya had hidden her fox-shifting abilities from everyone, just like her parents, and their parents, and their parents, and on and on as far back as the Todde family had possessed the ability.

But then, a week ago, she'd shown the boy down the street. Because she liked him. Because she trusted him. And he'd seen her in her fox form before that anyway, playing in the woods. She'd tried to deny it, but admittedly, not very hard. She'd been so excited to have someone to share it with, and the shock and amazement in his eyes had been so worth it.

Until now.

Tyson had betrayed her. Who else could it be?

Reya drew her legs up to her chest on the cot and cried, the fat, warm tears dripping down her cheeks and soaking the thin hospital gown. She was alone. Her family was gone, and it was her fault. What would happen to them?

The heavy door at the front of the small room clicked and creaked open. A woman with soft eyes, crimped hair, and a swishy skirt stepped in.

"Reya Todde?"

Her gentle voice and eyes made Reya want to like the woman, but she was scared. Her entire body trembled, and her bottom lip quivered, and no matter how hard she tried, she couldn't keep herself from blubbering like a baby.

"Where's my mom?" Reya wailed.

"Now then, she's safe. And so are you. I'm just here to do some tests to see what makes you so special. Because you are special, aren't you, Reya?" The woman came closer, kneeling beside the cot Reya sat on.

Reya gulped air and slowed her crying, her gaze locking on the beautiful color of the woman's eyes. "They're purple."

The woman smiled. "Yes. They are. They match my name. I'm Violet." She held out her hand.

Reya had never had an adult shake her hand before. She hesitated a moment before reaching out and taking the soft hand of the nice lady named Violet. The woman's eyes flashed with a bright purple glow, and Reya jumped, then giggled.

"You're magic!" Reya said.

"I am," Violet said, smiling. "I'm a witch. And I'm going to take care of you. I promise. Will you come with me?" She held out her hand.

Reya smiled and slid off the cot, taking Violet's hand in her own and following her out of the cell.

She passed all the tests. She sat still for every poke and prod, despite wanting to nip at the cold hands that touched her. She settled for glaring at the mean ones and smiling at the nice ones. The people who asked her questions made her shift again and again and again while they did scans, drew her blood, and gave her medicines to see if they could stop the shifting.

They couldn't.

For nearly three years, they performed their experiments. Reya felt her mind numbing to it, accepting it as her life. She hated herself for her complacency.

She saw her parents twice a year. Her birthday and Christmas. Violet wouldn't explain why Reya was kept away. When Reya saw her mom and dad, she'd gone from a little girl to a teenager, and her mother burst into tears at the sight of her baby girl half-grown.

Reya cried the first time. The second, she just leaned into her father's bulky warmth and sighed, letting the strains of the past year melt away. He felt skinnier than ever, and there were hollows under his eyes that suggested the experiments being performed on her parents as adults were different than the ones they used on Reya, and hopefully, her siblings.

Her heart ached for her twin baby brothers. They wouldn't be babies anymore. And what of Jake, her older brother, and Lisa and Laura, her older sisters?

All taken. All being tested like her. For what? For evidence of humanity?

Then one day, it all ended as abruptly as it had started.

Reya got up and dressed in the clean clothes provided for her—a cotton t-shirt and loose pants. She did her hair in a pony tail, brushed her teeth, washed her face, and sat on her bed, waiting to be taken back to the lab or the single-room classroom with one desk where a tutor on a computer screen had given her a bland glimpse into the world she was estranged from.

But that day, they didn't retrieve her at the normal time. And when they did come, they took her into a tiny room where they asked her to strip down, shower, then put on a hospital gown. Not too unusual, but Reya's nerves frayed easily after all that she'd been through, and her throat closed up as she put on the socks they provided to keep her feet off the cold tile floor.

The frigid temperature of the floor seeped through the socks anyway, and Reya rubbed her feet and stood waiting to be collected. Her heart beat loudly. Maybe today was the day she was set free. But then, why did they take her clothes?

She twisted her long red hair around her fingers, winding and unwinding. A clock ticked on the wall behind her, but she didn't look. It was sometime in winter, but she didn't know the date. It didn't matter anymore. Her life had become a singular experience for a singular, useless purpose.

Voices mumbled through the door. Reya walked to it and pressed her face against the crack in the doorframe, her cheek touching the icy cold metal.

"It's a shame, you know. A crying shame," said one voice.

"It's wrong. Straight up. Giving a girl a lethal injection. And for what? It's a waste of life."

Reya pulled away, her face twisting with confusion. She couldn't have heard that right. Were they talking about her? Lethal meant deadly. Were they going to kill her?

Her skin prickled, and her knees went wobbly. She needed to see Violet. To ask her questions. Violet always answered her questions.

When the two techs opened the door, they found Reya curled on the floor by the wall in the fetal position. They both had sympathetic eyes, but still they pulled her to standing, holding onto her arms to keep her from collapsing.

Reya mustered every ounce of her courage, looking at the woman with the soft brown eyes and skin, certain she was the one who had said this was wrong. She would be sympathetic to the teenage girl who had no control over her powers, who had never done anything wrong to anyone in her life?

"Please," Reya said, her voice cracking and her bottom lip quivering. She didn't have to act. This was all too real. "Please, can I talk to Violet?"

"Violet is waiting for you in the next room," the man holding Reya's opposite arm said abruptly.

The brown-eyed woman smiled sadly and moved Reya forward down the hallway.

Reya's heart plummeted. Violet was in the next room. Violet was part of this. She wouldn't save Reya. All the testing, all of Reya's compliance, had been for nothing.

It couldn't be for nothing.

"No!" Reya screamed. She yanked her arms away and dropped to the floor. In a flash, she was a fox, her spry body slipping easily through the loose hospital gown. Her claws clicked on the slippery tile as she ran.

The man shouted, his voice booming to her wide ears. Reya barked a warning as he lumbered after her, then darted down another hallway. She had to find a way out of there.

Ahead, a group of techs in white clothes spotted her as they came down the hall. There was nowhere to go but through. Reya zig-zagged, darting through their legs and tripping two of them. In the chaos and shouting, she managed to slip away, but she still had nowhere to hide. Her bright red coat, a muted brown in her own fox vision, was too easy to spot in the wide, white hallways. Where could she go?

Hands closed around her middle, coming out of nowhere. She hadn't even heard the footsteps. She'd been so preoccupied with finding a place to hide, she'd walked right into the enemy's hands.

The hands wrapped a jacket tightly around her, keeping her claws and snout away.

Reya whined. She didn't know who held her. She didn't want to know. They carried her through the building into a room with a metal table, and standing beside it with a clipboard was Violet.

"Reya, this isn't helping," Violet scolded.

Reya barked and growled. She was done helping. She wasn't going to lie down and let them kill her. Did Violet really expect…?

"Call in some back up. When she shifts back, she's going to have to be restrained." There was a measured coldness in Violet's tone and expression that threw Reya off guard. She squirmed in the man's hands, tugging one paw free of the haphazard restraint.

"I'll take her," Violet said. She gripped Reya with practiced firmness, not enough to hurt her, but too strong to wiggle out of.

If Reya had had a mouth that could speak, she would have been yelling. Cursing the witch and her betrayal so everyone in the building might hear. Anger coursed through her, hot and human, feeling too big for her fox body. It had nowhere to go, trapped as she was, so it cycled around and around until three more people entered the room, and one man held up a syringe.

Violet nodded. "Do it now."

The needle slid into Reya's fur, and she yelped, then pain flooded her senses. Ripping, shrieking, grinding, writhing, the serum forced her to transform from fox to human in an insane three seconds flat. Reya lay gasping on the floor like a fish out of water, limbs still coursing with fire and agony.

Hands lifted her up and carried her to the table. A gown was placed over her head and pulled over her body, and all Reya could do was sit there and try to remember how to breathe without feeling like she drew needles in with her air.

Straps tightened on her wrists. She grunted and tried to arch her back, but straps gripped both her shoulders and hips. She tossed her head, barely comprehending anything she was seeing. Gray and white blurs. The flash of blonde as a woman tossed her hair, glancing at Reya as she finished tying down a strap. A blur of brown as a dark-haired tech checked her leg straps.

Tears blurred Reya's vision, embarrassingly. She didn't want to cry in front of these people.

"Leave us," Violet said suddenly.

All activity froze as the techs stared at Violet.

"Are—Are you sure?" the male tech with the brown hair asked.

"She's tied down. What can she do?" Violet's voice dropped low and threatening.

The techs filed out to leave, the metal door banging shut behind them with a solid thud that made Reya wince.

Plastic crinkled. Reya glanced and saw the shiny, pointed tip of a long syringe, and immediately glanced away. Metal clinked on a tray beside her. She couldn't look. Not at the needle in Violet's hand.

The witch had promised to take care of Reya. Had advocated for Reya to see her family, to get more sleep when the lab rats wanted to keep testing, had brought toys and books and rocks and flowers from outside so Reya wouldn't get bored or feel so alone in her sterile prison.

And now Violet was going to be the one to kill her.

"You lied to me," Reya said, tugging against her bonds. But it was no use. They wouldn't budge. She squeezed her eyes shut, then blinked rapidly to get rid of the tears pooling in her eyes, but she couldn't stop them from coming, just like she couldn't stop what was about to happen to her. She was only fourteen. She should be thinking about boys, preparing for end-of-year testing at school, getting ready for summer. Instead, she'd be dead within the hour.

She turned her head away from Violet, unable to watch that needle descend.

"Reya," Violet said, her voice deceptively tender. As if she really cared.

Reya wouldn't fall for that trap again.

"Reya." Violet's voice changed, taking on an urgency that made Reya's eyes pop open.

"What?" Reya snapped her head back towards Violet. "Just get it over with. I know my family is probably dead already. Or will be soon. You betrayed your own kind. I hope you feel that guilt for the rest of your life."

Violet's brow creased. Her fingertips brushed Reya's wrist, then withdrew. "I'm not here to kill you."

"You don't have to pretend. I heard what the guy outside said," Reya said with bitterness.

"I'm not pretending. Now, shut up and listen." Violet's lips pursed. "We don't have much time to get this right, and once you're under, I can't wake you up until the perfect time. I've had a vision, Reya. It showed me the end of the world, and you were part of it. You're scheduled to be killed by lethal injection today, but I *am* going to protect you. You'll appear dead. I'll put a spell on you. The injection itself is only saline and will not harm you."

Reya's eyes widened. She lifted her head off the table. "What do you mean? I'll be asleep?"

Violet pressed her back down. She fiddled with something on the table beside her. It clinked against the stainless steel tray that held the needle. "Not just any sleep. The Hundred Years Sleep. Sleeping Beauty's nap, if you will." Violet gave a wry smile. "Your spirit will travel through the dream realm until someone comes and guides you back to your body and wakes you up."

"The dream realm? How long will I be gone? Will anyone else be there? My family?" Reya asked, her words choking in her throat. Oh, how she hoped she wouldn't be alone.

"I don't know how long you'll be there. It could be years. Your body will age, but your life will be preserved, so you won't need to eat or drink. The dream realm is expansive, and I can't guarantee you'll find anyone you know, but I'm attempting to get your family out this same way. Stay away from evil entities that will steal your light. I wish I could prepare you more, send you with protections, but the hasty ones I've set in place will have to do."

Reya opened her mouth to ask another question when the door to the room opened.

"Is something wrong, witch?" A man growled. Reya kept her face straight, staring at the cracks in the ceiling. Her arms trembled, and coldness seeped into Reya through the thin hospital gown she wore.

"Just double-checking the solution percentages. Can't be too careful when magic is involved. You can tell the others I'm ready to proceed," Violet said in a clipped tone.

The door shut in response.

Reya flexed her fists. "I'm scared," she whispered.

Moisture glistened in Violet's eyes as she raised the syringe in a blue-gloved hand, pausing over Reya's arm. "You're going to make it, Reya. You're going to survive. And you'll fight in a war for paranormal rights and change the whole world."

Violet raised her hand and plunged the needle into Reya's arm.

# CHAPTER ONE

## HARPER

HARPER'S LUNGS BURNED WITH each inhale and exhale, her throat parched and desperate for water. She ignored her body signaling for rest, sucking in more air and dredging up all of her energy. Her wings quivered, straining from her shoulder blades as if they'd launch her into the air at any moment.

She screeched, making the entire room stop and stare. Several people covered their ears, exchanging amused, even mocking glances with their training partners.

Her cheeks heated, but she squared her shoulders and faced her trainer, who blinked rapidly and pasted a smile on her oval face.

"That was, er, good. But not exact. When singing the Song of Breaking, notes go up, like this." The raven-born trainer, Nauja, opened her mouth wide and trilled a perfect rising scale. The same scale Harper had attempted a dozen times that morning and failed to reproduce.

Harper clenched her fists, then forced them to relax. It was impossible to sing the songs of her people when she was tense. At least, that's what Nauja told her. Along with every other bird shifter in this place.

Each tribe, or rather flock, of bird shifters had their own songs. Ravens could not sing the songs of the eagles, or the owls, or the blue jays. And there were blue jays here, among the rebels of the Transcendental Redemption Society.

Harper had seen the flash of blue wings in her first week and had left the training room without explanation. Over time, she'd grown used to the sight, but those blue, black, and white feathers never failed to bring Fletcher's face to the surface of her mind.

She forced herself to see his face. Not the broken body under a white drape. But remembering helped too. Helped her keep training, keep trying, despite the embarrassment she felt when she got the notes wrong. When she failed to sing even the simplest versions of the songs of the Tulukaruq people. Her people.

Remembering Fletcher reminded her why she had joined the rebellion. To fight. To make the world into a safe place for paranormal and human alike.

Nauja considered Harper's face, then nodded, as if she understood something. She clasped her hands behind her back and paced a few steps.

"The primary bars. Run through them again. Practice your voice control. You won't invite the river of magic until you get the notes right," Nauja said.

Harper breathed through clenched teeth and rolled her shoulders. Nauja meant well. But Harper had been singing the primary bars—fledgling songs meant to train the youth of the tribe—for weeks now, with little to show for it.

Where was the song she'd used at Camp Silver Lake to save Tyson from the band of rogue paranormals intent on killing him? Where was the power that had come so readily, so naturally to her in times of need? And why was she forced to bear the humiliation of singing the primary bars in front of everyone?

Even Quinn had advanced to the more complicated, full versions of the songs. There were eight in total, and he had already mastered three to their trainers' satisfaction.

Harper hadn't even mastered one. But she wanted to. She needed to. So, she shoved her pride aside and closed her eyes, swallowing past the dryness in her throat, unwilling to ask for a drink of water, to show any weakness or sign of fatigue.

Nauja seemed to read her mind and passed her a water bottle, but Harper pushed it away.

Harper cleared her throat and pursed her lips into a tight 'o' shape and whistled. Up and down, sharps and minors, trying desperately to feel the tone and invite the river of magic that Nauja claimed flowed through every raven-born individual.

"If you have the wings, you have the songs," she'd said during their past training sessions. "It's just a matter of bringing them out, making them second nature, rather than something that explodes from you in times of trouble."

Now, Nauja watched Harper, nodding as she hit the right notes and kept her pacing even.

Harper's hand slapped her thigh, giving her a rhythm to follow. She moved from whistling to singing and back again, the notes becoming wild, taking shape, flowing.

She was doing it.

Immersed in the music, joy surging at the flow she felt in the simple measures of music that emerged from her chest, it took Harper several moments to notice that the mutterings around the room weren't for her performance of the primary bars, but because someone important had entered the room.

Anna Aguta-King, raven-born daughter of the Tulukaruq tribe and leader of the council of the T.R.S., not to mention

Harper's own mother, strolled around the room, greeting the practicing avian shifters.

"Please, continue your training. Don't stop on my account," Anna called, and the room bustled once more as training efforts renewed.

Some practiced fighting, but more practiced their songs, like Harper. Most of them were much more advanced than she.

The bar Harper had been practicing caught in her throat. She watched her mother circle at the far end of the room, hardly hearing Nauja's praise and encouragement to keep going.

Anna's cold, dark eyes landed on her daughter, then slid away. She touched a lark shifter's shoulder, smiling as she said something, perhaps giving advice, then moved on.

Harper swallowed past the lump in her throat.

"Perhaps that's enough for today," Nauja suggested gently.

Harper's jaw tightened. "No. I want to do the Song of Breaking."

"But you haven't done your focus exercises, and given your current state, I don't think that's the wisest..."

Harper glared, her wings flaring, and Nauja's words faltered.

Ravens did not have alphas like the werewolves, but Harper had observed that there was still a natural hierarchy. Some of the ravens were more dominant, others more subservient. Her mother was clearly a dominant shifter, and Quinn had shown it as well. The others responded to Harper deferentially, but her position in the flock was still uncertain.

Nauja did not have much dominance, but she did have authority as Harper's trainer. Going against that authority was disrespectful, but Harper didn't care.

She had to show Anna what she was capable of. The woman had hardly looked her way, much less addressed her, in the weeks since they had stopped the witches from summoning Ragranoth several weeks prior.

Hadn't had time to even talk to her only daughter, who had been lost to her for almost twenty years. Hadn't offered a single explanation for her disappearance. So far, being reunited with her mother had turned out to be nothing special, and Harper's gut ached at the loneliness she felt, which had grown worse since she'd joined the T.R.S. and found her mother.

Even having Quinn back didn't help, since he spent all his time going on special missions for the rebellion and had no time to spend with Harper to rebuild the memories she'd lost to the beryllium orb.

Maybe, if Harper could show her mother the power she'd used instinctively before, maybe that would be enough to get her to notice, and Harper could be sent on a mission with Quinn next time one came up.

Harper ignored Nauja's attempts to dissuade her and opened her mouth, launching into the complicated Song of Breaking.

The notes cracked as they passed through her dry throat, but Harper persevered, focusing on the flow she'd felt during the primary bars. And to her amazement, the notes held. She raised her voice, the song rising above the chatter and the quieter tunes in the room.

Nauja stepped aside, wings folded against her back submissively, her eyebrows knit with concern, but she cleared the space around Harper.

Harper concentrated on the object she was meant to break with her song—a small glass jar contained in a box to avoid shrapnel striking anyone nearby if—when—the jar broke.

Harper focused on it, pushing her voice to its limit, letting the river of energy rush through her and into the jar. She imagined the song filling the jar, pushing outward.

Faintly, she heard a voice telling her to stop. Why would she stop? She would do it this time. She could feel it! She rushed the last four notes, holding the last high note as long and loud as she could, power coursing through her. The jar gave way, shattering with the telltale tinkle of glass. A heavy object thudded to the ground.

Someone screamed.

"Stop!" A harsh voice commanded.

Harper opened her eyes.

Nauja stood doubled over, her hand on her face, blood trickling between her fingers.

The table stood a few feet away, its legs broken from underneath it. The jar was no more than a pile of glass shards in the center of a flattened box.

Harper's song had broken too much. Too loud, too fast. She glanced breathlessly at those who gathered, their faces serious, even angry.

"I-I'm sorry, Nauja. I didn't mean—"

"What were you thinking!" Anna interrupted, stopping next to Nauja and taking her hand from her face to check the cut. It looked deep, the angry red line reaching from her mouth nearly to her ear. Anna passed Nauja off to another of the bird shifters to be taken to the healing floor. Then, she faced Harper again.

"I have rarely seen such irresponsible behavior. To disregard the safety of others, to ignore one's trainers. Again and again, you defy them, acting as if you know better. When will you learn?" Anna asked, her harsh voice cutting into Harper's mind.

Harper's wings drooped. She fidgeted. "I just wanted..."

Anna laughed. "Wanted what? To harm others? To ruin this entire operation? Next time, aim to bring down the entire Tower, if that's your goal."

Renewed anger surged through Harper. She'd fought harder than anyone she knew for the chance to live a normal life with her family, and now the only family she had left accused her of being a failure who would bring down the rebellion.

"You send Quinn on missions; you include him in the council meetings. Did you forget that I'm also your daughter? Don't I deserve a chance to serve where it really matters?" Harper asked.

Anna's hand balled into a fist, and her entire body shook as if she resisted lashing out.

Harper wished she would. She understood that kind of pain. Exchanging blows resulted in a clear winner, at least. The pain flaring in her heart didn't make any sense. No one could win in a war of emotions.

Especially if one side refused to engage.

Anna's hand relaxed, and she shook out her wings, brushing back a loose strand of dark brown hair from her face. She straightened her shirt and regained the impersonal expression that Harper had learned to recognize as her command face.

"As you've consistently shown, you're reckless and unreliable, I cannot send you on missions that require obedience, control, and discipline. Having a blood connection to me does not automatically qualify you for those positions." Anna drew in a breath and turned away from Harper.

Conversation over.

"What do I have to do?" Harper shouted. She panted, exhaustion settling into her chest and limbs from acting as a channel for the power of breaking.

Anna didn't stop, and Harper let the emotion surge out of her as a burst of sound, a cry of frustration and rage.

"Two weeks on double kitchen duty. Breakfast and dinner." Anna's voice carried clearly through the training room, and she didn't even spare a glance back at her.

Harper headed for the open-air patio attached to the training room. She had to let off some steam, or she'd break something else.

# CHAPTER TWO

## TYSON

TYSON SAT IN A windowless room, sweat dripping down his nose. His bare chest and back were slick with sweat and oil, and his head swam with hunger.

Ewu, the shaman assigned to train Tyson in the art of astral travel and war, insisted that fasting was the key to unlocking his full potential. Something about denying the carnal flesh and forcing his spirit to grow stronger.

Tyson just wanted a sandwich. Turkey and swiss, ham and cheddar, peanut butter and jelly...he wasn't picky; he'd eat whatever the cafeteria had that day. But he really, really wanted a—

A hand whistled through the air and clapped Tyson on the side of his head.

"Ow!" Tyson said, flinching away from the blow.

"If you were not so busy thinking about food, you would have blocked my strike, Tyson Miller," Ewu chided, adjusting his seat across from Tyson on a simple woven mat, legs criss-cross and arms relaxed on his naked thighs.

The man wore nothing but a thin pair of boxer shorts, his silvery aura gleaming like starlight around him. He insisted Tyson wear the same thing, claiming that shame was a barrier to ascension, and the energy that emitted from man-made fabrics inhibited truth, or something.

Tyson thought the guy was crazier than the online guru he'd studied when he first learned astral travel. Crazier than Charlemagne, the hippie auto-mechanic and soothsayer he'd run into what seemed like a lifetime ago. Before Alaska, before Harper's possession, before the Transcendental Redemption Society had taken over D.C. and captured the President of the United States.

Ewu's growl interrupted Tyson's thoughts. "Clear your mind."

Tyson straightened, attempting the impossible. Especially now that he'd thought of Harper. It frustrated her, not doing anything she considered important. Everything important in her eyes was inherently dangerous. And Tyson, for one, was glad that she'd been assigned benign tasks that contributed to the good of the residents of the Tower that housed the T.R.S. headquarters, even if it did make her cranky.

"Your thoughts are drifting, Tyson Miller." Ewu's growl became a bark, and he boxed both sides of Tyson's head with a ferocity that belied his frail appearance.

The polar bear inside of Tyson bellowed at this abuse. He clamped down on it, trying to control the shift like he'd been practicing. He wasn't here to work on that today. At least, he didn't think he was. He'd been sitting in this meditation pose for over an hour.

Tyson gritted his teeth. "Maybe if you told me what the point of today's lesson was, I wouldn't have such a hard time concentrating. It's hard to focus on nothing."

Ewu snorted. "Until you learn the art of focusing on nothing, you will not get anywhere. It took me three years in Vale do Javari to master that skill. Do not expect it to take you any less."

Tyson cleared his throat. "Master Ewu, I've been assigned to you to learn things that will help us win the war we're in now. We don't have three years."

"Such insolence. This is not a war. This is a stand-off. Each side showing what it can do, like territorial stags trying to frighten the competition. The war has not even started yet," Ewu insisted.

"But it will start, and in less than three years. What can you teach me before then?" Tyson asked, trying to keep his tone humble. His stomach grumbled.

Ewu certainly heard it. His laughter bounced off the walls in the dimly lit room, and he finally cracked open one of his ancient, crinkled eyelids to peer at Tyson with a single, clear blue eye.

He scanned Tyson from top to bottom, and Tyson got the impression that the old shaman had stripped him not only of the boxer shorts he wore, but his skin, muscle, and bone, all the way down to his soul.

Tyson shifted uncomfortably, feeling that stare in the most vulnerable depths of himself. He felt a bubble of gas build in his stomach and let it pass, the only sound in the small room.

Ewu chuckled, breaking the tension. "You are smarter than you let on, I'll give you that. So, you want to learn how to go to war in the realm between realms. I can teach you a thing or two. You know you cannot shift into your animal skins there. To face the demons that could besiege you seeking your life force, you must be able to form a weapon."

Tyson couldn't help the grin that formed on his face. Weapons. Yes. He would need weapons. Weapons were much more useful than meditation.

"Young men always think war will bring them glory. It only brings death and gore. But you will learn that soon enough. It is not something young men learn from old men. Only from experience. Do not be so quick to prove yourself. Hold back until you cannot possibly hold back any longer. Defend and protect. Do not seek to destroy, or you will destroy yourself."

Tyson's muscles cramped. He wasn't sure what Ewu was talking about. He didn't want glory. He wanted to be able to fight when the time came, to not always rely on people like Harper to defend him, or his polar bear form, which while destructive, was unpredictable and draining to use.

Instead of asking for clarification, he just nodded, hoping the old shaman would get to the part about weapons.

Ewu peered at him again with that same single-eyed stare, then smacked his lips and clamped his eye shut once more.

"Summon your spirit guide to enter the dream world, Tyson Miller." The shaman hummed a tone that Tyson had come to recognize. It was Ewu's way of putting his body into a vibration that allowed him to travel into the astral realm while awake.

Tyson had learned the tone, but he preferred his own method. He imagined the world yawning open, like someone had pulled a zipper in the air in front of him, and his spirit form stepped through into the astral realm.

*Todd?* Tyson called, summoning the fox-faced guide who had helped him come into his dreamwalker abilities during the trials in Alaska.

The astral world spread before him, the nearby area holding the shape of the room Tyson sat in with Ewu, before opening into a broad landscape filled with shapes and colors that only existed outside of Earth's limiting atmosphere.

It always seemed to be sunrise or sunset at the place where Tyson entered the physical plane. Never anything in between.

Ewu stood a few feet away, his frame skinny, but muscular. Here, he wore a loose orange tunic shirt and baggy leggings that matched, and his beard appeared about six inches longer, reaching his navel.

Tyson quickly imagined clothes for himself. He still struggled with changing his reality here. He could imagine anything, and yet, his mind often drifted back to reality—like the fact that he was sitting in a dark room, sweating and practically naked…

Ewu coughed, and Tyson glanced down to realize he had lost his clothes and was naked again.

Jeans and a t-shirt appeared in the blink of an eye, covering his intangible, floating form once more.

"Intention. Control. Clothing should be as innate as breathing. Do not let your emotions get the best of you. This is especially important when forming a weapon to attack."

A sword appeared in Ewu's hand. The glowing golden blade looked as if it had been formed out of the sun itself, its surface shifting with reds and oranges down to the ruby in the hilt. He swung it expertly, then paused. "Did you call for your spirit guide?"

The shaman's own guide, a gecko Tyson had learned was named Ohki, clung to Ewu's shoulder.

"I called him. Maybe he didn't hear me?" Tyson said, uncertain. Todd usually appeared soon after Tyson arrived in the astral realm. As a spirit guide, he had been assigned to Tyson and would always be with him, even after he'd mastered his dreamwalker abilities.

No one should travel alone in the astral realm, Ewu said. Tyson had done it before and didn't see the issue, though. He couldn't help it if his guide wasn't as attentive as others.

"He will find us when he's able. Come." Ewu snapped his fingers, and the world shifted, turning into a grassy field. A blue sky filled with white, puffy clouds appeared above. A single tree rose on the far horizon, but otherwise, Tyson saw nothing but grass and sky.

Ewu swung his sword around again and it turned into a spear. Still the color of molten gold with shifting red flames dancing across it. Still that ruby at the end. The appearance seemed tied to the shaman somehow.

Excitement filled Tyson. What would his own weapon look like?

"To form an energetic weapon requires immense concentration and effort. It does not come as readily as you might think..."

Tyson only half-listened as Ewu continued, picturing a spear like the one Ewu had. He imagined it made of green lightning at first, thinking of weapons from video games and movies he'd seen. A spark flared in his mind's eye, orange, like a 4th of July sparkler. He stretched the flame with his hands, forming it into the shape he intended.

*A spear. I want a spear.*

Something solid fell into his hands, as if dropped from the sky, and Tyson opened his eyes. They widened. Ebony wood, sleek and polished, mixed with patches of carved bone, and the tip of the spear gleamed obsidian, sleek and sharp and deadly.

It looked similar to his *ulu* knife, the gift from Nana that had once belonged to his grandfather Nukilik, and others who had come before him.

Ewu had stopped talking, his eyes narrowed. "You weren't listening, were you?"

"Er, no," Tyson admitted.

"Let's see if you can fight with it, then," Ewu said calmly, a voice that Tyson knew meant his mentor was angry, no matter what the man said about emotions clouding the mind.

Tyson braced himself. Here, it didn't matter if he knew how to fight. He could imagine his astral form doing anything he wanted it to do. His ability would depend on his energy levels and his focus. Right then, he trained all his focus on Ewu, and the spear thrumming with power in his hand.

"You still want that sandwich? Land a blow, Tyson Miller. A single blow, and I'll concede."

Tyson nodded, adjusting his grip on the spear. In reality, his stomach twinged, the thought of food drawing his attention away from this realm.

The spear in his hands flickered, and Ewu lunged.

Tyson stumbled back. He refocused, forcing his mind away from his physical body. He didn't have a body here. He didn't have a stomach, empty or otherwise. He was whole, here, without need, without concern, except to land a blow on Ewu.

Tyson held the spear in one hand. It was made for him and balanced perfectly. He tried a few different handholds, settling on one that felt right.

"Can we hurt each other with these?" Tyson asked, suddenly hesitant.

"Yes," Ewu said. "Strike with the flat of the tip or the butt only."

He raced forward, leaping into the air, and Tyson brought his spear up, wood cracking on wood. Grunting, Tyson thrust Ewu back, feeling a surge of confidence. The weapons had form to them. If Tyson reached out to touch Ewu with his hand, he would feel nothing. But the weapon, formed of a different kind of energy, could touch Ewu's weapon. Could touch and possibly harm Ewu himself.

That gave Tyson pause, and Ewu took advantage, spear swiping through the air, the flat side of the tip striking Tyson's shoulder.

The blow rippled through Tyson's astral form, and his physical body, sitting in meditation on earth's plane, trembled.

"These weapons influence your energy, your soul. If I tear into your energy, I can steal your life force. It will make me stronger. Younger. I will live longer. But it is an abomination to steal the life force of another. My soul will warp. My energy—and my soul—will darken. Eventually, I would become a demon. A lower vibrational being, eternally hungry, seeking always to steal the life force of others. Every soul that enters this realm makes a contract with the Eternal Source to protect life and never take it."

Ewu leapt into the air, rocketing far higher than humanly possible. Tyson got lost watching him soar, and then the man plummeted down, and Tyson scrambled to get into a defensive position. He breathed in, planted his feet, and imagined his astral form as a boulder, immovable, unshakeable.

Ewu's spear cracked against Tyson's, and the shaman was flung back by an invisible force. He tucked and rolled across the ground, coming up spryly as a warrior, not a creaky, old man.

He grinned at Tyson, his blue eyes bright. "You turned your defense into an attack! Excellent. Now, land a blow."

Ewu waited, and Tyson rolled his spear in his grip, wondering if this was a trick. It was undoubtedly a trick, one that Tyson would likely fall into. But before he made his attempt, he had a question to ask.

"Is this something I could form back on earth? You know, energetically?" He could see that being extremely useful in the war between the rebels and the humans that opposed them. To have the *ulu* knife and to be able to change it at will into a deadlier or more practical weapon.

"No," Ewu said, his voice harsher than Tyson had ever heard it. "Not unless the veil between worlds has torn and the energy lines get blurred. And that is something that we must avoid at all costs. Now, attack!" he shouted.

Tyson bolted, closing the space between them. He raised his arm, pulling it back as he flipped into the air. The staff twisted, the end now pointing down, and Ewu, who waited, seemingly frozen.

He was going to do it. There was no way Ewu could get out of the way in time. Tyson pushed himself to fall faster, like a bullet plummeting to the earth. He pulled back at the last second to soften the blow.

Ewu vanished. The green, swaying grass vanished, sucked into a void that opened up in the physical plane of the astral realm like a black hole.

Tyson tried to reverse his trajectory, but he couldn't escape the pull of the void. He screamed for Ewu, for Todd, for anyone. His spear flickered in and out of existence, then disappeared altogether as Tyson was sucked into the void-hole, and the blue sky above him winked out, plunging his vision into blackness.

The blackness was total. Tyson couldn't tell which way was up, or whether he floated. Time stretched, immeasurable here. He realized he could conjure a light.

Blue light flared, a little ball hovering next to his head. Darkness on all sides. No light, no variance. He'd been dragged into a true void, the likes of which he'd heard existed in the Lower Mental plane, two levels down from the physical plane where Tyson had spent most of his training.

Todd had shown him parts of the Lower Astral plane and the Higher Astral plane, gradually exposing him to the less stable, more unpredictable levels, but beyond that, Tyson didn't have much experience.

*Ewu!* Tyson yelled. Even his voice was different. It did not carry, swallowed by the void. There was no sound here, no color, nothing.

*Fool boy, you're going to draw the attention of every demon in the lower planes! Put out the light.* An impression of Ewu's astral form appeared, like an echo of his spirit.

Did Tyson appear that way to Ewu?

Tyson put out the light, obeying his mentor without thought. He could still see Ewu's form, a translucent outline, shifting and flashing in the impossible darkness.

*How do we get out of here?* Tyson asked.

Before Ewu could answer, a light blossomed, disrupting the void-light. It was dim, gray, unappealing, but any light seemed good to Tyson. He wouldn't go towards it without Ewu's word, though.

*Ewu?*

A dark chuckle responded, and Ewu's form shimmered, changing into a monstrous figure, black and gleaming as if covered in oil.

Tyson swallowed the scream that formed in his mind and reeled backward, away from the monster, away from the sickly light.

The monster grew in size, oily tendrils reaching for him.

He screamed, and a vision of Harper popped into his mind. He would see her again. He wouldn't die here, at the hand of this lower vibrational being.

Anger shot through him, clearing the panicked haze and allowing him to conjure an astral weapon. The spear appeared in his hands, eight feet long with an ethereal fire racing down its length.

Tyson swung, and the demon reared back, squealing in fear. He didn't need to eliminate it, just scare it long enough to get away.

The demon loomed behind him, closing in for the kill. Tyson waved his spear, frantically searching for a way out. He'd suddenly forgotten everything, fear clouding his inner vision.

A sensation like a giant hook grabbing his sternum yanked painfully inside his spirit-form. Spear and monster disappeared, the void reversing as something dragged him away. Back to life? Or another hell?

Tyson slammed back into his body, gasping and doubling over, his entire body quivering. He'd wet himself, and his stomach tried to empty its contents, but since he'd been fasting, there was nothing but yellow bile.

Soft, wrinkled hands grasped his arms with surprising strength, forcing him to kneel. Ewu's clear blue eyes searched his, frantic.

"You're still you, Tyson Miller." A statement, said with relief.

"Yes," Tyson replied, even though he knew it was unnecessary. The shaman had seen his soul, vibrant and still his, through his eyes. "What...happened..."

Tyson swallowed, gulping down the sweet, sweet air. He felt keyed up with adrenaline, his entire body rigid with terror, ready to fight should that monster follow him into the real world.

"You were sucked away by a void pocket. They can be maneuvered by an experienced demon. What did you see there? What did you hear?" Ewu asked.

"I saw you, first," Tyson said, gathering his breath and his thoughts. "It mimicked you. Tried to get me to go with it. Then it became...something. Something horrible. Oily. A demon." He shuddered at the memory of its chuckle, of its claws and teeth that he was only now processing.

"What did it want?" Ewu asked.

"To eat me, I guess. Consume my essence?" Tyson faltered. No. Yes, but no. It had wanted something else.

Ewu grimaced, then lifted his hand, passing it over Tyson's trembling body. A wave of warmth passed through Tyson, and his muscles stilled, relaxing at the touch of Ewu's power.

"The Mental planes are difficult to navigate, even for experienced walkers. Even we do not go there unless forced. Demons that live in the Lower Mental plane will reach into your mind and manipulate your fears, distract you with false realities."

Tyson nodded, sitting back on his heels and breathing deeply through his nose. Air swirled around him, cool on his sweat-covered skin. He needed to get out of this stifling box of a room, out of this tower.

Most of all, he needed to see Harper, to remind him of what was real.

# CHAPTER THREE

## ZEKE

ZEKE STOOD AT ATTENTION behind a twelve-foot electric fence surrounding the White House grounds, playing security guard for the President of the United States being held in the building behind him.

He shifted restlessly as a chick with blue hair screamed profanities at him through the bars, shoving her sign through and waving it in his face.

TAKE THESE PUPS TO THE POUND, the sign read. It included a rather artistic rendition of a snarling werewolf head, blood dripping from its teeth.

Zeke resisted the urge to shift and scatter some of the humans. It would only rile them up more. Every time one of these demonstrations happened, the human rebels attacked after dark in force. He needed to reserve his energy for dealing with those who acted on their feelings of discontent about the shift in power happening with violence, rather than just angry words.

To distract himself, he thought of Mandi.

He hid his smile from the raging protestors, but he felt as if he radiated with joy every time he thought about her. He wanted everyone to know his love for the talented witch who had given so much to the paranormal rebellion that would soon change the world for the better.

Mandi's unclouded, brown eyes unnerved Zeke more than anything else that had happened recently. More than the battle at the Washington Monument, more than Mandi being the only one of Lilith's coven that had survived the broken demon summoning, more than the violent humans raging outside the White House daily with their picket signs and megaphones.

She worked day and night to bring about change in legislation, contacting senators and chairmen and chairwomen, trying to persuade them to join the winning team before the T.R.S. sent agents to their homes and brought them in by force.

They would replace every person in the senate and the house if they had to, though they much preferred an equal split to show humanity that the paranormals didn't intend to destroy the government or take it over, simply to be part of making the laws that concerned them.

Clanging sounds at the fence jerked Zeke out of his thoughts, and his head itched where his wolf ears would have been in his shifted form, as if they were perking up to better take in the alarming sounds of the picketers turning into a mob.

Rocks pelted the gate. One got through and bounced harmlessly off Zeke's leg, but he growled anyway, showing fangs. He wouldn't go any farther than necessary to keep these humans in check. He was under strict orders to avoid violence.

They were building bridges, not destroying them. But damn, the humans could give a little and meet the T.R.S. halfway, couldn't they?

Zeke's growling and bared fangs only seemed to incite the humans further. He glanced to either side at the other shifters standing at attention forty feet away. They circled the White

House, preventing a daytime assault on the White House if the humans attempted to get the president back.

People at the back of the crowd pushed forward and the blue-haired girl flew into the fence, crying out at the force of the shock she received. She fell to the ground beneath the careless feet of the surging crowd.

Zeke cursed and pulled a radio from his belt, putting it to his mouth.

"We've got a mob situation out here. Is there someone around who can soothe them?" he asked.

"All soothers are busy elsewhere. You have permission to handle it, Z. We'll get some holding cells ready at the Tower," Jorge, another wolf shifter, said.

Zeke grimaced. "Copy that." He changed channels to talk to his team of mixed shifters. "Northside shifters, on me."

Hisses, howls, and words all echoed through the radio static as Zeke shoved the radio into his belt holster. He stayed in his human form and picked up the megaphone on the ground at his feet, raising it to his mouth.

"Security teams are on their way. I suggest you lot clear before they get here. Force will be used if necessary, and inciters will be arrested."

"Go back to hell!" a bearded man shouted. Cheers erupted around him.

Zeke let the shouted threats and profanities roll off his back as he stripped off his outer clothes and shifted into a large black wolf. He leapt the twelve-foot fence with ease, the crowd scattering, except for the blue-haired girl that had fallen.

She gaped up at Zeke, an abrasion on her head bleeding down the side of her face. Otherwise, she seemed unharmed, and Zeke relaxed slightly.

He approached, head down and ears back in a non-threatening position, then when he was certain the crowd would stay back, shifted back to human form. It was easy during the week of the new moon.

"You okay?" he asked. "I can call an ambulance if you need it."

Her face morphed from terrified awe to ugly fury in an instant. Her lip curled back over her human teeth.

"Eat my taser," she shouted. Her left hand came up and the taser she'd hidden beneath her body shot out and connected with Zeke's bare arm.

He barely even flinched. It took a lot more juice than a standard-issue taser could muster to take a werewolf down.

Damn. Why did these kids always think they could take on a fully grown shifter? And why was it always the small ones?

The pinch of the electricity vanished in a moment, and Zeke calmly reached out and yanked the taser from the girl's hand, then leaned forward letting his wolfish eyes and teeth come through.

"I really wish you hadn't done that," he said. And then he changed again, baring his teeth and joined the other shifters on guard duty herding the cowed humans that hadn't run into a tight circle.

A handful of witches and warlocks finally came on the scene, casting a cloud of confusion over the humans and making them more compliant for transport to the Tower via truck. Zeke was disappointed when none of them turned out to be Mandi.

Once the prisoners were recorded and settled, Zeke requested a replacement and headed upstairs to shower and get something to eat.

He hunted through several floors, checking Mandi's familiar haunts, but she wasn't in any of them. Her room, the witches' corridor, the lab, and the library were all void of his favorite person.

He didn't have a way to reach her, either. He hadn't gotten a cell phone yet, and neither had Mandi. Supply chains in a lot of areas were shutting down in protest of the paranormal takeover.

Getting groceries and clothing for the thousands of rebel members and prisoners now occupying the Tower after joining the T.R.S. was problematic enough. They'd had to open several hubs for the rebellion in other states across the U.S., and contacts from foreign embassies were pouring in.

The world was on the brink of war, each nation in danger of eating itself from the inside out as paranormals and sympathetic humans faced lash back from frightened, prejudiced humans.

Zeke wandered down to the cafeteria, hoping he'd run into her there but mostly just needing to satiate his growling stomach with a shredded beef sandwich. They didn't have any pepperoncini peppers or vinegar to dress it with, but he could forgive them for not perfectly mimicking his favorite food from his hometown of Chicago so long as they fed him.

He went through the dinner line mechanically, sliding his tray down the counter and accepting everything that was offered, except the chocolate cake at the end. Being a werewolf had its downsides sometimes, and chocolate did not sit well with most canine shifters.

"That's right! Werewolves can't eat chocolate. It's your lucky day. I saved one lemon bar just for you."

Zeke glanced up, gaping at Mandi as she slid the lemon bar onto his tray and gave him a small wave. The smells from the kitchen had masked her scent. He got a good whiff of it now, but he was embarrassed that his stomach had ruled him so thoroughly that he'd missed her, of all people.

Those playful brown eyes blinked at him, her smile stretching a little wider as he didn't respond. He was holding up the line, he knew, but he had to familiarize himself with that gaze. She had been blind the entire time he'd known her until her sight had been restored somehow in the magical backlash that sent Ragranoth back to the abyss the demon had tried to emerge from.

No matter what anyone said, Mandi was a hero. She'd risked her own life to break the pentagram and disrupt the summoning.

"Hey man, stop ogling the witch and let the rest of us pass, yeah?" A man with sandy hair flopping over his dazed expression nudged Zeke with his tray.

Zeke breathed deep to avoid snapping at the guy with his fangs and finally responded to Mandi.

"Thanks. For the lemon bar. Are you off duty soon?"

"I think I'm due for a break. I'll come join you once there's a lull in the line," Mandi said.

"Nah, go now sweetheart," Madge, head of the cafeteria, said from where she parceled out sandwiches. "I'm not one to begrudge young love. You need all the help you can get falling in love in these times. I'll ask Susan to cover. Susan!"

A twitchy, thin woman bustled over and took Mandi's place.

Zeke picked out a table and was joined a moment later by Mandi carrying her own tray of food. She still wore her apron and an air of fatigue as she joined him.

"You're off early. Did something happen?" Mandi asked, her gaze floating off over his shoulder, as if she were too tired to look straight at him. He didn't blame her.

"The picketers got a bit restless. We had to arrest a bunch."

"They'll come around. Some do, anyway," Mandi said, obviously trying to reassure him. She scooped applesauce from a small plastic container and spoke around the bite. "We're finding that cute, fluffy shifters help desensitize the prisoners to their preconceived notion that all paranormals are frightening or violent. You should apply."

Zeke started to object then cut off, giving Mandi an exasperated look. A look she never would have seen just a month ago, and it still amazed him that she reacted, her giggles the brightest sound he'd heard all day.

He placed his hand on top of hers, rubbing across it with his thumb. "How about you? How's your day going?"

"Oh, you know, typical rebellion stuff." Mandi waved her other hand, and Zeke realized the crystal bracelets she typically wore as protective wards were gone.

"Where are your bracelets?" he asked.

"Oh!" Mandi glanced at her wrist, as if this was the first time she'd realized they were missing. "I took them off to work in the kitchen. Didn't want them ruined or anything. Plus they kind of rub wrong sometimes, you know?"

Zeke didn't. He wasn't the jewelry or the crystal type, but it made enough sense that he let it go.

He bit into his sandwich, wolfing the entire sub down in just a few bites, washing it down with water and the applesauce from the container, which he finished in a gulp. He'd noticed that they'd reduced the amount of meat in the sandwiches. If they didn't solve the food supply problem soon, the packs would have to find a place to hunt.

Mandi seemed content to eat in silence, which was unusual for her. In fact, a lot of her typical behaviors had been absent lately, like the way she would twist her curly hair around her finger when she was thinking, and her laugh. When was the last time Zeke had heard her laugh?

Zeke didn't press the matter or spend too much time stressing over the changes. They'd both been under a lot of pressure lately, getting called into councils and sent out to subdue human rebels and raging paranormals alike. An endless cycle of politics and danger.

What they really needed was a break.

"Mandi?"

"Hm?" she said absently, turning towards him with her sunglasses on. She carried them with her to take breaks from the exhaustion and overwhelm of her newly gained sight. She still couldn't read, struggling to learn the letters, and headaches were a daily occurrence.

Zeke rubbed her hand, suddenly nervous. They'd spent time together at Camp Silver Lake, and since romantic relationships had been strongly discouraged there, they hadn't acted on their feelings. They'd slept together, but only with him in wolf-form at the end of her bed. He had a sudden surge of fear—what if her feelings for him had all been in his head? What if she'd never seen him as more than a seeing-eye dog and a protector?

He licked his lips and almost chickened out. But he hadn't run across the United States, getting attacked by monsters and mobsters, and risked life and family just so he could get intimidated by asking this woman out on a date.

"Do you want to go on a date with me? Nothing fancy, but there's this spot I know about...there's a garden that hasn't quite died yet. I thought...it would be nice for us to get some time alone."

A slow smile spread on Mandi's face. "That sounds nice," she said, and her voice had a far-off, dreamy quality to it.

Zeke's shoulders slumped in relief. It almost gave him the courage to ask the other question he'd considered over the past few weeks, one that came up every time one of them had their lives endangered by the work they did for the T.R.S, but a bustling cafeteria was no place for important questions like that.

Quiet, beautiful gardens, however, were. Especially if Zeke called in some of the favors owed to him and fixed it up a bit. A table and chairs dressed with a simple dinner, some candles and fairy lights around the gazebo he knew rested at the center...the image was turning into quite the incredible daydream in his mind, and he barely registered when Mandi said something.

He startled at the sound of her voice. "Sorry, what?"

"I said, 'what should I wear? And where should we meet?'"

"Oh! I'll, er, pick you up at the elevators at seven? Is that enough time for you to get ready? And wear something you feel nice in. Casual is fine." Zeke smiled at her, feeling like a sap but loving every second of it.

If his family pack caught wind of this, they wouldn't approve of the cross-species union, but since things couldn't get much rockier there, he let the twinge of guilt go.

Mandi kissed him on the cheek, then stood from the bench. "I've got to finish my shift. I'll see you in a couple hours!"

Her voice had a falsely cheerful tone Zeke's keen hearing picked up easily. Maybe just trying to psych herself up for the rest of her time volunteering behind the lunch counter. Serving food wasn't the most exciting job, and if she had a headache coming on, he could only imagine what another forty minutes of work would be like.

Zeke called in a few favors, asking for help setting up the garden the way he wanted it. He still had an hour left after he finished—his friends had insisted on doing all the work, leaving him to wander through the Tower, looking for something to pass the time. He had gotten roped into filling hygiene kits for the dozens of new recruits that came to the Tower every day, when Jack walked in.

Zeke dropped the travel-sized toothpaste he was stuffing into a zippered pouch and stood, knocking his chair back.

Jack's face lit up. "Z! My man! I've been looking everywhere for you!" He crossed the room and stuck out his hand.

Zeke shook it, stunned. The last time he'd seen Jack had been on his way to Chicago, when Zeke had gotten attacked by two Japanese Oni demons. Jack and his crew of rebels had saved Zeke from becoming dinner for the monsters and had given him what he needed to get to Chicago.

"How'd you get here? When did you get here?" Zeke asked.

"I've been here and there and back again. Portal travel. An absolute miracle. It'll change the world if the rest of my kind let it," Jack said, sticking his hands in his pockets.

Jack was the human leader of the rebellion running the Midwest branch of the T.R.S. The amulet that glowed under Jack's shirt made it so he could read people and know whether to trust them or not.

"You manage to recruit those Japanese demons?" Zeke asked.

"The Oni? Oy. Those two are a piece of work. We're close. We gotta help them get past their bloodlust in battle and make sure they're safe around our human recruits. But they're almost there," Jack said, positive as ever.

"That's good," Zeke said, at a loss for words. Greg and Steven had been Zeke's rideshare until it turned out they actually enjoyed eating people.

"Yeah! Humane rehabilitation is possible, even for the more violent paranormals. I think a lot of people will be relieved about that if we can get the message across. Speaking of," Jack said, eyeing Zeke. "You wouldn't happen to be interested in joining my team and helping us recruit more humans to our side, would you? You're likable and easy on the eyes, and I'm always looking for those who can keep their cool in a tense situation. I'd like you to lead one of my teams."

"Would I have to leave D.C.?" Zeke asked. It was an interesting proposition. More needed to be done on the human front; after the mob display today, he felt doubly certain of that. But he wouldn't leave Mandi if she wanted to stay.

"You would. But it's just a portal hop away, you know? We'd go all over. You could come back here often, if you've got someone you wanted to see." Jack looked curiously at Zeke but didn't pry.

"I need to talk to someone first. But I admit, I'm intrigued," Zeke said.

"That's great, man. I'll be here through tomorrow night, but then I'm out again, and you'll have to hunt me down. Let me know before then?"

Zeke nodded, and Jack turned to go, but Zeke snapped his fingers. "Hey, about your motorbike. It's in…"

"Chicago? Yeah, I managed to pick it up last week. We've got tracking on it, and your family was kind enough to hand it over. Thanks for taking care of it."

"Sure, man. Thanks for the ride." Zeke watched in a sort of daze as Jack left. He returned to stuffing the hygiene bags, more mechanically now as his mind dwelled on Jack's offer, and the last words his own mother had spoken to him before he left.

Find yourself a pack to lead, Zeke. A real pack.

He hadn't given it much thought since coming to the Tower. Most of his time had been consumed with training and fighting and guarding and council meetings and Mandi.

At the thought of the woman he loved, Zeke glanced at the clock on the wall. Ten to seven. His future as alpha of a werewolf pack would have to wait—he had a date.

# CHAPTER FOUR

## HARPER

FROM HER SEAT AT the top of the world, Harper watched the city burn.

Riot fires lit up the horizon. A dark patch loomed to the west, but smoke still rose. Those fires had been put out earlier that day.

From this distance, Harper couldn't hear the yelling that always accompanied these attacks, the screaming of profanities and "go back to hell, demons!" coming from humans who were furious paranormals had supplanted the president. Similar scenes filled the news, the papers, and both the World Wide Web and the ParaWeb.

Avoiding war seemed impossible, but Harper hoped the humans would gain some sense before the leaders of the Transcendental Redemption Society decided that more military force was needed.

The hairs on the back of Harper's neck prickled, and the air thickened slightly. Something approached, bending the molecules in the air. Harper whirled around a moment before a man materialized into view.

Tyson jammed his hands into his pockets. "You're getting better at recognizing when I'm coming. Still scared you though."

Harper narrowed her eyes. "Mildly startled."

"Your pupils are dilated." Tyson rubbed at the scruff growing on his jawline. He seemed troubled, a hollow look in his eyes, like he'd seen something terrible.

"You okay?" Harper asked cautiously. Talking about feelings never seemed to go well for her, just like her Singing.

Tyson crossed the space between them and sat down, dangling his legs over the edge of the skyscraper.

"That's a view," he said, ignoring her question.

Harper let it slide, guilty that she felt relieved she wouldn't have to help him parse through his feelings. She wasn't feeling particularly capable of that level of support at the moment, not after what had happened in training.

She had an overwhelming urge to give him the details of her day, and just how terribly wrong her training had gone, but he was just as stressed. He probably wouldn't appreciate getting her emotions dumped on him.

"Not exactly a sunset," Harper agreed, facing forward. The wind at that height was strong, blowing her hair across her face and into her mouth. She tugged it out, frowning. She would have normally cut it by now, but Tyson often commented on it, and some vain part of her wondered what he'd think if she grew it out longer. She wanted to find out. Even if it was inconvenient. She should have grabbed a pony tail holder.

"What are you thinking about?" Tyson asked, his brown eyes gazing curiously at her.

Harper shrugged. She wasn't about to admit she'd been thinking about her hair, of all things. And him. They still hadn't defined exactly what this thing was between them. Their trials in Alaska had revealed a connection between them, and her relief at having been reuninted with him after being demon possesed had seemed so strong. Time had expanded while they worked for the T.R.S., and those things seemed like they'd happened in a dream. Not to mention how he'd become some sort of dreamwalking shaman, she had found her mother, and they had both joined a rebellion. So much had changed. They had changed.

Harper blinked, realizing Tyson still waited for a reply. "Um, not much. Quinn isn't back yet, is he?"

"I haven't heard," Tyson said.

Harper squeezed her hands into fists, then relaxed them. "No one told me where he was going. He gets sent on these covert missions all the time. They seem important. I should be going with him."

Tyson put his hand over hers. "Your mother has a reason for not sending you. She probably wants to get to know you. You were younger than your brother when she left."

Harper stared at his hand but didn't pull hers away.

"Then why is she avoiding me? We're not exactly doing any mother-daughter bonding. She won't even talk to me except to criticize." She paused to swallow the emotion that blocked her throat. She hadn't meant to start talking about this.

"It takes time to build a relationship. And while you're getting to know your mom, you've got me, at least."

Harper looked at him, taking in the softness of his face in the orange-tinted evening light. He was sincere. Of course he was. Tyson never said anything he didn't mean whole-heartedly. Her heart fluttered like the wings of a moth against a porch light.

Tyson's finger caught her chin, tilting her face towards his. He leaned in, then hesitated, searching her face, giving her plenty of time to pull away.

Harper took the out and leaned back, widening the distance between them. She bit her lip, then glanced back over the dark, smoky city.

Beside her, Tyson sighed. Was he disappointed? She didn't have any experience with kissing.

And, if they started kissing, if they took this relationship any farther, they would forge more of a connection. A connection that could be broken any moment if one of them died in the war that raged across the United States, spreading to other countries like wildfire as paranormals, and a few humans, finally stood up for the rights of magic-users everywhere. She wasn't sure what she would do if even the tentative connection they already had was broken. The idea of making it stronger made her tremble, and she hated herself for the weakness.

Tyson's arm brushed against her back, and his hand cupped her shoulder.

Harper returned the gesture, draping her wing across his back. Her wing itched fiercely for a moment, and she shook it to get rid of the urge to scratch.

Tyson squirmed and laughed, rubbing at his neck with his free hand.

Harper withdrew her wing. "What?"

"Your feathers tickle." His eyes sparkled. "But I like it. They're soft." He dropped the arm around her and twisted, admiring her wing.

"May I?" he asked, holding up a hand.

Harper's breath caught. She didn't trust her voice to come out in anything more than a squeak, so she nodded. Somehow this seemed less intimate than a kiss, at first. But she was wrong, oh, how she was wrong.

Tyson trailed his fingers through her feathers, stroking the soft down, getting to the itchy part and soothing the irritation there.

A thrill surged through Harper from the base of her spine to the top of her neck, and a humming vibration started involuntarily in the back of her throat.

"Is this okay?" Tyson asked.

"Yeah," Harper breathed, barely getting the word out. She sounded like a vapid idiot. She'd known the guy for what, two months? Sometimes it felt more like two years with all that had happened. Her face heated.

"Tyson?" Harper waited for him to turn back to her.

His eyes shone. "Yeah?"

Her heart crawled into her throat, closing it up. She swallowed, pulse pounding, temple throbbing. The words wouldn't come. She shook her head and pasted on a smile.

"Thanks for being here."

A look of pleased confusion crossed his face. "Sure. Of course. I'm here because of you, you know. If you hadn't landed at Camp Silver Lake and shaken my whole world, I'd still be an idiot with my head up my...well, you get the idea." He laughed.

Harper resisted the urge to shake him off. It felt so *good* to be touched that way. She flicked at a piece of gravel on the rooftop, sending it soaring off the edge. Her stomach flip-flopped as she watched it fall. Not from the height, but from Tyson's proximity, the way his hand trailed up her arm and over her shoulder and rested there with a familiarity that Harper could scarcely believe.

Her lungs tightened up again. She needed to fly somewhere, get the wind back in her hair and clear this feeling out of her chest and head.

She opened her mouth to tell Tyson she wanted to go for a flight, when a figure rushed past, wings ruffling on the wind. A grin spread on Harper's face, and she stood before the figure dropped onto the top of the tower.

It was her brother, Quinn. He walked towards the two of them, flipping his long ponytail back over his shoulder.

"Where did you just get back from?" Harper asked him, swallowing past her jealousy.

Quinn smirked. "Wouldn't you like to know? You'll find out soon enough. Anna's called you to the council room. You, too," Quinn said, jutting his chin at Tyson.

Tyson groaned. "Break time is over."

Harper tugged on Tyson's arm. "Do you think they'll finally give me something to do? I've been sitting on my butt for weeks. Literally sitting in some stupid demon prison, then getting released to do more sitting here. It's a waste of talent."

Quinn raised his eyebrows. "I'll put in a good word for you."

Harper punched Quinn in the arm, then headed towards the stairs with Tyson.

Tyson stopped walking. "I know you want to fly. I'll meet you there."

Damn. He really seemed to read her mind sometimes.

Harper jogged back towards the edge of the building where Quinn stood looking down. Even cars looked tiny from that height.

"Ready?" she asked.

"Ready to beat your ass." Quinn jumped, tucking his wings to fall as fast and far as he could, aiming for the balcony the T.R.S. had installed for the aerials among them.

Harper leapt after him. She passed him as he spread his wings, and a moment later spread her own and slowed, then dropped onto the deck of the balcony, flinging open the sliding glass door and ducking in, breathless, just a second ahead of Quinn.

He shoved her shoulder. "That was insane! Are you trying to kill yourself?"

"Shhh!" A voice hissed from nearby. It was Zeke, but a smile flickered across his expression, and Harper knew he wasn't too serious.

"Nice of you to join us," Anna said, standing at the front of the room.

Harper stiffened and turned her gaze slowly towards her mother.

"Sorry," Quinn said, flashing a smile as he sat down in one of the wheeled office chairs and rotated it back and forth. Anna's stern expression turned into a shallow smile that straightened when she looked back at Harper.

"Sit down, please," Anna said, turning back to the papers in her hand. "Now then, before the interruption, we were discussing management of the southern quarter of the city. I think we should assign an aerial squad to distract them while we send some witches in on the ground. I—"

The door swung open, and a young warlock with curly, ginger hair burst in, breathless. "Channel 2 News, turn it on."

A projector cast an image at the front of the room, showing the Channel 2 News page where a livestream of a reporter played.

The door opened as Tyson ducked in, picking the empty seat next to Harper.

"Human residents of Texas took it on themselves to poison members of the Rio Grande werewolf pack today by lacing their herds with silver dust, resulting in a massacre that killed dozens in the hundred-strong pack. Once the second biggest pack in the United States, rivaling only the wolf pack in Chicago."

The room around Harper filled with gasps and even crying out.

"This is only the beginning, you know," Zeke said from his corner of the table, speaking over the information the news anchor continued to deliver. Mandi laid her hand on his arm, and he put his hand over hers. "We think we've got such an edge over the humans with our powers, but we're forgetting one thing—humans have survived for thousands upon thousands of years. They don't have to kill us with knives and guns. They have wit. They have patience. And if it comes down to an all-out war, I think they'll win."

Harper's heart beat so loud she was convinced everyone could hear it. Zeke's words seemed insane at face value, but it was true. They couldn't afford war.

"Then it's a damn good thing our numbers just grew," Anna said, gesturing to Quinn. "My son Quinn has returned from the first of several excursions to retrieve members of project FT1X. If this is the first time you're hearing it, that is intentional. We didn't want to get anyone's hopes up that the paranormals Violet hid from the government ten years ago would still be alive, but my son brings good news. The best news. Quinn?"

Murmurs broke out from the other people in the room.

Harper's shoulder feathers itched. She sensed Tyson looking at her, gauging her response through the lens of a psychologist and counselor. She wouldn't give him the satisfaction of a reaction.

She folded her arms, trying to subtly rub her itchy shoulders on the back of her chair, and put her focus on Quinn, who now stood at the front of the room with Anna.

"I was privileged to be selected as part of the team to wake the first wave of survivors. These people are like us—magical beings, shifters and witches and enchanters, diviners and beings who were in hiding before their magic was exposed and they were taken by the government."

Angry mutterings moved around the room.

"At the time, Violet worked for the government. Many of you know this. But what most of us didn't know—what I didn't know until just a week ago—is that Violet hadn't turned against her kind. She worked for the government to prevent the devastations that happened. The government-sanctioned executions of those deemed too dangerous or too difficult to manage within the Naturalization program."

Quinn's voice rose above the growing volume in the room. "Violet used magic to save as many of those individuals as she could, by preserving them in a Hundred Year sleep, and she left instructions to find them and wake them."

A woman stood so fast she knocked her chair back. "And they're here? Right now?" Her voice trembled, and she wrapped her hand anxiously in her long red hair.

Harper recognized her as a shifter, although she didn't remember which kind.

Anna came forward. "Yes, they are here. And I know many of you, and those who live in our headquarters, are eager to see if your loved ones are among them. But I urge caution. They are not who they were when you knew them."

Anna steepled her fingers together in front of her. "They were held in limbo in the astral realm, unable to reside in their bodies, fighting off beings who intended to steal their forms. We must continue to observe them for any demon possession. Healers are asked to report to the fourth floor immediately after this meeting to assess not only their physical health, but their mental and spiritual health as well. All others are asked to wait for a day or two until the survivors are settled in further. Respect the time and space they may need to adapt to living in the real world again."

The red-head nodded and sat back down, still tugging at her hair.

Anna held up her hands to quiet the questions that started to rise up. "I know you all have many questions. Let's focus on getting the newcomers settled in for now. We know of three other groups like this one across the United States. There may be more. If you'd like to volunteer to waken those that are still sleeping, speak with Quinn. Otherwise, proceed with your current assignments. Until tomorrow." Anna flipped her hand down into the loyalty gesture over her heart, thumb to pinky, the three other fingers outstretched.

Everyone in the room copied her. Even Harper, though making the sign felt unnatural, even childish.

As soon as the meeting ended, Harper bolted out of her seat and beelined for Quinn.

"I'm signing up. I'll go with you to get the next group," she said breathlessly.

"I said I'd hook you up. What do you say, captain?" Quinn turned to Anna.

Harper's breath caught.

Anna smiled and rolled her eyes. "No one calls me that."

"But they should. That's what you are," Quinn insisted.

"The T.R.S. is run by council. As it should be. We are all equals here." Anna shuffled through some papers on the table in front of her.

Harper cleared her throat. She bounced on her heels, then forced herself to stand still and tall, trying to look like the adult she was.

Quinn caught her earnest glance and rolled his eyes at her, but he turned back to Anna. "Anna, Harper really should come on the next mission with me. She's eager, she's doing well with the Songs, she's familiar with the danger. I think she'd be a great asset to the team."

"No," Anna said without looking up from the paperwork.

Tears stung Harper's eyes. She swallowed hard, balling her hands. "I'm just as capable as Quinn. I found him, after all. All on my own."

Anna faced her, eyes flashing. "I never said you weren't capable, but the answer is still no."

Harper changed her approach, making her voice more plaintive. "If you'd just let me…"

Anna slammed her hand down on the table. "I am a senior officer here. I don't have to give you a reason, Harper. But you do have to listen to me if you want to keep working for this cause."

Harper looked desperately at Quinn, whose large black wings moved as he shrugged his shoulders.

"Mom's right, you know. What's got you all fluffed up, anyway? You get to stay here all safe and cozy with your boyfriend while the rest of us risk our lives. I don't get why you're so eager to be in danger."

"Oh, now it's 'Mom'? You guys have gotten really close while plotting your secret missions. Easy to see who the favorite child is." Harper threw her hands up and stood, stalking towards the door.

"I don't show favorites among my children or the members of T.R.S. We're all working together to bring peace to our corner of the world. We share that mission. You have to do your part," Anna chided.

Anger exploded from Harper. "I am doing my part. I've done everything you've asked of me without complaint. Have you once sought me out? Asked me about my life, the risks I took to reunite our family? Now I wish I'd never found you."

Harper's arms and wings quivered as emotion thrummed through her. Not just emotion. Notes. A song. A song she didn't dare Sing in that moment because she didn't know what her anger would do.

Quinn and Anna stared at her with stunned expressions, but they said nothing.

Harper spun on her heel, walking to the balcony. She flung open the doors and launched herself into the dark sky, not bothering to glance back.

# CHAPTER FIVE

## TYSON

TYSON WALKED THE FAMILIAR pathway through the physical level of the astral realm, setting his intention to land on the fourth floor where the healing rooms were. He felt fragile after his encounter in the astral realm earlier and wasn't eager to reenter it this soon. Fortunately, inside this pathway that Tyson had created himself, he was protected. Nothing could enter this pathway unless he gave permission.

The ethereal walls gleamed a pale, pearlescent green, pulsing with waves of light. Pride squeezed Tyson's chest; for a man who hated portal travel, he'd come a long way. And he could traverse both the astral and physical planes. He was a dreamwalker, capable of becoming a polar bear and a raven at will, and could heal magically inflicted maladies.

Sometimes, he could hardly believe he was the same person as the hesitant camp counselor from Camp Silver Lake.

Tyson reached the bubble-like end cap of the astral pathway, stepping into the stagnant air of the hallway outside the healing rooms. The doors were open. Tyson stepped into the nearest one.

Two rows of bodies were arranged on the floor, and a third row extended down the middle. A thin blue or tan blanket covered each body up to the neck, leaving their faces exposed. None of the bodies seemed to even be breathing, and the silence in the room reminded Tyson of a tomb, except for the hushed whispering coming from his right.

A large African man, Lethabo, stood beside a shorter, red-headed woman with freckles. She grinned widely when she saw Tyson, her mixed pink and blue aura pulsing around her.

"Tyson Miller, it's good to see you alive."

"Melanie! Er, Jackie?" Tyson said, flustered but thrilled to see the chimera nurse that had helped him in the hospital after he'd injured his head. Interesting that chimeras had two-toned auras.

"Most people call me MJ," MJ said dryly, shaking her head.

"Sorry you got stabbed. I think that was my fault."

"Naw, that bitch Sonia had been on my trail for a while. Luckily some friends were nearby, and they got me out."

"And now you're here. How? We're a long way from where I met you," Tyson said, jamming his hands in his pockets.

"Portal. I requested the transfer. I needed to get out of the public eye for a while. It can be traumatizing working on the front line, and I couldn't take much more of trying to be two separate people."

"That really does sound difficult. Thanks for everything you did for me," Tyson said.

"You found your friends? Everything work out?" MJ asked.

"Not everything. Yet. But it's going pretty well," Tyson said, smiling as Harper came to mind. "You'll have to meet Harper."

"If you like her, I'll like her," Melanie said, a southern accent creeping in that Tyson recognized as the voice she used with Jackie.

Tyson clapped and rubbed his hands together, looking at Leth, noting his healthy yellow aura. "I'm ready. Where do you need me?"

"I am grateful to have another shaman to work with," Leth said. "We have a lot to do."

"I can see that," Tyson said, glancing around the room filled with sleepers. Their auras looked muted, as if the preservation spell they were under dulled their life force. He rested his hands on his hips.

Leth rubbed his hands together. "Where would you like to begin?"

Tyson walked down the rows of bodies, looking into the faces. He didn't expect to recognize anyone, but he figured it would be easier if he felt some sense of connection.

At the end of the second row, he still hadn't felt anything, and he wondered if maybe he should just pick someone. Leth patiently walked beside him. If he felt any rush, he didn't push it on Tyson, simply pausing where Tyson paused, and followed him when he started walking again.

Tyson glanced across the inert bodies to the third row, and his gaze caught on a woman with bright red hair splayed beneath her head. He tilted his head, eyebrows furrowing. Something about her seemed familiar, and his memory flashed back to the image of a fourteen-year-old girl laying on a steel table, seemingly dead.

Could it be...?

Tyson stepped in the space between two bodies, crossing over the rows and walking down towards the woman. He stared into her face, but no other sense of recognition came to him. She looked to be in her early twenties, just like him.

It had to be a coincidence, and yet, he couldn't shake the feeling that he knew her.

"I'll start with her," Tyson said, settling on the floor in a cross-legged position.

Leth joined him on the floor, nodding towards the woman on the floor. "Her soul must be called back to her body. There is a tether connecting the two. Find it, follow it, convince her soul to return. Defend it if necessary." Leth's dark brown eyes glittered fiercely.

Tyson swallowed past a sudden lump. "Defend it?"

A golden light flashed in the depths of Leth's gaze. He snorted. "The chiwanda will be drawn to your life force and hers. In English, you call them demons—beings with the lowest vibrations and energy sent to suck the life force from beings with living essence. Like our friend here. Surely you have experience with them in your dreamwalking?"

Tyson thought of the terrifying being that had impersonated Ewu and dragged Tyson down to the Mental plane. He shuddered.

Leth eyed him, as if he was suddenly unsure whether Tyson measured up to some standard he held.

Tyson straightened. "I can make an energetic weapon. I just learned how."

"Then you know that you must have absolute faith in it in order to strike an energetic being. And you know that chiwanda cannot die like beings of flesh and blood." Leth's mouth widened, revealing two rows of brilliant white teeth. "They cannot die, they can only be banished. You, on the other hand, can die, my friend. Even in the astral realm. If they drain your living essence, your body will perish."

Tyson tightened his lips and breathed deeply. "I understand. And I'm ready. Find the tether, follow it, bring the spirit back."

He clenched his fists, trying to keep from shuddering again. He'd have to enter the astral realm. What if Todd didn't respond again? What if Tyson was taken back to the Mental Plane where that lower vibrational being waited to feast on his life-force?

Leth jutted his chin at the unconscious black-haired man. "And make sure you have the right spirit, lest another try to trick you to get into this body."

Tyson blew out forcefully. "Anything else?"

Leth clapped him on the shoulder. "You will do great. I would go with you, but we need as many of us working at a time as we can. If you need me, call for me in your mind. I will try to answer, but the astral realm is not linear. We may not be in the same place, and I may not hear you."

"Got it." Tyson rubbed his hands together and bounced in place, hyping himself up. He could do this.

After some thought, Tyson stretched out on the thin, scratchy carpet. He still felt off after his last walk through the astral realm, and he didn't want to fall over while dreamwalking.

He breathed deeply, losing himself in the rhythm of it. His right hand drifted to the *ulu* knife on his belt. He didn't need it to cross into the astral realm, but he'd found that it helped, especially when a violent tingling sensation took over his limbs. They fell asleep, and he imagined he was getting buried in a deep hole, suffocating.

The *ulu* knife burned against his thigh, and a glowing, orange symbol flashed before his eyes, vanishing before he could get a good look at it. He hadn't seen it before. Then again, he was still new to all of this.

His consciousness drifted towards sleep, and just when he thought he'd succumb and take an unintended nap, the familiar zipper appeared in the air, and he leaned forward, his soul swooping straight out of his body.

Tyson stared down at himself for a moment, the elation at his success fleeting. He glanced around to get his bearings.

The breath-taking view he normally saw on the physical plane of the astral realm appeared dark and murky now. Sepia and gray tones covered the ground, the dead trees, even the sky, and the horizon stretched on in an endless and depressing eternity.

*Where am I?* It didn't feel like the physical plane, either. Then again, he'd set out with the intention to find the soul of the woman that his body lay next to. What if that woman's soul had been consumed by a lower vibrational being? What if her tether led Tyson to the lowest abyss?

Tyson's skin crawled. Not really, since he didn't have a physical form there, but a sensation like it seemed to consume him, and fear rose up in his chest.

A golden strand of energy, thin as a spider's silk, lit up and spun from his chest into the ether beyond. Tyson immediately relaxed, fear bleeding from his mind. That golden strand pointed to Harper, connecting them somehow.

He didn't know exactly how it worked, but he'd used it to find her when her soul was trapped, and her body was possessed by Lilith's dark magic. It comforted him to know that if he lost his way in the astral realm, he could use it to return to her.

Tyson visualized the woman with her high, thin cheekbones, reddish-orange hair, the curve of her chin, the shape of her head. Tyson didn't know anything else about her, but on the off chance he was right, he added his memory of the girl on the steel table, the same girl he'd known at age ten, the one who had trusted him and shown him she could take the form of a fox.

The one he had unknowingly betrayed.

A faint, flickering blue line lit up through the gray mist covering the wasteland in front of him.

That had to be the tether. A thrill rushed through Tyson, and a great, rushing wind pushed against his back, sending his soul rushing through the air in the direction the tether stretched.

Tyson panicked at the otherworldly intervention, then remembered that his emotions had a greater impact in the astral realm, and he needed to tighten the reins on them. He neutralized his thoughts and slowed to a swift glide above the ground. He didn't even have to move his legs, only concentrate on that tether and not get distracted.

The line wasn't straight, not like the golden one connecting to Harper, which followed him wherever he went. This line curved and twisted around rock features and dead trees, like a trail of vines. Every so often, it glowed brighter for a moment, pulsing with life, then it became dull and nearly invisible.

Tyson had to pause to make sure he still followed the same line every time it nearly vanished. The wind that had urged him along before died down to nothing, and despite attempts to will his spirit form back into the air, he trudged on the ground, mist swirling around his legs. The bleak landscape hung around Tyson, unchanging.

He would never find this soul here. Nothing existed here except the color gray.

A desperate cry split the aether.

Tyson startled, then launched himself into a sprint. A new energy coursed through his astral form, lifting his feet off the ground and speeding him forward. He drew the *ulu* knife, the handle fitting his hand like it had been made for him.

He rounded a cluster of dark rocks and caught sight of a terrified person with wide eyes cringing against the back of a shallow cave.

"L-L-Look out!" The black-haired man shouted.

The sound of a weapon whistling through the air drew Tyson's attention, and he spun around as an ax stopped a breath away from his skull.

Todd blinked in surprise, his fox head tilting as he stared at Tyson. "What are you doing here?"

"I thought you were supposed to know when I entered the astral realm. Where have you been?" Tyson asked. "And why are you attacking this man?"

"That is no man," Todd growled, shoving Tyson aside.

Tyson whirled around, confusion and shock coursing through him and making it difficult to move, like he was wading through thick mud. He needed to clear his mind.

The man cowering against the rock started to chuckle, and his human-like body shredded as tentacles erupted and he changed forms.

One of the tentacles shot towards Tyson, and he tried to move out of the way, but too late. The tentacle wrapped around Tyson, pulling him into the air.

The creature deafened him with an ear-splitting shriek. His ears rang. The beast charged forward, holding Tyson aloft. Swung upside down and racing over the ground at highway speeds, Tyson saw the flash of orange again.

At least Todd was here.

Tyson tried to summon an energetic weapon like Ewu had taught him, but all he managed was a shower of sparks. He concentrated, but getting flung around didn't help much.

Todd launched into the air with a yell, and the monstrosity reared back, spitting a purple substance at Todd just as his ax flew through the air and struck the monster with a squelchy-sounding thud. The creature slammed to the ground, its tentacles releasing Tyson mid-air.

Tyson struck the ground hard enough to rattle his entire being. He sat up with a groan, and the blue flickering soul tether brightened at the edge of his vision. The soul he sought was close.

He focused, following the tether to where it ended.

Right in Todd's back as he plunged his ax into the creature again, splitting its skull with a spray of purple blood-like substance.

Something wasn't right. Tyson's gut told him this was an illusion of some kind.

He looked closer, tuning into his aura vision, striving to see the true form beneath the illusion he sensed. The aura around Todd darkened, and his form flickered. He tossed his head back, and the fur on his head became hair, long, curly woman's hair. Todd's muzzle shrank, forming the same high cheekbones, the same heart-shaped face Tyson had seen on the floor of the healing room of the Tower.

"You're not my spirit guide," Tyson said. "Who are you?"

The woman's face was covered in a splattering of the creature's purple blood, obscuring half of her freckles and coating her hair. She dragged two clumping strands apart and made a disgusted face. With a swipe of her hand, the blood disappeared, and she tossed her hair over her shoulder.

"What? Never seen a girl before?" She dropped her hair and stood, dragging the ax off the ground. It shrank a bit, and she rested it on her shoulder.

The red-haired woman seemed familiar, and a memory tickled the back of his brain. Where had he seen her before?

"How is this possible? I thought spirit guides held one shape," Tyson said, confusion making his own aura pulse green.

"They do. Unless they're dead, and someone has taken their place." The woman grinned, leaning forward on her ax. "Come on, remember me. It's no fun unless you remember whose life you destroyed."

Her face and tone darkened, and Tyson drifted back from her, reaching for that sense of familiarity that whispered in the back of his mind. He knew this woman. He did.

"Are you Todd? Have you always...been my spirit guide?" Tyson asked, mind spinning as it scrambled to put the pieces together.

The woman's face twisted in disgust. "No, I consumed your spirit guide and took his place."

"But...why?" Tyson asked, shock filling him. She had *consumed* Todd? Like, his essence? His life-force? How long had she taken his form?

Her lips lifted in a snarl. "Maybe it was too much for me to expect of someone like you to remember me. It was, after all, more than ten years ago that you destroyed my life and murdered my family."

Tyson didn't have time to internalize the horrifying truth of what she'd said as she crouched in front of him and reached her intangible hand into his chest, yanking somehow on the line that tethered Tyson back to his body on the physical plane.

Tyson screamed at the burning that erupted and threatened to tear him apart. It rattled him, inside and out. A wall of darkness crashed over him like a wave.

His spirit surged into his body, then hit a wall and bounced out. He tried again, straining to escape the darkness that held onto him like glue. It stretched him thin, trying to tire him out, to make him give up, but he took the knife from his belt and sliced backward, severing the unnatural bond that held him in that dark plane.

He came gasping to life in his body and immediately became aware of hands clamped around his throat, cutting off his air supply. He grabbed at them, but the fingers were locked in place.

The woman crushing his esophagus sat up in the bed, her hair askew and her face twisted in an expression of pure, terrifying rage.

# CHAPTER SIX

## HARPER

HARPER WHEELED TWO IV poles down the hall, walking as fast as she could with her wings tucked against her back. Orders for more blood had come from the healing rooms, where paranormals were being woken from the Hundred Year Sleep Violet had put them into years ago.

Apparently, a fair number of them were vampires, and they were thirsty.

She ignored the slight itch at the base of her feathers. It seemed to have spread since the day before, and despite cleaning her wings thoroughly, she hadn't been able to figure out the cause.

She tried to get her mind off the discomfort as she passed Quinn, who nodded, but seemed focused. He'd volunteered to help with transporting blood for the vamps, and she was grateful. Double kitchen duty sucked.

But at least she had a chance to see Tyson, since he was working in the healing rooms.

Harper picked up her pace, wondering if Tyson would be working in the room she was headed for. She checked the room numbers, scanning the open doors for him.

Shouts echoed down the hall ahead of her, urgent, terrified.

Harper rolled the poles faster, pushing them into the room the shouts were coming from, taking in the scene in an instant.

A woman with red hair gripped Tyson by the throat. His face was reddish purple, his mouth wide and gasping for air. She was strangling him.

Harper launched herself across the room, spreading her wings to act as a glider as she jumped over the middle row of unconscious people lying on the floor.

Harper landed on one knee and leaned forward, grabbing the woman around her middle and pulling her back. The woman kicked and screamed, throwing her head back. Harper dodged, barely avoiding getting her nose bashed in.

"Calm…down, lady!" Harper shouted. The woman was slightly bigger than her, but Harper had a smidge of supernatural strength on her side. It worked until the woman jammed her elbow into Harper's ribs, and she folded, releasing the madwoman, who lunged for Tyson again.

Her human form shifted in a blur of orange, and a fox darted out from where the woman had crouched. She snapped at Tyson, growling from deep in her throat.

Tyson yelled and tripped over the legs of the unconscious person behind him. He had nowhere to go. He frantically formed a symbol in the air, one that Harper vaguely recognized as a healing symbol, but it *bounced* off the vixen and disintegrated.

Tyson's eyes widened in panic. His magic didn't seem to be working.

The vixen paced in front of him, black lips curled viciously back, revealing glistening fangs.

Pushing through the sharp pain in her side, Harper opened her mouth and Sang. The notes drifted over the occupants of the room, and despite her intention to direct the sleep-song only at the crazed woman, Harper realized others were dozing off. Too much. She always put too much into the Songs.

The fox staggered to the side, panting and blinking slowly.

The totem hanging from Harper's neck warmed against her chest. The fox stumbled. Tyson blinked, then disappeared. He must have dreamwalked into the place where he traveled between worlds.

Harper's tune trailed off with a final pealing high note, and the vixen circled once, twice, three times before tucking her face into the tip of her tail and falling fast asleep.

The room fell silent. Harper dragged herself upright, wincing at the ache in her ribs. That woman had come out from her astral slumber fighting, but why?

She glanced around the room. Both Leth and the other attendant, an apparently human woman, plus the vampire they'd already woken, were snoring where they sat. She rubbed the back of her head and flushed, grateful no one was awake to see her mistake.

The hairs on the back of Harper's neck rose, and she turned as Tyson emerged from thin air, hair blowing back in some ethereal wind she couldn't feel.

"Thank you," Tyson said, voice hoarse. He rubbed the front of his throat.

"We need more people working on this with you if they're going to go insane," Harper said, eyeing the sleeping fox again.

"I don't think they'll all be like her," Tyson said, sitting back on his heels.

There was more to this situation than Tyson had let on. Harper waited for the explanation, her breath hitching.

Tyson turned his glistening eyes towards Harper, and when he spoke his voice had tightened. "I knew her. No, damnit." He closed his eyes for a long moment. "I turned her and her family in a long time ago."

Harper blinked. A roaring filled her ears. He knew people called on their neighbors, their friends, even their family. Hell, some turned themselves in. But Harper had never met someone who admitted it.

She forced herself to think past her gut reaction, which was to yell at him and run. She'd changed. Tyson had changed, too. He wasn't the camp counselor anymore.

Fletcher's face flashed into Harper's mind, and her gut clenched. She squeezed her hands tight, nails digging into her palms. A thousand feelings tore through her at once, and it took all of her self-control to breathe in and out instead of rage.

She'd learned to trust Tyson, that he wasn't always what he seemed on the surface. He'd changed.

Tyson dragged his hands through his hair. "I know what you're probably thinking. It sounds pretty bad when I say it that way, but it's true. I was a scared kid, and they told me my friend needed the government's help. I didn't know what they'd do to her, that they'd take everything from her."

A sort of orange glow surrounded Tyson, coming from the knife hung from his belt. Tyson didn't seem to notice the magic, but he noticed Harper's shock. Tyson furrowed his brow, his lips tightening into a thin line.

"Harper?"

"I-I'm okay. It's okay," Harper said, licking her lips. She cleared her throat. "It was a long time ago. I know...I know you're not like that, now."

Tyson nodded, hands dropping into his lap as he eyed the sleeping fox. "I would never do it now, knowing what I do. Knowing the truth."

Anger melted inside Harper, replaced with a warm sensation that flooded her throat, choking away any words she might have said.

Tyson had changed. For everyone he'd ever wronged, for everyone he'd thought he was helping as a counselor at Camp Silver Lake. For this fox shifter, for himself. For Harper.

"How long will they sleep?" Tyson asked, looking around. He didn't seem like himself, but she didn't blame him. Getting strangled by someone from his past...that would put anyone off.

"Could be hours. I'm not..." Harper sighed. "I didn't mean to put them all under. Just her." She jutted her thumb towards the fox shifter.

Tyson gave her a look of stunned awe. "You put all of them to sleep by yourself? Is that normal?"

"Most ravens can control their Songs better," Harper muttered, scuffing her shoe on the carpet. "I'll go find someone to wake them up. If I do it, everyone in the building might wake up."

"Those on night shift won't like that," Tyson said, chuckling, his voice still scratchy. He swallowed hard. "I just need Leth and MJ awake."

Harper moved towards the poles she'd left standing near the door. "I've got to deliver these first. Will you be okay here by yourself?"

Tyson scratched his eyebrow, then gestured. "I'll try not to get mauled by a sleeping fox while you're gone."

Harper opened her mouth, then closed it again. She hadn't meant for it to sound like he couldn't take care of himself. The words had just come out.

Tyson seemed to sense her concern and waved it away. "Go. I'll be fine."

Harper dropped the IV poles off in an adjacent room. Fortunately, she ran into a group of bird shifters at the end of the hall, and among them she found Kallick, another raven shifter. He stood a whole head and a half taller than Harper. She explained what had happened, and he wasted no time following her to the room where Tyson waited.

"I'll show you what to do this time, but you should practice more with the primary tunes so you don't inadvertently murder an entire battlefield," Kallick said, his expression stern.

Harper bobbed her head. "I understand. I'll be sure to practice more."

Tyson stopped pacing at the back of the room as they entered, watching as Kallick Sang Leth and MJ back to consciousness.

Harper heard the notes that had fallen flat in her own song, the ones that directed the Song more accurately, that didn't allow the magic to escape on either side. She ran over them in her head, determined she'd do it right next time.

Leth woke with a start. "Why was I asleep? Is everyone all right?"

MJ put a hand on her chest and took several deep breaths. "I'm fine. Tyson? Oh!" She exclaimed, noticing Kallick beside her. She tucked a hair behind her ear and visibly swooned at the tall native raven shifter.

Tyson stepped up to the group. "I woke one of Violet's sleepers, and she turned out to be someone I knew-someone I turned in-a long time ago. Her name is Reya. Four years at the hands of the government and at least six more years in the astral realm gave her plenty of time to nurse a grudge."

Leth frowned, but nodded, standing up out of the chair. "I assume that little fox over there is the one responsible for attacking you?"

"Yes," Harper said before Tyson could speak, irritation prickling against her forehead. "She shouldn't be woken up with Tyson in the room. And another healer should work with her."

MJ stood straight. "I'll go get Bunny. She's an absolute dear. They had her working in the room a few doors down, I think. Come with me, Tyson. You can take her spot in the other room."

Tyson looked like he wanted to argue, but wisely, he didn't, following MJ out of the room with a final glance over his shoulder before he disappeared through the doorway.

Harper gazed at the sleeping fox on the ground. After hearing Tyson's side, her hatred was clearly justified, and yet Harper was convinced Tyson had changed. It would take time for the fox to see that, if she ever did.

"Ready?" Leth said, startling Harper from her thoughts.

Bunny, a thin blond woman, had arrived. She jumped when Leth spoke, then laughed nervously. Her nose actually twitched, and her name suddenly made sense.

Harper took her hands out of her pockets, shaking the tension from her wings, and moved closer to where the fox still slept.

Leth joined her on the opposite side, another layer of security in case Reya got violent again.

"Don't crowd her, but don't let her hurt anyone else," Leth cautioned.

"Maybe we should take her somewhere else for this?" Harper suggested.

Bunny interjected. "No, she could wake up during the transfer." She crouched on the ground in a sort of child's pose. A moment later, her head drooped to the floor, and a strange humming sound vibrated from her body.

Harper shifted her weight, wary of what would happen when the fox shifter woke. To her surprise and relief, there was no sudden explosion of violence, no screaming or kicking.

The fox blinked and lifted its head, then stretched its body and yawned similar to the way a cat would.

It was too cute, really. Hard to believe the fox was a woman. Until it turned its amber eyes on Harper, and she saw the fury smoldering inside.

The eyes stayed the same as the fox became a woman. Bunny draped a blanket over her bare shoulders.

A shudder ran through Harper, making her feathers quiver, and the aggravating itching sensation started up again.

Reya's eyes burned with a deep hatred. Not for Harper, but for anyone that would stand in the way of her revenge.

Harper flared her wings, making herself look more intimidating, and the fox shifter blinked a few times, as if confused. Harper crossed her arms over her chest and glared.

The woman had another thing coming if she thought she could take her revenge on Tyson with Harper around.

# CHAPTER SEVEN

## MANDI

MANDI WATCHED ZEKE WALK out of the cafeteria through filtered eyes, the demon's darkness obscuring her full view, as usual, but it was a view she never thought she'd have, blurred and somewhat distorted as it was.

Behind her eyes, she was haunted by a gruesome vision of Zeke's blood-soaked body laying prostrate, his arms and legs bound to a metal table, everything that should have been inside him exposed through cut skin and a broken rib cage.

*You'll never have him,* Mandi raged at the demon hiding in her soul, shoving the strongest parts of her consciousness up against the darkness, trying to corner it and gain some control over her body.

*In time, I'll have them all,* Ragranoth said. *And once my consort joins me and I give him the body of your lover for his own, we will reign over this pathetic floating rock. Turn it into something truly glorious and terrible. You could join me, you know. With your will combined with mine, we could do great things.*

*Never,* Mandi replied. To anyone looking at her, she would appear lost in thought, her fork halfway to her mouth, a blank stare on her face.

*Very well. Then I will crush you into oblivion.*

Mandi nearly vanished, then. She nearly gave into the waves of darkness that beat on the shores of her soul, but she saw Zeke in her mind's eye, all the parts of him that her body knew. The way his fur felt against her fingers when he was in his wolf form. The warmth of him as he lay next to her. His lips against hers.

And now, the new sense that had opened to her, the one that had always remained empty and dark, filled with the soulful, golden brown of his eyes, the way his mouth quirked up on one side when he smiled at her, his strong, broad frame.

Lilith's foolish summoning had given her this, at least. And it was those images that made her hold on when she wanted to give in and fall into the oblivion Ragranoth offered.

Something had gone horribly wrong when Mandi broke the ritual meant to summon Ragranoth. She'd done it too late, and the summoned demon had surged into her body.

Mandi hadn't noticed at first, relishing in her newfound sight, which brought more challenges with it than she'd expected, from learning to read to the agonizing headaches that pounded in her head each night, to the fatigue that wore at her eyes as she strained muscles she'd rarely used to move her eyes and see.

And then the headaches had become constant, and Ragranoth had revealed herself, commanding Mandi to act as if nothing had happened, to tell no one of the demon inside of her.

She shuddered to think of the threats Ragranoth plied her with, sending her vivid, tortured dreams where she watched as demons gutted Zeke, peeled off his skin, took out his organs one by one, and tortured him—like the one she was seeing now. In many of them, Mandi herself performed the torturing. All the visions ended with Zeke recognizing that the woman he loved—the one he'd chosen to be his pack in place of the family that had displaced him—was the one causing him unimaginable pain.

As the days wore on, Mandi resigned herself to merely holding on, her existence the only rebellion she could manage other than the times when the curtains of her mind parted. When Zeke was kissing her.

The Demon in Mandi's head hated it when she kissed Zeke. Ragranoth, Autarch of the Lowest Abyss allowed it only because the time had not yet come to take complete control, and the demon needed Mandi to avoid arousing suspicion. So, she allowed the kissing, allowed Mandi moments to be herself, so long as she behaved, so long as she didn't attempt to reveal the demon in her soul.

Selfishly, Mandi basked in the stolen moments of peace when the demon quieted, watching, waiting for her time to arrive. Mandi didn't know what lay in store, she only knew it couldn't be good for her or the rebellion, but threats of taking Zeke's life kept her from taking any meaningful action.

Mandi knew the day was swiftly arriving when she would no longer be able to hold Ragranoth back from killing the love of her life. She had decided that tonight would be the night she told him.

She sat on her bed, forcing her conscious thoughts to be as blank as possible. Ragranoth could hear her thoughts much of the time, but Mandi had discovered that the demon had to be listening. As long as Mandi kept her thoughts in check most of the time, Ragranoth wouldn't catch her thinking such rebellious thoughts.

If she did, no doubt the demon would make good on the threats in those vivid, nightmarish visions she sent.

At 7:00 p.m., Ragranoth's presence flooded her mind, tendrils of darkness seeping through and tainting everything they touched.

Mandi forced herself to stay sitting, wishing she'd gone slower getting ready, wishing she had an excuse for delaying other than the fact that she was trying to get Zeke to notice on his own, trying to help him see that something was off. The less she acted like herself tonight, the easier it would be for him to kill her and destroy the vessel the demon needed to exist on the physical plane.

She held out for twenty minutes, until Ragranoth sent her a vision so horrific, Mandi almost ran screaming from the room. But she couldn't push the demon any further. The demon could control her limbs, had proved it on several occasions, and Mandi didn't want tonight to come to that, not until the last possible moment.

In the elevator, two friends talked and laughed about their plans for the evening. One of them waved to Mandi as they left, and Mandi lifted her arm half-heartedly. She didn't even know the girl's name. She hardly had space in her brain for remembering.

Through the filter of the sunglasses she was forced to wear, plus the blurring and shifting of her new vision, Mandi watched the elevator doors open on the first floor and stepped out into a shifting sea of people. The rebellion had grown, and dozens arrived every day. Soon the tower would be full.

*Soon they'll all be mine,* the demon in her mind projected.

Something nudged Mandi's arm, and she jumped, even though it was just Zeke. He hadn't surprised her—he'd touched her that way when she'd been blind, and it felt as familiar as blinking. But she wanted him to feel like something was off, wanted him to suspect something was wrong with her.

"Sorry," Zeke said, offering his arm. "Shall we?"

Ragranoth roiled in the back of Mandi's mind, watching her every move. When she didn't immediately reach for Zeke's arm, the demon's awareness grew stronger, impressing on Mandi's, urging her to act normal or there would be consequences.

Mandi reluctantly took Zeke's arm. "Is it very far, where we're going?"

"Not too far. But don't worry, I got us some transportation." They walked out the front of the Tower to where a fancy blue car idled on the street. A nice car for the current state of the world. Zeke had to have pulled quite a few strings to get a car this fancy.

A large man squeezed his way out of the car and fast-walked to open the back passenger-side door for them.

"Hey, Will," Zeke said. "Thanks for doing this."

Mandi forced a smile on her face. *Look normal. Act normal.* She had to maintain the charade a bit longer.

At least when she told him the truth on this date, no one else would be around to witness what Zeke would have to do. No one else would get hurt. No one but her.

"No problemo," Will said, grinning back. He wiped his hand on his pants, then gestured for them to get inside the car.

It smelled of french fries and cheap coffee, and the cloth seats had some sort of film on them that made Mandi want to wash her hands after touching them. Zeke slid in beside her, the narrow middle seat between them.

Will got back in the car, huffing a bit, and fiddled with the phone he had connected to the car stereo system, shuffling through a playlist. Blaring saxophone music filled the car.

Zeke whimpered beside her, holding his hands over his ears. "Could you turn it down a bit?" he shouted, glancing at Mandi.

Ragranoth didn't like the romantic music, which made Mandi not mind it so much, even if her sensitive ears were getting blasted.

"Sorry!" Will said, nudging the volume button.

Zeke picked up Mandi's hand. She rested it heavily in his, not grasping, not stroking, as if she wasn't interested at all. It felt like betrayal to not respond to him when every cell in her body wanted her to lean into it, to scoot closer, lay her head on his shoulder, to kiss him.

She resisted. It would be easier if she didn't, she told herself.

He glanced over at her several times, his thumb still stroking rhythmically across her hand, but if he thought something was wrong, he didn't ask.

She needed him to not ask. Not yet. Ragranoth still seemed to think everything was fine, that Mandi was acting as she should. The demon knew little about human courtship and social rules. The only way she could tell if Mandi was acting strange was if the people around her reacted.

The car ride was short, only ten minutes to a local park. Zeke climbed out of the car and helped Mandi through her door, and Mandi froze, too stunned to act like she didn't care.

Twinkling lights wove around rose bushes, making the last of the bloomed flowers glow, and she could make out the flickering candlelight in the pavilion where dozens of candles had been set up on the ground and hung from the pavilion itself.

"You-you did this all yourself?" Mandi asked breathlessly, resting her arm in his and letting him lead her down the glowing pathway.

"I had some help. A few friends from the T.R.S. helped me make it extra special. Otherwise, we'd be sitting on that concrete slab surrounded by dead flowers in the dark." He chuckled.

Mandi licked her lips and swallowed. She wished more than ever that she'd never agreed to be part of Lilith's coven, that she'd never stepped into that circle, even if it meant that she never could gaze into Zeke's handsome face like this.

"Is something wrong?" Zeke asked.

Mandi wiped at the dampness in her eyes. "It's just...thank you."

She wished she could enjoy it more, but all she could think was how she was about to ruin this night and this beautiful place with her request.

A small round table in the pavilion held two plates loaded up with food, along with drinks and everything needed to enjoy a meal.

Zeke pulled Mandi's chair out for her, and she sat, Zeke taking the chair opposite her. He rested his hand on the table, palm up, inviting her to put her hand in his.

She folded her hands into her lap and tilted her head down towards the table.

"I kept the lighting dim. I hoped you'd be able to take off your glasses," Zeke said.

Mandi reached for them, but Ragranoth stopped her hands.

*Leave them on*, the demon hissed. *He'll see my presence.*

Mandi hesitated, straining for just a moment before dropping her hand back into her lap.

"I can't," she said, speaking as much of the truth as she could manage.

The moment had arrived. She'd hoped to at least enjoy one last evening with him, to tell him she loved him before she asked him to do something so terrible, she knew she'd never manage it herself. But looking around at how much effort he'd put into this date, seeing the care and concern in his eyes, Mandi knew if she didn't say it now, it might be too late before the next time she'd gotten up the courage.

"Maybe you should see a doctor, then. I'm sure we can find one—"

"No!" she said loudly. "I'll get used to it."

"All right," Zeke agreed. "No doctor. But tonight…are you mad? Did I say or do something wrong?"

"No," Mandi said desperately, biting her lip. He was so close. She just had to open her mouth and tell him that yes, she was mad. He hadn't done anything wrong, she had. Her selfish actions had led to a demon entering her body, and she was furious and terrified, and he needed to kill her.

"Are you upset? Grieving? A lot has happened, losing your coven, joining the rebellion—"

"No!" she said, shouting this time. The word died in the still night air, seeming to echo down the streets. Why couldn't she say what she needed to? Her tongue seemed petrified, and yet she didn't sense Ragranoth behind it. She was stopping herself.

Mandi reached out and grabbed Zeke's hand, holding it as if it were a lifeline and she was a drowning person. She was drowning. Drowning in darkness.

Tears slipped down her face.

"Do you want to talk about it?" Zeke asked, in a voice so soft and tender, Mandi felt her heart break.

"No," she said again, choking on the word, hating herself for it.

Zeke pulled his hand back from hers, unwrapping his silverware from the cloth napkin holding them, then cleared his throat. "Are you hungry? I got us some chicken."

"Not hungry," Mandi said, her hands clenched in her lap. She stared down at the plate of food, then slowly looked up. "There's something...important I need to tell you."

"Okay," Zeke said, setting down his fork and putting his face in his hands, focusing intently on her.

Mandi closed her eyes for a moment, gathering her strength. Ragranoth had drifted away slightly, hadn't noticed Mandi's distress, but how long until the demon returned and choked Mandi out for her disobedience? If Mandi failed, would this be enough to trigger the demon's promise to torture Zeke?

"Would you do anything for me?" Mandi asked.

"If there's something you need, you just have to ask," Zeke said reassuringly. His eyebrows furrowed, and his head tilted. "What is it?"

Mandi took a deep breath in. "Zeke, there's a—" her throat closed off, and she choked, coughing. Ragranoth surged into the forefront of her mind, seething with fury.

*Did you think I wasn't paying attention?* The demon screamed. *It is you who have damned him.*

Mandi's head shook, the movement directed by Ragranoth. A smile pulled at the corners of her mouth. Words spilled out of her mouth, untrue, insincere, inadequate.

"Sit down. I'm sorry, I didn't mean to ruin our night. The food looks tasty." Mandi trembled as she pushed against the demon's control, trying to take back her vocal cords, her mouth, her face. Nausea roiled in her stomach. The demon could make her say anything, do anything. What if she acted out one of the torture scenes the demon had sent her?

Zeke straightened and picked up his fork. "If you say so. I'm here if you need to talk, you know that, right?"

"Of course," Mandi's mouth moved, her own voice betraying her.

Her hand closed around the sharp knife next to her plate, while inside of her mind, she screamed for him to run.

# CHAPTER EIGHT

## ZEKE

ZEKE WATCHED MANDI'S EXPRESSION carefully. She had been upset to the point of being distraught, acting as if each of his well-meaning questions was a kind of torture. She'd flinched away from him, hardly smiled, hadn't flirted. Her only normal reaction of the evening had been when they got out of the car, and then she'd seemed to shut down.

He didn't know what to make of it. The evening hadn't gone at all to plan. If it had, they might have finished their meal, teasing back and forth about the food, about this or that happening back at the Tower, trading stories from before they knew one another.

After dinner they might have danced. Zeke had a decent voice, he would sing a song they could waltz to, and he would spin her around under the stars until it got too cold and Mandi started to shiver. He would hold her in his arms a bit longer until the candle flames sputtered as they touched the melted wax pooling at the top. And he would ask her to come with him to work for Jake, to stay with him. Maybe even to marry him.

But not tonight. Because tonight, he wasn't sitting across from Mandi.

He stood and in a rude, rash move, yanked the sunglasses off her face.

Mandi gasped, surprise turning to rage as her amber eyes sparked with anger.

"How dare you!" she shouted, her voice far more guttural and furious than he'd ever heard it.

He didn't reply, too busy staring at her eyes. They had changed. The dark splotches were gone, as was the roundness of her pupil. Instead, an hourglass shape had formed in the center, black and unnerving in its otherness.

He dropped the sunglasses on the table and reeled backward, stumbling on the uneven cobblestones beneath his feet.

Mandi recovered her sunglasses, placing them back on her face, then cocked her head. "What is it?" Her voice had returned to normal.

He could have imagined it, couldn't he? He tried to level his breathing. He glanced around, looking for the shifter friends he'd asked to stick around for protection, trying to make eye contact, to signal them without letting whatever had possessed Mandi know what he was doing.

*Pull yourself together*, Zeke told himself. He closed his eyes and breathed deep.

"Sorry, I shouldn't have done that."

"No, you shouldn't have," the thing inside Mandi said. And it grinned, spreading Mandi's face too wide. "Because now I have to kill you."

She held the sharp knife meant for cutting chicken high in the air and shouted something that sounded like Latin.

Zeke didn't wait for her to finish. He ripped off his belt and shifted, letting his wolf form explode through his t-shirt and jeans. He couldn't attack—it was still Mandi in there, no matter what sort of being had presented itself in her stead.

He howled as he fled, signaling to anyone still around that they should run.

He ran for Will's car, but when he got there, it was empty. Glancing around frantically, Zeke saw the body sprawled face-down on the pavement.

It was a trap. Somehow, his date with Mandi had been a trap. And whoever was behind it had killed Will and would kill him.

He took off running as fast as he could, still in wolf form, headed for the Tower so he could warn the rebellion that some kind of monster had stolen his girlfriend's body.

And there might be more of them.

# CHAPTER NINE

## TYSON

FOOD. TYSON NEEDED FOOD. His stomach clenched in response to the thought. He hadn't had much appetite since the events with Reya the day before, but he'd promised Harper he'd meet her for lunch.

He forced himself to walk to the lead nurse at the front of the room to request a break. She smiled and nodded, handing him the checkout chart.

Tyson signed his name, then handed the chart back and glanced around the room. He'd woken six people that morning. All of them had been confused, and all of them had complained of headaches. One had cried, and one had claimed a sort of amnesia.

None of them had tried to strangle him.

Tyson stepped from the relative calm of the healing room to a sea of auras and emotions as he entered the stream of people heading down to the cafeterias. He still couldn't believe Reya had consumed his spirit guide and impersonated him. He hadn't even known that was possible. How long had she taken Todd's form without him knowing? He'd never guessed something was off about Todd, except he seemed crueler than Tyson had expected of a spirit guide. Harsher. Had it always been Reya? But then why help him at all? Why not kill him then?

Unless some part of her had hesitated before?

Tyson rounded the corner and was immediately overwhelmed. After a morning spent around magically brain-dead individuals, whose auras were dim or nearly non-existent and their projected emotions even dimmer, the flood of auras in the cafeteria caught him off guard, and he staggered to the wall for support as he put his protections back up.

The auras around him dimmed, and the bombardment of emotions lessened. He tugged on his t-shirt to straighten it and hiked up his cargo pants.

Harper waited for him outside the cafeteria doors. She had her wings folded against her back—she hadn't drawn them inside since arriving here, which made sense given that she didn't need to hide anymore.

Admiring Harper was a good distraction from his distressing thoughts about Reya. The crowd moved around Tyson as he took a moment to calm his emotions.

Harper leaned against the wall in a black racerback tank top and jeans, her short black hair curling under her chin.

She almost never looked relaxed, and this might be the closest he'd ever seen her come...except for the rooftop the night before, when he'd stroked her feathers and could have sworn her eyes actually closed.

He'd felt something through their bond, a sort of comfortable acceptance from her, and then stronger feelings had pulsed through, and despite the fact that she'd pulled away from his attempt to kiss her, he knew her feelings went deeper. Stronger.

She didn't seem ready to face them yet, and Tyson wasn't sure how long he could wait. He wanted to say he could wait as long as it took, but what if she was hesitant because she didn't know what to do? He didn't think she had much experience with romantic relationships. What if all he needed to do was make his move with more confidence, show her what she was missing?

Just like his magic, he needed to take initiative and not be afraid of the potential consequences.

Her eyes scanned the crowd almost lazily, watching passersby, then her gaze landed on him and a smile touched her lips.

Tyson's heart skipped a beat. He swallowed and walked over.

Unfolding her wings slightly, she raised a hand to greet him. "Hey."

"Hey yourself," he said, catching her hand in his and pulling her close for a hug.

Harper squirmed against his arms. "What is this for?"

Tyson squeezed her a little tighter, willing her to relax, to let him embrace her. He wanted to nuzzle in her neck and breathe in her unique dusty sunshine smell, but she seemed to have reached her max for public affection. So far, initiation wasn't working the way he'd hoped.

"You've been sorta...touchy-feely lately," Harper noted, looping her arm through his as they entered the cafeteria.

Tyson chuckled. "One of these days, when we're not fighting a political or literal war, I'm going to sit you down in a dark room and do nothing but cuddle with you. No talking allowed. No crises. Just you, me, and maybe a movie." From what he knew of her life before he'd come into it, she hadn't been touched nearly enough. Did he need to move slower? He could curb his own desires for her comfort.

The witty comeback Tyson expected from Harper didn't come, and she stayed quiet until they joined the line to get food.

"I think movie night was my favorite part of Camp Silver Lake," she said quietly.

She never talked about what had happened there. She didn't talk about her feelings in general. Tyson recognized the trust she showed in him just sharing that small tidbit.

"What did you like about it?" Tyson tried, knowing she might not say, but he hoped...

The cafeteria line moved forward several paces, and Tyson bridged the gap.

Harper moved with him, hands in her pockets. "My last placement before I ran away was a group home. We had a movie night once a month, and I guess it felt like that. It didn't matter that I was some angry girl with no family or friends. On movie night, no one could see you, no one made fun of you. We existed in the same story for an hour or two. Those were some of the happiest times I can remember."

Tyson reached over and wrapped an arm across her back, squeezing her in towards him in a sort of half-hug.

"I know I can't possibly make up for everything you ever experienced, but I hope we get a chance to have more fun than that together," he said, searching her brown eyes.

"I have a feeling you could make just about anything fun," Harper replied, nudging him with her shoulder. Then she sank in towards him and looked up, face getting closer and closer and Tyson realized what she wanted and leaned in...

"The line moved," a man said from behind them.

Sure enough, the line ahead had moved so much that it was their turn to grab trays. Tyson mumbled an apology, face burning, as he took one of the plastic trays and some utensils, letting Harper go first. She seemed nonplussed at their kiss getting interrupted. So much so, he thought he had imagined her desire.

Tyson had to wonder if she felt this as deeply as he did. Curious, he tuned his aura vision, feeling a bit like he was cheating at the whole relationship thing, being able to see emotions through auras. Harper's normally orange aura had gained a subtle blush. Could auras get embarrassed?

His own bright teal aura had a purple hue at the edges, perhaps indicating his fading embarrassment...or passion. The purple deepened when he realized that.

"Corn?" The older lady on the other side of the lunch counter interrupted him, and he had to ask her to repeat herself before he understood what she meant.

Yes to corn. No to salad. Yes to sandwich, turkey and swiss. Yes to a cookie. He felt like he was in elementary school again as he grabbed a bottled water and turned to look for Harper, who had already taken off towards a table.

Her aura had cleared, all the blush gone from it, and the moment was also gone. He knew Harper cared about him, and he really liked her, maybe even loved the stubborn woman with her determination and her raven wings and a protective streak a mile wide. But this rebellion, this war, didn't give them any time to figure out what they were, much less how they really felt for each other.

And Tyson knew all too well that after it was over might be too late. He dragged himself over to the table where Harper sat, good feelings evaporated by the depressing thoughts. He mindlessly chewed his sandwich in silence while Harper dug into her food next to him, neither of them saying a word.

Tyson's eyes wandered until they caught on a head of red hair. It was Reya, sitting down by herself at a table across the room.

He startled, nearly choking on his sandwich, and he had to put it down and take a drink.

"You okay?" Harper asked, staring at him.

Tyson finished drinking and wiped his mouth, still watching Reya.

Harper followed his gaze and glowered. "She shouldn't be allowed in public without an escort."

"It's okay, I've got you," Tyson joked, but it fell flat as he fixated on her.

"Are you sure you're all right? Do you...need to talk to someone about what happened with her?"

Tyson's gaze flicked back to Harper, and a smile tugged on the edge of his mouth. "Are you going to play counselor for me?"

Harper flushed. "I didn't mean it like that! I just...I'm here, you know? If something is bothering you..."

Tyson swallowed and looked down at his tray. "It's just...what she said keeps haunting me. That I murdered her family. Does she know they're dead? Maybe if Reya made it, they did too."

"That's what you're worried about? Whether or not you killed her family? Not the fact that she as good as killed your spirit guide and tried to kill you? That's messed up."

"No, it isn't," Tyson said defensively. "That's bothering me too, but if I hadn't turned her family in, she wouldn't have done any of that. In a way, it's all my fault."

Harper stared at him. "But you can't blame yourself for her actions. She's the one who tried to kill you."

Tyson sighed and set his sandwich down, poking at the other food on his plate. He'd lost his appetite and his desire to talk about the situation with Reya. Harper didn't get it. Probably because to her, the world was black and white. There were no gray areas. But Tyson had learned that when he saw the world so starkly, he made mistakes. He chose the wrong side. It had to be grayer than that, and he had to accept responsibility for what he'd done to contribute to Reya's desire for revenge.

He picked up his cookie, hoping the slight sugar rush would help fight the depressing thoughts in his head, when a pulse of energy washed over him. His mind spun, making him dizzy, and nausea gripped his stomach. He stood as if to make a dash for the bathroom but stopped when he saw the crowd gathering at the front of the room. A dark-skinned, curly-haired woman stood at the center, and everyone seemed to be asking her questions. Mandi shook her head in response.

Was her aura darker than usual? Or was his aura sense getting messed up by his emotions? And where was Zeke?

Another wave of the strange energy came over Tyson, and he doubled over, holding onto the table for support.

"Tyson!" Harper exclaimed. Her wing draped across his back protectively, and from the corner of his eye, Tyson saw her looking around for the threat.

"Some..weird...vibes in here," Tyson managed to gasp. His throat seemed to close, and his vision narrowed.

The lights in the cafeteria flickered, and someone shrieked, then laughter broke out. Did no one else notice the suffocating presence?

Tyson turned as much as his neck would allow and watched Reya. Her aura hadn't changed, still dark enough to suck in the light around it.

What if she was the source of the pulsing, dark energy?

Tyson straightened. He had to do something...tell someone...

The lights flickered again, the fluorescent bulbs growing brighter this time, buzzing loudly over the chatter as it quieted to concerned murmurs.

A bulb burst, sending a shower of sparks over a group of tables. The occupants screamed, ducking and scattering. Another light broke, and another, until the room was plunged into darkness.

"Stay calm!" Anna shouted. Where had she come from? Tyson hadn't seen her in the cafeteria, but then again, he'd been distracted. She stood on a table, face lit by a glowing orb. A witch stood on the floor nearby; she must have cast the orb.

"Someone has gone to look at the breakers. Meanwhile, I ask you to finish your meal and remain here. The fewer people we have walking the halls during this brief power outage, the fewer chances there are for accidents." She climbed down from the table.

The noise volume rose as excited and anxious conversations started. Nearly everyone's aura had tinged yellow, which indicated fear or nervousness.

He sat down, nausea still roiling in his gut. Whatever force was causing the energy surges and his discomfort was still at play.

Harper's feathers rustled as she sat beside him, the warmth of her wing radiating into his back.

"I don't like this," she said.

"Watch Reya," Tyson replied.

"Did you see something?" Harper asked, dropping her voice.

He dropped his hand to cover hers, and the table beneath their fingers vibrated. The vibration grew, and the tables creaked.

"Earthquake!" someone yelled. Chaos and screams erupted. Everyone stood to run from the room, but the entire building was shifting, and people were falling. They would get injured.

Tyson stood up to yell, but his breath caught as the floor rolled beneath him, almost liquified with the movement of the building's foundation. He reached for something to grab onto, but only found Harper, who yelped when he grabbed her wing.

He grasped her shoulder instead and pulled her down to the floor, ducking under the cafeteria table. Bits of debris fell from the ceiling, cracking on the table's surface.

The lights burst again. No, this time it was lightning. Supernatural energy built until a ball of light exploded in the center of the room, and five monstrous figures dropped onto the floor, glowing red, purple, and yellow light emanating from their horns, claws, and mouths.

People scattered like roaches to escape the reach of the hideous monsters that had landed in their midst.

A sulfuric stench sent Tyson gagging, and his knife burned against his hip.

Several silvery witch light orbs hovered closer to the five figures, illuminating their terrible faces.

Demons. With twisted horns and eyes that glowed like molten rock. Two had snouts. One had a human face so beautiful it hurt to look at. Another had tusks. And the last had a wicked black beak. It turned its head, golden eyes shining towards Tyson. He flinched and hit his head on the metal table leg.

The demons laughed, their voices echoing strangely in the deathly still room.

"Welcome to the end of the line," the tusk-faced demon said, voice gravelly and deep. He raised a clenched fist.

"What do you want?" Anna asked, pulling herself off the floor and facing down the demons.

Tyson had to admire her courage, facing five demons alone. But then, she wasn't alone.

Bodies stirred around her. Several sat up, hands glowing with magic or growing fur and fangs if they had them. Her army was ready to defend their leader.

"To quench our unending thirst for revenge. We've been locked up in the pit of the realms for millennia. It is time we feasted on mortal flesh and made a new world for ourselves. And it begins now." The tusk-faced demon bellowed and turned, slashing the air with a massive ax. The air tore, and through the slash two clawed hands appeared, prying the slit apart. A bat-winged female demon climbed through, hissing and spitting with a snake-like tongue.

Another demon spilled out, and another.

"To me!" Anna yelled.

Her army burst off the floor and hurled themselves at the demons in a cacophony of shouted spells, gunshots, shrieks, and growls.

The demons met them with fire and acid, iron weapons, and brute strength.

A bear-shifter flew across the room, shattering the glass partition between the cafeteria and the kitchens. A bird shifter screamed as a bull-like demon wrenched its wing, snapping the delicate bones.

Harper lunged out from their hiding place, leaping on the back of the bull demon and locking her arms around its neck.

The demon hardly batted an eye, slamming its back on the table over Tyson and smashing Harper.

Her gasp, more of a wheeze as all the air was crushed from her lungs, woke something in Tyson. Something primal and protective.

The polar bear inside him roared, but Tyson didn't release it. He wouldn't last much longer than Harper against the insane strength of the demons. He had to be smarter than that.

Tyson darted out from beneath the table and helped Harper up. She held her ribs, wincing, but obviously trying to hide the full extent of her pain. She moved towards the fight again, but Tyson clamped his arm around her and held her to his side. She wasn't going anywhere.

Quinn rushed the bull demon, kicking it in the face as it bore down on Tyson and Harper.

Tyson concentrated, chanting words to open the portal into the astral realm. A spinning disc of light widened in front of him. The tunnel formed between the planes, and the disc widened as the connection on the other side was made.

He focused on the wide, grassy fields between the Washington Monument and the Lincoln memorial. A lot of people could fit there, and it wouldn't take as much energy to send them somewhere within the city.

He forced the portal to open wider. Most portals were made for one person to pass through. This one could fit four across. The edges flickered as Tyson's concentration wavered, but he held on, breathing deep into his core and accessing the energy that pulsed there, somehow fed by the power of the knife.

"To me!" Anna called, flying over the fighting and pulling up in the air over Tyson's portal.

Everyone surged towards the portal.

The tusk-faced demon slammed its fist down on the floor. A fiery red crack spider-webbed through the tile. The stone cracked wide, and demons poured from the rift. Several people fell into the pit, while others backed up, scrambling and scream-ing.

A handful of people made it through ahead of Tyson, but most of them were engaged in demon battles or trapped on the other side.

Tyson grimaced, straining to hold the portal open.

"I could use a little help!" he yelled, looking around for a fellow shaman, dreamwalker, or witch to lend their power to him. None were near enough, and perhaps they couldn't hear him over the roaring and bellowing and screaming, though he thought he caught a glimpse of a second portal opening on the other side of the room.

Three demons advanced towards them.

Harper jerked against Tyson's grip. "You can't open this and defend against the demons," she insisted.

"I can't hold it much longer, period," Tyson said. "Go through. Now."

"I'll hold them off," Harper said.

"No," Tyson said through gritted teeth. Two more people had made it through. The rest were holding the demons back. He wasn't going to be able to save everyone like he'd imagined. He had to convince Anna to go through. Perhaps her people would follow then.

"Anna!" he shouted. "Go through the portal!"

"I won't abandon my people!" she called back. She raised a spear and thrust it downward, fending off a bird-like demon.

"You won't have any people if we don't get them through the portal!" he yelled back. He glanced at Harper. "Grab someone and fly them through."

Harper nodded and darted away. To Tyson's relief, she came back carrying a young leopard-shifter and flew the woman through. Tyson felt their travel through his portal like a ripple through his body, and then a smaller wave as Harper flew back.

More demons spilled from the hole in the floor. They outnumbered the paranormals and humans two-to-one, and the room was packed to standing-room only, people getting crushed and trampled as the demons rose. The air thickened with flying demons.

Quinn, standing nearby, grabbed the closest human and tossed them through, shoving and forcing them despite their insistence that they could stay and help.

They wouldn't win this battle. It was a massacre. But how had the demons gained access? Tyson couldn't think about it now. He couldn't do anything but hold the portal open, and his strength was failing.

Sweat dripped down his temple. The portal flickered, shrinking, and Harper had to duck to enter as she passed him again. He'd only saved a couple dozen at most. He had to try harder.

Tyson fell to his knees, body trembling. His head burst with pain.

The portal vanished.

"No!" he screamed. He took out the ulu knife and frantically drew runes in the air, letting the knife guide his arm. A red-lined doorway appeared. He didn't know what location he thought of, he just let the magic guide him and hoped it would be enough.

Quinn flew through, carrying a red-haired woman. A man raced for the doorway, but a demon intercepted him, and the man's screams cut short as the demon swiped a claw viciously across his throat.

Tyson gathered his strength and stood. "Now or never, Anna!"

The bird woman glanced his way from her position in the air, her face a desperate tangle of emotion.

Leth appeared, his black face gleaming with sweat as he charged. He leapt into the air, inhumanly high, grabbing Anna's ankle and bringing her down. He locked her into his arms, even as she thrashed and struggled, her wings beating against his face and shoulders. His face remained a mask of determination, undeterred by her frantic yelling.

"Harper!" Leth bellowed.

Harper swooped down, grabbing her mother under her arms, and flew towards the portal.

"Let me go! I won't leave them! I won't!" Anna's screams cut off as Harper entered through the doorway with her.

Tyson crawled towards the door, passing Leth, who spared a glance at him and simply nodded. Tyson understood—Leth would risk his own life to keep the demons away from Anna and the portal she'd gone through.

Tyson's arms and legs collapsed beneath him, putting him halfway in, halfway out of the portal. Someone grasped his wrists and pulled, dragging him onto a cold, filthy cement floor in a dark and relatively silent room, except for haggard gasps from one corner.

Tyson pried his face off the floor and looked around. He smelled engine oil, and a car sat not too far away, wheels missing.

Where had he brought them this time? There were only six of them gathered here, but he knew more had gone through his first portal. Hopefully that meant they had landed where he intended in the memorial fields.

Had the second portal dropped them somewhere nearby? A mechanic's garage on a different block, perhaps? His mind puzzled over why the knife would have brought him to a car maintenance building until his eyes landed on a toy laying on the floor just out of reach.

A small naked troll doll with spiky green hair grinned up at him with a wicked, gleeful expression.

There was only one person Tyson knew who collected troll dolls and worked in a mechanic shop.

# CHAPTER TEN

## HARPER

"What's crackin', Dreamwalker?" A woman with mechanics coveralls covered in neon orange and pink flowers stepped into the room, tilting her head to peer at them over her rose-colored glasses.

Harper blinked at the woman in her neon overalls and long braids. It felt like it'd been a lifetime since she'd seen the hippie mechanic. She remembered how she and Tyson had threatened the RV-driving goblin couple until they had dropped them off at the place where a mysterious soothsayer could interpret Tyson's visions—Charlie's Auto Shop.

"Charlemagne!" Tyson exclaimed, scrambling to his feet. He brushed his hands on his jeans and held one out to the Seer.

Charlemagne shook her head. "Out here we hug. You oughta know that by now." She crushed him in a strong embrace and stepped back, nodding a more reserved greeting to Harper, who she'd met before, and the others, who she hadn't. "Well, look what the cat dragged in. Y'all are here to see the Troll collection, I reckon."

The soothsayer had been less than helpful, in Harper's opinion, but she didn't mind being here rather than T.R.S. headquarters at the moment.

Charlemagne—also known as Charlie—scanned the new occupants of her shop. Tyson, Harper's mother, Quinn, and Reya.

Harper's eyes narrowed at the red-headed woman, who was too busy eyeing the tiny green troll laying in the middle of the lopsided circle of people to notice Harper's scrutiny. She wished Quinn had grabbed anyone other than the fox shifter that wanted Tyson dead. Harper would have to watch her closely to make sure she didn't take advantage of the chaos to take her revenge.

"We're not here about the troll collection, unfortunately," Tyson said. "We were escaping a demon attack at the Transcendental Redemption Society headquarters in D.C."

Charlie's eyes widened. "My, my. You've been busy since we last saw each other. I assume my Jeep is a lost cause?"

Tyson ducked his head sheepishly, exchanging a glance with Harper. "It's in a parking lot in Kennewick, Washington. Or it was when we last saw it. I meant to call you, but between going through a dreamwalker initiation in Alaska and joining an international paranormal rebellion, I kinda forgot. If it helps, I still have the keys. I think."

Charlie stared at him a long moment, then burst into laughter. Her hand waived through the air. "Never you mind. It'll all balance out in the end for the favor I need to ask you."

"Favor?" Harper said. "We just got here. And you didn't know we were coming."

Charlie looked at Harper and tapped her temple. "Ah, but I did. I didn't know under what circumstances, but I saw you all arriving in a vision. What was it? Six days ago, Bo?"

The office door swung open behind Charlie, and a man emerged. He wore grease-stained blue overalls, and a bandana tied around his head. He looked at Charlie and at the group of people in his auto shop, then thumbed his nose and stuck both hands in his pockets.

"Guess you were right, Charlie. A whole crowd of 'em," Bo said.

"Looks like we have some acquaintances to make," Charlie said. "The office is a bit small for this crowd. We'll head to the house."

She made ushering motions, but nobody moved.

Charlie held up a finger. "Ah, yes. That way, everyone. Up the stairs." She pointed to the left, where a door stood with a wrinkled, handwritten "PRIVATE: DO NOT ENTER" sign taped to its chipped surface.

The group filed up the narrow stairs. Even Anna was uncharacteristically silent. Harper had expected Anna to demand who Charlie was and how Tyson and Harper knew her, but when the raven woman passed Harper, she seemed as glassy-eyed as one of Charlie's trolls. She hadn't thanked Harper for saving her, hadn't said anything since they'd passed through the portal.

A second door at the top of the stairs opened into a cramped and cluttered living room with attached kitchen. Brown panels lined the walls, and all the furniture was brown, yellow, and orange with flower and duck patterns.

And of course there were trolls. Every flat surface had a troll and several other vintage knick-knacks.

Unable to shake the feeling that Anna needed someone to talk to her, Harper waited for her to come up the stairs, then leaned in towards her.

"Are you all right?"

Anna blinked as if waking up. "I left them," she said, her voice trembling.

"You did what you had to do. Now at least one leader made it out alive, and we can get you back to help them," Harper said, feeling awkward, but knowing the words were right.

Anna breathed in and nodded, as if she agreed with Harper, and for the first time since they'd been reunited, Harper felt hope for their relationship.

Harper sank into a couch covered in ducks in flight. She felt a sharp pinch and shrieked, standing up to release the wing she'd just sat on.

Tyson coughed. Quinn didn't bother covering up his laugh. Typical.

Heat filled Harper's cheeks. She pushed her wing tips forward with her arms and sat again, letting her wings cup her shoulders and touch the ground by her feet.

Anna sat daintily next to Harper, crossing her legs and draping her wings around herself gracefully. "You simply need more practice," she said. Her tone sounded much warmer than usual, and Harper actually considered that Anna meant it kindly.

Tyson sat on the carpet near her legs. Harper met his gaze, and he smiled, but the smile faded when he glanced over where the red-headed Reya slipped through the doorway behind Charlie.

Reya's eyes moved from the empty spot on the couch next to Harper to the floor where Tyson sat. She inched closer to Quinn but stopped a few feet away and folded her arms tight against her body.

Reya seemed far too shifty, and Harper found herself scooting to the edge of the couch, muscles tensing, prepared to jump between the fox shifter and Tyson if she decided to attack. The fact that she hadn't yet made Harper wonder if she was simply biding her time, or if she'd decided not to kill Tyson. Perhaps the shock of the demon attack had been enough to put Reya on the same side as Tyson, but until Harper could be sure, she would be vigilant.

Plastic cups clacked together in the kitchen, and the faucet ran several times. Bo ferried the cups to the living room, offering them to each person there.

Harper took one, rubbing her fingers on the bumpy design in the cup before drinking. The lukewarm water didn't seem to want to go down her throat. She swallowed her first gulp painfully, then took another one. The second went down easier.

Charlemagne entered the living room and sat at the front of the group on the floor next to the yellow-brick fireplace.

"There now," Charlemagne said, slapping the tops of her thighs and rubbing her hands together. She gazed expectantly at each of them in turn. What could the soothsayer read in their faces?

The skin of Harper's wings prickled beneath her feathers, and she rolled her shoulders back as subtly as she could manage to try to get rid of the itch, but it didn't go away.

"What do we do now?" Tyson asked from his seat on the floor.

"We return and eliminate whomever is responsible for this mess," Anna said, a hard edge to her voice.

"That's great. Except we don't know who it is," Quinn said.

Tyson's hands moved as he spoke. "Any of the newcomers to T.R.S. could have been exposed to demonic influence while in the astral realm. Demons could have consumed their essences and occupied their bodies, waiting for the right moment to strike. But from my understanding, opening the rift in the cafeteria would have taken an enormous amount of power, involving one of the lowest vibrational beings in the known universe."

Reya had come out from behind Quinn and now leaned against a wooden desk on the back wall. She kept her eyes on the floor, and didn't try to enter the conversation, or even react to what Tyson had said about the possibility that Harper could be right, and that Reya or one of the others might be possessed.

"Ragranoth," Anna breathed the name out slowly.

Charlemagne startled. "You've been dealing with the Autarch of the Abyss?"

Tyson cocked his head. "Autarch? I haven't heard that word before. But then, I'm new to all this."

Harper had no idea what Charlamagne meant either. Being a shifter, even one with ancient powers and songs she still needed to learn, seemed far simpler than all the alternate plane of reality stuff Tyson had to figure out as a dreamwalker.

"Autarch means ultimate ruler, essentially," Charlemagne explained. She placed a finger on her squarish chin. "We should be careful uttering the names of any demons. Names have power, and we don't want to draw the attention of those beings here."

"But Mandi shut down the pentagram and stopped R—the demon Autarch from coming, didn't she?" Quinn said.

"I'm going to need to hear that story," Charlamagne said, eyes gleaming with interest.

Tyson launched into it, with Anna interjecting the parts she knew about because of the involvement of the T.R.S.

Harper had heard it all, and with the itching in her wings driving her nothing short of crazy, she leaned back on the couch and closed her eyes, forcing herself to think.

Her eyes drifted to Reya, who seemed to inch behind Quinn. Except for Tyson, none of them knew Reya before she'd entered the astral realm, and he'd been ten.

Reya seemed normal enough, but Harper couldn't rule her out as a threat.

"I think Reya knows something," Tyson said, finishing his description of the events that had led to that point. It was almost as if he'd read Harper's mind, picking up on her suspicions.

"I don't know anything," Reya said, rubbing her arm in a rapid, nervous motion. She laughed. "I-I just got here. I've been in limbo, remember? How could I—"

"Her aura isn't right," Tyson said. He glanced at Harper, as if hoping she'd back him up, but her thoughts were still catching up, and she wanted to hear what Tyson knew.

"A dark aura isn't always an indication of evil," Charlemagne said.

"She tried to kill me back at T.R.S. headquarters," Tyson said.

"After you tried to have her and her family killed!" Quinn shouted, stepping between Tyson and Reya. "Of course you would accuse her. You've had some grudge against her from the beginning."

Anna stepped forward. "Let's not get ahead of ourselves with accusations. Tyson, have you compared notes with the other magic users waking others from the Hundred Year Sleep?"

"Other magic users have reported similar effects in the others woken from the Hundred Year Sleep. It could be a side effect of being in the astral realm so long, not necessarily possession or impersonation by a demonic influence. Or they all betrayed us," Tyson added.

Reya stood up. "Whatever you think of me, I'm not possessed. There's no demon inside me."

"Then why did you try to kill Tyson?" Harper glared at Reya. "Why not even give him a chance to prove he'd changed?"

"If your family had been murdered because of his actions, you'd be helping me kill him instead of kissing him," Reya spat.

Harper bolted off the couch, anger flaring through her. She wanted to punch Reya's freckled nose in, but Tyson grabbed Harper's arm from his seat on the floor, holding her back.

"Um, Harper?" Tyson said, his tone off.

"Your wings," Quinn said, pointing.

Harper glanced down and gaped. A small shower of feathers had cascaded onto the couch and floor behind her. She grabbed one wing, several more feathers falling. What was happening?

"You're molting," Anna said, her face moving oddly, like she was...

Harper dropped her wing, clenching her fists and her teeth. "It isn't funny."

Quinn burst out laughing.

Anna joined him, actual tears streaming from her eyes. "You're having your first molt! I can't believe it's happening now. You haven't spent enough time in your raven form before for it to happen. You really are a fledgling."

"I'm a grown woman!" Harper shouted. "When will you start taking me seriously?"

Anna's face darkened, a reproach or a lecture no doubt ready on her tongue.

The others stared, glancing at Harper and Anna then away, as if they didn't know where to look or how to avoid the feud building in the room.

Harper didn't wait to be scolded. She jumped over the back of the couch with her inhuman strength, making for the dark hallway at the back of the room. She threw open the first door she came across and found a bathroom.

Entering, she flipped on the light and slammed the door, feathers drifting onto the linoleum floor. She locked the handle, then leaned against the counter, gazing at her reflection in the mirror. Her face had filled out a bit since arriving at the Tower. Her wings looked ragged, but as she shook them out, only a few feathers fell, and none of them were primaries. She was molting. A normal rite of passage that she'd somehow missed, like puberty, though she'd definitely already hit that.

Gripping the cold counter, she bowed her head and gritted her teeth. She might be learning the most basic Songs her tribe could teach her, and she might be molting, but she was no fledgling.

And no matter what anyone thought of her, she wouldn't remain blind to Reya as a potential threat in their midst. Not when the fox shifter threatened the family Harper had been through hell to find.

# CHAPTER ELEVEN

## ZEKE

ZEKE NEVER MADE IT to the Tower after his date with the thing that had taken Mandi from him. All he remembered was a bright, flashing light, and all the muscles in his body had relaxed, causing him to fall mid-leap to the road. His eyes had stayed open, but all he'd seen were booted feet walking up to him. Everything after that was a fuzzy blur.

He'd woken in an extra-large wire dog kennel, transformed from beast to man, his human form almost too big for the kennel. He'd panicked, knocking over water and food dishes, and nearly tipped the cage over.

There were others trapped with him, but they remained in their animal forms, and none of them spoke. He counted four werewolves and a bobcat shifter. The cat hissed at him whenever he looked at it.

All of them wore thick collars with some sort of digital device attached to them. Shock collars.

Zeke shouted and raged. He tried bending the bars of his cage, working at breaking the hinges on the door or removing the pins, but none of it worked.

When his human muscles cramped so painfully, he couldn't take it anymore, he shifted back to his wolf form, feeling defeated. Whoever had caught him and brought him here had experience capturing paranormals. They'd thought of everything.

What he didn't get was why the others didn't talk to him. He didn't recognize any of them to know whether they were part of the rebellion or not.

Three days after he'd been captured, someone entered the room. Zeke had licked up every drop of water and every scrap of dog food, gagging each time he took a bite of the spilled, grain-laden kibble.

A large, red-haired man with a full beard walked into the room with an air of superiority, peering into the kennels.

One of the werewolves growled at him, and the man barked, snapping his jaws and growling right back.

The werewolf laid back its ears and cowered at the back of its kennel, and the man laughed.

"What day is the new capture on?"

"Day three." A reed-thin man entered the doorway, dragging a massive bag of dog food behind him.

Zeke drooled in spite of himself. No, he had to keep it together here. These sickos were, by all appearances, torturing these shifters. He needed to find a chance to escape, and there'd be no better moment than when one of the men opened his cage.

"He's a beautiful specimen. You saw him shift?" The red-haired man said, coming close to Zeke's cage.

Zeke kept quiet, appearing docile. He whined a little at the back of his throat, even gave his tail the slightest wag and looked up with all the hopefulness of a dog at the pound.

"He seems more doggish than the others," the red-haired man said.

The thin man finished dragging the dog food to the far wall on the other side of Zeke and ripped it open.

"We haven't seen him shift, sir. But we heard him shouting soon after we brought him in. The new ones always give themselves away."

Zeke's tail stopped wagging. He wouldn't fool them into thinking he was just a dog, but he could still make them underestimate him.

The red-headed man crouched down, making eye contact with Zeke.

"Come and talk to me, beast," the man said. "I know you can."

Zeke withheld a growl. He didn't want to change for this man. He wasn't a circus animal or a tame pet. But perhaps he could accomplish something by talking with him.

He shifted, muscles and limbs groaning, his human body filling the cage, the wire biting into his shoulders.

"If you don't mind, I'd appreciate being let out to walk around. My muscles are killing me," Zeke said, taking the polite approach.

The man whistled. "This one's ripped, isn't he? Quite the specimen."

Zeke gritted his teeth. "This is inhumane for an animal or a person, and I'm both."

The red-headed man laughed. "It makes jokes! Maybe we shouldn't waste this one in the pit."

"Highly inadvisable, sir," the thin man said dryly. He had scooped up a bowlful of dog food and carried it to the nearest cage, where a thin gray wolf skittered to the back of the kennel, trembling as the thin man drew near.

"Who makes the decisions, Drew?" the red-headed man asked.

"You do, sir." The thin man, Drew, muttered, opening the cage door.

Zeke expected the wolf to attack, assuming it wasn't a regular dog that happened to look like a wolf. He was starting to doubt his initial assessment that these were more than mere animals, but by the satisfied look on the red-headed man's face, he had a sinking, sickening feeling that this man took pride in capturing and breaking shifters.

"What's your name?" Zeke asked.

"I'll tell you mine if you tell me yours," the big man said, turning his attention back to Zeke.

Zeke hesitated. He didn't really have anything to lose by giving this man his name. And exchanging names would create familiarity and give them a connection.

"Zeke,"

"Zeke," the man said, as if tasting the name. "That does suit you. We'll keep it for now. I need to come up with a real good one for you."

Zeke didn't know what that meant. He hooked his fingers through the wire rectangles of the kennel. "And your name?"

"Boris DeLuca."

"And your purpose?" Zeke asked, eyes flashing in challenge. He had tired of the game already. He didn't want to pretend anything, and he certainly didn't want to sit in a cage talking to this man who didn't know the definition of respect.

"Build an army of you to fight against your own kind. Teach them a thing or two about who is master here," Boris said.

"We're not animals for you to train," Zeke said, snarling.

"Could have fooled me," Boris said, shrugging. He stood with a sigh. "As lovely as it is speaking with you, Zeke, it is inevitable that our conversation come to a close. Drew!"

Kibble scattered as Drew jumped, standing in front of the bobcat's cage. Apparently everyone got dog food, dog or not.

"Yes, sir?"

"Water only for this one, three more days. Then bring him to me." Boris walked towards the doorway.

"Wait! You can't do this! There's something in the city—something bad. I have to warn the others. You have to let me go," Zeke shouted, rattling the door of his cage.

Boris turned, leering. "You're right. There is something bad in the city. You and your kind. I figure, since your kind isn't going away, I'll make you into something I can control. I'll make this city safer for everyone. And once I have enough of you, we'll go after the President. Your kind won't know what hit 'em when they've got werewolves attacking their own." Boris's laughter echoed down the hall as he left.

Zeke eyed Drew. "He's mad, isn't he?"

Drew clenched his jaw. "I'm not supposed to talk to you."

"You just did," Zeke pointed out.

Drew's eyes darted from Zeke to the bobcat's cage and back. He opened the door, ignoring the bobcat's frightened hisses. Similar to the werewolf, it didn't attack, didn't even try to swipe with its claws, only cowered in the back of the cage until Drew finished filling its food and water and re-locked the cage door.

"What did he do to them?" Zeke asked.

"You'll see," Drew said. He came around to Zeke and poured water through the top of the cage, filling the bowl and splashing Zeke in the process. He kept glancing at Zeke with curiosity, but he didn't respond to anything else Zeke said.

Zeke didn't trust the two men. He tried to sleep in short bursts, but with no food and nothing to pass the time, he eventually shifted back to wolf form to give himself more room and fell asleep, curling into a tight ball.

The creak of his cage door cut into his dreamless sleep and his head shot up. A sharp pinch of a needle plunged into the back of his neck, and cold liquid shot into his body. A moment later, Zeke slumped over, unconscious.

# CHAPTER TWELVE

## HARPER

IT NEARLY KILLED HARPER to draw her wings back inside her shoulders, but she didn't want to deal with leaving a trail of feathers everywhere she went. She hadn't drawn them inside in weeks, and she felt a bit unsteady on her feet as she opened the bathroom door and crossed into the living room to rejoin the others, who were catching Charlie up on the rest of the details about how they'd come to be in her garage.

Harper sat on the floor next to Tyson and leaned into him, trying not to make eye contact with Quinn or her mother.

"They'll grow back," Anna whispered, leaning across the couch towards her. "It only lasts a day or so."

Harper shrugged to show she'd heard, but she didn't feel like responding. She felt exhausted and embarrassed at her outburst.

"What'd I miss?" she asked Tyson.

"Charlie scanned Reya with her magic, and there's no demonic influence. She said there's 'something else,' but even Charlie didn't know what it was."

"What do you think about it?" Harper asked, scanning Tyson's face.

He grimaced, glanced around at the others still discussing something with Charlie, then lowered his voice. "I think being in the astral realm for so long changed her. Tainted her, darkened her soul. She might not be possessed, but that doesn't mean she's fully on our side."

"But we're fighting for her rights, too," Harper said, glancing towards the fox shifter, who leaned against a wall on the far side of the room with her eyes closed like she was resting.

"She's angry. There's so much anger. I can't seem to sense further than that without being obvious. Her fury feels like a pacing animal, and every time my magic reaches out towards her, it snaps and snarls." He closed his eyes, his brow furrowing. "Does that make sense?"

The room went quiet, and Harper glanced around at the others.

They were all staring at Charlie, who stood by the fireplace, scanning the trolls along the mantle, patting their hair, and adjusting their positions by the tiniest fraction. Then she clasped her hands behind her back and faced the group, expression grim.

"If you're really up against the demon Autarch, and I don't doubt you are, then there is only one place you can go to get the help you're gonna need, and that's the Eternal Source."

"We can go there?" Tyson said. "I heard it was nearly impossible for a mortal to reach."

Charlie nodded. "It is. Traveling through the planes of the astral realm is treacherous, especially for the uninitiated. Then there are the harpies who guard the gate leading to the pathway to Utopia, not to mention confronting the Eternal Source themselves. Fortunately, I have a ticket to the doorstep, so to speak, which will cut down on travel time and the dangers you would otherwise face. I'll gladly transport you there if you'll do one thing for me."

"What is it?" Tyson asked.

"Save my husband," Charlie said. Her eyes glistened, and she clasped her hands in front of her, breathing deep before continuing. "Five years ago, Randy died. Heart failure. Even my healing abilities have their limits, and he went so suddenly I had no chance to save him. To lose him so early, when I thought we'd have another thirty or forty years together...well, it wasn't as devastating as realizing later that he never passed on."

"He became a gaunt," Reya said from her corner, her eyes open and gleaming.

Harper didn't know what a gaunt was, but even the thought of the word left a bad taste in her mouth.

Charlie's eyes clouded over with grief. "He's not a spirit, properly crossed over and connected to Utopia. And he's not a living being visiting the astral realm. He's become a lower vibrational being that can suck the life essence out of anything living that draws near. He cannot be reasoned with. He often does not recognize me. And no matter how much light I pour into him, his status does not change. Last time I tried..." Charlie drew in a shaky breath.

"He nearly killed her," Bo continued. "Sucked her almost dry. I had to pull her out." The man shifted, as if the memory unnerved him, and he crossed his arms defensively over his chest.

Interesting. Bo had some of his mother's gifts, then.

Tyson coughed. "You know I'm new at this, Charlie. I didn't know what a gaunt was until a minute ago, and I don't know the first thing about healing them or changing them or whatever needs to happen."

"But I know you are the one I need to take with me," Charlie said, her tone pleading. "I saw you. I painted you out of one of my visions, long before we ever met. And I helped you, and you promised to return the favor one day. Just...will you try?" Her eyes glistened.

"Isn't the fate of the world more important than your husband?" Harper cut in. "No offense, I'm sure Tyson would love to save him, but what if we don't have time?"

Charlie stared at Harper without flinching. "He is your ticket into the Eternal Source. Escorting his soul to the Harpies who guard the gate to Utopia is possibly the only way you will get close enough to convince them to let you in as well. Otherwise, you could spend days, weeks, months, even years wandering the astral realm and facing the dangers there before you reach the entrance, and it will certainly be too late by then."

Harper ducked her head, slightly ashamed that she'd questioned Charlie in her grief.

Tyson put a hand on Harper's shoulder. "I'll do what I can, Charlie."

Harper had the sudden urge to hug him. She might not much appreciate physical displays of affection, but she knew Tyson did. She snaked her hand into his and squeezed. When he squeezed back, her heart fluttered.

Anna cleared her throat. "And what are the rest of us expected to do, ungifted as we are in the ways of the astral planes? While you and Tyson go on this dangerous mission into the realms beyond to seek the advice of this Eternal Source, are we meant to...play monopoly? Watch movies?" There was a tone of sarcasm in the woman's voice that shocked Harper. Anna usually kept herself poised and professional. Could she be just as frustrated as Harper at being left out of the action?

"You're not going there without me," Harper said, her head lifting as she gazed fiercely from Tyson to Charlie.

"You don't have the gift, honey," Charlie insisted. "As much as we could use someone with your fighting spirit, we just don't have the power."

"I can take them," Tyson said quietly. He lifted his chin. "Anyone who wishes to come, can. I brought them here through the astral realm, after all."

"You would have to bind their souls to you. Even as experienced as I am, I wouldn't dream of binding so many. Though," Charlie said, scanning Tyson as if she could see beyond his physical form. "I have a feeling your power is strong enough."

"With all due respect, you're not a dreamwalker." Tyson said. "Besides, I only have to tether those who cannot tether themselves. You can tether yourself, I assume?"

"Hold up. Maybe Reya shouldn't come," Harper argued, glancing at the red-haired fox shifter leaning against the back wall.

At the mention of her name, Reya straightened, her expression darkening. "Why not? I know more about the astral realm than all of you put together. I lived there for six years," she snapped.

Tyson cleared his throat. "Harper has a point. You spent so much time there, it might have...damaged you somehow. Going back so soon after spending six years there might not be such a good idea."

"The only damaged one here is you!" Reya shouted. "Who tells the authorities on their best friend? Who betrays those who confide in him? You made a career out of it, from what I hear!"

Harper stepped swiftly between Reya and Tyson and noticed Quinn moving towards Reya. She readied herself to shift, should the fox shifter attack.

"If you can't keep your petty squabbles to yourself, I can't trust you to work as a team. You certainly won't go if that's the case," Anna said in a voice that was all leader. "Tyson is right to be concerned, and Reya is right that we could use her expertise. I say we let her try if she's willing to take the risks."

The prickling hairs on Harper's neck calmed as the tension in the room diminished.

Reya snorted, crossing her arms and glancing away. "I don't want to be left here to do nothing."

"Fine. Will working with Tyson be a problem?" Anna asked sternly.

"No," Reya muttered, eyes flicking up to meet Anna's for a moment.

It hardly sounded sincere to Harper. She felt off about the whole interaction, but if Anna decided Reya should go, she wouldn't be able to stop her. She would have to be more vigilant than ever, and it didn't help that the only time she'd been in the astral realm, she'd been possessed, her soul imprisoned in one of the lower planes. She wouldn't have any of the advantages Reya would have once they were there.

Anna seemed visibly relieved. "Good. Now that's decided, I suggest we rest before taking off into unknown realms. Time is not on our side, but if we haven't slept or eaten properly, we might as well quit now."

"I just ate," Harper said, holding a hand over her stomach. "We were eating lunch when the demons attacked."

"I'm not hungry either," Reya added.

Quinn murmured his agreement, and Tyson nodded.

"It's seven o'clock here. Wherever here is," Anna said, looking at Tyson expectantly.

"Oregon," Tyson said.

Anna seemed a bit stunned to discover they were on the opposite side of the country but continued, "So, four o'clock back at the Tower. You'll be hungry in an hour or two. Those who are tired now can rest, and we'll have a meal before we leave. How long can we remain in the astral realm before our bodies require our return?"

"In the astral realm, time moves differently," Tyson explained. "You could return in a day, having done far too many things for it to have been only a day in the astral realm, or you could pop into the astral realm and come back and find your body aching with hunger, thirst, and other needs."

"A day, then," Anna said, pursing her lips. "We essentially have a day to find this woman's husband, get him to pass through the veil, or however that works, get past the harpies, and convince this Eternal Source being to aid our cause."

"Sounds about right," Charlie said, then clapped her hands together. "Who needs a bed? There are three available. You can take turns napping. I'll get dinner started. Do ya'll like tacos?"

Several hours later, the smell of spiced meat wafted through Harper's consciousness, and she dragged herself off the couch. She'd dozed in the name of getting 'rest' but hadn't really slept. After all, it was still early evening in the time zone her body was adjusted to.

Anna stood at the table, crushing chips over a heap of food on a paper plate. She glanced up as Harper entered the kitchen.

"Go wake your brother," she said. After growing up without her around, it still sounded odd to hear those familial words from her mouth.

Harper resisted the urge to refuse. *You're not the boss of me.* She licked her lips, tasting salt. But she didn't want to pick a fight at the moment, so she carried the storm cloud with her down the hall and peeked in both rooms.

In one, Tyson was up and putting on his shoes. His smile faltered when he saw the expression on her face.

"Harper? What's wro—"

She didn't let him finish but crossed the hall and threw open the other door. Quinn slept on a pillow on the floor, the fox shifter curled up in human form in a fetal position on the bed.

Harper nudged Quinn's toe with her foot, feeling oddly satisfied when Quinn startled awake, sitting bolt upright and glancing around as if looking for an attacker.

His shoulders slumped when he saw Harper. "Why'd you wake me?" he muttered, pulling the blanket up and laying back down.

"Tacos. And *mom* said I had to," Harper said.

Quinn groaned but tossed the covers off, rolled onto all fours, then stood. He glanced at the bed.

"Should we wake her?"

"I'm awake," Reya said without moving.

Harper shrugged to Quinn, and they both left the room, heading for the kitchen.

Quinn ruffled Harper's hair. "Is Tyson up?"

Harper ignored his attempt to goad her about Tyson and headed for the kitchen, immediately grabbing a plate from the island counter and loading up several tacos.

Tyson emerged a few moments later. He smiled at Harper, coming up behind her and kissing her cheek—a peck so subtle Harper hardly felt it, but it made her burn from her face to her toes. She avoided looking at Quinn as she moved away from Tyson under the pretense of reaching for the salsa.

"Does it ever feel odd to anyone else when you do something totally normal—like eat a taco—right before doing something spectacular, like travel to another realm?" Tyson chuckled, picking up a plate and digging into the spread.

"It amuses me every time," Charlie said from the kitchen area. "The mundane and the magic. I could be cooking pot roast for dinner and painting a vision at the same time, and it never ceases to amaze me that I actually have magic. Like something from the movies."

Harper had no idea how one "painted a vision," or what Charlie meant by it, but then, she was fairly certain she was less sane than the rest of them.

"I felt like that when I learned to fly," Quinn said. "Really fly, not just swoop down from a high place. We had to go at the crack of dawn to this ravine. I was so sore after, but I remember walking back to the house and going to school and realizing that no one around me knew I could *actually* fly. How would they react if they did know? All the kids at school would be jealous. If they'd stop being afraid for a few moments, they'd realize what a gift our abilities could be."

Harper's memories of that time were gone. So much of her childhood was missing, sacrificed to the beryllium orb in order to escape the camp. She'd lost what she'd fought so hard to find.

She wasn't sure the humans would ever stop being afraid. The world had broken, and the more she considered it, the more she realized no one could fix it. Not with talking, not with fighting. And yet, she couldn't bring herself to give up, either.

Reya walked into the room, stretching her arms, and everyone paused eating and talking and stared at her. Harper resisted the urge to stand up and put herself between Tyson and the fox shifter.

Reya narrowed her amber eyes and went the long way around the table, opposite the side Tyson and Harper sat on, to get her plate.

Quinn cleared his throat, watching Reya. "Sleep well?"

She shrugged. "Well enough." After a moment's pause, Reya lowered her plate. "You know, I had a thought before I fell asleep. Why not just send a small, efficient team into the astral realm? Charlie and me, for obvious reasons, Tyson because apparently Charlie thinks we need him, but what about you feathery folks? You going to be gaunt fodder? Distract them so we can get through?" Reya inquired, tilting her head with curiosity. A hint of smugness turned up the edges of her eyes.

Harper stood up, hands pressing into the table so hard she felt it shift as if it would tip, but she pulled back on her strength, and it remained on all fours.

"I've been possessed by a witch channeling the power of the Autarch. If nothing else, I know what the demon feels like. And you don't know anything about what I'm capable of, or my family, so back off."

"Harper," Anna said, sternly.

Harper glowered at Reya, then at her mother, but backed down, keeping her wings put away and the Songs hidden in the back of her throat.

Anna dabbed at her mouth with a paper napkin. She stood, more reserved, her wings ruffling and tucking delicately against her back. "Harper is correct, Reya. We can do more than just fly around. Despite our inexperience, I believe our Songs might prove useful. If nothing else, perhaps we can serve as distractions if things get dire enough. There will be no more talk of who is staying or going. We're all going."

Tyson nodded. "I'm ready when you are. Charlie, do you have a specific place in the astral realm we need to travel to?"

Charlie appeared from seemingly nowhere—Harper hadn't even noticed she'd left the kitchen—lugging a massive painting that was nearly as tall but wider than she was. She propped it against the kitchen counter, gazing lovingly at its textured surface.

A mountain cliff dominated one side of the painting, with a narrow, winding path leading up to a ledge through mist and trees. The rocky ledge had a house on it, no bigger than Harper's thumb. Like a pimple on a giant's face.

"This will serve as your anchor. If you reach out to it with your mind…" Charlie stared at the painting, and paint swirled and blended together, a light glowing from the center.

Charlie reached out and a blue strand of light shot from the painting to her palm, connecting the two. She grabbed the strand.

"As long as I hold on to this tether and hold the image of that location in my mind, my magic will take me there. I suspect yours will work similarly. Try it." Charlie dropped the tether, and the painting became stationary, the glow disappearing.

Tyson remained seated. Within moments, a faint glow appeared around him, and then the mountain scene blurred, a glowing swirl pulsing in the center of the painting. He raised his hand, and the blue tether shot from the painting, connecting with his palm. He grinned, raising and lowering his hand, testing the connection.

"That's incredible," he said, cutting off the connection by closing his hand. The painting went inert once more.

"Well done," Charlie replied, smiling at him. "You're a quick learner. Now, if we all lay near each other on the floor, Tyson can thread the tether through us and bind us together. Any questions before we begin?"

"No way in hell I'm letting his magic anywhere near me," Reya said, bristling.

"His magic saved your life when the demons attacked. That was his portal Quinn flew you through," Harper said.

"Yeah, and it wasn't my choice to go through. White knight over there just grabbed me," Reya said, shrugging.

"Would you have rather been ripped apart by demons?" Tyson asked incredulously.

"This argument isn't helping. Reya, I know you're familiar with the astral realm. But Violet is the one who sent you there. Can you go through on your own?" Charlie asked.

Reya smirked. "It feels like it's just…right…there." Her hand grasped at the empty air in front of her face, and then her body crumpled.

Quinn yelped and caught her, staggering back at her dead weight before lowering her to the floor.

Harper glanced at Tyson. "Have you ever seen anyone do that? Go through while awake?"

"I mean, technically I'm awake when I go through, but I usually have to get into a sort of meditative state or visualize my entrance. She just…wow," Tyson said, looking impressed.

Charlie crossed her arms. "Reya, I think you proved your point," she called out.

Reya's body jerked, then sat up. She smiled at Quinn still hovering nearby. "I knew you'd catch me."

Quinn rubbed the back of his head. "Uh, you're welcome?"

"Now try to connect to the painting, Reya. Just like I showed Tyson," Charlie said.

Reya raised her hand and concentrated. It took much longer than it had for Tyson, the seconds dragging on, and Harper felt a bit smug until a flickering blue line connected with the painting.

Reya dropped her hand, panting slightly. She tossed her red hair. "See? I got this. No need to be tethered to anyone."

Tyson and Charlie exchanged looks, and then Charlie nodded. "All right, then. If you want to take that risk on, you do that. Just know, it'll feel different traveling there on your own power, rather than the power of a spell. If anything happens to you, you'll have a direct line to your body. Use it."

"I will," Reya said.

Harper still didn't want the fox shifter to come with them at all, but she didn't say anything. She wanted to get there and get this over with; the idea of entering the astral realm didn't appeal to her at all.

"Do the rest of us have to fall asleep?" Harper asked.

"Yes and no. I will be in charge of that," Charlie said. "We don't have time to teach you the art of successfully traveling to the astral realm, so I will put you to sleep, and Tyson will pull you through."

"Will we be in our bodies?" Harper asked.

"No, we won't," Tyson said. "Astral travel is different from portal travel. Our bodies will stay behind, binding us to this world, and our spirits will enter the astral realm on the physical plane, right Charlie?"

The soothsayer nodded. "Yes, that's correct. It's in a very far reach of the physical plane."

"How far is it from your husband's house to the Eternal Source?" Anna asked.

"This pocket dimension is positioned at a jumping off point, if you will. Normally, a traveler intending to visit the Eternal

Source would have to travel through the upper planes of the astral realm sequentially. The Higher Astral plane, the Higher Mental plane, and when he reached the Formative plane, he would find his journey unmade and be sent back to the beginning because it is most likely his cause would not be found sufficient for the attention of the Eternal Source."

Harper crossed her arms. "And what if our cause is not deemed sufficient?"

"We will deal with that if it comes to that. But I believe that the Eternal Source will hear us. After all, while Earth is not the only world with life on it in all existence, it is one of the most populated, and if it were consumed by the Autarch, then it would throw the universe out of balance and result in potentially devastating consequences for other worlds." Charlie scooped up several items from the table and headed for the fridge. "Help me clean this up."

After straightening the kitchen, everyone gathered in the living room. Bo pushed back the couch, giving them more space. Quinn pulled his wings inside his shoulder blades, and Anna did the same, lying where everyone else put their feet. Charlie took her place by the fireplace.

Bo stood near the mantle. "Have a good trip, ya'll. And mom? Tell dad I love him."

"I will, Bo." Charlie reached her hand up from where she lay on the floor and took his hand, squeezing it.

"Bo isn't coming?" Harper asked, adjusting her head on the fluffy carpet.

"Someone has to watch the shop," Charlie explained. "You ready, Tyson?"

Bo brought the painting over, putting it in front of the fireplace.

"Ready," Tyson said. "Hold hands, everyone. It makes the tethering easier."

Harper grasped Tyson's hand and found Quinn's on her other side.

Her body shuddered in anticipation, and Tyson's hand squeezed hers.

Words bottled up in her throat, and pictures crowded her mind. Pictures from Camp Silver Lake, that first time she fought with Tyson, and he stormed off into the woods, and she had found him hanging beneath a vampire's fangs. What if she couldn't protect him in the astral realm like she had there?

The words she wanted to say, just in case something happened in the astral realm, in case one of them didn't return, got stuck, blocked by the lack of privacy and her nerves.

A vibrant glow emitted from the painting, the blues, greens, and grays of the paint merging together.

Harper steadied her breathing. A weight dropped over her mind, and she suddenly felt as if she were drowning. Her instinct was to panic, but she calmed herself by thinking of the two hands she held, even as her sense of them faded.

Tyson's voice carried through the room. "Traveling in three...two...one..."

Harper's soul stretched. It clung tight, stretching until it seemed she would snap. The opposing force pulling it towards the swirling light yanked harder, and Harper's soul let go.

Charlie's living room hovered around her, and when she looked down she found her own body, appearing to be asleep.

Reya, with her spread of fiery hair, peeled away from her body. She sat in a yogi position in the air, and her eyes opened, lighting up with a bright orange glow. She smiled, her teeth glowing, then uncurled her ghostly form and shot across the room into the portal.

Quinn and Anna seemed to have already gone. Charlie passed through next, nodding to Harper and Tyson.

Tyson waited, his spirit hovering next to the painting, the tether glowing in his palm, his other hand reaching out towards her, a strand extending from it for her to grab.

The moment her hand touched it, an electrical current surged through her, and an irresistible pull dragged her towards the portal. She let go of the urge to resist it, allowing the supernatural force to take her from the only world she'd ever known into the realms beyond.

# CHAPTER THIRTEEN

## TYSON

TYSON NODDED AT BO, who watched from his spot beside the painting, somehow able to see everything that happened in that limbo space between realms.

Bo saluted him, and Tyson squared his shoulders and dove into the darkness.

When he emerged, he had no sense of place or direction except for the five tethers that he held connected to that place in his palm. He oriented himself upright, vision blossoming from darkness to a blurred mass of shapes to clarity.

A canyon yawned below and above, cliffs stretching on either side seemingly to eternity. The sky was a slit at the top, gray and sunless. The ravine on his left had a river of darkness at the bottom, without the soothing sound of water. Tyson couldn't be certain it even contained water.

He glanced around to his five companions, each of their forms glowing with aura light. Harper's familiar orange shone at him, along with the golden line connecting their chests.

She eyed it, dragging her eyes along the line to where it met Tyson, and she smiled, drifting towards him.

"Can we touch anything here?" Harper asked, reaching for him.

Her hand passed through his body at first, and she frowned, then pulled it back and looked at it. The color of her skin darkened, becoming less transparent, and she tried again.

Tyson *felt* something. A tingling, buzzing, trembling of his soul. His astral form quivered with pleasure.

"I didn't know you could do that," he admitted, trying it with his own hand. He held it up and met Harper's raised one, the tingling intensifying.

"There's a lot you don't know about these realms," Reya said, passing them and pulling a massive spear out of thin air. Blue lightning crackled, rallying at the tip, and she spun it around. She seemed taller here, her hair drifting around her face, lashing like living flames in a current Tyson couldn't see or feel.

She had become something else. Not human. Not a soul.

He gaped at her, his hand dropping from Harper's.

Charlie's lips pursed. "Very impressive, Reya. Where did you learn to change your astral form?"

Reya shrugged, a smile tugging at her lips. "Anyone can do it. Just takes practice."

Charlie raised her eyebrows, but didn't say anything else, instead orienting herself towards a steep path that wound up the side of the craggy mountain cliff.

"The fog hasn't descended as thick as usual. Good. Fewer monsters that way," Charlie said.

"Monsters?" Anna said, stepping up beside Charlie and scanning the path. "What dangers do we face here, soothsayer?"

"We're full of life force that the lower vibrational beings long for. It's simpler to refer to them as monsters; that's what they are."

"Most of them used to be people like us," Reya challenged.

Charlie met her gaze calmly. "Yes, but they chose to make oaths with Ragranoth. They chose darkness. That is the difference. We shouldn't soften our blows should it come to that."

Tyson noticed that Charlie had dropped her cheerful hippie demeanor. Her face was drawn, serious, reflective. Facing what they had come to do was taking its toll. They had to convince her husband to take them to the Eternal Source, where he would pass through the veil of life and death for good. Not a joyful reunion, to be sure.

"Let's go," Tyson said, moving forward on the path.

"I don't get it," Harper said, following Tyson. "If we're just spirits, why can't we zip up there like it's nothing? Why can't we fly?"

"We can move faster. But you'd risk losing control and jumping realms. Walking, or floating as we are, is better when you're new," Tyson explained. He'd had enough experience traveling where he hadn't intended to go in his few weeks of training.

"The rules are different here. This is a pocket dimension," Charlie said from behind, her voice drifting up, muted and flat. "In a pocket dimension, whoever created it can force certain rules. Such as gravity or denying all laws of physics. This dimension was created by my husband, Rudy. He's made it nearly inaccessible from the outside. You can fall off the edge of this path, and the river below will drag you into lower planes of existence. You could attempt to climb out, but you'd go mad trying. The cliffs have no end; the sky is an illusion. This path we're on loops back around, so even if you pass the cabin up there, intending to see what's beyond, you'd eventually find yourself exactly where we are now, walking up to the cabin again."

Tyson couldn't help but feel awed, despite how terrifying that sounded. The astral realm defied all Earth physics, and he still didn't have his head wrapped around everything that was possible here.

"It takes a lot of energy to develop a world this thoroughly," Reya said from somewhere behind. Judging by her tone, she sounded impressed, but Tyson didn't want to risk his balance to glance back and read her facial expression. Had Reya created her own pocket dimension while she was here?

"He's had ten years to develop it. And there will likely be traps, so be alert," Charlie said, her voice hushed.

No wind blew through the canyon. The lack of air stirring unsettled Tyson, even though he'd spent hours in the astral realm lately, trying to acclimate himself. He had no physical cues to go off of, either. No skin prickling. None of the minute body signals he relied upon heavily on Earth.

Just his intuition. Fortunately, over the past several weeks, he'd spent time honing his intuition to sense the danger creeping on them from below.

A gurgling sort of rattle filled the canyon as Tyson turned his head in time to see six monstrosities with multiple legs spider-crawling up the rocky cliffside, their pupils red and dilated.

"Mortu!" Reya yelled, at the same time Tyson shouted, "Watch it!"

Tyson drew his astral weapon out of the air. It appeared as a spear, and he threw it, the tip glowing orange. It sparked as it struck the first monster, who squealed, but kept climbing. The mortu were lower-vibrational denizens that could send a casual realm walker into a coma state, dragging their souls into the mortu's nests in the first abyss, allowing the entire colony to feed off their life force until their body eventually died and their spirit disintegrated.

Tyson called his spear back, gritting his teeth. He needed to put more energy behind the throw, like...

Another spear, crackling with brilliant blue lighting, shot past and speared one of the black mortu straight through, leaving a smoking hole. The spear shot back up and into Reya's hand.

Tyson stared at her. He wasn't the only one. He'd seen her spear in action before, but it still amazed him how powerful she was here in the astral realm.

"How do I get a weapon?" Quinn asked, eyeing their spears.

"We don't have time for a lesson. Fight the mortu with whatever you have," Charlie said, a glowing fuchsia bow in her hands, and a quiver of arrows on her back. She set an arrow on the string and aimed.

The monsters rattled and hissed, jumping in tandem as Charlie fired. Her arrow lit up with a neon pink flame, but soared past the nearest creature.

The group scattered. Tyson scrambled up the path as the mortu crashed onto it behind him. The path crumbled, sending rocks scattering down to the river of darkness the mortu had crawled out of.

The others were trapped on the opposite side, three mortu between them and Tyson.

Tyson wished he'd spent more time learning how to fight the lower vibrational beings of the astral realm. He didn't even know what the mortu were, much less how to banish them.

The closest mortu turned on him, hissing. It was shaped like a moose, if a moose had six legs, insect jaws, and pointed antelope-like antlers. The mortu's insect-like jaws clicked together, making that horrible, gurgling rattle.

It charged along the cliff wall, its feet gripping the stone as it skittered towards Tyson.

Tyson scrambled back, hefting his spear again. He shouted and threw the spear. The weapon cut through the air, piercing the mortu's black, shell-like hide between its head and front left leg.

The mortu lost its footing and howled, crashing onto the path, its legs thrashing frantically. Its movement caused it to roll off the edge of the broken mountain path and down into the dark depths.

A glowing fox the size of a bear leapt on the two remaining mortu, snapping at them.

Reya had changed her human form for her fox one, eyes aflame and looking like a god. How had she shifted in the astral realm? Even Tyson hadn't learned to do that yet, and he'd been told it wasn't possible. Then again, he'd been told that by Todd, who was Reya, and perhaps that had been part of her plan. How much of what she'd told him in that form could he consider true?

Quinn, Harper, and Anna soared above the spider-like monstrosities, flying over the fight and landing behind Tyson.

"Head to the cabin! I'll bring up the rear," Tyson said.

Harper's eyes ignited. "I'm not leaving you here."

"I'll be right behind you!" Tyson snapped. "Go!"

He pushed her, earning another glare, but she finally obliged, racing up the path with her brother and Anna just ahead.

Tyson turned back, looking for Charlie. He'd lost sight of her fighting the other mortu, and with Reya and the last two mortu blocking the mountain path, he couldn't see beyond.

One mortu clung to the upper part of the cliff, hissing and darting at Reya, holding her attention while the other one darted down and around, coming up behind the fox.

Where was Charlie?

A few pink arrows shot through the air, sticking into the mortu's hide.

Tyson chucked his spear, but it flew wide past the mortu Charlie faced and came back to him.

He threw it again, wildly, desperately, and it skimmed over Reya's back before striking the cliff face. Her back legs slipped off the path, and she yelped, paws scrambling, claws digging into the stone but finding no purchase.

Both mortu lunged for Reya at the same time.

Tyson soared through the air and screamed, thrusting his spear at the nearest mortu, hoping his aim would be true and he wouldn't hit Reya.

His spear struck one of the mortu and as it fell, one of its flailing legs shot out and hooking around Reya's midsection, pulling her down into the ravine.

Tyson watched in horror, waiting for Reya to miraculously save herself.

"No!" Tyson shouted, and he leapt from the cliffside without thinking. He dropped his spear, and it blinked out of existence as he plunged down into the ravine.

He willed his form to change into a bird, but his astral form didn't respond to his panicked thoughts. He didn't know what lay at the bottom of this ravine, but he wouldn't die from the impact. In his spirit form, there wouldn't be an impact. But the monsters at the bottom might rip him apart.

Arms gripped beneath Tyson's armpits, wrapping around his chest and yanking him upward. It would have hurt if he'd been in his physical body. He glanced up and saw Harper's determined, and furious, expression.

She hadn't gone into the cabin, like he'd said, but had turned back, seen his idiotic attempt to save Reya, and came to get him.

They landed, Harper dropping Tyson a moment before her own feet hit the ground, and she immediately turned on him.

"Never do that again. Never."

"Why didn't you jump when Reya fell? Why save me?" Tyson said, spinning on her.

Harper froze, her expression shocked. "That's what you're worried about? I just saved your life!"

"If you would have gone after Reya-"

"I started running when I saw Reya fall. I was too far away to catch her. I knew before I jumped. And you're lucky I jumped when I did, because I would have been too late for you too," Harper snapped.

"I'm sorry I'm such an idiot for wanting to save someone's life," Tyson shot back.

"Don't send me away like you have it handled when you clearly don't!" Harper shouted.

"In my defense, I should have been able to shift, or at least float," Tyson said, holding up his hands.

"Not here," Charlie said, her voice strained. "There are different rules in pocket dimensions. Here, there's gravity. Or some semblance of it. And in the ravine itself, the darkness is oppressive. Not all of your abilities will work here at all times."

Tyson opened his mouth to attempt to salvage some of his pride but was stopped by Charlie raising her palm.

"Additionally, Tyson, you are tethered to three other people. If you had fallen into that ravine, which ends in another plane of the astral realm, your tie to them would have severed, stranding them here in this pocket dimension. You would have essentially killed three people trying to save one. You can't take risks like that."

Tyson gaped at her. Why hadn't he considered that? Because he'd been too driven by the need to save Reya to consider the consequences.

"She's not dead. We have to go down there and save her. There are probably more mortu and who knows what else," Tyson argued.

"She wasn't tethered to you, and she knows her way around the astral realm. I've seen that girl fight. I'm sure she can handle herself," Charlie said with a soothing tone.

Tyson drifted away from her, glancing over his shoulder at the ravine. "What if she can't handle it herself? We can't just let her life-force get...get consumed by those things."

He glanced frantically around at the others, each one meeting his gaze with compassion and concern, but none of them offered to follow Reya into the ravine.

"The only ones who know how to fight in the astral realm are you and Charlie," Anna said abruptly. "We need you for obvious reasons, and Charlie is the one who can get through to Rudy and convince him to give us access to the harpies and the Eternal Source. It doesn't make sense to sacrifice the most experienced among us to go after Reya when there's a strong chance she'll make it back to her body on her own."

"Besides, we don't have time," Harper said.

Anger and guilt grew in Tyson, threatening to explode. Reya wouldn't even be there if it hadn't been for him. He was the one who had woken her up. He was the one who had built the portal and agreed to let her come with them to the astral realm.

"Stop blaming yourself," Harper insisted, her brown eyes resting on his. She stepped forward and took his hands in hers.

"How did you know—"

Harper tilted her head to one side. "You get a look when you're thinking too much, and you always blame yourself. Reya made the choice to come with us. She knew the risks. We have to move on without her."

"I agree with Harper," Quinn said.

"As do I," Anna agreed.

Tyson looked at Charlie, who gave him a sad smile. "If it were as simple as jumping down and getting her back to the top of the cliff, I would do it in an instant. But she's entered one of the lower planes and retrieving her and returning here could take hours or days of Earth time. We'll talk to Rudy, get through the harpies, and when this is all over, we can go back to the house and find her. Bo will be there when she wakes up, and he'll keep her company."

Tyson wanted to believe that Charlie was right, and Reya would make it out of that pit of mortu on her own. But his own encounters with the lower planes had been terrifying, and it was difficult to let go of the urge to jump in after her, and assuage his guilt at the harm he'd caused her and her family.

"I don't like it. In fact, I hate it. But since none of you will agree, I guess I'm outvoted," Tyson finally said.

"Then let's go," Charlie replied, leading the way up the path and across the porch, stopping at the front door.

"I don't know what we'll find when I open this door. Some days he rages, burning this dimension to the ground with his grief. Other days, he's like a ghost, unresponsive and impossible to communicate with. Tyson, I'm hoping your ability to see beyond the surface and heal will come into play. Your intuition is strong. Trust it."

"Unless it says to jump off a cliff. Then don't," Harper said.

Tyson resisted the urge to shoot her a glare. He wanted so badly to prove that he was capable of fighting for himself, not just healing people. This recent stunt hadn't helped Harper's view of him.

Charlie put her hand on the doorknob and twisted.

The door flew open with a bang, and a wind rushed from inside, threatening to push them all back down the stairs.

Charlie grimaced, bracing her astral form, then walked in against the wind.

The rest of the group followed.

"Hello? Rudy?" Charlie called. "I've brought some friends to meet ya."

The house was dark and appeared to be covered in a thick layer of dust.

A creaking sound came from the right.

Charlie led the group into the living room, where a figure with its back to the doorway rocked in a wooden chair.

The figure stood. A man in his early fifties faced them; a stern face with sagging cheeks and a dead expression in his eyes stared back at them.

"Hell, Charlie. You ought to give a man warning before bringing company over." The man's face split into a wide smile that did not reach his eyes. He extended his hand to Anna, who stood closest. "If I'd have known you were coming, I would have rolled out a welcome mat."

Harper leaned towards Tyson, voice hushed. "If he means more mortu, I'm glad he didn't."

Tyson nodded, recognizing that she was trying to reconnect with him, trying to help him feel better about what had just happened, but his pride still ached that she'd had to save him.

He kept his eyes on the man Charlie called Rudy. Her husband.

Something was off, and it wasn't the dead eyes, but a feeling in Tyson's chest. A tightening, a warning.

The man—or spirit, Tyson supposed—gestured into the dark, cobweb-filled living room. Lights flickered on as he gestured, turning the place into a more vibrant and welcoming version of itself.

"Since you're here, come in, make yourselves at home," the thing called Rudy said.

Harper stepped forward and Tyson flung his arm out, blocking her from getting any closer to the spirit standing in front of them. She looked at him like he was crazy but didn't challenge him.

Tyson opened his mouth to warn the others, but Charlie beat him to it.

"You aren't my husband," she said to the spirit. "Where's Rudy?"

# CHAPTER FOURTEEN

## HARPER

FEAR SURGED THROUGH HARPER. Without her physical body cues to focus on, her emotions were stronger than ever. She could hardly focus, much less interpret each sensation that flooded through her. Everything felt dangerous in this place, even the floor and walls.

So, when Tyson's arm flew across her chest, barring her from moving forward, she froze, letting him prevent her from doing something stupid. Like she had done at the cliffs for him.

The spirit in front of them chuckled. "Not your husband? Charlie, it's me, Rudy! I can't believe it. I don't booby trap the place one time and she thinks I've been usurped."

Charlie's face contorted, and she scoffed. "You got everything right, from the accent down to the last mole as far as I can see. Everything except the eyes. Rudy's are brown, not blue."

"I've always wanted blue eyes. How do you know I didn't change them?" Rudy's blue eyes narrowed, his tone gaining a dangerous edge.

Harper flexed her hands. She didn't know what to do here. She had limited physical abilities—she'd only caught Tyson because of their connection allowing her to touch him in this insane realm. She'd only ever known the physical world. What could she use to defend those she cared about if this unsettled spirit attacked them?

"What did you do with Rudy?" Charlie demanded.

"Hell if I know!" The spirit tossed its arms in the air, exasperation taking over its expression. "He told me to mirror him, see, said he'd be gone a few days and that some people might come looking for him. He was tired of fighting with you, the way I understand it."

"So, he ran away? It's been months since I last visited. It's not like I'm hounding him," Charlemagne snapped.

Harper glanced around at the group. They all wore the same bewildered expressions on their faces that she was certain she had on hers. Was this an enemy or not?

The spirit posing as Charlie's husband shook his head. "In the scheme of eternity, once every ten years would have been too soon. But you couldn't leave him alone."

"That's because he's making a mistake!" Charlie shouted. She ran a hand down her face. "Enough. I don't need directions."

A look of concentration passed over her face. She focused on something in the air in front of her, a few feet from her chest.

The soul-bond. Harper could see the line connecting her to Tyson out of the corner of her eye. It brightened as she focused on it, the other end disappearing into Tyson's chest. As if sensing her focus, Tyson glanced at her, shooting her a quick smile, and the line pulsed with waves of golden light.

Charlie must have a similar bond with her husband.

After a moment, Charlie slumped, putting her hands on either side of her head and shaking it back and forth. "No. No, no, no, no, no. What has he done? What have you done?"

Tyson approached the distraught seer, hands out but not touching.

"Charlie? What is it?"

She turned her head and looked at him with red-rimmed eyes. "Use your power of sight, dreamwalker. See what isn't there."

Harper didn't have Tyson's abilities. All she saw was Charlie's astral form, glowing slightly fuchsia.

Tyson raised his hand as if tracing something in mid-air.

"The bond...it's missing," he muttered out loud. "I can see its absence, like a ghost of the connection that was once there. Even that impression fades the farther I try to follow it."

Harper's hand flew to her chest. What would it feel like for that comforting warmth to be gone? If she couldn't sense Tyson there all the time?

"It's been weakening the longer he remained here without passing on, but I didn't think it would ever sever," Charlie said, sniffing loudly.

"How is that possible?" Tyson asked, louder. "You can't just...end a soul bond, can you?"

"Even when one of you dies, the bond is still there, leading the other into the afterlife. I didn't...I didn't notice when it stopped." Charlie's voice trailed off, her face going blank. "He's blocked it, somehow, to prevent me from finding him."

Charlie's brown ponytail whipped behind her as she swung around to face the spirit in her husband's body.

"Lose his face and take me to him now!" Charlie demanded.

Rudy's face melted, his 6-foot frame shrinking until a 4-ft tall goblin-looking creature stood in his place. He grinned toothily.

They didn't have time for this. Back on Earth, their bodies were getting thirsty and hungry. There was no telling how long they'd already spent away. A minute, a day.

Harper's anxiety rose, and her control vanished. She growled and rushed the goblin-like spirit, but her body passed through his. She snarled, whirling around.

The goblin's high-pitched laughter choked off with a gurgle as a trilling whistle sang through the room.

Anna's hair lifted, the silvery glow around her astral form expanding as she Sang the Song of Binding.

The goblin flew back, slamming into the wall of the cabin and sticking there, its arms trapped by its sides. It wriggled and grunted, gasping and growling in turn as it struggled against Anna's binding.

Her Song ended, but the glowing did not. She stepped towards the goblin-spirit, stopping just below where it hung.

"Tell us where Rudy is. And do not lie. I know other ways to use this Song that are not nearly as pleasant."

Harper could have kicked herself for not thinking to use one of the Songs. Not that she knew any of them well enough to use them like this. Like a warrior. Unless they needed something randomly and unpredictably blown up.

Tyson had backed up when Anna started singing, and his hand bumped Harper's. He interlocked her fingers with his, and Harper's anxiety diminished. At least she had him. For the first time in a while, they were working towards something together rather than being split up.

All her thinking had almost made her miss what the goblin said.

"...there's a tunnel in the basement. It contains a portal to his location." The goblin hissed and writhed as soon as it finished speaking.

"And what does he owe you for this farce?" Charlie spat. She stood next to Anna now, a whole head taller than the raven woman.

Anna sang a bar, the rising notes creating an almost visible vice around the goblin's neck as it hung suspended in the air.

"Gack! It—urg—h e agreed to pay me in soul essence." The horrid thing flicked its tongue between its teeth and tasted the air.

"No!" Charlie gasped. She turned to the others. "If what this cretin says is true, my husband is literally selling pieces of his soul, still trying to circumvent his inevitable crossing. This setup was to dissuade me from following him."

"I imagine it's done the opposite," Tyson said.

Charlie's face set with a determined grimace. "Convincing Rudy to cross is still our best chance for getting to see the Eternal Source."

"Lead the way, seer," Anna said.

Harper admired Anna's control—able to hold the effect of her Song in place until the group of them reached the stairs. Anna sang a descending tone that Harper felt as an odd, downward tugging sensation in her navel. The Song of Release.

The goblin thudded to the floor and skittered across the room towards the front door.

Harper reeled around to face it in case it tried anything funny, Quinn in front of her doing the same.

The thing's tongue tasted the air once more and laughter rattled in its throat. "You will all be dead before long. A waste of life source, if you ask me. A waste—"

Quinn lurched towards the goblin creature and it jumped, eyes widening, its back ramming into the door and rattling the tiny windows at the top. It fumbled for the door handle and flung the door wide, racing across the porch and down the path on all fours.

The door swung wide on its hinge. Quinn crossed the room to close it, shrugging at Harper's stare.

"It felt weird, keeping it open at our backs," he said. "The little creep might bring some friends if it returns."

Harper nodded and turned back to where Anna and Charlie were halfway down the stairs already. Tyson waited at the top, holding out his hand, and even though it made her feel childish, Harper took it, wanting any familiarity she could get in this strange place.

Harper followed Charlie, Anna, and Tyson down the creaky wooden staircase. No drafts emerged from the open doorway on the basement landing. No sound emerged, either. If Harper had had hair on the back of her neck, it would have been raised.

She tucked her astral wings in close out of habit, grateful that here, at least, she didn't seem to be molting. It made sense, as her wings weren't technically tangible. She walked through the doorway and into what appeared to be an endless tunnel.

"Where do you think it goes?" she whispered ahead to Tyson. Magic swirled around her ankles, urging her forward.

"We're definitely crossing planes," Tyson replied. He glanced over his shoulder, smiling reassuringly, but his eyes glowed faintly orange and Harper nearly reared back. It was just his dreamwalking ability, activated by this tunnel.

"We're descending," Tyson said a moment later, loud enough for the entire party to hear.

Harper grimaced. She still didn't know much about the astral planes, but Tyson had mentioned the different levels a few times, and she knew that going down wasn't good, especially since she'd spent some time caged up in one of the lower realms during her possession.

A light blossomed at the end of the tunnel, and a tiny pinprick rushed to meet them like a light on a freight train. Harper leapt into the air to avoid getting struck, but the white light swallowed Tyson, then her, then everything.

The house was gone, the ground and sky were gone, and then she was somewhere else.

The images around her blurred and shifted, slowly coming into focus. A man sat in an armchair with a newspaper, the room so small that he could reach the walls on either side if he spread his arms.

Harper's astral form overlapped with Tyson's, Quinn's, and Anna's, a crowded sensation filling her mind, but she couldn't actually feel any of them, except Tyson.

The man shook his newspaper and lowered it. He looked exactly like the goblin impersonator had while wearing his form, except for his muddy brown eyes.

"Damnit, Charlie. Why do you insist on following me everywhere? Don't I get a few centuries of peace before I'm stuck with you eternally?" the real Rudy asked, his voice gruff, but his eyes seemed to gleam and Harper realized the roughness was a mask, one that she herself wore sometimes when emotions became too large to handle.

Charlie stepped forward, reaching for Rudy with outstretched arms. "We promised each other that forever, Rudy. Fought for it, once or twice. Why are you turning your back on it now?"

Rudy grunted, then jutted his chin towards the cluster of spirits behind Charlie. "Who'd you bring with you this time? I don't see Bo."

"Bo's watching the shop. I don't think he wanted to come, to be honest. He's tired of seeing you like this."

"Seeing me like what?" Rudy snapped. "I have everything I want here. Everything except peace and quiet."

"And family," Charlie said softly. "You don't have that here. Your parents, your grandparents. Miles."

Harper had no idea who Miles was, but Rudy visibly startled at the name, and then his face and the entire room darkened.

The lighting didn't change—a glow still emanated from the lamp on the table beside Rudy's armchair. But Harper suddenly felt drained, her limbs heavy, as if she hadn't slept for days and needed desperately to lay down.

Tyson gripped Harper's arm. "Stay alert."

Harper shook herself, straightening, and forced herself to watch the spirit in the chair.

Rudy gritted his teeth, tears falling down his face. "Stop mentioning them!"

"They miss you. You're meant to go to them. I don't understand why you refuse," Charlie said. She gestured for Tyson, and he moved forward.

Harper pinched herself to hold the drowsiness at bay, catching Charlie's words to Tyson.

"Do a scan or whatever it is you do. Can you see anything?" she asked.

"Stop whispering!" Rudy bellowed. Long, shadowy tendrils shot out of his body and reached for them. The thing that was Rudy screeched and rose from the chair, using the lower tendrils like legs to lift himself up.

Tyson sketched something in the air—a symbol that glowed and drifted towards Rudy's torso, then vanished.

An acrid stench filled Harper's nose. How could she smell here? She gagged and stumbled back from Quinn, who seemed similarly affected.

Harper tried to plug her nose and straighten, but her fingers just went through her own face.

"Tyson!" she gasped, a burning sensation filled her mind, and she couldn't think of anything else.

Tyson glanced over, worry and concentration creasing his face. He drew another mark, this one all swirls and dots, and sent the rune-like figure floating towards Rudy.

Rudy lashed out at it, cutting it in half and hissing as it burned him, but not as badly as the first.

Charlie whirled around, eyes wild, hands splayed out before her. "Don't hurt him!"

Tyson sketched two more marks in quick succession, pushing them through the air at Rudy. They enveloped the thrashing, tentacled creature, surrounding it with pulsing light until they exploded.

Harper ducked but felt nothing touch her. She lifted her head.

The darkness and the fatigue immediately lifted, and the cozy reading room had transformed into a blank-walled room with sparse, crumbling furniture. The paradise Rudy had created for himself had broken like his spirit.

Tyson lay on the ground, grimacing in pain but slowly getting up.

Rudy did not.

Prostrate at the foot of the armchair, Rudy's size and energetic presence had shriveled to almost nothing. The shadows had gone. Fled or banished by Tyson's power. Only the spirit remained, a sagging-faced gray-haired man with stubble and deep circles under his eyes.

Charlie rushed to her husband's side. She knelt and dragged his head into her lap, apparently still able to touch him despite how their soul-bond had nearly vanished.

Harper ached at the sight of Charlie dry-sobbing over her husband's ruined form. Was this how he had died? His mortal body ruined with age and medical complications? To have to relive this...Harper could hardly imagine. But there was love in Charlie's eyes, alongside the despair, and Rudy looked at her with pain and adoration both.

"I d-don't...want you...t-t-t-o...see me this...way," he spoke in stutters and pauses, each one more labored than the last.

"Shhh," Charlie said, rocking slightly. "Don't waste your energy talking. You know what we have to do."

Tyson approached the couple, crouching down to be on Charlie's level. "I don't know what it's called, but there were several...beings attached to him, leeching off his soul essence, changing him. Warping him. They're gone now."

Harper blinked. Was Rudy...disappearing? The spirit in Charlie's arms seemed more translucent than ever.

Charlie noticed, too. Her hands roved over her husband's face and shoulders. "You're fading. No, no, no! You can't go here, Rudy. You have to cross over. Show us the bridge. You have to take us with you to confront the Eternal Source."

"Not...strong enough," Rudy gasped, his voice nothing more than a wheeze.

"What happens if he disappears?" Harper asked, approaching.

"I'm not sure. Souls are supposed to cross into the Eternal Source using the bridge that appears to those who have died when they first leave their physical bodies. If they wait too long, the bridge disappears and the only way back to the Eternal Source is through the bridge in the harpy's domain. That's my understanding, anyway," Charlie trailed off, gazing into her husband's eyes.

Rudy reached up and stroked her cheek. "You tried to tell me...for so long."

"You're a stubborn old goat," Charlie replied.

Tyson cleared his throat. "I have an idea for preserving him. If he can tell us how to get past the harpies, that is. I'm not sure it'll work, but it's the best shot we all have."

Charlie's eyes lit up with hope. "Please, Rudy?"

Rudy gestured for Tyson to lean in. Tyson did, bowing over the man's frail spirit and listening intently as those thin lips whispered words only Tyson and possibly Charlie could hear. Then, Rudy slumped back into Charlie's arms, his form diminishing in both size and appearance until Harper could barely make out his outline.

Tyson stood, making a motion like brushing his hands off on his pants, then glanced at his hands looking a bit lost.

"What did he say?" Harper asked, nearing Tyson. She wanted to touch him, to ask if he was hurt, to ease the worry lines from his face, to rub the knots from his neck and shoulders, but now wasn't the time, even if he had a body for her to embrace.

Tyson glanced from the couple back to Harper. "I'm dreamwalking into the T.R.S. to get the harpy egg so we can barter with the harpies guarding the Eternal Source."

# CHAPTER FIFTEEN

## TYSON

TYSON TRIED TO IGNORE Harper's dagger-like glare, her crossed arms and stiff wings a sure sign she was angry with him. Instead, he drew in a breath and called the others over.

Anna and Quinn came together, their faces interested and open. He'd earned their respect and trust, at least, despite his stupid mistake at the cliffside.

Tyson cleared his throat, but Quinn spoke first.

"Is he going to make it?" He jutted his square jaw towards Rudy and Charlie.

"Yes. Probably. At least across the bridge to the Eternal Source. But we have to get there first and fast. Charlie says it's guarded by Harpies, and the only way across, according to Rudy, is to barter with them," Tyson explained.

"What do we have that they could want?" Anna asked, tapping her chin. "You know, the T.R.S. has a treasury of both magical and non-magical items. If I could get a hold of an inventory sheet, we could offer any number of those items to them."

Tyson nodded. "I like where your thoughts are going, but we can't guarantee any of those items are still accessible with the Tower taken over."

"And how is that any different from your idea?" Harper said, gritting her teeth. "If Anna wants to go, let her. Her items are likely as good as some harpy egg."

Anna's eyes widened. "A harpy egg? Where did you get something like that?"

"It was a gift," Tyson said, exasperated at Harper's lack of support. Why didn't she accept that they all had to take risks, and she couldn't be the only one in action all the time?

Harper threw her hands up. "You're walking straight into a demon-infested building. What could go wrong?"

"A lot," Tyson admitted. "But I'm safer alone, and I'm traveling straight into my bedroom using a tunnel through the astral realm that I built with my own mind. That makes it very low risk. I doubt the demons are occupying my room."

"Why not take someone with you?" Quinn asked.

Anna cut in. "Tyson should go alone. Anyone else will only slow him down, and there's the added risk of them getting left behind if Tyson has to leave in a hurry. Not to mention if the demons attacked both of you, we would lose two in our party instead of just one."

Harper's wings shuddered, the feathers tickling Tyson's arm.

Irritation overrode Tyson's inclination to reassure her. Irritation that in every instance she seemed to care about him, except when he had to enter danger for the good of everyone else. She had no qualms about doing the same herself.

It irritated him even more that he didn't have time to unpack this insecurity with her. He would just have to show Harper that she could have confidence in him by proving that he could do this.

"Charlie, can you hold the others here in the astral realm while I'm gone?" Tyson asked.

"Holding them here should take less energy than bringing them here would have, and you already did that," Charlie said. "Just be quick. My energy isn't at its highest right now."

"Understood," Tyson said. He lifted his hand and held it near Charlie's, focusing on transferring the energetic anchors he'd used to bring the others there.

Charlie grunted and her magenta aura dimmed, but she gave Tyson a quick, strained smile as if trying to reassure him.

"Sure you'll be all right?" Tyson asked.

"Go," Charlie replied, nodding.

Tyson concentrated on the heat in his core, the place his magic resided. He used to think the *ulu* knife was his magic, but it was more like a focal point, a way for him to train. He was still getting used to the magic just being there, ready to use at any time whether he had the knife out or not.

"Are you sure this isn't about Reya?" Harper asked, stepping towards him.

Quinn caught her arm, and she tried to shake him off.

"Tyson!" Her voice was low, urgent, almost pleading.

He couldn't look at her. He had to focus on the tunnel he'd built in his mind, the one that was forming right in front of him. None of the others could see it unless he intended to take them with him.

The opening yawned and stretched, the walls a pearlescent shade of green, glossy and glimmering, a color that Tyson always thought belonged in the ocean.

"Let me go! Ty—"

He stepped through before Harper could shove Quinn off. Her broken-off shout garbled into nothing as he entered the stillness of the tunnel. A heart-beat like sound pulsed through the walls, rhythmic and haunting.

He had to go get his body first. Then, this tunnel would take his physical form to the T.R.S. Tower. Without his body, he wouldn't be able to pick up the egg. The tunnel acted like a shortcut, personalized just for him and tied directly to his body and any other location he attached to it. Currently, it was just his room at the Tower.

Tyson concentrated and felt his essence slide through the tunnel. A split second later, he was in Charlie's living room, where Bo slept in an armchair, head tilted back and snoring. Tyson slipped into his body, laying down and sitting up in an instant. He shook out his limbs, breathing deep to stave off a wave of hunger.

The clock on the mantle said it was after three a.m. Based on his body's cues, they had been gone in the astral realm for about eight hours. Most likely.

He glanced around at the sleeping bodies on the floor of the living room. Reya's form, with her long, red hair, still lay near Charlie, and Tyson's chest clenched with guilt. He should have gone after her, whatever the others said. He could have transferred their tethers to Charlie, could have...

He didn't have time for this.

Tyson called the tunnel he'd created, this time stepping inside. It sucked him in and flung him across space and time.

He fell out of the tunnel onto his bedroom floor inside the Tower, the cheap industrial office carpeting rough on his hands and knees. He breathed for a moment, making sure his breakfast wasn't going to make a reverse trip, then sat back on his heels and glanced around.

He froze when his eyes landed on a figure sitting cross-legged on his bed in the dark room.

"Who are… Ewu?" he asked, recognizing the man's lean body and long beard, even in the shadows.

The man's eyes opened with a yellow flash that illuminated his face in a sickly glow before dimming and darkening to normal.

"Tyson." He croaked, climbing from the bed and staggering forward. He gripped Tyson's shoulders like a pair of clamps, his arms trembling. "You weren't possessed."

Tyson shook his head. "No, we escaped."

"Thank the gods!" Ewu gasped, tears springing to his eyes. He drew himself up, sniffing and trying to regain his composure. "We? Who is with you? Where are you?"

Tyson glanced around the room again, even though he knew they were alone, something felt off about the Tower, and he couldn't be certain they wouldn't be overheard.

"Oh, it's safe in here. For now. I've put up some protection. They haven't found me yet, and they've searched this floor three times." He held up three skinny fingers and grinned.

"All right. I've got Harper, of course. Her brother, Quinn. And Reya—" His voice choked and broke off, but he forced himself to continue. "And Anna."

"Anna!" Ewu's eyes widened. "You have her! Praise all life. I will tell the others. They were worried she'd been captured and that the demon queen was waiting for something before revealing that she'd gotten one of our leaders."

"What about Jack and the others?" Tyson asked.

"Most of them escaped underground and are hiding out in the safe rooms in the city. The tunnels were destroyed. I was sent back here to try to find anyone else who might be hiding," Ewu said.

Tyson hesitated. He didn't have long, but he had a chance to find out how things looked for the T.R.S., and he knew Anna would appreciate the update. "How is it looking?"

Ewu shook his head. "Bah," he spat. "We were caught totally unawares. None of us expected attacks of a supernatural nature. We were too busy dealing with attacks of technology and warfare from the other side. We forgot we still had enemies among our own kind. And that shock cost us dearly. I don't have proper numbers, but I estimate only one in ten of our men and women got away. The children, fortunately, received enough advanced warning and were far enough from the attack that most of them were rescued and hidden in time. But I've already had to face those left behind, and they fight their friends without mercy."

Tyson shuddered, remembering when, not so long ago, Harper and Quinn had both been demon-controlled and had fought him with the intent to kill. He'd tried to forget the blank, glowing stares and the ruthless expressions on their faces, but he woke up at night in a cold sweat still, those eyes flaring at him.

"We're doing everything we can to get them back and take care of R...the demon Autarch before it's too late," Tyson said.

Ewu's eyes lit up. "Come up with a plan, have you?"

"I have a contact who knows...things. It's a lot to explain, actually. But we're going to see the Eternal Source. We've just got to get past these harpies. I have a harpy egg, and..." Tyson trailed off at Ewu's sudden change in expression, from mirthful and celebrating to rearing back, eyes wide with terror.

"The Eternal Source? Tyson, your training has barely begun. You think you can traverse the upper planes without losing your way, much less your mind? I've elevated to the Higher Mental Plane myself but at great cost. Attempting to go higher without proper training will only get you killed or make you go mad, which will have the same end result."

Tyson squirmed. "Well, we've found a shortcut of sorts. Hence the harpies." A sudden realization struck Tyson, and his legs went weak, one hand going to his forehead and rubbing through his hair.

"What is it?" Ewu asked.

"The egg. I just realized I won't be able to take it into the astral realm with me without dreamwalking. And where I'm going...I probably shouldn't risk using my physical form."

"No, that would be unwise. But have you considered that the harpy egg belongs to the harpies and therefore isn't of this world? It is tangible, yes, but in my experience similar items tend to change forms as they're brought across the veil between realms. Not an issue at all."

"But I also need a vessel for Rudy—that's Charlie's husband. You don't know him. Nevermind," Tyson said, rubbing his face in his hands. "Is there something I can do about getting some kind of vessel into the astral realm? Something I can bless with my magic and use to put a degenerating spirit inside?"

Ewu's jaw worked up and down, little grunts and high-pitched noises coming out, as if he were starting words and stopping without finishing their first sounds. Finally, he clamped his jaw shut and held up his hands.

"I do not think it is important that I understand what you are trying to accomplish. But this I may be able to help you with. How did you travel into the astral realm?" Ewu asked.

"Through a vision painted by a soothsayer," Tyson said automatically.

Ewu raised his eyebrows and whistled. "That's some talented friend you have there. I hope you treasure them. This makes it simple—paint an image of the vessel on the painting. When you return, the vessel will be where you painted it, and it will be in a spirit form."

Tyson glanced around the room. He didn't have anything here he could use as a vessel to protect Rudy's spirit. Not even an empty shampoo bottle. But Charlie's house had to have a jar or something...

Ewu cleared his throat. "I do not wish to deter or discourage you, but I know you, Tyson Miller. I've been as close to inside your mind as one can get. And I know that you're not ready to face the Eternal Source. No man is meant to face them and live."

"No man has ever had need like I have now," Tyson insisted.

He shoved away the anxiety that rose in his chest, trying to make him believe he was an imposter, that he didn't have strong enough magic, that he wasn't much of a dreamwalker at all, if he even was one.

"All mortals on the earth will be either destroyed or changed irrevocably if I don't do this. The demons will finish the bridge between the Final Abyss and Earth and more demons will cross over, and they will swallow our world and everyone in it. If the Eternal Source is all-knowing and all-powerful, if they are what we came from and will return to, won't they know all of this? Won't they be expecting us to seek their aid and willingly offer it to save their creations?"

Tyson's chest heaved up and down as he finished. He searched Ewu's gaze, noting the way the old man struggled to hold his eyes in one place, the way his shoulders gradually sagged inward, as if he were caving in on himself.

"There was a time," he started, then coughed, clearing his throat. "There was a time when man could access the Eternal Source simply by going to a mountain and meditating. Many things have widened the distance between our world and the up-permost planes. Technology, pollution, and war have laid waste to the sacred places. Pride and hate have laid waste to the places within our minds and hearts where the Eternal Source used to rest. They got tired of waiting for us to get our act together and have turned their back on us."

Tyson got the impression that the sage didn't think that Tyson would return from the meeting, if he even made it in the first place. But Tyson couldn't afford to give any of those thoughts a chance to root in his mind. He would return. And so would Harper, and Quinn, and Anna, and Charlie...

Ewu coughed. "Wasn't there something you came here for?"

Tyson shook himself. "Yeah. The egg."

He headed for the closet and dug into the back on the floor where his backpack slumped. Stained with dirt and who-knew-what else, the sun-bleached blue nylon ripped a bit as Tyson undid the zipper. The Harpy egg nestled inside a white t-shirt he'd wrapped around its softball-sized surface.

Once he handed the egg over to the harpies, he might never know what lay inside, and part of him couldn't help but wonder if he was giving away a weapon that could potentially win this war for them.

As soon as that thought landed, it was like a bur in his sock. He shrugged it off as he gripped the egg and turned back to Ewu, who sat back on the bed in his cross-legged position, readying himself for meditation.

"You could come with us. We sure could use your wisdom," Tyson said.

Ewu didn't even open his eyes. "I have a purpose here."

Tyson sighed, but he'd expected as much. He readied himself and concentrated on opening the walkway between realms to carry his physical form back to the relative safety of Charlie's house before he returned to Rudy's place in the astral realm.

Ewu's ancient voice crackled from the corner of the room again just as Tyson stepped out of this world and into the next.

"We will not meet again, Tyson Miller."

Sea-green light glimmered past Tyson's peripheral vision as the tunnel drew him onward. He turned around out of reflex, but Ewu had vanished, and the walkway entrance had closed.

Had Ewu meant that Tyson wouldn't see him again because Tyson's mission would fail? Or because Ewu would eventually get caught by the demons? Tyson had no way of knowing, and his confidence wavered.

The bright light appeared at the end of the tunnel like a train coming down tracks, and Tyson stumbled out into Charlie's kitchen, nearly knocking a chair over at the table.

Bo woke with a startled shout, arms and legs flailing as he shoved his way out of the yellow armchair by the fireplace. He whirled around, somehow managing to not step on the bodies of their astral-bound companions as he lurched towards the intruder in his house, only to come up short as he finally recognized Tyson.

He blinked, then frowned, his forehead creasing. "Tyson. Why are you back? Are the others…?"

"I'm just passing through," Tyson said in a rush. His stomach growled. He needed to eat something.

He ran to the kitchen and opened the fridge, grabbing a package of pre-sliced cheese, and shoved it into his mouth, chewing as fast as he could. He took a wad of curled ham from another package, grabbed the milk carton from the door and chugged to wash it all down.

Wiping his mouth, Tyson glanced into the living room and saw Bo, standing frozen behind the couch as if he'd seen a ghost.

One of the bodies on the floor was moving.

Reya sat up, stretching, then glanced up at Bo. Her eyes wandered past him into the kitchen where Tyson stood with the carton of milk in one hand and the harpy egg in the other.

In the blink of an eye she shifted into her fox form, bounding over the couch and darting towards Tyson.

Tyson swung the carton of milk in front of him. "Reya! Stop!"

She skidded, her claws scratching on the linoleum, and snarled at him, creeping one way, then the other, then launching herself at him.

Tyson dodged and banged his hip on the counter, then lurched through the dining room into the kitchen.

"Go!" Bo bellowed, raising his arms. Troll doll eyes lit up the entire living room, glowing neon orbs of terror. A whole army of trolls.

Tyson threw himself over the couch, gripping the harpy egg as tightly as he could, and laid on the floor. He lifted his hand, concentrating on the painting, trying to ignore the howls and yelps of pain as the troll dolls zipped from their stations towards the mad fox in the kitchen.

Just before he felt the portal connect, Tyson dropped his hand. He still needed a vessel.

"Where does Charlie keep her paint?" Tyson shouted, standing and jumping back over the couch.

"This isn't the time for painting!" Bo said, grunting as something struck his stomach. Reya had head-butted him.

A heap of trolls piled onto her back and seemed to be pulling her fur. She snapped and snarled at them.

"Bo!" Tyson shouted again.

"Cupboard in the hall, middle shelf. Can't miss it," Bo said, voice strained.

Tyson flung the nearest door open and immediately saw the paint. He grabbed the first colors he saw that would match, or come near enough, then headed for the portal painting leaning against the fireplace.

"Bo, I need a troll." Tyson glanced at the tubes of paint in his hand. "Er, a green one?"

One of the glowing little toys zipped over and started climbing his pants. Tyson dropped the paint and set the Harpy egg down, keeping it from rolling away with his foot, then grabbed the troll.

He drew a symbol over the troll with his free hand, watching the symbol float down into the troll's belly button. Orange light blossomed in the toy's eyes, then vanished. Its eyes went dull.

Tyson hoped it would work.

He squirted the two colors straight onto the tile next to the fireplace and picked up a paintbrush.

"Sorry, Charlie," Tyson said, dipping his paintbrush in the paint and stroking the colors onto the painting, placing the troll doll at the bottom of the path leading up to the tiny house at the center of the painting. He hoped intention was more important than accuracy, because his rendition of the troll doll looked like little more than a splotch.

Behind him, the fighting sounds escalated, chairs scraping across the floor, cups clattering to the floor as Reya fought the trolls and Bo tried to subdue her. The sound of shattering glass startled Tyson into looking up from the painting, and he saw Reya in her human form climbing over jagged glass shards in the kitchen windowsill, her eyes glowing amber.

Tyson dropped his paintbrush and stood, but it was too late. She was gone. Going after her at this point would only cause more trouble or get him killed.

"What's that for?" Bo asked, breathing heavily as trolls marched past him back to their places.

"Your dad," Tyson said, heading back to lay down in his spot on the floor, the harpy egg and the troll doll each in one hand.

He reached into the painting, sinking into his own subconscious as he was pulled onto the astral pathways back to where Harper waited for him.

# CHAPTER SIXTEEN

## ZEKE

ZEKE WOKE SOME TIME later, drowsy and wearing one of the bulky shock collars. A bowl full of food awaited him, a bone with bits of meat still clinging to it resting on top of the kibble.

His wolfish jaws clamped around it before he could stop himself. His human mind shouted at the wolf to put it down. He growled at himself. The ridiculousness of him growling at himself almost broke him down, but he held onto sanity and forced his jaws to open, dropping the bone with a clatter on the cage floor.

He sat back on his haunches and concentrated on shifting. With hands, he could remove the collar and see what he was up against.

An electric current went through his body, and he yelped, jumping and hitting his wolfish head on the cage.

Tentatively, he tried to transform again.

Again, the collar sent a shock rippling through his body. He howled and thrashed in the cage.

They'd taken his shift from him. The collar was somehow tuned to detect when he attempted to shift, to keep him in his wolf form.

Zeke beat his body against the cage door, trying to break the hinges. The cage flipped on its side. Water and kibble splattered all over Zeke, and he lay panting, defeated.

Slowly, he rolled upright in the turned-over cage, shaking the spilled dog food onto the floor. His stomach pinched and grumbled, and his body trembled with exhaustion and pain.

He had to keep up his strength. These men wouldn't care if he starved.

Zeke let himself lick up the scattered kibble, then chewed on the meaty bone. He licked up what little trails of water he could manage off the cement floor through the bars.

Moments after he finished the meal, his tongue went numb. It lolled out of his mouth, and the numbness seemed to go to his head, making his brain fuzzy. What had been in that food? Something on the bone? He hadn't tasted anything.

The door of the room opened, and Boris walked in, all swagger. He stopped in front of Zeke's cage.

Zeke tried to stand and wobbled but managed to get his feet under him. They'd drugged him, but why?

"Now you see. We have the power here. You're nothing but a mutt, and before I'm done with you, I'll teach you some manners. We'll see who's the master here." He turned to Drew, who stood behind him with a leash in hand. "Bring him out to the training pit."

"Who do you want in there with him?" Drew asked, inching towards the kennel.

Boris moved out of the way, giving Drew access to the cage.

"Get Cookie," Boris said, giving Zeke a wicked smile. "She'll teach him a thing or two."

Drew opened the cage door. Zeke tried to lunge, but he somehow misjudged the direction, and his nose ran into the side of the cage. He blinked. He'd never been so befuddled in his life. Something in whatever drug they'd given him was messing with his depth perception, sense of direction, and muscle control.

Drew grasped the collar and clipped the lead onto it, then tugged. "Come on, get out here."

Zeke sat on his haunches, something he could do without falling over. The collar dug into his neck, but he refused to be led around like a dog.

A shock blasted through him, and he yelped, standing up. Drew yanked on the lead again, dragging Zeke from the cage.

Zeke's head came up past the man's waist. He snapped at the man's leg, but another shock rippled through him.

He backed up, whining in pain, clawing at the collar around his neck.

*Get it off. Get it off. Get it off.*

His animal brain shrieked in pain and fear. Zeke's human mind wasn't faring much better. He couldn't think clearly. He didn't have full control of his limbs.

Drew tugged on the lead. "Come on, don't make me shock you again."

Boris laughed in the background, and Zeke snapped at the sound. He leapt towards the man, relying on scent more than sight, jaws open and aimed to close around any part of the horrid man that they ran into.

Another shock brought him down, a higher voltage this time.

It was a thousand times worse than anything he'd faced at the naturalization camp.

Zeke's breath wheezed in and out of his mouth as he lay on the ground with his eyes closed. Back in the camps, he'd chosen compliance. Do what he had to do to get out some day and return to his family. Eventually, he'd been given trust and responsibilities, and he'd met Mandi, and things hadn't felt so bad. He might never have left if it hadn't been for that raven shifter killing Violet and James and breaking the camp wide open.

He both hated and appreciated what that event had done for him. But at that moment, lying on the cold cement floor with Boris bearing down on him and the shock collar on his neck, Zeke wished he was back at Camp Silver Lake.

"Get up, pup," Boris said, his voice a harsh growl. The lead jerked, choking Zeke, and he was forced to stand or have his air supply cut off.

His body trembled against his will, and his tail hung low.

"Come," Boris said, clicking his tongue.

Zeke couldn't move. He didn't want to move. He wasn't sure his body would obey him if he tried.

"Come, dog," Boris snarled.

Another shock went through Zeke, this one smaller than the last but still like a thousand pinches all over his body. He took a step forward, then another, his body betraying him to avoid getting another shock.

He allowed himself to be led, humiliation, hunger, and hatred coursing through him in equal measures. He held onto his thoughts of Mandi, refusing to let these men turn him into the dog they saw him as.

Mandi laughing at something he'd said. Mandi running her fingers through his fur, scratching his ears. Mandi, white-eyed and stunning. She'd been perfect before her sight had been restored. Was she still inside her body? Or had the demon or whatever it was consumed her? Was anything left of the woman he loved?

He replayed the memories of the last few weeks that he could recall, searching for her, his despair growing. He couldn't tell. And if he couldn't tell, did that mean he didn't truly love her? Or was the demon just that good at mimicking her?

A heavy metal door swung open in front of Zeke, and scents assaulted him. Blood, sweat, humans, and the overwhelming odor of a female alpha.

Zeke glanced up, meeting the gleaming yellow eyes of the werewolf Boris had called Cookie.

*You will obey or you will die,* her voice sounded in his head, and Zeke startled.

*Make me,* Zeke replied, lifting his top lip in a silent snarl. He drew himself to his full height. Cookie was big, but he was bigger.

Boris chuckled. "Now, now. Have some patience, Zeke. You'll get a piece of our girl in the pit. If you don't die, maybe you'll even get chosen to breed her."

*I would rather die!* Zeke shouted.

Cookie's laughter filled his mind. *That can be arranged.*

Zeke fought against the lead. Even as they shocked him into unconsciousness, he fought. He would not back down. He would not let them turn him into an animal. He would not lose Mandi again.

# CHAPTER SEVENTEEN

## HARPER

HARPER WISHED TIME WOULD have passed like a blink before Tyson got back from retrieving the harpy egg, but instead it stretched out painfully long.

At first, she paced, but the repetitive motion did nothing but throw her into a frenzy of worry. The more time that passed, the more her worry turned to anger. She wanted to punch something, but given that the astral realm was intangible, she had nothing to take her agitation out on.

Tyson had gone alone into a den literally crawling with demons, and no one had listened to Harper about what a bad idea that was. Even Tyson had seemed more pissed off than anything at her protests.

He was still mortal despite his powers.

Agitated and distracted as she was, Harper didn't sense Tyson's return until he'd popped out of his dreamwalker tunnel almost on top of her.

He stumbled into her, holding an egg and a troll in his arms.

Harper caught him, fingers digging into his arms. Noises came from her throat that sounded so desperate with relief, she flushed with embarrassment.

Tyson cleared his throat. "Hi, Harper."

Harper cut off the strange whimpering sound that betrayed her concern and glanced over his entire body, scanning for injuries, and making sure he had none before she let him go and stepped away.

"Just bruised. Good news is, Reya made it back."

Harper studied his face. "And the bad news?"

"She kind of attacked me?" Tyson said.

"Attacked you?" Charlie said, lifting her head from where she sat with Rudy.

"When I got back with the egg, she woke up. Bo sicked your trolls on her, and she jumped out the window," Tyson explained.

"Good riddance," Harper snapped. "If she dared stick around after that, I'd—"

"Did you get the vessel?" Charlie interrupted.

"And the egg," Tyson said, holding the smooth black egg up. It gleamed in the low illusion of light in Rudy's astral hideout.

Harper held out her hands, and Tyson handed her the egg without hesitation.

"It's so light," Harper said, breath tightening. "Is it viable?"

"I'm not sure," Tyson said. "My magic revealed that there is something inside, but the previous owners never got anything to hatch."

"Harpy eggs used to be poached, centuries ago, when harpies had nests on the physical plane," Charlie said from her seat on the floor where her husband's spirit rested. "Not for the child inside, but because the child in its fetal form held a potent magic that could be changed through the intention of its caretakers. In times of war, the infant inside could be turned into a weapon. In times of peace, harpies would allow their children to hatch and flourish. A very useful evolutionary adaptation, if you ask me, but at high risk of being exploited by outsiders."

"So, a harpy child could be in there, just waiting to hatch?" Harper asked, shuddering at the thought that there were people in the world who would destroy a life to manifest something they desired. No matter what weapon could be forged through intention, she couldn't bring herself to even imagine altering the life within the warm egg she held in her hands.

Quinn finally sauntered over from where he'd been napping and crouched down in front of Harper, eyeing the egg.

"Aside from the obvious disturbance of an innocent life, is there any reason we shouldn't use this to wipe the demons out for good? I mean, it could potentially solve all our problems."

Harper glared at him, but a glance around the group showed her that they had all been considering it, and guilt flooded her. She had considered it, too, even if she'd rejected the thought instantly.

Her gaze lingered on Anna's face, taking in the almost hungry light in the rebellion leader's eyes. In her mind, everything was a tool. Her own son and daughter were no exception, why would an unborn child be any different?

Harper's hands moved protectively around the egg, covering more of its surface from view.

Anna glanced up, raising her thick eyebrows. "It must be considered. We don't reject any possibilities when the lives of millions are in danger. When the existence of our very world could—"

"We reject the possibilities that we can't live with," Harper snapped, pulling away from the circle that had tightened around her and the egg.

Tyson caught her by the arms, not caging her, but holding her in solidarity. Warmth flowed from his body to hers, and she stopped trying to back away, breathing through her nose and glaring at her mother, daring her to respond.

Charlie piped up from outside the circle instead. "If we had time, we could consider imprinting on the egg more seriously. We're saved from this ethical dilemma by the fact that imprinting a harpy's egg takes weeks, months, even years of concentrated intention. And at the end of that very vague time range, the egg could still refuse to hatch with what we needed. Our safest bet is to travel to the harpies and offer the egg to buy passage."

"Why did we need your husband if all we had to do was approach the harpies and offer something to trade?" Quinn asked. "We've wasted precious time as it is, and this seems like a useless detour."

Charlie's smile seemed more like gritted teeth. "You forget we didn't know how to get to the harpies; Rudy knew a shortcut, which he's now told Tyson and me."

"And I owed her a favor," Tyson cut in. "Charlie helped me get to Alaska and understand what I needed to do there. I owe much of my power to her, and certainly my life."

"The time has been spent either way," Anna said. "Charlie, will you be telling the rest of us how to reach the harpy nest?"

"We open the pathway with my husband's soul. It's slipping away further and further as we speak. When it's at the brink, a portal will open to take him away, and we will take advantage of it. We will have to work fast." Charlie looked to Tyson. "How did you manage to get it here?"

"What's the troll doll for?" Quinn asked, glancing between the two of them with confusion.

Harper had to admit she had no idea what the creepy toy was for either.

Tyson passed the troll doll to Charlie, its wicked little eyes gleaming lifelessly. "Ewu met me in my room and told me I could paint the image of it on the portal painting. I might have ruined it, sorry about that."

"No, it's perfect. He'll hate it," she said, sniffling and smiling as she turned the troll over in her hands. "Serves him right."

"So, the plan is to just...wait until he's nearly gone?" Quinn asked, rubbing the back of his head.

Charlie looked down at her husband's head in her lap. "It won't be long now," she whispered.

Rudy's head turned towards her, his image flickering.

"Pass me their tethers, Charlie," Tyson said quietly. They held up their hands like before and Harper felt a slight tingling, then suddenly more secure as Tyson's power took hold of her astral-linked spirit.

A howling wind rushed into the room, the first evidence of air Harper had found in the astral realm. It screeched past her, rushing down towards Rudy.

Tyson shouted words Harper didn't understand, his eyes glowing with orange ethereal power.

Charlie held the troll over her husband, and the wind ripped harder through the room as if it would shred all their souls into nothing. It seemed to fight with Charlie's grip on Rudy, and then it turned into a whirling vertical tunnel of wind and slashes of light, towering higher and higher. Harper felt herself drawn upward and gripped Tyson's hand even harder.

Rudy groaned, astral form rising, and for a horrifying moment Harper thought he'd be sucked up the vortex and the rest of them would be left, but the enchantment won, turning Rudy's soul into a thin ribbon of golden light and pushing it into the tiny plastic troll body. The jewel-like eyes flared with a golden glow, and the hair took on a wavering life of its own.

Charlie grabbed the troll doll without ceremony and shoved it in her pocket.

She didn't have much time to consider it as she rose with the others through the vortex, her soul getting thrust from one realm into another like the most insane roller coaster ride ever.

The vortex dropped them on a rocky cliff just as a spray of sea water rose up and spattered their faces.

Wind ripped at Harper's clothes and caught her wings, threatening to throw her off the cliff. She tucked her wings into her back and leaned into the wind, grabbing onto Quinn's arm in front of her to keep her feet on the ground.

Ocean waves struck the rocks and sent their spray to soak the high rocks they stood on.

After the utter stillness of the lower plane they'd just come from, Harper gasped that she now felt cold and wet. Every sensation seemed magnified, from the salt water stinging her astral skin to the high-pitched screaming of the wind.

Except the screams weren't coming from the wind.

Figures circled in the air over the cliffs and ocean nearby, reminiscent of vultures circling a corpse. They were some distance away still; a narrow, slick-looking natural bridge of stone reached from the rock Harper and her companions had landed on to the cluster of cliffs where the harpies flew.

Anna led the way across. Hunched against the wind, the leader of the rebels looked small and almost frail as she shuffled along the narrow path, pausing when the wind gusted and threatened to throw them off.

Tyson gripped Harper's hand from ahead, his other hand clutching the backpack that held the egg.

Harper squeezed his hand, wishing they had the option to turn back and try something else, but they couldn't fight a demon horde on their own. But even after they defeated the demons, there was still a war to be fought, to establish themselves among the humans on earth, to be seen as equals...maybe they ought to let the demons wipe everyone out and just start over.

Harper's dark thoughts were interrupted by shrieking so loud her eardrums ached. A second call, different in tone, broke through the harpies' harsh tones and brought relief to Harper's ears.

Anna stood, wings out, confronting the six harpies that had flown down from the sky. The harpies landed on a slightly wider part of the bridge, each woman taller than the average human by at least a foot and dwarfing Harper's mother.

Their wings were connected to their arms, their skin textured with feathers. They had human faces, except for downy feathers, and their hardened lips, more like beaks than lips, protruded slightly. They wore no clothes, and Harper noticed their chests were flat and covered with down.

Far more bird than human, unlike the raven tribe Harper came from. The two groups glared at each other, all screeching stopped. The harpies tilted their heads back and forth, considered the intruders.

"Only the dead are welcome here. What brings the living to our eyrie?" A harpy with gray and white patterned feathers called out over the howling wind.

"We come seeking aid for the mortals of earth," Anna replied. "The demon Autarch has brought demons through a portal and will destroy all living things if they are not stopped."

"We care not for your mortal troubles," another harpy said, more brown in her feathers than gray. "We have two tasks, and two alone—keep the living out and make sure the dead cross over." She lifted her chin and sniffed at the air. "You have one dead among you. Which is it?"

Charlie moved past Quinn, holding up the troll that held the wasted spirit of her dead husband.

"He is here."

"That is a toy," the gray harpy hissed. "Do not make fools of us, witch."

"I am not a witch, though the difference doesn't matter much to you, I suppose," Charlie said.

"Whatever you are called, you are mortal, and you try our patience. We could dash her on the rocks, Lyvaphe. We haven't seen the color red in so long," the brown-gray one said.

Lyvaphe, the gray harpy, flung her winged arms out, blocking the other harpy's access. "No, Mynera. They have something. Let's hear them."

"We aren't supposed to hear them," a third harpy said, this one with vivid black markings around her eyes. "We're supposed to warn them, then kill them. That's what They said."

The way the harpy emphasized "They" made Harper assume she spoke of someone above them. The Eternal Source or a god, if those actually existed.

"We want to talk to Them," Harper shouted. "We have your egg and a soul that needs to pass on. Let us through."

Tyson glanced at her, wide-eyed, his head shaking slightly. "What are you doing?" he whispered.

"Hurrying things along. They want to kill us, if you didn't hear. I'm just telling them what we have to bargain with."

The one called Mynera clapped her hands. "Oh, a bargain!" she squealed. "Let's consider it, Xynis. Please?"

The one with the dark around her eyes glared at them. "Bargains bring trouble. As do mortals. The last mortal to touch our shores killed many of our sisters, or have you forgotten?" Her yellow eyes flared with anger. "Stole many of our eggs, too. This must be one of them. Why would we accept in trade something stolen from us? The soul belongs to the Source and is not a bargaining chip."

"Then they have nothing," Lyvaphe said, folding her wings over her chest.

"Do any among you need healing?" Tyson asked. "I have some healing gifts."

The harpies hardly glanced at him before rolling their eyes and muttering to one another, their discontented words carried away on a gust of wind so strong, Harper had to grab onto Tyson to avoid stumbling off the edge of the path.

"We are immortal and injuries are rare. There is nothing you have to tempt us. The egg is ours, give it to us now," Lyvaphe insisted, holding out her hand towards Tyson.

He leaned back into Harper, gripping the straps of the backpack.

"I brought it here to you. Surely that would count for something."

Xynis bared wickedly pointed teeth and screeched. "Hand it over and leave immediately, and we will not kill you!"

Charlie raised the troll. "Wait! I could paint a vision for you. Predict your future..."

"We are prisoners!" Xynis turned on her, stalking past Lyvaphe and beating her wings together in a show of anger and strength. "We have no use for your parlor tricks!"

Charlie stammered something that Harper didn't quite hear, an apology, maybe.

Lyvaphe pulled Xynis back with a firm hand on her shoulder.

"That's enough, Xynis." She cleared her throat. "You have nothing to trade, and we have little patience remaining. Your desperation only makes us hungrier for something to break our eternal boredom. Go." She raised a winged arm, pointing back the way they had come.

"If you do not give us the soul and the egg, we will take them," Xynis said.

"I prefer bargains, but smashings are nice, too," Mynera said, shrugging, her face morphing from calm to vicious in an instant.

As a whole, the six harpies stepped forward, hissing and shrieking and beating their wings, forcing Harper and the others to walk backwards on the precariously narrow bridge.

"Wait!" Anna shouted, wings flinging outward, her arms shooting forward, palms up. She glanced away from the harpies for a moment, looking at Quinn then making eye contact with Harper, who stared at her, confused at the calculation clearly happening in her mother's head.

Anna turned her attention back to the harpies, who looked pissed at having their "smashing" interrupted.

"What happened to your songs?" Anna asked.

"Songs?" Mynera echoed. She must have been a younger harpy, or at least Harper assumed. She didn't seem to know how harpies should act compared with the others, who came off as more confident.

Xynis scoffed. "Harpies don't sing. We don't have songs."

"No," Lyvaphe agreed. Then she added, "but we used to."

The other five harpies protested loudly. She was mistaken. She was wrong. Songs? We have no songs.

Lyvaphe raised her arm in a fist, silencing the chattering and shrieking.

"It was millennia ago. Back when the old gods held power, before they merged into one. I was a hatchling, but my mothers told the stories, and I remember. Our beautiful voices were taken by the Source, another way for them to control us. Now we only scream, so all the damned might know what horrors await them, and the elevated will know what they have avoided." She lowered her feathered fist and turned her brilliant yellow eyes on the short raven woman. "You have the Songs?"

"We have our Songs," Anna said. "Taught to us by Raven. We have kept them, and our voices are strong."

Xynis shook her head. "Their having Songs means nothing to—"

"It could mean everything," Lyvaphe said. "If they have the Song of Breaking."

Harper's heart leapt into her throat. She touched the totem that rested on her chest, the hard edges of the bird skull warming against her fingers. She'd used the Song of Breaking herself in practice, the one that had gone wrong and exploded the glass everywhere and caused someone injury. What use was such a song here, in the wastelands of the astral realm where the dead went to cross over?

"We have such a song," Anna said. "We can break bonds of all kinds. Bonds such as yours."

"No song could break a bond of the gods," Xynis said bitterly.

"Our songs are of the gods," Anna insisted. "And there are three of us here who can Sing it for you. Our combined strength will set you free, and when you are free, you will allow us to cross."

"And you will give us the egg," Lyvaphe insisted.

"And the egg," Anna said solemnly.

"What of the soul?" Mynera piped up.

Charlie held the troll tight against her chest. "I will take him in myself, if you don't mind."

Xynis looked about ready to boil over at the comment, but Lyvaphe touched her sternum with two fingers. The odd gesture stopped the harpy in her tracks.

"We find these terms agreeable. But if the Song of Breaking does not work..." she paused, making eye contact with each of them before continuing. "Then I suggest you run."

Harper edged past Tyson. He squeezed her hand and let go, letting her by. Charlie moved aside as much as she could, nodding at her. Harper stood by Quinn, staring at Anna.

"Can we really do this?" Harper asked, keeping her voice low. "I've never broken anything other than glass. I didn't know the Songs could be used for...for concepts." Oaths? Ideas? How did one break something intangible? Harper's insides flip-flopped as she scanned her mother's face.

She didn't expect the smile that broke out on Anna's face, or the hand she reached out to rest on Harper's shoulder.

"I've never seen the Song of Breaking so strong in another Tulukaruq," Anna said. "Truthfully. The way you shattered that jar...it needs honing. That's why I will Sing with you. And Quinn," she glanced up at her son, who closed the circle by reaching his wings around the two women. "You have the focus she needs."

"Should we be doing this?" Quinn asked, eyes darting to where the harpies stood. "They must have been chained for a reason."

"That reason wasn't necessarily good or fair," Anna said. "We can't know the minds of the gods when they bound these creatures. But we have little choice if we wish to speak to the Eternal Source."

"We should have bargained for them not to kill us once they were freed," Quinn said. "They won't be bound by any limitations once this is done."

"Perhaps balance will be restored, rather than destroyed. Consider that," Anna said, raising her eyebrows at him. "Will you do this with me?"

Harper shifted uneasily. "I've only used the song a few times. And last time...that was an accident. I lost control."

"Reach inside and let the song out. I'll give you the primary bar. Just clear your mind, and follow my lead. Quinn and I will send our power into the bond, and together, we will succeed. I feel it," Anna insisted.

Harper wanted to believe her, wanted to listen to the advice that was like a balm to her lonely, rebellious soul. She would try.

She nodded. "All right. Let's do this." She breathed in several steady, slow breaths.

Anna hummed the notes of the primary bar, and Harper joined in, Quinn's lower tones starting at the exact same time and startling her almost into stopping, but she managed to keep going.

Thoughts crowded Harper's mind as the momentum of the song built in the air. A wall of sound constructed around them, blocking out the wind, blocking out everything. Harper tried sending the thoughts away, releasing her fear of someone getting hurt, of Tyson getting hurt, of her family breaking apart again, of the rebellion failing and Earth being demolished by the demon she had failed to stop from coming to earth. The demon she had, in a way, helped, by helping Lilith in the beginning at the lake.

She raised her voice, trying to drown out her thoughts. Trying not to think about what would happen if they failed, if the harpies killed Tyson.

Images of his life ended on the sharp rocks below made her voice tremble. Quinn gripped her elbow, lending her strength, and Harper clung to the totem on her chest, striving to activate the power she'd felt before when she sang to protect those she loved.

*Sing out of love, not fear.* She didn't know where the thought came from, but she let it shine at the forefront of her mind and finished the bar, then started again, more strength in her voice now.

The three voices reached a crescendo, and power surged through Harper from her core through her heart, getting caught there. It throbbed, forcing its way through her. She tried to cut off the song, tried to say it was too much, and she needed to stop before something broke they didn't intend to break, but the words were trapped by the song.

A pain exploded in Harper's chest, and the last note of the song turned sour as she screamed, falling to her knees on the hard rock.

Like a bubble bursting, the air seemed to pop around them. An invisible force crashed into the harpies, sending them flying backward. One went off the cliff, screaming in terror, but she used her wings to pull herself back into the air and by the time they saw her again, she was grinning.

Harper breathed, hand on her chest. The pain had only lasted a moment, but she was certain something had broken. Only, she didn't know what. Distantly, the harpies cackled with glee, and Harper assumed their bond was gone, that the Song of Breaking had succeeded.

But what had it cost? What had she done?

"Harper?"

The familiar male voice floated into her consciousness. She sat up, turning slowly through her shock. She met Tyson's gaze and reached for his outstretched hand and watched in horror as her own hand passed straight through his.

Their bond.

She'd broken their soul bond.

# CHAPTER EIGHTEEN

## TYSON

TYSON'S FINGERS MET AIR, and he nearly fell forward in shock. He pulled back at the last moment, righting himself, and he stared at Harper in horror.

Something had happened to their bond.

The golden strand that had connected them was gone—he couldn't see it threading from his chest to hers anymore, and where they could touch one another before in this intangible place, that ability had been taken away.

Harper looked a moment away from losing it, her aura throbbing, waves of pain coming off her that Tyson couldn't even begin to shield himself from, because his aura was doing the same, their pain crashing into each other and creating a turbulent storm that threatened to sweep them both away.

Tyson shoved his panic down and tried to smooth out the concern on his face.

"Hey, it's—"

"Don't you dare say okay," Harper said, backing away from him, her aura throbbing. Terror, guilt, anger all crossed her face. "You don't know it's going to be okay."

"Then we'll figure it out," Tyson said. His own emotions threatened to swallow him, and he felt his grip on the astral realm slipping. No, he couldn't let that happen. He held four tethers with his power. If he left, they would all leave, and they would lose this chance to see the Eternal Source.

"How? We were already struggling. You have to have seen it. I don't know how to do this, and you—" Harper stopped and shook her head, turning away from him.

"Me what?" Tyson asked, unable to stop himself. His de-escalation training didn't seem suited for a situation like this.

"You're so busy trying to prove yourself you don't listen when I have concerns. You're always going off on communication and how important it is, but you never talk about when things are hard. You gloss over them like we can sweep them under the rug, and they'll go away. This isn't going away, Tyson. As far as we know, it's permanent."

Her eyes didn't leave his, and the confusion and sorrow in them made him long to hold her. *Damn this intangible form.*

And damn her logic.

"What if…What if without the bond, we can't make this work?" Harper looked as if she wanted to shrink in on herself, as if all her confidence were slipping away.

"Hate to interrupt, but we have a bigger problem," Quinn said, putting his hand on Tyson's shoulder and pointing up at the sky.

A multitude of screeches filled the air, and Tyson realized the number of harpies had doubled.

"Are they…circling?" he asked.

"You never gave them the egg," Harper said.

"Run!" Anna's voice thundered, and she barreled past them all and raced down the narrow stone path, wings tucked at her back to keep from being buffeted off the cliffs into the sea.

Harper took off without question, and Tyson followed, glancing behind to make sure everyone had heard the warning.

A split second later, the harpies began to dive.

Tyson raised the egg over his head while running. Could the harpies kill them while they were intangible? He had a feeling it wouldn't matter to them, considering their earlier threats. If they ripped into his soul, would he die or simply get banished back to his body? He didn't care to find out.

The harpies pulled up at the last moment, beat their way back into the skies, and fell again, dive-bombing the group with piercing calls, hurling insults and small rocks. The rocks, at least, went straight through Tyson's astral form without harming him. The insults were ridiculous.

Ahead, Anna reached the far cliff and skidded to a stop, turning with her palms raised, yelling for them to stop.

Tyson skidded to a halt with so much momentum, he almost couldn't stop before the edge of the yawning portal. A giant eye stared up at him, glowing with a blue iris and a fiery orange pupil. It stared straight through Tyson, stripping him of all his pretenses, protections, and shields, reaching into his core.

"We have the egg!" Tyson yelled, spinning away from that eye and holding the egg in front of him.

"We had a bargain, harpies!" Anna shouted.

One of the harpies from before—Lyvaphe, Tyson thought—touched ground in front of Anna, reaching out with two fingers to touch the raven born's sternum.

"Do not begrudge us our fun. We've had so little in the past thousand years. Yet, we do honor our agreements, Raven Born. You and your party will pass into the Eternal Source without any more harassment from us. Hand me the egg."

Tyson walked forward, hoping he wouldn't meet the wrong end of those wicked talons the moment he passed her the egg, but the harpy merely used them to grasp the egg's oval surface, taking it from him.

He edged away from her, those bright eyes watching him.

"I feel compelled to warn you that it is unlikely you will leave once you enter," Lyvaphe declared. "The Eternal Source will test you, and if you do not pass, They will absorb your souls to be recycled for a later life. You will not return to your precious Earth to see it saved. So, if you wish to die with the rest of your kind, you should turn back now."

The harpy's yellow eyes were not cruel, and Tyson knew she intended to do them a favor by telling them this truth. His heart clenched, and he glanced at Harper, realizing that without their bond, if they died they might not find each other again in the existence beyond. And if their souls were "recycled," as Lyvaphe had put it, would they still be soulmates? Would their new selves find each other without the golden line to connect them?

The full implications of Harper's song breaking their bond washed over him, and he felt as if his heart would tear apart. Perhaps they could ask the Eternal Source to restore their bond?

"Thank you for this information," Anna said. "We'll take our chances."

Lyvaphe bowed her head. "Then, enter the Eternal Source." She gestured behind her, towards the cliff edge and the portal that looked like an eye.

Harper drew close to Tyson, leaning towards him despite knowing they could no longer touch. Tyson held up a hand, and after a moment, she held hers up right beside his. If he concentrated, he could feel something...a buzzing between their palms, their energies combining. The tingling washed through him, and he smiled at Harper.

"Together?" he asked.

She nodded. "Together."

They stood beside one another and on three, they leapt into the unblinking eye.

# CHAPTER NINETEEN

## TYSON

A SWIRLING MAELSTROM OF glittering energy ripped through Tyson, and he lost sight of Harper. He lost form, he lost all sense of meaning, he lost consciousness.

When he regained awareness, he lay on his back in an entirely white room. Four white walls, white ceiling, and a hard white floor. None of it was made from any substance Tyson recognized. He sat up and walked to each wall and pushed, learning it was solid. He tried to imagine a way out, something that would work on the physical plane of the astral realm, but nothing happened.

His vision telescoped, zooming in on the wall across the room, then zooming out of its own accord, as if someone had control of his eyes. As his vision widened in scope, the room extended, and in the distance a wall appeared, then disappeared, opening into a comfortable-looking room where a man sat in a chair holding a clipboard.

The man motioned for Tyson to come, and the distance flashed. He found himself standing in the middle of the comfortable room, the wall replaced to hide the white place that Tyson had just come from.

"Tom?" Tyson exclaimed, blinking and shaking his head.

Tom, his old counseling mentor at Camp Silver Lake, sat across from him.

"Tyson Miller," Tom said, smiling wide. He stood and reached out his hand, which Tyson took without thinking.

Their hands passed through each other, and Tom laughed.

"Got ya!" Tom said, making a finger gun and winking at him.

Tyson only stared at his old counseling mentor, a thousand questions flooding his mind. He didn't know which to ask first, and it must have showed on his face because Tom sat down and leaned forward with a concerned expression.

"What's on your mind, son?" Tom asked.

"You're dead," Tyson blurted. He sat down on the edge of the couch behind him, still in shock. He had never expected to see his mentor again, and certainly not in a place like this.

Tom chuckled. "Yes, I died. And yes, it was at Lilith's hand. She killed a lot of people. You're not dead, though." His eyes glittered with something…it couldn't be admiration. Tom had been disappointed in Tyson at the end, considered him enough of a failure to terminate his internship early.

"I have to hand it to you, Tyson. You sure know how to go out with a bang. I deliver the message that you've been fired, take your badge, and next thing I hear you've helped Violet's and James' murderer escape the camp and go into hiding." Tom interlocked his fingers and rested them on the clipboard. "I want to know what you were thinking."

There was no accusation in his tone, only curiosity.

Tyson swallowed. He had dreaded the day he'd have to justify his actions at Camp Silver Lake to someone. He'd started to believe that day would never come as long as the rebellion won, but it had caught up to him after all.

"Did the Eternal Source send you? Am I being judged?"

"I volunteered for this position. There were a few candidates, and I'm honored to have been chosen. Do you know how many paranormals and humans died because of decisions you made?" His eyes still gleamed, but this time Tyson didn't pretend there was anything kind in the expression. Pure, unbridled hate shone through his old mentor's gaze.

Guilt surged inside Tyson. He licked his lips. "I never meant for any of it to happen. I just…" *Did my best*. The words felt entirely inadequate, but they were true. He'd done his best with the information he'd had. He knew better now. He regretted every moment. But saying it was pointless.

"Tell me what I have to do to make it right," Tyson said, spreading his hands. "I'll do anything. I'll sacrifice everything I have, my power, my life. Just tell me what I have to do."

"Oh, there's nothing you can do," Tom said casually. He clicked the end of a pen that had appeared in his hand out of nowhere. He jotted something down, biting his lip as he did.

"What are you writing?" Tyson asked.

"You're suffering from a severe savior complex. You think you can fix your past by throwing yourself in front of the bus, so to speak. But nothing can compensate for what you've done. Those people are still dead. Lives ruined. You're still alive, and you are what you are. By the way, how is that going?"

"What?" Tyson asked, confused by the sudden change of topic.

"Discovering your powers. Learning that you're the same as those you condemned to a life without magic," Tom said, his gaze ruthless.

Tyson struggled to get the words out, emotion clogging up his ability to speak. "I-I learned that it's part of them. Whether it's shifting or spells or singing—It's all magic, and it's as much a part of them as their blood, and just as essential for survival." He hung his head, staring at his hands and thinking of Fletcher, who had died because Tyson hadn't understood this one crucial point.

Except that was a lie. He'd known, somewhere inside he'd known, and he'd refused to acknowledge it until Harper came along and challenged him because it was easier to go along with what society wanted and believe that he was making a difference.

He closed his eyes, wishing he had the comforting rhythm of his breath to ease the discomfort of the emotions washing over him.

Tom tsked. "You've certainly come a long way. The question is, are you ready for what comes next?"

Tyson brought his head up. "What do you mean?"

"I mean exactly what I said," Tom replied. "Are you prepared to deal with the result of your actions? You've indirectly murdered dozens of people. And you've fallen in love with one of them."

Tyson stared at Tom, wondering if his mentor had gone insane after death. "But Harper isn't...she's not..."

"Oh, but she will be," Tom said, standing. The pen and clipboard disappeared, and he walked around behind the couch Tyson sat on.

Tyson turned, trying to keep his eyes on Tom, distrust rising like bile in his throat. "Tell me what you mean! Nothing is going to happen to Harper. She's smart and strong and resourceful, and..."

"It's already happened. *You* already happened. And Harper won't be able to resist protecting you now that you have her heart. The moment your life is in danger, she will risk it all to save you, and you'll have one more death on your hands. Are you prepared for that?"

Tyson stood, facing Tom. "She's not going to die. She doesn't have to protect me anymore. I have magic. I can protect myself."

"But she doesn't understand that, does she? If you want her to live, you're going to have to step up your game. Throw yourself in front of the bus before she has the chance. Are you willing to do that?" Tom asked, raising his eyebrows.

"Are you saying that a moment will come when one of us will have to die? And it should be me?" Tyson asked,

"Sometimes we're called to do things in our lives, and the journey we embark on is not the journey we end up taking," Tom said, smiling.

Tyson recognized the words. They were almost the last thing Tom had said to him before everything blew up at Camp Silver Lake. And he found that as they sank deep into his soul, he knew the answer to Tom's question.

Yes, he was willing to die for Harper. For the world. When the time came, Tyson would give up his life. Even though the thought of it terrified him, he hoped they could find a way to avoid anyone dying.

"But what's going to happen? Are you going to help us?" Tyson asked desperately.

Tom's smile widened, and then he pushed on Tyson's chest, sending Tyson reeling backwards, his soul flailing into a place between time and space, where everything had started and nothing began.

Tyson ignored his first instinct, which was to panic. Instead, he withdrew, finding the core part of himself that existed no matter what form he took. Human. Polar bear. Immaterial spirit. The part of him that made him, him.

He found it burning at his center, brilliantly glowing orange in his mind's eye, pulsing with life and purpose. He sat with it, content to just be, sending away every doubt, every thought that tried to derail him from being centered and calm. He waited, letting go of pretense, letting go of fear and guilt and lust and everything that normally drove him.

All of it burned away, leaving just him.

*You are ready*, a voice said, the same one from before.

A brilliant white light lit up the space Tyson was in, and it snatched him from the womb-like space he'd created for himself, dragging him into paradise.

Or, what he assumed was supposed to be paradise.

He'd heard somewhere the idea that paradise would look different for each person that encountered it. Something about paradise meaning something unique to everyone. Looking around at the empty road and the flat, white expanse with nothing on the horizon and a silver ball mimicking the sun in the sky, Tyson hoped that person was wrong. Because if not, his paradise sucked, and it would be his own fault.

Tyson turned around. "Hello?"

Behind him, a cloud of mist gathered, blocking out the road beyond.

*Hello*, the disembodied voice responded.

"Where am I?" Tyson asked.

*A place we meet with souls like you.*

Not exactly a comforting response, but Tyson felt some relief that someone had replied.

"Who are you?"

*You can call us the Source.*

"There's more than one of you?" Tyson said, confused. He'd thought Tom was the Eternal Source, or a representation of them.

*We are the whole. We are the Source,* They said, as if that explained anything.

"We need your help. Earth needs your help," Tyson rushed to say.

The cloud of mist agitated as if a wind had blown through and disturbed it, but Tyson didn't feel anything.

A sound like laughter echoed around Tyson.

*We will wait for the others. There is no point in repeating what we have to say.*

Fair enough. And it would give Tyson a chance to practice letting go, he assumed. He let the hundreds of other questions he had fall to the side in favor of one that he needed the answer to.

"Where are the others?"

*Coming.*

The word hung in the air, and then Tyson felt a familiar tingling sensation spread from his palm to his chest and down his trunk and legs, then up into his head. It filled him with a sense of exactly who would be coming through next, and his aura pulsed in anticipation.

Harper. Harper was coming.

# CHAPTER TWENTY

## HARPER

HARPER STAYED CONSCIOUS THROUGH the eye-portal until she struck the hard white floor, and then she lost all sense of time and herself.

When she woke, she was entirely convinced that she might, in fact, be dead, which wouldn't be so bad after everything that had just happened.

She had severed her soul bond with Tyson, and the pain of knowing it was her erratic magic that had caused it muddled all the feelings in her chest and head and made her wish that she could be dead and not have to deal with all the mortal emotions flooding through her.

Those emotions were ultimately what made her decide that she wasn't dead yet. Wouldn't she feel some release from all the stuff mortals cared about if she had died? She hoped so. Facing the thought of an eternity with all the conflict warring in her soul made her want the oblivion of being possessed, which had been peaceful in comparison.

She rolled over and pushed her way to her feet. By the time she was standing, another presence had entered the white-walled room.

Harper blinked, trying to clear the blurred form materializing in front of her. Blue and white and black and gray merged together, then sharpened, coming together all at once and shocking Harper into jumping back.

Harper gasped. She brought one hand up to cover her trembling mouth. "Fletcher?"

"In the flesh. Well, spirit. Best I could do." Fletcher smiled at her, tossing his frosted blonde hair back, hands jammed in his loose, ragged jeans and the tank-top he always used to wear. His bluejay wings, more vibrant than ever, flared out on either side of him. Whole and complete.

He was the last being she'd expected to see here. Whatever she'd believed about death being the ultimate end before was gone in the face of Fletcher standing before her now.

"This isn't a trick, is it? You're not some god taking on Fletcher's form because you know it would get me to trust you? Because if it is, I'm going to make you regret your immortal—"

"Whoa, there," Fletcher said, holding up his hands and laughing. "Let's stop you before you start blaspheming."

A laugh bubbled out of Harper's throat, tinged with sadness and regret and guilt. She didn't even know where to start. Before she could say anything, however, Fletcher walked across the room, arms stretched out, and enfolded her in a hug, strong arms flexing, wings cupping around her.

She didn't know how it was possible in this intangible place, and she didn't care. She only cared that she had her friend. He was here. She could touch him, giving him the final hug that had been stolen from her when he took his own life.

That memory soured the embrace, and she pulled away, mourning Fletcher's loss all over again.

"Why?" she asked softly.

"Why what?" he asked, confusion on his face.

Harper squirmed. As hard as it was to remember what had happened, it was harder to say it out loud. "Why did you do it, Fletcher? So many of us...we cared about you. We would have supported you through it. We were trying. Did we...did I say something wrong? Was it too much, being around me after they took your wings?"

Fletcher's head cocked to one side. "That hurt, yeah. But it wasn't too much for me. I just needed to be away for a bit. Take a walk. Let the wounds—Inside and out—heal while I figured stuff out. I went out to the cliff. It was a bit harder on foot," he laughed bitterly, hollowness in his gaze.

Fletcher continued. "But I didn't jump. That's what you're implying, isn't it? I thought about it. Not gonna lie. But then...Lilith was there. And she said something about persuading, and how she needed you to run to her because she was losing you." Fletcher's blue-eyed gaze seemed to pierce Harper, and her breath caught. "What did she mean, Harper? Why did she kill me?"

The ground seemed to fall out from under Harper. Everything she'd assumed—that Fletcher had killed himself over the sorrow and pain of facing a future without flight—was a lie.

Lilith had killed him, had pushed him from that cliff where they first kissed. And she'd done it to convince Harper to use the beryllium orb and kill Violet and James, the witches running camp Silver Lake.

"Lilith killed you? She...she was there? No, I..."

"Even when the facts are presented to you clearly, you reject them. What a tormented soul," Fletcher said, and his face morphed into an expression entirely unlike his own, his astral form glowing.

"Fletcher?" Harper said, not sure her heart could take much more of this encounter.

"Yes, and no," not-Fletcher said. "We have met before. Do you remember?"

"W-was Fletcher real? Just now? Was he here?" Harper demanded, while also trying to pinpoint where she might have met this otherworldly, possibly eternal being. There was *something* familiar about it, but she couldn't quite put her finger on it...

"Yes, and no," the being said again, this time dissolving Fletcher's form and appearing to her as a glowing orb of light.

The Beryllium Orb.

"No!" Harper shouted, grasping air. Her legs wobbled and then wouldn't hold her anymore. She collapsed, wings slumped around her on the white floor, the light that had simply existed in the room dramatically reducing to a single spotlight.

"You can appear as anything. Say anything. You're just trying to frighten me," Harper said, grasping onto whatever shred of courage she had left. Seeing the orb made her entire frame quake and fear rise in her throat like bile, choking her, but she held on, squinting into the orb as if she could see past it. Was it real? Or another illusion?

"It is your fault your friend Fletcher died. Lilith wanted to control you, and you let yourself be controlled, all while thinking you were in charge. And you haven't learned anything. You're here to convince the Source to help you at all costs. But are you truly willing to pay the cost?"

"What are you saying?" Harper asked. She didn't want anything to do with the orb after what it had convinced her to do to Violet and James. Had the Eternal Source been inside the orb this whole time? Had they taken her memories of Quinn, forcing her onto the path she'd gone down to get to this point?

"You know Tyson would do anything for you. Even die for you. Are you willing to let him?" the being in the orb said.

"I'm not letting Tyson die!" Harper shouted.

Laughter filled her mind. "Excellent," the voices said, then faded.

"What's going to happen? Don't leave! Tell me!" Harper demanded.

The room around her stretched and reformed into a long hallway, and at the end of it was a door.

Harper dashed for the door, throwing it open to find Tyson standing alone in an empty white room similar to the one she'd left.

She drew close, but didn't try to touch him, afraid of what it might do to her heart if she passed through him again. She wanted to get back to earth and fill her senses with him. She was sick of this lifeless, senseless place.

A presence filled the room, swelling until Harper thought she'd implode, and Tyson pointed behind her.

"Someone else is coming," he said.

The wall opened and Anna emerged. She nodded in greeting, her expression unreadable. She stopped next to Harper.

"I assume this is where we meet the Eternal Source?" Anna said.

"I think we've already met Them," Tyson said.

"Tyson, it's the orb. The Beryllium Orb. It—They—said I'd met Them before." Still shook, Harper hunched over, unable to draw comfort even from her own body, since it was back on the physical plane.

Tyson frowned. "Are you sure?"

"That's what They said to me."

"They must have some purpose...some reason..." Tyson murmured.

The room pressurized a fourth time, and Quinn stepped through the door, his expression so hollowed out, Harper wanted to run and hug her brother, but she couldn't here, and again, it frustrated her. She wanted this conversation to be over with, and with or without divine help she was going to go back to earth and give every person in this room a damned hug.

She never thought she'd miss those; after a lifetime of living without them, she'd adjusted, or so she thought, to not having much in the way of physical expressions of affection. Tyson had changed that for her. Having her family back had changed that for her, not that they ever hugged her. Well, she was going to change that just as soon as...

"Is Charlie coming?" Quinn asked, wings flexing.

They waited a bit longer in silence, time stretching before them as a meaningless thing in this space. There was no way to know how long they waited, but just as Harper's restlessness became unbearable, Tyson spoke.

"Hello?" he called. "Where are our friends? Where is Charlemagne?"

*They are still in their own test,* the voices said, void of emotion.

"Where are they?" Tyson tried again.

*They are safe, for now.*

"Depends on your definition of safe, I'll bet," Harper muttered darkly. If They really were responsible for what she'd experienced with the Beryllium orb, then she couldn't trust Them.

*We are the creators of life, not the enders. Each life must end, but life will always find a way,* the voice insisted, this time with a sharp edge.

Cryptic as hell. Great. Harper crossed her arms, still disoriented by the fact that she couldn't feel her own arms. Having Fletcher show up and then mystically fade away hadn't exactly put her in a good mood.

"Let's cut straight to it," Harper said, butting in before Tyson could ask another unnecessary question. "Earth is in trouble, and I'd wager that you already know that. Ragranoth wants to do away with all mortals, human and paranormal, and make Earth into another hell. So, what are you going to do about it?"

Stunned silence followed her words.

"Harper!" Tyson hissed, glaring at her. "You can't talk to the Eternal Source like that! Maybe show some respect?"

"They already know what we want. The rest of this is just messing with us. Mind games." She would have spat if her astral form had the ability, but she didn't even have any spit in her mouth. She settled for glaring back at Tyson, then at Anna and Quinn in turn.

Anna had a hand on her forehead, looking exasperated.

Quinn just shrugged. "Someone needed to say it. Doesn't matter how nicely you put it. Earth is screwed. Why else would we come all the way up here to talk to a god?"

*Mortals have it all wrong,* the Eternal Source said. *We are not a god in the way your gods are gods. We simply create, and are, and keep life in balance.*

"Well, it's about to get unbalanced," Harper said. "Are you the kind of god that doesn't care? Are we just numbered souls lining up to be reabsorbed into whatever you are? Or do we matter?"

She had been afraid, before. Afraid of confronting an immortal, supposedly all-knowing, all-powerful being. After talking to Fletcher and learning the Eternal Source was a glowing ball of prideful energy, she was just pissed. No one had protected him.

No one had warned Harper what using the orb would do. How had that balanced things?

*All things matter. It is not our place to intervene. If we get involved, the power becomes imbalanced. Balance must be maintained above all things.*

Harper had some choice words ready on her tongue to respond to that, but Tyson jumped in, giving her a look that practically begged her to be quiet and let him salvage the conversation.

For once, Harper backed down, recognizing that he needed this chance to try to convince this immortal being to care about mortality. But their short lives were no doubt as significant as the lives of insects were to most mortals. Harper was unimpressed and ready to go back so they could at least go down fighting.

"Please, there must be something you can do. We're willing to fight, willing to do anything to save the rest of mortality and preserve Earth for future generations. Just tell us what to do, and lend us some of your power to do it," Tyson said.

Moments ticked by, and Harper circled the room, longing to look at something other than the bland white walls surrounding them. She passed her mother, who gave her a concerned look but didn't speak.

Finally, the Eternal Source released their voice into the room.

*Earth has been cleansed before. When the imbalance between good and evil grew too great, we covered the Earth with water and washed it clean. We could do so again, if you prefer.*

"No!" Anna, Quinn, and Tyson all shouted.

Harper threw up her hands. "You know, I had high hopes that this would work out. Thanks for nothing, I guess, because we would very much like it if most of us, and those we care about, and the rest of mortality made it out of this alive."

"She has a point," Quinn cut in. "Is there a solution that gets rid of the demons for good but doesn't also kill the rest of us?"

Anna cleared her throat. "We just need to keep Ragranoth from finishing the bridge between realms, and a way to send them back. We'd need the world's entire population of witches to begin to have enough magic to cast the demon out, and that's assuming we could survive the demon army long enough to make the attempt."

*To close the portal requires a sacrifice.*

Everyone in the room seemed to pause as if holding their breath, waiting for the Eternal Source to go on.

Tyson cleared his throat. "Is...that it?"

*It is.*

Just like the Source had told Harper when it was the orb, convincing her to be willing to sacrifice herself. Had they all been told the same thing? Had they all had someone from their past appear to them?

She glanced around at the others and saw her own thoughts reflected in each of them.

Any of them would give their lives, she knew. But she wasn't convinced yet that they should.

Harper flung her arms wide, turning around the room and addressing the ceiling, the walls, even the floor, wherever the god was hiding.

"A weapon? Greater power? Do you have anything *useful* to give to the only mortals willing to travel this far and converse with a being that could pulverize them in an instant?" Energy pulsed through her in waves, conviction pouring off her. She stopped, waiting for a response, and when it came it was exactly as disappointing as she expected it to be.

*You have your answer, mortals. Pay the price and the portal will close. Continue in anger and fear and all of mortality will perish, and the Earth cleansed as in times of old.*

Before any response could be made, the room dissolved around them, turning into a barren clifftop in the middle of a literal wasteland.

Charlie rushed towards them, eyes concerned and eager.

Charlie reached them first. "Did you meet with Them? The Eternal Source? What did They say?"

"They said 'Go to hell,'" Harper replied bitterly. "We're on our own."

# CHAPTER TWENTY-ONE

## MANDI

EVERYTHING HAD GONE PITCH black for Mandi. It must have been days, because when she woke, there were demons everywhere. People were dying.

Some of them, Mandi killed, her hands ripping out throats and hearts, the demon inside her relishing the violence.

She watched, for a while, both hoping to see Zeke and praying that Ragranoth did not come anywhere near him again. If Mandi didn't see him, she could believe he was still alive.

After some time—time stretched oddly without control of her body or mind—Mandi withdrew from the devastation, not wanting to remember anything her hands were made to do. She went into the dark places of her mind, going so far she almost forgot herself. She almost disappeared.

But the one thing Mandi did do, the one thing Ragranoth couldn't take from her, was listen.

She listened, curled up as she was in that black place in the back of her mind like a child hiding from a monster under its bed. She drifted, but every time Ragranoth spoke, Mandi heard. At first, it was nothing but the command to kill. And then several different demons emerged, robed demons wreathed with dark power, and they sat in council with Ragranoth.

Mandi emerged from the depths of subconsciousness during one of these councils, listening for anything that might help her escape, or that she could tell Zeke if she managed to find him. If nothing else, someone would know the demons' plans.

"Autarch," the demons said, speaking their guttural language.

Mandi shouldn't have been able to understand it, but somehow sharing a body possessed by Ragranoth enabled her to hear the words in English.

"Moraxxon," Ragranoth said, the demon name sounding odd coming from Mandi's mouth in a voice warped by the demon. "Report on the progress the portal has made."

"It grows, your infinite darkness," Moraxxon said.

The two robed demons sitting beside them across a table from Ragranoth all muttered in agreement.

"How fast does it grow? How many demons are let through in one Earth day?" Ragranoth asked, clasping Mandi's human hands together.

Looking out from her own eyes at the demons, Mandi felt tiny, like a fly on the wall.

"Hundreds, mistress," one of the other demons said.

Ragranoth snapped her gaze to this demon. "Jezebeth. You are coordinating our forces to spread through the city and recruit magic users to be sacrificed. How goes the hunt?"

Jezebeth ducked her cowled head, shifting smoke beneath the hood obscuring her features. "It continues, my dark mistress. The ones with magic hide well, but we sniff them out. But..." the demon trailed off.

Ragranoth's being filled with a crackling, furious energy. "But? What excuses do you bring me? I see the evidence of your lack of effort, Jezebeth. The portal is not widening fast enough. The speed increases with each magical sacrifice we make on the altar connected to the portal. I need more sacrifices, and you are meant to bring them to me."

"Why not use some of the sacrifices to shed your human skin? Then you could aid us, mistress," the third robed demon hissed.

Ragranoth rose, standing in Mandi's slight form, somehow still managing to make the demons across from her quake.

"My actions are not for you to question, Hela. I put building our demon army and bringing through my most loyal counselors before my own comfort. I will emerge with my true form when the time is right. Do not question me!"

A thunderclap tore through the room, and the three robed demons wailed and writhed in their seats as if tortured.

A torrent of power rushed through Mandi's soul, through Ragranoth, and into the three. Mandi wished she could stop it. Watching even evil beings suffer the way Ragranoth made them suffer was terrible. Mandi wanted to curl up in a state of oblivion, plugging her ears and closing her eyes.

But Ragranoth still controlled her body and much of her mind. Mandi could only watch and listen from the backseat of her own mind, and though she could have burrowed deeper into her subconscious to hide from the horrors, she knew she risked losing the ability to return if she did so.

"If the portal does not widen by the time the stars align in these heavens, we will not have enough power to bring my consort through," Ragranoth hissed, digging the sharpened fingernail points on each of Mandi's hands into the table.

Mandi felt a vague sensation of pain, but she was so far removed from the sensations in her own body that Ragranoth's wrath drowned even that small sensation out.

"You will increase your efforts. Hela, join Jezebeth in the hunt. Search every building. Go underground, if you have to. And if the demons in your command are so out of control that they kill those with magic in their blood before bringing them to the altar, you are to bring them to me that they might be tortured. And you will be held responsible for any that are allowed to murder unchecked. The humans are yours, I have given them to you to satiate your bloodlust! Do not take what is mine," Ragranoth finished with a lip-curling snarl, and all three robed demons startled, then bowed frantically.

"Yes, Autarch."

"Yes, mistress."

"Yes, your dark eminence."

Pleasure came through the connection Mandi shared with the demon. Pleasure at their deference to her, their queen.

"Go!" Ragranoth commanded.

The three robed demons fled from the room, either with true eagerness to carry out their dark queen's wishes or fear of what she would do to them if they hesitated.

Ragranoth stood in the dimly lit room—Mandi didn't know where they were—and she raised one human hand to her eyes, turning it this way and that, examining it.

*Your body has served me well, human. But it will be time soon to take another form. What will we do with you then?* The demon mused.

Mandi waited, paralyzed in her own mind. She could respond, but she did not know what to say. Did she plead for her life? Would anything she said change the demon queen's decision?

*Do you wish to die, mortal?* Ragranoth asked. *Or do you wish to serve me?*

Death would mean release from this hellish existence. But death would also mean that she would never see Zeke again, and never know if he'd survived. Never tell him she was sorry for the mess she'd gotten them all into. And his grief over her death would consume him. She wouldn't get a chance to tell him to move on, to not let her death mean the end of his life.

But service to a demon...she mentally shuddered at the thought of what that would entail. She didn't want to kill people. Didn't want to have more blood on her hands. And yet, selfishly, she knew that choosing to serve would mean that she lived, and she could find Zeke or he would find her, and she could tell him what she knew and perhaps save him.

*I would serve you,* Mandi said, with as much conviction as she could muster. Could she fool the demon into thinking she was willing?

Ragranoth laughed. *I chose my vessel well, it would appear. You have enough magic to become a portal yourself. It is one of the highest callings a servant of mine could have. You will birth my demons into being with your magic, mortal.*

*I don't know how*—Mandi started.

*Oh, you won't have to do anything but exist,* Ragranoth said.

Mandi realized they were moving, the meeting room door closing behind them, a darkened hallway extending before them.

Ragranoth opened another door where a woman lay on a metal table, gleaming under a single exposed light bulb.

Ragranoth stroked the woman's arm, and she woke with a start, screaming as if in agony, her eyes rolling with terror.

"Come forth, Baalpeor!" Ragranoth shouted above the woman's screams.

The woman bucked like she was having a seizure, choking and gagging as energy filled the air.

Her body stilled briefly, and Mandi thought she had died, but then a form peeled itself from the woman's—a demon with elongated, insect-like limbs and a face like a greyhound dog's—emerging like a nightmarish butterfly from its chrysalis.

The demon jumped down from the table, flexing its limbs. It bowed to the Autarch.

"Mistress," it said in a deep, rumbling voice. "Thank you for choosing me."

Behind the newly emerged demon, the woman sobbed and gasped for air, writhing against her bonds.

"Baalpeor, I need you to take control of a contingent of my demons. Find the ones that run amok and command them to capture the mortals with magic in their blood. Take them to the altar to open the portal large enough for my consort. Mortals without magic are yours to consume."

"As you wish, Autarch," Baalpeor said, and a pair of transparent wings flicked out from its back, flexing powerfully.

Ragranoth watched as the demon left the room, then stroked her hand down the arm of the woman on the table again.

The woman whimpered.

"Thank you for serving me," Ragranoth said sweetly in Mandi's voice. "Your service will not go unrewarded."

Ragranoth gestured, and a demon came out of the shadows holding a pitcher of water and a plate of food. It came to stand next to the woman and gave her water, which the woman gulped greedily, then fed her the food bite by bite, each piece held between enormous talons.

Mandi felt sick.

*Regretting your decision, mortal?* Ragranoth asked. *It will be your turn as soon as we secure the President.*

Mandi didn't know what the President had to do with it but didn't dare respond. She had chosen her fate, and all she could do was hope that she'd made the right decision.

# CHAPTER TWENTY-TWO

## ZEKE

ZEKE WASN'T PREPARED FOR Boris to suddenly start dragging him to the edge of the pit a few feet from where he stood facing down the werewolf they called Cookie.

He yelped as the shock collar dug into his neck, and his clawed feet scrabbled uselessly on the slick flooring.

A booted foot met Zeke's side and his back feet slid back over the ledge. He slid down the sloped side of the pit in an awkward, pained sprawl, bolting to his feet the moment he reached the bottom.

Above him, Cookie sprang in a graceful arch over Zeke's head, landing behind him.

He whirled around, expecting an attack, but Cookie looked to Boris, who stood at the edge of the pit and eyed the wolves with eyes glittering like beetle shells above his puffy red cheeks.

"Cookie here is a good dog. She knows her place in the pack, and she's here to teach you a thing or two about obedience. I'll shout a command, and if you don't do it, you'll get a shock and a lesson from Cookie," Boris shouted.

Zeke's ears flattened against his skull. He pulled his lips back, growling and baring his teeth at the brown-furred wolf waiting patiently for her master to give her permission to attack.

*Why do you let him do this?* Zeke sent his thoughts out to her, hoping she was still human enough to receive the telepathic message.

*He is the alpha*, Cookie responded, her face impassive.

*Humans can't be alphas*, Zeke returned.

She didn't posture, didn't snarl, didn't try to cow him or correct him. She just waited. Her passivity bothered Zeke to his core. Any self-respecting werewolf would defend their alpha's honor with the appropriate threats. The way she sat so perfectly and waited for her cue was exactly the way any simple dog would act. It demeaned her, and it worried Zeke.

How many werewolves had Boris caught and trained the instincts out of?

Zeke shifted his weight, feet itching to run and try to jump out of this place, to get back to Mandi.

"Sit, dogs!" Boris yelled.

Zeke almost obeyed out of reflex, but he clenched his haunches just in time and stiffened.

The collar delivered a painful zap, and Zeke cowered in spite of himself, almost missing Cookie's lunge.

Zeke leapt out of the way, a warning growl erupting from his throat as he spun to keep the female werewolf in his line of sight. The collar on his neck sent another charge through his body, stronger this time, and he flinched.

At that moment, the female attacked again, nipping Zeke's soft underbelly.

Zeke yelped and barked, backing away and snarling. His entire body trembled.

He couldn't do anything against the collar. But he could try to do something against this female.

He jumped for her, aiming for her throat.

The collar zapped him hard enough his muscles seized, and he landed in a crumpled heap at Cookie's feet.

Her jaws closed softly around his neck, and she growled, low and threatening.

Zeke relaxed completely, surrendering. He thought about those teeth sinking into his throat, how quick it would end the nightmare his life had become overnight.

But Mandi needed him. If she had any chance of coming back, she would need him. She might not have ever said it out loud, but Zeke knew she loved him, and he loved her. He would make it through whatever Boris handed him, even if he had to bend over backwards and act like a dog to do it.

He closed his eyes.

Boris tsked loudly from his platform. "Aw, now Cookie, you've overdone it."

Zeke heard movement as Boris no doubt made his way down into the pit.

"Release," Boris commanded.

Cookie whined, showing her first sign of disobedience. Whether she got a shock of her own or not, Zeke didn't know, but she trembled briefly and then her jaws released.

His head slumped to the ground. He forced himself to not move, to act weaker and more frightened than he was.

"Come on, you. Up." Boris nudged Zeke's side, not too softly either.

Zeke grunted and staggered to his feet, hating that he didn't have to fake weakness. Those shocks, plus several days' starvation, had done a number on him.

Boris re-clipped the lead on and jerked Zeke towards the sloped wall. As they drew nearer, Zeke's eyes adjusted, and he finally saw the hidden staircase built into the wall.

At the top of the pit again, Zeke glanced back at Cookie. She sat at attention, staring straight ahead, waiting for Boris to call her.

He whistled twice, and she laid down, head in her paws, a perfect example of an obedient dog.

If she hadn't spoken in Zeke's mind, he would have wondered whether her humanity had broken entirely, but she had enough for speech. He just needed a chance to convince her to blow this joint with him.

*How long has it been since you were in your human form?* Zeke asked, watching her body for a reaction. She gave none, and she didn't respond.

Back in the concrete room he'd first woken up in, Zeke paced around in a larger kennel—metal fencing pressed into the concrete so he couldn't bend it out or dig under it, but at least he could pace, and a bowl of kibble waited in the corner.

His stomach simultaneously pinched with hunger and churned with nausea, so he avoided it and only lapped at the water briefly before he resumed his pacing, fully aware that Boris watched him from the corridor between the kennels.

"You're more restless than most, boy," Boris said, coming close enough to lace the fat fingers of one hand into the chain-link fencing of the door to the kennel. His other hand grasped the coiled lead, jostling and fidgeting with it. He gazed at Zeke with narrowed eyes, as if Zeke were a puzzle he hadn't figured out yet.

Zeke stopped pacing and stared at Boris, projecting as much humanity and pleading out of his eyes as he could. If there was any moment he could try to reach this thick-hearted man, he knew this was it.

Boris barked a laugh and shook the gate, making Zeke's ears flick back.

"Hah! You think those sad eyes are going to make me have a sudden change of heart? I was pitting dogs in the arena long before the monsters came out of the woodwork. Werewolves just made the game more exciting. There's a big tournament coming up in a few days. It isn't much time to train you, but I'd wager a lot of money to watch you fight for your life." Boris's laugh echoed loud and obnoxious in the small cement room.

"The guys won't know what hits them when my dogs rip theirs to shreds. Werewolves are bigger, faster, and more vicious. Must be the man in you."

That sickened Zeke more than anything the man had said or done so far. Not just that he was a dogfighter, but his comment about Zeke's split identity as both man and wolf making him more suited for cold-blooded killing. Maybe it was his naturalization training, but Zeke had learned that he was more than his basest instincts. It didn't matter, human or not, monsters were found everywhere.

He looked pointedly at Boris, wishing he could have a real conversation with the man, rather than this one-sided, ego-stoking drivel.

Zeke stared at Boris until the man kicked his cage and walked away muttering to himself.

Then, Zeke got to work assessing his prison mates.

Two wolves, a bobcat, and the massive bear shifter at the end. He wondered for a moment where Boris kept Cookie, then had an image of Cookie sleeping on a dog bed in Boris's own room that made him sneeze so hard it hurt.

That wolf had been seriously damaged, worse than anything he'd seen even in naturalization. If he wanted to get out of here, he'd either have to convince her to leave with him, kill her, or knock her out. None of those things sounded easy, much less possible, but he had to try. Mandi's life, and the lives of the rest of the T.R.S. and even the humans in D.C. if not the world were at stake.

Zeke had no pretense that he'd be able to get back in time to warn the T.R.S. about the evil lurking in their midst. No doubt the being using Mandi's body as a puppet would have moved by now. But he had to hope that Mandi would still be alive when he got out. That she hadn't died when the pentagram had exploded those weeks ago at the Washington memorial, that she wasn't actually dead.

The thought was horrible enough to freeze Zeke's mind for a solid few minutes, making him forget what he'd been about to do, but he finally shook himself free.

If he was going to escape, he'd have more success if it wasn't just him trying to break out. He had to try to get through to the others, though if they were at anything like Cookie's level of brainwashing, he had his work cut out for him.

He'd been able to link thoughts with shifters outside of his pack before—it was a tentative link, one both parties had to be open to. Getting through could take some effort, but he had to try.

He targeted the scrawny black werewolf nearest to him, across the row and two cages down, licking at the last scraps of kibble in the metal bowl.

*Hey there, friend,* Zeke said.

The werewolf paused, licking its jowls, glancing furtively around the room. Zeke trained his eyes on the werewolf, making it as clear as he could that he was the one reaching out.

*What's your name?* Zeke asked. *Remind them of their humanity. Convince them escape would be worthwhile. Then look for an opportunity to get the hell out of this place.*

The black werewolf circled a few times, then curled up, tail over its nose, back towards Zeke.

Ignoring him.

Zeke snuffed, irritated, and turned his attention to the next wolf, a silvery gray just as thin and bedraggled looking as the black.

*Hey,* he said, wagging his tail a bit as the gray wolf looked at him.

*There's no point in getting friendly,* a distinctly female voice snapped in his mind. *I've been forced to kill more than a few of our kind in the past few weeks.*

Zeke's tail dropped so low, it almost went between his legs. *Boris made you fight others? And you...you killed them?*

*It was kill or be killed,* the female gray said, a twinge of sadness in her mental connection. She shut it off with a snap Zeke felt in his head, as if she didn't want him sensing anything about her. And perhaps Zeke couldn't blame her, but he wished she'd told him her name.

He nudged the bobcat, but they were well and truly asleep.

Zeke thought it might be a guy, judging on the musky scent he'd caught several whiffs of, but he didn't want to make any offensive assumptions. He moved on to the bear.

He hadn't known any bear shifters in his time at Camp Silver Lake, and he'd only spoken to one other at the T.R.S. He didn't know if they had any sort of protocol for mental conversations, so all he could do was dive right in.

*Hey, I'm Zeke. What's your name?*

The bear grunted out loud and rolled over, pushing to its feet. It was in a reinforced cage with thick iron or steel slats wide enough Zeke could only catch glimpses of the bear's brown hide through the small spaces. It seemed huge now that it was standing. Was it a grizzly?

Zeke stared in awe for a moment before the male voice rumbled through his brain.

*The new one. Should have guessed. The others stopped talking to me weeks ago.*

*How long have you been here?* Zeke asked, trying to hold his paws still. He wanted to prance, his excitement rising that the bear shifter was actually talking to him.

*So long I've lost track. I counted more than seventy days before Shira came. I lost track before Mike. The cat still won't talk to me.*

*That's because you're annoying.*

Zeke startled as the sly, higher-pitched voice of the cat entered his mind, and he realized the bear had been projecting his thoughts for the entire room to hear. Even Shira—the gray wolf, Zeke assumed, and the black wolf the bear had referred to as Mike—stirred, opening their eyes into slits.

*You could at least tell me your name,* the bear shifter insisted, addressing the big cat.

The big cat yawned and stretched, its tail lashing across its hindquarters as it turned its slitted, lamp-like eyes on Zeke.

*Names don't matter when you're all going to your deaths.*

*That's an extremely pessimistic point of view,* the bear said indignantly. *Have some humanity.*

That comment sent the two listening werewolves into howls of laughter that startled Zeke.

He grinned, tongue lolling, listening to the banter between the bear and the cat.

The door to the kennel room swung open and the scrawny man, Drew, peered in at them.

Everyone slumped over, pretending to sleep. Zeke sniffed at the floor of his cage casually, then lifted his leg and peed, staring at Drew with a dumb expression on his face.

Drew screwed his face up and slammed the door shut.

*That was stupid, you guys,* Shira said, her head coming up off her front paws. *We can't let them suspect we're anything other than dumb animals.*

*That's dumb,* Mike said, sniffing in her direction. *They know what we are.*

*Yeah, but if we pretend to play their game, they'll underestimate us,* Shira said, licking her paw a few times before setting her head back down. She sighed. *Just...stop talking. It's better that way.*

*Better for you, maybe,* the bear shifter's voice piped in again. Zeke had a feeling he would really like meeting this guy in person.

*I didn't catch your name,* Zeke prompted the bear, pressing up to the corner of his cage closest to all the other shifters. He let his tail wag, sending out that universal signal of "friendly" dog. Maybe his plan would work after all.

*It's Edgar,* the bear shifter said, voice sounding eager. *Edgar Allen Poche.*

*Seriously?* Zeke asked, taken aback by how closely that name resembled the famous gothic poet.

*Yeah, my parents were literary nuts. We're all named after famous authors. I have a sister named Emily, and another brother named*

*Alfred. When I left they had one on the way we all hoped was a girl. She would have been Jane. Or Virginia, perhaps.* The bear finished with a wistful tone in his gravelly mind-speak voice.

*That's actually really neat,* Zeke said, grasping onto anything he could that might convince the bear to trust him. *I have eight siblings.*

*That's a big family,* the bear shifter, Edgar, said. *You must miss them.*

*I do. Terribly. But at least they're safer than I am,* Zeke said. He kept his thoughts projecting out to everyone now, following Edgar's example.

Shira seemed to be ignoring them, but every now and then her ears flicked, as if she were, in fact, listening.

Mike bounced around his cage like a golden retriever who just got told they were going for a walk, as if waiting for his chance to speak. And sure enough, when a few moments had passed without Edgar or Zeke speaking, Mike took his chance.

*I'm Mike. Sorry about ignoring you earlier. I'm used to Shira trying to bite my head off, and I didn't know what kind of wolf you were. If you'd been like her, I wouldn't have bothered.* He fake-growled in the she-wolf's direction, a growl with a tone Zeke had heard only among young wolves that had crushes on each other.

He grinned in spite of himself, amused at how pointedly Shira ignored Mike, clearly disinterested or at least playing the part very well. Mike had his work cut out for him.

*Good to meet you, Mike. I'm Zeke. And I'm going to try to get us out of here.*

Everyone gaped at him. Not mouths-open the way that their human forms might. Well, except Mike, who seemed incapable of closing his mouth when he was excited, but their eyes all fixed on Zeke, and a chorus of objections and insults avalanched into Zeke's mind.

Fortunately, he'd had enough experience as an alpha that he knew how to handle this.

He barked. Not the alpha bark—these weren't his pack, and he had no hold over them. But it was an authoritative bark, and the rest of the shifters fell silent in its wake.

Zeke wagged his tail slowly, showing that he wasn't a threat. *Sorry. That was overwhelming.*

Shira stared at him, hatred in her gaze. *You're an alpha.*

*Not anymore,* Zeke returned.

*I heard it in your bark. Not everyone has that, you know. First borns and rebels and rogues.* Shira spat the last word with so much venom, Zeke wondered if she'd been wronged somehow.

*Cookie is her sister,* the big cat said dryly.

Shira stood up, snarling in the cat shifter's direction. *You have no right!*

*We might as well get the tragic backstories out of the way. He won't leave us alone until he knows everything he can exploit. Look, I was sold out by my clan for a promise of protection. Edgar bumbled into Boris on a camping trip. Cookie and Shira were captured on their way to join that rebellion thing, and Mike...I don't actually know what happened to Mike,* the cat shifter finished.

*He bribed me with treats,* Mike said, then paused. *That sounds worse than it is. My parents are human. I got turned and they kicked me out. Boris found me on the streets in this form and treated me like he thought I was just a stray dog. When he offered me food, I took it.* Mike shrugged his wolfish shoulders in a very human way.

*And I was just stupid,* Zeke said. *I was running...from something evil. Something that plans to take over the city, maybe the world.*

*It doesn't belong here, it's not like us. It's actually evil. And it has possessed my girlfriend.*

Mike doubled over. Shira and Edgar snickered. Even the big cat rolled over, an amused expression on its feline face.

*You were running from your evil girlfriend?* Mike howled.

Anger rose in Zeke. It was stupid to feel angry, as it was his fault he'd said it that way. He should have found different words, but he couldn't take them back now.

*You know, when you really boil it down, that's what happened,* he said, making Mike collapse, rolling on the ground with laughter so violent he'd gone silent. Which was for the best, considering Drew was still listening outside and could come in any moment.

Zeke didn't know what would happen if Drew caught them talking, but he assumed it would be painful, and he'd had enough of that today. Parts of him still ached from his fight with Cookie.

Speaking of...he turned his attention to Shira, who had turned away from all of them, her head facing the back of her wire-wrapped kennel.

*Shira, I'm sorry about your sister. Is her real name Cookie?*

Shira didn't answer for a long moment, and the entire room fell silent, almost ashamed in the face of her obvious emotional pain.

*No. She was Sasha before that bastard warped her mind so badly she doesn't even recognize her own sister,* Shira said quietly.

*That must be really hard,* Zeke said. *I know a little of what that's like.*

*Your girlfriend?* Shira asked, lifting her head and turning to glance at him. *Is she possessed or something?*

*I think so,* Zeke said. *She got roped into helping another witch summon a powerful demon. We thought we'd stopped it, but it might have backfired instead.*

He hadn't put it together until he'd said it out loud, but he realized that's what made the most sense. Ragranoth must have possessed Mandi instead of Lilith, escaping as the monument exploded. They thought they'd destroyed the spell in time, but the magic must have been strong enough to allow Ragranoth to cross. He still couldn't be sure, but he was certain that it hadn't been the woman he loved staring out of those amber eyes that night.

*The cat's name is Francis,* Edgar blurted into Zeke's mind.

The werecat hissed and spat, clawing at its cage, rattling the bars as if it could get through them to rip the bear shifter to shreds.

Edgar only chuckled at the fit the werecat was throwing. *It's only fair. He knows about everyone else.*

*No one calls me Francis,* Francis spat, ears flat against his skull.

*Fine,* the bear shifter sighed. *Frank.*

Zeke bit back his own desire to laugh. *I'll call you whatever you want me to call you, as long as you agree to help me get out of here. I have to warn the T.R.S. about the demons. It might already be too late.*

*We can't help you,* Shira said bitterly. She stood, stretching in her dog-like way, then shook out her body. She turned her blue eyes on Zeke. *My sister has us under the alpha call. We answer to her, and only her. She's specifically ordered us not to try to escape. We're lucky she didn't tell us we couldn't talk to each other. But it's possible she's been listening to this whole conversation.*

*She didn't put me under her control,* Zeke said. Was she waiting for something? Or had she done it deliberately, to get him to try to escape so she could punish him?

*She'll try. Soon,* Shira promised.

Zeke lifted his lips in a snarl. *I'd like to see her try.*

*You're the only one among us who could challenge her,* Shira said.

Which wasn't technically true. Any wolf could put out the challenge call. Few would without the strength of the alpha genes flowing through them to help them control the pack after the fight was over. Back at Camp Silver Lake, werewolves Gavin and Mavis had challenged Kamri and Zeke as alphas. Their combined strength as fighters had helped them win the challenge.

*You want me to challenge your sister?* Zeke asked. *You know what that means.*

Shira cast her eyes down. *I do. But you don't have to kill her, right? Just get her to yield.*

Remembering the way the female wolf had stared him down and the fierceness in her words to him, Zeke doubted he'd be able to convince the she-wolf to simply "back down" and let him have the pack so they could escape. But maybe, armed with the knowledge Shira had given him, he could get under Cookie's—no, Sasha's—skin, and she would make a fatal mistake.

Zeke looked around at the roomful of friends he'd managed to make in the space of an hour, considering his words carefully. He didn't want to promise something he couldn't deliver, but he knew he would do everything in his power to take as many of these shifters with him as he could when he got out of here.

*I will challenge the alpha the next time we fight. If I win, we're busting this joint.*

Yips, growls, and hisses of approval met his ears, and Zeke's tail wagged. For the first time since his capture, he actually felt hope.

# CHAPTER TWENTY-THREE

## TYSON

"WHAT IS WRONG WITH you?" The words flew out of Tyson's mouth before he could stop them.

Harper faced him, arms crossed and eyes flashing. Her aura shot off flickers of light, like flames coming off the sun, turning from pale teal to orange.

"You heard what the Eternal Source said same as I did. They're not going to help us. We're on our own."

Tyson cupped a hand around his ear. "Hear that? Your trauma is calling. It wants to talk to you."

Immature? Yes. Necessary? Dubious. But Tyson's irritation with Harper had grown every time she'd chosen to communicate violently instead of calm down and reason through what the Eternal Source and everyone else was saying. Couldn't she be reasonable for *once*?

Harper's hands went to her side in fists, and her aura flared again. Light flashed in her eyes, the storm of emotions inside of her causing her aura form to react.

"Maybe if you were a real therapist, you could have healed my so-called trauma," she snapped. "Instead, you decided to play mage and join a rebellion and fall in love with me."

"Who says I'm in love with you?" Tyson snapped back. The moment the words left his mouth, Harper's aura dampened, the fire disappearing and her glow diminishing to almost nothing.

She stepped away from him, looking smaller than he'd ever seen her.

"Harper, wait. I didn't—" He broke off, regret choking him. Tyson hadn't meant the words. He'd let his frustration run his mouth. He'd meant to jar her out of her sour mood so they could have a real conversation about what the Eternal Source had said, maybe even help her understand it better since it was obvious that she was too caught up in her belief patterns about being left alone to come up with a real solution.

The entire group had gone silent, watching the drama unfold. He never should have started this conversation while they were emotionally exhausted and so far from the anchoring of their physical bodies.

"Harper? I'm sorry," Tyson said softly.

She didn't speak, turning away from him and walking over to stand by herself at the edge of the cliff.

Tyson moved to follow, but Quinn stepped in front of him, shaking his head.

"I wouldn't, if I were you. She needs a moment." His brown eyes were piercing, angry, even. He'd just watched Tyson break his sister's heart, and Tyson didn't blame him for being upset.

Tyson turned back towards the group. He kept his eyes on the ground, unwilling to see the disappointment he knew he'd find in the others' gazes.

He cleared his throat. "The Eternal Source said that it can't get directly involved because it would throw off the balance between good and evil, which is essential to keep for life to exist. If the balance gets thrown off too far in favor of evil, the Eternal Source will cleanse the earth, presumably through flood or fire, wiping out all life and starting the planet over. So, in essence, Harper is right. We're not getting divine help to solve this problem for us."

"You forgot the most important part," Harper spat, clenching her hands into fists as she stalked back towards them. "They demanded a sacrifice. They claimed one of us has to jump into the portal to close it."

Charlie gasped in horror.

"The Eternal Source can't be trusted," Harper said.

Tyson closed his eyes. Did Harper trust anyone? "The Eternal Source said the portal needs a sacrifice. We don't have to assume that person will die."

"I can't believe you're considering this at all," Harper shouted. "The Eternal Source as good as admitted to being the Beryllium orb, which, if you recall, made me kill two people and stole my memories of my only brother. I don't think I'm being unreasonable to say we should think twice before trusting Them."

"We have nothing else to do," Anna said in a surprisingly soft tone.

"What did the Eternal Source say would happen once one of us entered the portal?" Charlie asked, her voice strained.

Tyson glanced up, looking into his friend's eyes and noting the deep sorrow there. She had the brightly colored troll clenched tightly in her hand, but he could tell by the lack of glowing that the soul of her husband no longer resided inside the plastic body.

He'd passed on, and Charlie had lost her husband all over again, for real this time.

Despite her sorrow, she seemed to be looking at Tyson like she felt sorry for *him*, and it was enough to almost send Tyson off the edge.

He wanted to get back to earth, curl up, and sleep until this was over. He hadn't signed up to save the world. He'd just wanted to be part of the solution. But the world wasn't going to fix itself.

"They said the portal would close," Anna replied. "Which we need to happen in order to stop Ragranoth's plan."

"By now hundreds, if not thousands, of demons could have come through," Charlie said thoughtfully. "How are we going to deal with them even if one of us sacrifices ourselves to close the portal?"

"So who's jumping in?" Quinn asked. "Do we draw straws or..."

"We all need to be willing to make the necessary sacrifice," Anna said stiffly. "If any of us are near the portal and have the chance, we should take it."

"No, we don't. That's exactly what the Eternal Source wants. We can build an army and fight the demons on our own. If we take down the Autarch, maybe the portal will close by itself," Harper said.

"I don't believe, from what you've told me, that the Autarch is the source of the portal. She's fueling it with some other power," Charlie said, rubbing her chin.

"If she's not the source, then the only way to close it is to do what the Eternal Source said," Tyson argued. "None of us want to die, but if it's the only way, we have to be willing."

"No one is sacrificing themselves, least of all you," Harper growled, stalking back and forth with agitation.

Did she realize she treated him the same way her mother treated her? Refusing to let him do important, dangerous things because she was afraid he would get hurt or killed?

Anna held up her hand again, stopping Tyson's response. "We will do our best to find another way. But if we reach a point where we realize there is no other way, whoever is closest to the portal and able to reach it will give their life to close it. Are we all agreed?"

Heads nodded. Tyson bobbed his furiously up and down, despite Harper's glare.

Anna nodded her approval. "We all have our roles to play. Beliefs will be challenged. Power will be extended. We will go until all our contacts are exhausted, every avenue tried. I will return to D.C. and gather what is left of the T.R.S., instructing them to reach out to the humans and ask them to fight the demons with us."

"What about the Songs?" Harper's aura flared with excitement. "I've seen them persuade, bind, even break. Couldn't we use them to force the demons back into the portal? Even close it?

Anna hesitated, breathing deeply, then letting it out with a sigh. "If we had more of the raven tribe with us, we might have the power to sing the Song of Binding and force the demons to walk back to their own realm. Other songs could potentially close the portal they've opened, although this is not something that has ever been attempted." She nodded, almost to herself. "Yes, this could be exactly what we need. Harper, Quinn, you will return to the tribe and seek their aid."

"Come with us," Harper blurted. Some of the fire had returned to her gaze, and she focused it on her mother, glaring and pleading at the same time.

Tyson admired her for it. All his earlier anger had been swept away with the regret of what he'd said, and he knew that, despite her stubbornness, his love for her remained. The breach between them was more than just the broken soul bond. They would have a lot to rebuild once they returned and after this battle was won. If they won.

Anna's face hardened. "No."

"Grandfather won't listen to us. We tried before," Harper said. "He needs to see his daughter, and you need to forgive each other, or the tribe will refuse to leave the village. They won't let go of their traditions because everyone who does gets banished. They're afraid of losing their family. But if you come, and the chief lets you come back, then we can prove that it doesn't matter where we go. The village is wherever we are. We don't have to banish anyone."

"You don't understand," Anna said, her voice low and tinged with anger. Her aura shook as if trembling, but it didn't turn to rage, only sorrow. "Change is their greatest enemy. We went back, once. We wanted to make amends, to have a safe place to bring our children. We planned to repair our relations, come get you and your brother, and return to the village to live in safety and obscurity from the government."

Anna took a shuddering breath, then continued. "The moment we crossed into Tulukaruq territory, we were attacked by the scouts. We surrendered and were brought to the chief. He claimed we were traitors returning to destroy the village, that the government would follow and discover our people. We had endangered them, and we had to be punished. He challenged your father to the *Ilau Toqu*. A duel to the death. Only if your father won would we be allowed back into the village. But your father refused to fight, and the chief struck him down."

Tyson startled. He'd met the chief, Harper's grandfather. Could it be true that Chief Aguta had killed his own son-in-law rather than make amends for the safety of his daughter and grandchildren?

Harper made a choked sound. "Grandfather wouldn't do that. He's stern, but he wouldn't kill his family."

Anna's wings flared out. "He never saw Stephen as family!" she shouted. "He hated him from the moment we revealed that we were courting until the day we left. He's the reason we left, and he's the reason I will never return."

"Then maybe it's time for a new chief," Quinn said. "I'll challenge him to this *Ilau Toqu*. If he would truly kill you simply for leaving the village, if he killed our father out of fear of change, he doesn't deserve to lead our people."

Despair passed over Anna's face. "No. It's not worth the trouble. We will find other bird shifters. Other raven born. It isn't worth the cost of your life."

"No one has to challenge anyone," Harper insisted, standing between Quinn and Anna. "We will approach the village, request an audience with the chief, and we will plead for our lives without shame. We will plead, not to become part of the village, but for the village to fight with us. We will ask them to approach the villages around them and bring them to D.C."

Anna scoffed. "He will say no. They will kill me on sight."

"We won't let them," Harper insisted.

"Can we bind the Autarch and send the demons through the portal without them?" Tyson asked, tentatively entering the conversation. He barely glanced at Harper, not wanting her to reject the idea out of her anger at him.

But it was Anna who shook her head and replied. "I do not know another way. Perhaps enough witches could do it, but covens are difficult to join, and the way Lilith recently used them to bring the Autarch here, they will be hesitant."

Her wings drooped, but her head lifted high, and moments later, her wings followed. "I will come with you. If for no other purpose than to prove to you that some things cannot be healed."

Tyson waited to see if Quinn or Harper would respond, but they just exchanged looks, then nodded at their mother.

Anna drew in a long breath and turned to Tyson. "Dreamwalker, you can build us a path to the Tulukaruq village?"

"We need to get back to our bodies first," Tyson said. "But then yes, I've been there once, and if you describe it to me, I can form a portal." His fingertips tingled, as if ready to form a portal right then and there. He stepped back from the group and used the gathered energy to draw a circle in the air, thinking of his own body and Charlie's old-fashioned living room.

They went through one at a time, Tyson hanging back to keep the path through the astral realm open, and as Harper passed him, she hesitated. Sea-green light from the portal washed over her face. She glanced up at him, a longing and a question in her eyes.

"Did you mean what you said before?" she asked at last, her voice almost too quiet to hear.

"No," Tyson said, with all the earnestness he could muster. He couldn't manage anything else as a tidal wave of emotion overwhelmed him, choking off his words. After their bond had broken and the damage his words had done, would she still choose him?

He tried to convey more of what he felt through his eyes, hoping she would hear it from his lips before anything worse happened.

*I'm sorry. I love you. Please trust me.*

Harper squared her shoulders and marched through the portal without saying anything else, and Tyson watched the swirling light of the portal opening for a long moment before he, too, returned to earth.

# CHAPTER TWENTY-FOUR

## HARPER

HARPER FLOATED TO THE surface of her consciousness and then burst through, gasping like she hadn't taken a breath in days. Her bladder immediately complained, and her stomach ached with a deep hunger she hadn't known since her time living on the streets.

She rolled over, running into Bo, who looked at her with shocked, wide eyes, a syringe in one hand and a cup of some thick tan liquid in the other.

Harper wiped at her mouth, realizing something had dribbled out. She looked at the back of her hand at the dribble.

"What is that?" She asked, tasting a gritty, creamy sweetness that did nothing to quench her thirst.

Bo stammered a moment. "It's, uh, it's this mixture, like a protein vitamin powder. Supplement! It's a supplement." He seemed relieved to have found the right word. "You've been gone for two days, I had to do something."

Harper sat up and groaned, grabbing at her abdomen. Two days? How had she not peed her pants? She doubted she'd make it to the bathroom, but she had to try.

She peeled herself off the floor, using the couch for support, and staggered to the bathroom.

Feeling like death and doubting she looked any better, she left the light off, not even bothering with the bathroom door, and she peed longer than she ever had before. She'd have to stay extra hydrated and pray that she hadn't done anything to her kidneys. The last thing she wanted was to get a kidney infection before fighting a demon queen.

Harper splashed a bit of water on her face after washing her hands, dried off, and headed for the kitchen.

Others had sat up in the living room. Quinn passed Harper with a familiar grimace on his face, shutting the bathroom door behind him.

Harper froze in the space between the wall and the island countertop that cut the kitchen and dining room in half.

Standing at the window, just finishing off a glass of water and reaching for the faucet handle to fill it up again, was Tyson with several days' worth of stubble on his jawline and hair tousled like he'd already run his fingers through it.

She wanted to touch him, ached to run her hands over his arms and down his face, to assure herself he was real, but their recent argument made her hesitate. How could she love someone so much and be so hurt by a few stupid words he'd said in a moment of idiocy?

She'd believed him when he'd said he was sorry, that he hadn't meant to say it. But they hadn't really talked about it, and she wanted to clear the air before they muddled this thing between them any further.

Tyson turned around, and Harper thought she recognized a similar storm of debate and desire flashing in his eyes.

He ripped his gaze away and turned back to the sink, filling up his glass for a third time, then handed it towards her.

Harper forced herself to step forward and take the glass, their fingers brushing as he passed it off. Her skin tingled where they'd touched, and she had to concentrate on swallowing to avoid spilling the water down her front.

"Thanks," she said, handing the cup back to him.

"More?" he asked, raising his eyebrows.

Harper nodded.

"Coming through," Quinn said, and Harper moved for her brother as he went to the cupboard and got out a cup for himself.

Tyson stepped aside to clear the way to the sink, passing a second cup of water to Harper.

"Thanks," she said again, feeling stupid that all she could manage was that single-word communication. She wanted to talk to Tyson. Really talk. But with Quinn right there and a dozen ears listening across the room, there wasn't much opportunity.

Not that they had time for things like determining their relationship. Not when the world's existence hinged on her taking her mother back to the raven born village and convincing her grandfather to not only *not* kill them, but to leave Alaska and come to D.C. to sing the song of binding and force Ragranoth back to her abyss.

The thick plastic cup cracked in Harper's hand, and she stared at it in shock. She hadn't even noticed the shift, but her wings were out, sweeping across the fortunately clean kitchen counter behind her, and the cup had broken as she'd squeezed it with her superhuman strength.

She set the cup on the counter, avoiding Tyson's stare.

A few stray feathers scattered on the counter and the floor as she turned, and Harper groaned. She'd forgotten she was molting. Part of her had hoped that would be over by the time she got back from the astral realm.

"Please tell me this doesn't last much longer," Harper said to Quinn, reaching to scratch a particularly itchy area on her wing.

Quinn laughed loudly, then cut it off to answer. "Yeah, it's a pain. But lucky for us we molt much faster than actual birds. They take weeks or months, we take days. You'll be itchy for a bit and lose a few feathers. I'm due for my molt soon, too."

"It doesn't affect our magic or anything, does it?" Harper asked, forcing herself to stop scratching.

"You'd have to ask mom. I don't know that one," Quinn replied. He tipped his head and the cup in his hand back, chugging the last of the water, then headed for the fridge.

"It won't affect your Songs," Anna said behind Harper, making her jump. "But it can make it harder to concentrate on shaping your will, so be extra conscious of where you direct your intention while Singing."

"Great," Harper muttered. She wasn't good at that to begin with. Just powerful. Now she had to worry extra about maintaining her focus, right as they were about to try to save all of mortality.

Her stomach constricted, distracting her. She found Quinn straightening from the open fridge, arms stacked with sandwich items.

"I restocked the fridge," Bo said from the other room, where he sat beside Charlie on the couch. Her eyes were red-rimmed from crying.

Harper averted her gaze. She felt for the woman, having lost her husband all over again. But surely she felt some relief knowing he'd finally passed on?

Thoughts buzzed around in Harper's brain, none of them really landing long enough for her to ponder them. Hunger made her light-headed, and Tyson's proximity distracted her. He stood beside her preparing a sandwich, and it wasn't until his elbow bumped hers for the third time that she realized she'd just been standing like a statue at the table, bread in hand but nothing on it.

"Do you want me to make you something?" Tyson offered.

"No, I'll get it," Harper said, moving as if through molasses to get the pre-sliced cheese and ham. Anything to fill her stomach.

She ate standing up, and a few minutes later, the fog in her brain cleared.

Anna stood up from her seat, clearing her throat. All eyes turned to her. "As much as I'm sure we'd love to rest, time is not on our side. We have two tasks before us—recruit the Tulukaruq raven tribe to aid us in binding the demons and convince as many humans as possible to join our cause. Tyson, you'll portal Harper, Quinn, and myself to Alaska."

Tyson nodded. "I'll gladly join you there."

"No," Anna said firmly. "You'll return here immediately and go back to D.C. Contact anyone you can find still alive and unpossessed from the T.R.S. Check the backup hideouts. Contact Chicago and Wyoming. Get every seer, dreamwalker, witch you've got who can contact others through portals or other means to reach out to their network and get as many people to D.C. as possible. We're going to repeat the same stunt we pulled to stop Lilith's pentagram to stop this demon, but we'll need more manpower this time."

Harper's breath caught in her throat. Not that Tyson wouldn't be coming with her to Alaska—she'd expected as much. But he would be working alone in a city filled with demons.

"I don't like it," Harper murmured to Tyson, leaning in.

"Anna has a point," Tyson said. "I'll be a lot more useful on the recruiting-humans front. I'll be fine."

But he had a point—up until now, Harper had treated him like he was helpless. She had to trust that if he were attacked, he could hold his own. After all, he had found her soul in the depths of the astral realm when she'd been possessed.

Harper held Tyson's gaze, trying to convey that she trusted him, not having the words to say out loud. Her heart beat fast in her chest, making her want to run, but she only pushed away from the table and stood up.

"Let's do this," she said, moving to stand next to Anna.

Quinn drew closer, too. "Do we have a plan for getting back to D.C. after? If Tyson isn't with us, we'll need a way back."

"We can fly if there's no other option," Anna said. "It will add a few hours, but we'll manage. Charlie," she said, turning towards the living room where Charlemagne still huddled on the couch next to Bo.

Charlie lifted her head and sniffed. "Yes?"

"Do you have any weapons?" Anna asked casually, the way one might ask a host for an extra blanket.

Charlie blinked, her mouth working for a moment before the words came out. "I do, actually. Bo, my closet, tucked behind my old formal dresses. The ones in the bags."

Bo left the room, and after a few moments and plenty of loud banging sounds, he came back with an armful. He dumped it all on the kitchen table, knives skittering across the wooden surface and a heavy-looking pistol thudding hard in the center of it all.

"Nothing particularly magical, but I've been collecting these just in case," Charlie said, standing and joining everyone around the table. She eyed Anna. "Do you expect trouble with your tribe?"

"I'm preparing for anything," Anna said simply, picking up a knife and pressing the pad of her thumb to the blade. She put it back and selected another. "If nothing else, we might need these to get food."

"A good knife is never misplaced," Charlie agreed, picking up an ornate sheath, pulling out the blade to admire it before passing it hilt-first to Harper.

Harper took it, and the sheath that followed. She knew some knife moves, but she'd never had to use one against a person, only threatened.

"Thank you," she said, holding the knife awkwardly.

She considered her clothes—a racerback tank top and jeans—wondering where she could possibly store the knife. Her front pockets were useless. If she stuck it in the back, she wouldn't be able to sit down, and it might fall out, anyway. Eventually, she jammed the sheathed blade through one of her belt loops and hoped it would stay.

Tyson moved into the living room, and Harper followed.

Anna gave Tyson a description of the approximate location of the village, and Charlie brought up a satellite map on her phone so Tyson could get them as close as possible. Then, he opened a hole in space and time wide enough for all three of them to go through.

Harper took a breath in, not letting herself consider whether or not she'd see him again. She would. She refused to accept any other outcome.

She moved to enter the portal, but a hand landed on her shoulder, turning her around.

"I know you probably want nothing to do with me right now, and it would be so warranted after what I said." Tyson's voice cracked. He cleared his throat, his fingers flexing into her shoulder. "But I'd really like to hug you before you go, if that's all right."

Harper leaned into him without saying a word, pressing her face into his chest and breathing in his scent. He smelled like a man who hadn't showered in a couple days, but it wasn't a gross smell, just...natural. She liked it. And she liked the way his arms wrapped around her, careful of her wings.

It ended too soon. Her body yearned for more, while her heart warned against letting him in again. Harper pulled away reluctantly, then walked across the portal threshold, a frigid Alaska wind banishing the warmth of Charlie's living room.

Quinn and Anna stood looking out over the valley where the Tulukaruq village lay. It was late afternoon in September, and a few snowflakes drifted lightly down around Harper. She felt the cold, even welcomed it after the nothingness of the astral realm, but it didn't bother her. She'd been made for this climate.

"There aren't any fires," Quinn said, pointing at the village.

Harper watched a little longer, noting no smoke rose from holes in thatched roofs, and no one walked the worn paths between homes. Her eyes turned to the sky, where she caught sight of a hawk wheeling around, no doubt searching for dinner.

"Where is everyone?" she asked.

"They could be in hiding if something threatened the village," Anna said. The skin around her eyes was creased, tightening with concern as her thick eyebrows came together in the middle.

The sudden, keening note that pierced the air caught Harper completely off-guard. The second note wrapped around her wings and arms as if to pin them to her sides, and she opened her mouth to counter the attack, but her starting note faltered. Her singing caused more trouble than it was worth, and she didn't want to chance hurting any of her people.

Anna and Quinn must have had the same thought, because neither of them sang or even struggled as the song wrapped around all three of them, binding their wings, arms, and legs and making them fall to the hard-packed ground.

Boots thudded around them as six tall, male raven born landed. Strong hands hauled Harper to her feet, holding her upright as a man with the tribe's familiar brown skin, dark eyes and hair, and round face peered at her.

"You've returned," he said with shock, glancing over to his companions, two of each holding Quinn and Anna.

Harper didn't know this man, but she noticed how wide his eyes got when they landed on Anna. He must know of her, and her supposed betrayal of the clan.

"We came to speak with Chief Aguta. My grandfather," Harper said, hoping a reminder of the familial connection would convince the man to relax the hold of his Song on her. "I didn't meet you last time I was here. What's your name?"

"I am Luca." He turned his attention to his men. "We will take them to the chief."

Harper recognized none of them. But then, she hadn't spent much time among them, a fact that still made her insides twinge with guilt. These were her people, and she didn't know any of them.

"If you release us, we can fly," Anna said. "We won't try to leave until we've gotten what we came for."

"Try anything funny, and you'll be killed," Luca warned. At his command, the other five tribe members sang to release the song's hold.

Harper was finally able to relax. She shook out her arms for good measure, then lined up next to Anna and Quinn.

"Follow closely." Luca spread his wings and walked to the edge of the cliff. He jumped off without saying anything else, and Harper followed, diving and angling until she flew alongside the cliff face. The wind rushed past her, bringing with it joy unparalleled, even through the tension that hung in the air.

Luca tilted and disappeared inside the cliff. Harper almost pulled back, but as she flew the crack he'd flown into came into view. She followed, bringing her wings in so they wouldn't hit the cliff walls on either side, and landed on a ledge.

A dark cave entrance yawned before her, only slightly higher than she was tall. Luca would have to duck to enter.

He waited in silence until the others had landed, the ledge now crowded with eight wing-bearing individuals.

"Where is the tribe?" Quinn asked.

"In hiding. Local human villages have grown suspicious since hearing of the paranormal attacks in the US and the capture of the president. We've been forced to withdraw from our homes for fear of attack," Luca explained. He gestured into the cave. "Come. I will take you to our chief."

Strands of electric lights hung on the cave walls, no doubt run by generators. Even with the lights, Harper had to watch her footing on the uneven ground.

Somewhere, water dripped. A child's laugh echoed down the tunnel, and Luca stiffened beside Harper, seeming even more anxious than before. Things had to be pretty bad for the tribe to hide themselves this way.

The stone corridor opened into a wide chamber with natural light filtering in from a crack far above them. Women in one corner fried pancakes on electric griddles. A mixed group of men and women chatted while cleaning tools and weapons, their lively conversation dying down as Harper's group passed.

Whispers followed her out of the first chamber, down a set of splitting corridors, to another, smaller hollowed-out room with only a few people inside.

Chief Aguta sat on a blanket at the center of the room. He looked older than when Harper had last seen him, his gray hair turning white, his face paler and thinner. He looked up as the rest of the group fanned out behind Luca and Harper.

Chief Aguta's eyes flicked from Luca to Harper, and his face split into a wide grin. He spread his arms, then stood with only a moment of effort.

"Granddaughter! You have returned! And my grandson as well! This is a happy day indeed."

Anna stepped up beside Harper. The face that Harper shared with her looked foreign in its blank sternness, and she wondered how Anna had mustered up such a cold expression.

Chief Aguta's smile faded, and his arms slowly returned to his sides.

"Why have you brought death with you?" he whispered, glancing from Harper to Quinn and back at Anna. "Why have you brought our greatest enemy among us?"

# CHAPTER TWENTY-FIVE

## MANDI

SEVERAL DAYS AFTER MANDI swore herself into the service of Ragranoth, Autarch of the demon legions, she met the queen's consort for the first time.

Ragranoth locked herself in one of the deepest rooms of the White House, practically giddy with pleasure. Something had happened, and she wanted to tell her consort. That was all Mandi knew after she'd woken from a period of oblivion.

It was getting harder and harder to stay aware.

Ragranoth used Mandi's hands to renew a pentagram on the floor with blue chalk, sketching symbols both familiar and foreign to Mandi. Some of them were ones she'd used in her witchcraft, others were so arcane they must have been lost to the knowledge of mortals. The lines squiggled in Mandi's blurred, backseat vision, looking as if they came alive as the demon drew them.

Finished with the summoning circle, Ragranoth stepped into the center and called out in her guttural language.

"I summon you, Issachar! Appear before me in your glory."

Their connection translated the words so Mandi understood them. Immediately, she was filled with terror and confusion. Ragranoth had said she needed more power to bring Issachar to Earth's plane of existence. How could she summon him here without any sacrifices, just the circle?

A transparent image flickered to life, revealing a towering monstrosity with a bull's head, scorpion tail, and lion paws. Its eyes glowed silver, round like moons, and they looked straight through Mandi.

"Issachar," Ragranoth crooned, stepping closer, her hand—Mandi's hand—passing through the image.

She had summoned his likeness, his spirit form, so they could converse. Mandi relaxed, but only slightly, realizing that the time was swift approaching that this demon king would be flesh and blood far too soon unless someone stopped it from happening.

The demon swiped at her hand, but it passed through, and he growled.

"How dare you come to me wearing that form!"

"It is the only form I can manage. All sacrifices must go to widening the portal for you, so you can be with me and reign over this realm. Our children work through the night to bring you here."

"Surely you can spare the blood for your own transformation," Issachar snarled, flexing his claws.

"Soon, soon," Ragranoth crooned. "We have obtained the President. I will appear on the mortals' television, broadcast to the world. We will convince those with magic to gather here. They line themselves up for the slaughter."

Her laughter filled the room, and Issachar's deep chuckle followed, then cut off abruptly.

"It has been too long since we last spoke. You missed much. The mortals came, just as we expected. The feathered ones, and the ones who walk in dreams."

Ragranoth's excitement increased, a sensation that washed over Mandi and made her feel sick in her own mind. A demon's excitement was never a good thing. But what did Issachar mean, feathered ones and the ones who walked in dreams?

"You were able to fool them? To appear as their loved ones and strike their hearts with guilt?" Ragranoth asked eagerly.

Issachar nodded. "They were fooled. I told them the Eternal Source could not help them, that balance had to be kept. But they asked how they could close the portal, and I told them one of them must sacrifice themselves."

"The raven born and the dream walker have magic strong enough to crack the portal wide enough to let you through. But are you certain they felt convinced? Did they have any suspicions?"

Raven born? There were two people Mandi had met in her lifetime that matched that description. Harper and her brother Quinn, raven shifters from a northern tribe, had both been at Camp Silver Lake.

Somehow, they had met Issachar and believed him to be the Eternal Source, a powerful entity of the upper planes that Mandi had learned about in her training on the astral realm with her coven.

"One of the female raven born did not trust the Eternal Source, but she trusts no one. Her companions will persuade her, and even if they do not, they feel trapped and without options. One of them will sacrifice themselves, and the power of that sacrifice will connect the final pieces of our bridge."

"Let it be so," Ragranoth hissed, pacing. "We should capture them, bring them here and throw them in rather than leaving it up to chance."

"You forget that the sacrifice must be willing," Issachar bellowed. "That is where much of the power comes from, such as how that witch puppet of yours sacrificed herself and her coven to bring you across."

"Yes, yes," Ragranoth said impatiently. "I know how it works. I just worry for you, my consort."

"Do not fret. The humans have a strong sense of duty. They will do what they've been told is the only way to save their loved ones. I have ensured that we have at least five willing sacrifices. Now we must watch to see how it unfolds and trust the fates have swung in our favor for the first time in the history of this planet."

"And what of the true Eternal Source?" Ragranoth snapped. "What if they interfere?"

"They have not interfered with these mortals in thousands of years. They have abandoned them. We will not have any interference from the Creator of All."

Mandi's being tremored. It was so much worse than she'd thought. If the Eternal Source couldn't be bothered to step in and help the mortality they had created, was it even possible for them to survive?

Maybe, if Mandi got this information to the right person, she could make a difference. No one else knew the Autarch's plan to bring her consort to Earth.

It struck Mandi then that she'd never tried to enter the astral realm. After all, in order to enter, one had to put themselves into a subconscious trance, not awake, not asleep. Technically, that's where Mandi existed all the time now, hovering at the back of her own mind.

She concentrated. She'd only entered the astral realm a few times. Surely it would be easier now?

Like a zipper opening in her mind, Mandi watched the astral realm appear, vaguely aware of Ragranoth's attention moving to her and noticing what she was doing.

The demon might punish her, might leave her body and kill her for what she'd done. But Mandi didn't care. She would likely be killed anyway the moment the demon considered her usefulness to be over. She would do everything she could with her time to warn those she cared about and possibly help save humanity.

The physical plane of the astral realm had dulled to muted colors, the brilliant sunset and vibrant colors of plants and buildings gone. Demons roved everywhere Mandi looked. It was so different from what she'd seen before, but one thing remained the same. The golden strand vibrating from her chest, connecting her to her soulmate.

Zeke was alive.

Why hadn't she done this sooner? Mandi berated herself as she willed her astral form forward, moving over the city, a spirit-version of Washington D.C. that constantly shifted and changed. The line led her into a back-alley underbelly side of the city, only a short distance from the park where Zeke had taken her the night of their disastrous date.

He was nearby.

Mandi moved faster, soaring down to the place the soul bond led her, the line disappearing inside a building that pulsed with a darkened aura of some kind. The dark energy clung to Mandi as she passed through the exterior of the building, her aura form landing in a darkened room filled with sleeping animal figures.

One of them looked like a bear, the others wolves, and one big cat asleep on a perch.

The biggest, darkest form was on the other end of the golden thread connected to Mandi, and she floated towards the cage.

He was trapped in a space far too small for him. Fear and pain emanated from him as he snuffled and whined in his sleep. He tried to roll over and rattled the cage as he ran into the mesh bars.

Mandi tugged on their soul connection.

"Zeke?"

Zeke snorted and his golden eye opened, then closed.

"Zeke," Mandi tried again. "Wake up. I need you."

The spirit form of a man with long dreadlocks stood up from the wolf and approached her.

Relief flooded through Mandi.

"Mandi! What is this? Are you really here? Am I dreaming?" Zeke asked, reaching for her hands.

Mandi expected them to go through her spirit form, but there was a tingle where he touched her, almost like the feel of his skin on hers. She lifted his face towards his.

"I'm really here. Well, in the astral realm. I don't know how long I have, so I need to make this quick."

"I'm listening," Zeke replied.

"When the pentagram broke in D.C., I was possessed by Ragranoth," Mandi began, and the entire story unfolded, as quickly as she could tell it, including everything she knew about Ragranoth's consort and how the demon had tricked their friends.

Zeke watched her the entire time, nodding along, silent. When she finished, his brow crease deepened.

"I'm grateful you found a way to tell me, Mandi, but I can't do anything about it." He swept his arm around at the kennels and the smaller cage behind him. "This insane dog fighter caught me. I'm working on a plan to escape, but I don't know when or how, and meanwhile I can't tell anyone else about this. Why didn't you go to Anna or one of the other leaders of the T.R.S.?"

Mandi stood there, stunned for a moment. "I-I needed to know you were alive. And I didn't know you weren't with them. You could have made it back. And finding you...it's easier. I don't know if I can find Anna, I barely know her. You and I have a bond."

Mandi raised her hand to Zeke's chest where the golden line from her met him.

Zeke held her hand in his. "I'm going to find a way out, Mandi. I'm going to find my way back to you."

Mandi swallowed. She'd left out the part about Ragranoth's ultimatum—serve the demon queen or die. She didn't have the heart to tell Zeke that by the time Ragranoth was done with her, there might not be anything to find. She pressed her astral lips to Zeke's hand.

"Be safe," she said, not making him any promises.

"Find Anna," Zeke said, stepping back towards his body. He slowly sank back inside, watching her as he re-entered the wolf.

When the spirit had been fully absorbed, the wolf's golden eyes opened, and it stood, tail wagging at her. Mandi waved one last time and flew from the building into the star-studded sky, taking up a yogi position in mid-air as she concentrated. She didn't think she could trace Anna's soul signature in the astral realm. She barely knew the raven born leader. She knew Anna's daughter Harper vaguely, having met her once or twice. Harper was in a relationship with Tyson, a dreamwalker, and Mandi knew him better from their time working at Camp Silver Lake. If she could get through to anyone, it would be him, and he would likely be close to Anna.

"There you are, mortal," Ragranoth's voice echoed through the physical plane of the astral realm, seeming to come from everywhere. "I'd wondered where you'd gone off to."

Mandi didn't see anything, but a sensation like claws hooking around her stomach yanked her out of the sky, down, down, down towards the ground and back into the body that had become a prison.

# CHAPTER TWENTY-SIX

## ZEKE

ZEKE WOKE FROM THE dream with a start, sneezing in his wolf form and puzzling over how vivid it had been. Mandi was there, and she'd talked to him about demons and one of them impersonating a god...

It hadn't been a dream.

The realization filled Zeke with dread and hope simultaneously. She was still trapped by Ragranoth, still held captive in her own body. But she'd found a way to contact Zeke through his dreams, and she would find Tyson. She had to because Zeke couldn't do anything from his cage.

The door to the kennel room creaked open. Zeke woke immediately, brain fuzzy with sleep. He couldn't be certain it was midnight down here, as there were no windows, and the lights were automated. He hadn't gotten enough sleep to really recover from his fight the day before. The lights were still out as booted feet passed in front of his cage, and keys jangled in the lock before it clicked and the kennel gate swung open.

"Come," Boris's gruff voice pulled Zeke the rest of the way into his consciousness, and Zeke staggered to his feet, stumbling forward.

He must not have been fast enough, because he received a mild shock that sent him yelping and scampering forward, past Mike's and Shira's cages, both of them looking at him, unmoving.

Frank stirred on the ledge in his cage, glancing down as Zeke passed, giving him a sort of thumbs-up gesture with his paw.

Or maybe he was trying to flip him off. Zeke couldn't be sure with Frank, who had proved to be as irritable and contrary as a house cat.

Edgar was the only one who slept through Zeke's passing, or at least Zeke thought he had until the bear's voice echoed in his head.

*Give her hell, Zeke.*

*Hey, that's my sister you're talking about,* Shira argued, the door shutting behind Boris as Zeke trotted forward, trying not to let the grin show on his face.

He had *friends*. Even in this hell of a place, he'd managed to make friends. Now he had to make good on his promise to those friends—challenge the alpha without killing her or getting himself killed and get everyone out of their cages and back on the streets.

Back to Mandi.

He let all other thoughts vanish from his mind except that singular goal. Mandi's face had kept him going all the way across the United States when they'd been separated before. She would keep him going now as he faced the terrifying, brain-washed she-wolf that Boris kept at his side.

Zeke wasn't afraid of Sasha; he wasn't even afraid of the demons. More than anything in the world, he was afraid of not returning to Mandi.

He forced himself into a higher state of alertness out of sheer will, picking up his paws from dragging on the floor to a pace that made Boris curse and walk faster to keep up with him.

Boris chuckled, slightly breathless. "Eager to get to the killing, eh dog? Well, who am I to keep you? Cookie is looking forward to spilling your guts. Prove to her you can hold your own, and she might let you into the pack."

Zeke bared his teeth and ran forward, jumping into the arena. He wouldn't be kicked around today.

Cookie walked out of the shadows, already waiting for him. She held her head high, as if showing off her glossy coat, the ultimate sign of health for any canine creature. The gleaming fur covered rippling muscles. She'd clearly trained well to become Boris's pet killing machine.

Zeke resisted the animal instinct that wanted to snarl and attack, instead drawing himself up. He was a mess after almost a week imprisoned in the kennel, starved and kept from any physical activity, but his coat still shone beneath the grime. He'd been strong before this, and he still had plenty of that to fall back on. He would meet Sasha posture for posture, blow for blow.

But first, he had to issue the alpha challenge, putting them on equal footing.

He opened his mouth to give the challenge cry, when a shock arched through his neck. Zeek reeled back, scraping at the collar with his forepaws and whining at the pain.

"Get him, Cookie," Boris said, and Sasha charged forward.

Zeke crouched low and rolled beneath her leap, sending her sailing past him. He stood on trembling legs and launched himself at her hindquarters, mentally scrambling for control over the instincts that demanded he lock his jaws around her throat and not let go.

Instead, he bit her haunches and darted away as she whirled around.

*Hey, I learned your real name,* Zeke taunted.

The wolf's yellow eyes flashed, and she lunged again, ducking under his chest and throwing him before he could dodge.

Zeke sailed through the air and landed on the hard cement floor, sliding with the momentum from her throw.

She was using the strength of her pack to outmatch him. He had to issue the challenge and bring her down to his level or he'd never be able to best her.

Zeke jumped to his feet and raised his head, managing the first note before Sasha cut him off, her teeth snapping dangerously close to his throat.

They locked together, snapping and barking, front claws scratching and thrusting, each one trying to get their heads around to the others' neck.

Sasha's sharp teeth pinched the skin on Zeke's scruff and he yelped, then attacked with more fury than before. He bashed his skull into her over and over again, hitting her side, her back legs, her chest, her head.

She reeled back after that last strike, seeming a little dazed.

Zeke took a brief moment to catch his breath. *Your sister says she'd like Sasha back.*

He tried again to raise the challenge howl, but Sasha, despite the numerous cuts and the bash to the head she'd just received, didn't let him take a deep enough breath. She barreled into him, efforts doubled from before.

Zeke went on the defensive, biting as little as he could, staying away from her throat. He couldn't win like this, fighting an alpha borrowing the strength of her pack.

"Cookie, enough!" Boris bellowed over the snarling wolves, but Sasha didn't back off the way she had before. She was beyond her master's call, and since she didn't have a shock collar like Zeke's, Boris had no way to call her back except for his own voice.

"Cookie! Down!" Boris shouted again, panic creeping into his voice. "Don't kill 'im yet! We just got 'im!"

Zeke caught a glimpse of the large man moving at a run around the fence above the arena, heading for the stairs on the far side. What the human thought he could do to separate two enraged werewolves, Zeke could only imagine as he fought for his life, dancing around Sasha's blows.

*This isn't you,* Zeke tried, seeking again to help Sasha find her humanity. *You're not Cookie, you're Sasha. You have a sister, Shira. I've seen her. Talked to her. She misses you.* He kept his tone earnest, without guile or mocking, but it didn't seem to help.

Sasha was in a killing frenzy, attacking him without letting up, barely pausing to catch her breath each time Zeke managed to separate himself before she sank her teeth into him again.

Boris was nearly to the stairs. Zeke had to stop Sasha before Boris entered the arena—the big man presented a factor Zeke wasn't prepared to deal with while he fought the alpha.

Zeke straightened, arching his neck up, exposing it to Sasha as he opened his jaws and sang the song of the alpha challenge.

Sasha's jaws were inches away from his throat when he finished, and Zeke flipped backward, his back leg catching her under her chin.

The challenge rippled through Zeke, and Sasha must have felt it too because she immediately slumped forward, legs splaying on the floor as all the strength of the pack left her.

Zeke took his chance and ran forward, putting his jaws around the back of her neck tight enough she couldn't thrust him off, but not so tight he crushed her. He growled, commanding her to stay down, to not make him kill her.

Sasha whimpered, squirming and struggling.

At the sound of her whine, Boris glanced up and caught sight of Zeke holding his prized wolf in a death grip. He yelped and mashed his finger down on the remote for Zeke's electric collar, zapping him over and over again.

Zeke held on through the pain, each shock weakening his muscles more and more until he knew he would drop Sasha, knew he would lose this fight after all he had done. And then Boris would let Sasha kill him, or Zeke would be starved again, maybe beaten.

He closed his eyes, keeping the rumbling, commanding growl going in his throat, sending it to Sasha.

*I don't want to kill you. I just want to get out of here. I just want to save my mate.* He sent Sasha an image of Mandi at her best, a favorite memory he had of her laughing, her milky-white eyes gazing sightlessly back at Zeke as she ruffled his wolfish ears. She hadn't pet him like that since she'd survived the pentagram collapsing. Maybe because she had been possessed by a demon. It actually relieved Zeke to know that perhaps nothing had been wrong with their relationship, that a demon had just gotten in the way.

Sasha stopped struggling, and Zeke dropped her, panting as another blast of current went through him. He'd almost gotten used to the voltage now, and it tingled painfully but didn't make him convulse.

Boris jogged down the stairs.

*Fine. You win,* Sasha said bitterly into Zeke's mind.

At her words, power flooded Zeke. He suddenly felt every member of the pack Sasha had led. Mike and Shira perked up, their minds linking effortlessly with his, and he felt what they felt rather than just heard their voices.

The foreign feel of the bobcat, Frank, and Edgar the bear shifter followed more slowly, as the pack link hadn't been intended for other species, but the connections were there and Cookie—or Sasha, rather—had managed to bring them into the pack regardless of their biological makeup, which showed her incredible strength.

A bolt of electricity ran through Zeke so strongly that his entire body stiffened, and he groaned, losing complete control of his muscles to the crackling, invisible power. Boris had increased the voltage to an insane height. Any regular dog would have been permanently damaged by that shock.

The shock ended and Zeke gulped for breath, chest heaving.

"I'll show you what happens to mutts that threaten my Cookie," Boris snarled, his booted foot digging into Zeke's side with a sharp blow on his ribs, sending him sliding across the arena.

# CHAPTER TWENTY-SEVEN

## TYSON

Opening the portal onto the Lincoln Memorial in D.C. turned out to be much harder the second time around. He was tired, and he worried about what waited for Harper in her village, but he forced himself to concentrate, dragging the image of the memorial platform up in his memory.

He gasped and separated himself energetically from the portal, almost collapsing it. He held on through the pain until a second river of magic flowed into him. Neon yellow bursts flashed behind his eyes. He smelled sage and bubblegum.

Charlie had joined her magic with his to keep the portal open.

"Thanks," Tyson said once the portal was stable. It would hold on its own until he went through now, but he wanted to say goodbye before he left Charlie.

He cleared his throat. There was too much to say. "I'm sorry about Rudy. It seemed like he was good to you."

"He was," Charlie said, tears brightening her eyes. She tugged on one of her freshly done braids, then hung her thumbs from her coverall pockets. She rocked on her heels.

"You're good, you know. Powerful. Just as I assumed when I first saw you in one of my visions. Thank you for what you did."

Tyson had stripped Rudy of the power he'd built up to maintain his personal astral paradise and healed the darkness inside him, reducing the spirit to his true state of crumbling consciousness and essence. It didn't feel like it had been a good thing, but Charlie's words sounded sincere, and he trusted that she meant them.

"You're welcome. We're even, I guess."

"Hardly," Charlie scoffed. "You're going off to save the world. Least I can do is come with you."

Tyson blinked. "You're leaving your garage?"

Bo stepped up to Charlie and handed her a bulging backpack.

"It'll be here when I get back," Charlie said, waving her hand. "I've got protections in place against intruders and the like. Plus, Bo will be here. It'll be in much more trouble if the demons actually win, so I figure you'll want all the help you can get. I can be pretty useful in a fight." She waggled her fingers, shooting off little neon sparks and patting a bulging bag slung over one shoulder.

Tyson caught a glimpse of a fringe of neon hair coming out of the bag and grinned. "Of course."

Bo hugged Charlie. Tyson turned away to give their goodbye some privacy, watching the glowing swirls within the portal pulse rhythmically, troubled by his thoughts. He liked Charlie, and he knew she would be helpful in the battles to come, but he worried that losing her husband had made her emotionally unstable. He could easily see her giving herself up as the portal sacrifice the Eternal Source had demanded, if she'd lost sense of the meaning of her life with the final death of Rudy. He'd have to watch her.

A moment later, Charlie joined him in front of the portal, wiping her eyes and sniffing as she adjusted the backpack strap on her shoulder.

"Ready?" she asked.

"Yep," Tyson said, stepping forward.

Charlie put a hand on his chest, stopping him. "I'll go through first. Just in case that fox had any smart ideas about jumping you on the other side."

Tyson didn't like it, but he allowed her to pass through first.

"Take care of her," Bo said quietly.

"I will," Tyson promised, giving Bo a reassuring smile before he, too, stepped through time and space, crossing miles in the blink of an eye.

He was barely even nauseated when he walked out onto the Lincoln memorial platform, face-first into a cold wind. Flashbacks from the last time he'd stood there assaulted him. His charge as a polar bear, falling from the sky, waking Harper from her possession, the thunderous crack as the Washington Memorial broke.

He could still see what remained of the dark crystal from here, the ruins hadn't been cleared from the memorial grounds. The pentagram on the ground had been carefully scrubbed away, however, to prevent any further use, and it was usually under guard. Tyson didn't see anyone now, not even a demon.

"Tyson," Charlie said, her voice thick with warning.

Tyson dropped to the ground, crouching behind the pillar next to the one Charlie looked around, and what he saw made his blood chill.

Demons crawled across the grounds, scurrying, lurching, flying, leaping, whatever their deformed and unusual limbs allowed them to do. Some had goat legs, some had lizard legs and scurried along the ground. Others had massive arms they used to propel themselves forward. The air filled with chittering, buzzing, shrieking, and roaring so terrible it grated on Tyson's mortal senses and made everything within him clench.

And then, dawn broke across the horizon, lighting the city up with reflections of gold and pink fire. Tyson hadn't even noticed the sky lightning.

The instant the sun broke out, the demons scattered, filling every shadow, melding into them until only their glowing eyes were visible, and then even those winked out. Could they teleport from the shadows back to their masters? Or would they emerge from the same places after the sun had retreated again?

Either way, witnessing the demons vanishing brought Tyson immense relief. They stood a chance if they made their move when the demons were at their weakest.

Charlie came up beside Tyson. "Well, that was *illuminating.*" She smirked at her pun.

Tyson snorted quietly. "Yeah, at least now we know we're safe to walk through the city during daylight hours. Though the human rebellion could still be at large, and we'll want to avoid running into them."

"I thought we wanted to talk to them?" Charlie said, furrowing her brow.

"Yeah, but I'd prefer to have the numbers on our side when we approach them to talk. Otherwise, we'll just get captured."

"All right, captain, where to?" Charlie glanced sideways at him.

Tyson shifted uncomfortably.

He'd never gotten used to his role as a member of the staff at Camp Silver Lake, and he'd never had an opportunity like this to lead a group, even a small one. He scratched the back of his head as he neared the bottom of the Lincoln Memorial, glancing back on a whim to see that the stone president's face was half gone.

"The Autarch would have started killing and possessing anyone within reach. I'm sure that means most of the hideouts are compromised, but if we find one that isn't crawling with demons, we can use the resources inside to contact the other hideouts and find out who else survived."

"Can we walk to any?" Charlie asked, glancing at the sky before looking at Tyson. "And can we get there before nightfall?"

Tyson nodded. "I think so."

The streets remained empty and void of any sign of demons, and all other life forms for that matter.

Tyson hitched the backpack he'd gotten from Charlie's house to carry supplies up on his shoulders, fiddling with the strap to adjust it while he glanced nervously around at the too-bright, too-empty streets. It ought to have been filling with tourists and protestors, even at the early hour, but there was no one.

Had Ragranoth possessed or killed so many people? Or were they simply frightened and hiding in their homes?

"I don't like this," Tyson muttered, rounding another corner, his skin prickling all over. He couldn't tell if it was paranoia or a premonition of some kind.

"Me neither," Charlie responded.

A wind blew garbage across the street, the paper scratching on the pavement. The hairs on Tyson's neck rose. He whirled around.

The empty street flooded with over a dozen people. They came in from all sides, swinging nail-studded clubs, brandishing guns and tasers, some even had slingshots and chunks of cement.

Tyson did the only thing he could think of that wouldn't get them killed. He threw his hands up and knelt on the ground. "Don't shoot! We're friendly!"

Charlie knelt beside him, the troll raised high in one hand.

He could transform into a polar bear and hope to kill a few of the heavily-breathing, furious-looking people closing in a tight circle around them, but that would only succeed in getting him and Charlie killed. Even if they did survive, it would draw the attention of every other being in the vicinity, and no doubt another gang would discover them before they made it to the backup hideout for the T.R.S.

A man stepped forward, dirty blonde hair tied back in a black bandana, sleeveless leather vest over a black shirt, and several gun holsters on his belt. He rubbed his square jaw, pinning Tyson and Charlie with a narrowed, suspicious gaze.

Tyson would bet a hundred bucks these people were human rebels. He didn't recognize a single one, and while there had been thousands of recruits in just the past few weeks, he didn't think they would be quite this hostile to two strangers walking down the street.

"Ya might be friendly. But friendly to who?" The man said, walking closer and crouching down to look Tyson in the eyes. "Look at me," the man demanded.

Tyson licked his lips and glanced up. Fortunately, his eyes had remained the same blue, even after his magic came on. There was nothing about his outward appearance that would suggest he was magic, nothing in his backpack. Except the *ulu* knife Nana had given him, but even that just looked like a really cool knife. He could tell them it was an heirloom.

Charlie, on the other hand, looked human enough, but other than a ridiculous number of plastic trolls, had she packed anything that could incriminate them?

The man nodded, leaning back in his crouch as if satisfied, but his eyes still held a suspicious glare.

"Name your business. Who are you with? Why risk being out where the demons can get ya?"

Tyson slowed his breathing before answering, giving him time to search for the best response.

"We were separated from our group when the demons attacked a few nights ago. We've just been surviving since," Tyson said. He nodded towards Charlie. "We came to join the cause."

Technically, nothing he'd said was a lie, but he was certain this man would see through Tyson's vague generalities and insist he deliver a more specific answer.

The man didn't seem to notice. He just nodded. "Yeah, we've had a few of your type come through and try to join us. Liberalist yokels who don't know the real nitty gritty of what we're dealing with here. But let's get somewhere more secure before we talk. You don't mind coming with us, do you?" He eyed the two of them, as if expecting them to suddenly leap up and attempt to run away.

Tyson swallowed the lump in his throat. Adrenaline coursed through his body, and he definitely wanted to get away, but saying no to such a reasonable request after he'd just said they were interested in joining them would give them away in an instant.

"Of course not. We'd appreciate it," Tyson managed to say.

"Don't mind my guards. They're a bit touchy," the man said, gesturing to the three women and two men that stepped up and surrounded Tyson and Charlie, each one holding a semi-automatic rifle that looked like something the henchmen of a crime syndicate would have on hand.

The man, obviously some sort of leader for the group, signaled his team and they moved out, those not guarding Tyson and Charlie melding into the background of the city so smoothly, Tyson might have thought they'd vanished.

Except these weren't magic-users, witches, shifters, or vamps. These were humans. Trained and highly dangerous humans.

Without even trying, he'd found the human rebellion. Now he just needed to survive long enough to convince them to join T.R.S. in ejecting the demons from their world, because he doubted anyone would find them where they were going.

# CHAPTER TWENTY-EIGHT

## HARPER

HARPER'S BLOOD ROARED IN her ears. She hadn't thought to this point. What it would be like to hear her grandfather deny her mother. His daughter. Why did it have to be like this?

The chief stared at Anna with wide, horrified eyes. "Do you know what you have done in bringing her here? Our ancient laws dictate her death."

Quinn stepped up on the other side of Anna, putting an arm around her shoulders. "I've learned that some laws weren't meant to be upheld."

The chief's face morphed into something ugly, all the bitterness and guilt, too, showing through. He raised a shaking finger.

"She's your daughter," Harper said, touching the totem on her chest. It warmed beneath her fingers, and that somehow lent her strength.

"I lost my daughter long ago. She cannot return. She is dead," Chief Aguta said.

"She's standing in front of you!" Harper shouted, gesturing to Anna. "I know you can see her. Don't act like this."

"If I acknowledge her, then I must acknowledge the fact that she has come to kill me, and I will order my warriors to attack," Chief Aguta said, gesturing to Luca and the men blocking the exit behind them.

The warriors shifted as if uneasy, but they hadn't been given any orders yet, and they kept their faces carefully composed so Harper couldn't tell whether they would remain loyal to the chief if he asked them to kill their own tribe members.

Anna lifted her chin defiantly. "If I had come on my own, it would have been to avenge my husband. You are correct there. But I didn't come for him, and I didn't come for you. I came for my children." She raised her hands, indicating Harper and Quinn. "Fate has seen us reunited for the purpose of bringing the world to its senses, and we will do the same for you. Let go of petty laws and customs and help us fight the evil that threatens the entire world."

"Last I heard, the only thing threatening our world was your foolish rebellion," Chief Aguta growled, clenching his fists.

He seemed to sway, and Harper worried that he would fall. Her muscles tensed, ready to lunge forward and capture him if he crumpled. Their visit was putting too much strain on him.

The chief accused them all with his gaze. "You went with that man, and you joined this cause to better the world, but we are more oppressed than ever. The humans we once traded with, lived in peace with, now shun us. They shoot at us. We've lost so many..." his voice went hoarse and cracked at the end, and he took a moment to collect himself before continuing. "Our tribe's numbers have been reduced so drastically that we will barely survive, and we will survive only if we remain in hiding, but there is little food and few supplies here. That is what your precious rebellion has done, after all this time. Was it worth Stephen's life? Is it worth yours and your children's?"

Anna's wings quivered with her rage, trembling against Harper's arm. "It is for them I fight. It is for them we have always fought. You had your chance to accept us back into the tribe. Years ago, when I brought Stephen back here. You chose to murder your own family and forever banish your daughter and by extension, your grandchildren, rather than to help them and welcome them home. I am not the one who should be asking the difficult questions, *father*." Anna spat the word like it tasted dirty.

"You will address me by my title or not at all," Chief Aguta snapped.

"I will address you how I see fit!" Anna replied. "Titles mean nothing after you die."

"Then you do threaten me, after all," the chief said, his gaze darkening, eyebrows sinking like hoods over his eyes.

"Do you wish for death?" Anna asked. "Because if so, there is a better use for what remains of your life than to throw it away fighting your family or starving in this cave."

"We are not the enemy. There are demons," Quinn said, cutting in. "Their leader was brought to earth by a powerful coven of witches and is building a bridge to the lowest abyss in another realm, bringing all the hordes of hell down on our heads. She will lay waste to the earth and every living thing in it if she's not stopped. We stand a chance if the Tulukaruq use the Songs to bind her, to make her walk back through the portal. We've gained a lot in leaving the village. Like new friends and allies who will help us survive this attack." His chest heaved, and he glanced at Harper, who tried to make her expression look assured.

Chief Aguta's expression remained skeptical. "And what of the humans? They've suddenly decided to forgive us? To let their world be inhabited by aberrations like us?"

Quinn hesitated, and Harper jumped in. "We're working on that. We've sent others to gather reinforcements and persuade the humans. This situation with the demons could finally show the humans that not all paranormals are bad."

"What of your new allies, then? Are there no flocks among them?" Chief Aguta asked.

Harper nodded. "There are. But none of them have magic or numbers like ours. Too many of the world's shifter flocks have been reduced to almost nothing, and none of them have preserved their songs as well as ours have been."

She'd gained that understanding from her training, watching the other shifters struggle to use fragments of song, or try another species' songs in order to regain some of their abilities. She hadn't realized then, frustrated as she was by the difficulty she had controlling her power, what a gift it was to have had her traditions passed down so clearly and faithfully.

"You understand the advantage we have gained by keeping to ourselves, and yet you ask me to give it all up for a world that would see us destroyed?" Chief Aguta said. "Leaving the village would mean death for us all. And what of the little children? Would you have us bring them into battle?"

"I will stay with the children, Aguta. I'm of little use in a battle." The female voice came from a dark recess at the back of the cave that Harper had assumed was merely shadowed over. She hadn't noticed the form moving within, a form that now hobbled into the light.

Scars twisted across the old woman's face, but they didn't prevent Harper from recognizing her.

"Ahna!" she cried, rushing forward past the chief to hug her grandmother, slowing as she approached so she didn't knock her over.

Ahna reached a trembled arm around Harper, her cheek damp with tears she had already shed.

When Harper pulled away, Ahna patted her cheek, then craned her neck to peer around her.

"Is she really here? My Anjij?" Ahna asked. "I heard her voice, but I could not see her from where I lay."

Harper hadn't heard her mother's birth name—she must have changed it to fit in, or perhaps forget her past. But she knew it was Anna her grandmother spoke of, especially by the expression on her mother's face.

"She's here," Harper confirmed, taking Ahna's arm and leading her towards Anna.

"Stop!" Chief Aguta bellowed, and he motioned to his men, two of which split off from the entrance and moved to separate Harper from her grandmother.

"What are you doing?" Harper cried, letting Ahna go so her struggle with the warriors wouldn't inadvertently hurt her. She batted at the men's arms as they pulled her back to where the rest of them stood, leaving Ahna looking bereft.

Chief Aguta approached her, looking cross. "Ahna, it is forbidden for one who has betrayed their tribal oaths to return after leaving. You know this. Do not greet her like a long-lost child! We have no child."

"Yes, we do!" Ahna said, her voice rising in pitch and turning into a wail. "I have never forsaken her as you have. I could never, and I will never. Let go of your pride, old man, and see your daughter standing before you like the miracle she is."

That seemed to fluster the old chief. His mouth opened and closed, anger still evident in his eyes. But pride, it seemed, won out.

Chief Aguta raised his hand and flicked it forward dismissively. "Take her away."

Warriors closed in around Anna, but Harper and Quinn took up defense positions, one in front of their mother, one behind.

"We are outnumbered," Anna said. "The only way is the Songs. Harper?"

Fear ran through Harper like the blood in her veins, saturating every part of her. What if she broke their family the way she'd broken her bond with Tyson? But maybe they didn't have to Sing the Song of breaking.

"Don't do this," Quinn said to their grandfather.

What was he doing? A final plea for them, for their mother? Harper glanced away from the circling warriors to glimpse the chief's face. His expression hadn't changed, his heart apparently untouched by this plea from his grandson.

Ahna's weeping filled the brief silence in the cave.

"I can do nothing else," Chief Aguta replied at last.

"Then you leave me no choice," Quinn said, and he reached up to the totem hanging from his neck, grasping the bones and feathers in one hand.

"I, Quincey King, challenge Chief Aguta King to the Ilau Toqu."

"No!" Anna cried out hoarsely, surging forward to grab Quinn's shoulder, turning him to face her. "You can't do this! He'll kill you."

Quinn's brown eyes had hardened beyond recognition. He looked from Anna to Harper, and his words chilled Harper's blood. "The killing will end with him."

"What did he do?" Harper asked, uncertain of what had happened. She didn't know any of her family's native tongue, but the words sounded ancient. Ancient and binding.

"He has invoked the Invitation of Death. The challenge for leadership in the Tuluqaruq tribe," Anna said, looking desperately from Quinn to Chief Aguta. "Call it off. Refuse to fight your grandson."

Harper spun on Quinn, fury springing from her heart. "We could have fought them! Why do you always have to reach for glory by doing foolish things?"

"Guess we're related," Quinn said, shrugging. He gave her a small, sad smile. "Your heart isn't in the Singing, is it, little sister? Without your voice, we'd fail. This will be quick. I'm younger, stronger."

"My father knows the Songs," Anna interrupted, putting her hands on Quinn's face. "You don't understand how well he knows them. He—he's changed some of them. I've never seen anyone wield them the way he does."

Quinn tugged her hands down, holding them a moment. "Believe in me," he said, and then he squared his shoulders and looked back to the chief, who had a dazed look on his ancient face.

Their grandmother's crying had stopped. "See what your pride has done now? Will you fight your own blood?"

"I will fight anyone who defies our ancient laws. Do you know the rules of the Ilau Toqu?" Chief Aguta removed the heavy robe he wore and tossed it to the side, revealing a bare, muscled chest. His wings unfurled from his back, seeming too massive for the small chamber. He gestured, and the warriors opened their circle to let Quinn through.

Quinn rolled his shoulders, stretching his wings. "I don't." If he was nervous, his face didn't show it.

Harper's mind raced. What could she do? Could she challenge her grandfather at the same time and help Quinn? She doubted the rules allowed two challengers.

"Very well," Chief Aguta said. "In an Ilau Toqu, only the Songs are used. No weapons, no physical attacks. You may only attack with your soul and the Songs within. Your training has surely been limited in this area. Withdraw your challenge, and I will allow you to train with our warriors to learn dozens of variations, to hone your power to what it truly ought to be."

"I won't withdraw," Quinn said without hesitation.

Chief Aguta inclined his head.

A small sound of protest escaped Anna. She looked at Harper with fear in her eyes, but she didn't speak.

It struck her then, as she watched Quinn step into the center of the cave to face their grandfather, that she understood some of Tyson's frustrations with her. She had been projecting her fear that he wasn't strong enough to protect himself, and in doing so had driven a wedge of resentment between them. It was possible that her distrust and his resentment had weakened their bond and caused it to be broken by her misdirected song in the first place.

"There will be no taking turns," Chief Aguta announced. "In the Ilau Toqu, we Sing our songs together at once. The stronger Song will overpower the weaker, and thus the victor will be decided."

"You could end this. Decide to release these toxic traditions that pit family against family," Quinn said.

"Our traditions have kept our tribe alive, our blood strong and pure," Chief Aguta argued. "If we abandon them, we will fall into oblivion."

"That's where the tribe is headed anyway," Quinn said. "Can't you see? You have a dozen men and only a few more women. A handful of children. Our people are dying. We must adapt or your worst fear will come true. Those who adapt survive."

"This challenge is a good thing," the chief said, rubbing his hands together. "I will subdue you, your sister, and your dangerous ways of thinking. We will find a way to carry on for decades more because of our traditions."

He was delusional, Harper realized. So caught up in his beliefs and traditions he couldn't even consider another point of view that would take them away from him. He was afraid, and that was why he saw his own daughter as his greatest enemy.

"Ready?" Quinn growled.

The Chief smiled. "Let it begin."

# CHAPTER TWENTY-NINE

## TYSON

BLINDFOLDED, TYSON AND CHARLIE were led to the human rebels' hideout in the underbelly of D.C. A musty smell permeated the air, and water dripped somewhere.

When the dirty strip of cloth was pulled off his head, Tyson confirmed that they were underground. A network of pipes made up the ceiling, and they were surrounded by four cement walls.

The leader of the ragged band that had intercepted Tyson and Charlie had introduced himself as Terran, no last name, no explanations. The dark-haired woman at his side was Robyn, Tyson had heard one of the other rebel team members whisper it during a conversation, and based on their similar features, Tyson guessed she was related. Maybe Terran's daughter?

Terran motioned for the door to be closed. It shut with a heavy thud, and the dead bolt clicked into place, leaving Charlie and Tyson alone in the cement room, with the leader and his people on the other side.

Tyson ran forward, pounding on the door. "What are you doing?"

An intercom crackled to life in the room. "Don't worry. All new recruits go through this. Relax. It'll be over in a few days."

The intercom shut off and a hissing sound filled the chamber. Tyson glanced around frantically. What was that? And what did the leader mean by a few days? They didn't have a few days!

"What do you think that is?" Tyson asked, glancing at Charlie.

Her brow furrowed. "I don't think it will kill us. It wouldn't make sense for them to kill everyone who became a recruit. I'd wager it's a harmless gas that might knock us out for a bit. If we fight it, or try to use magic to escape, they'll know what we are and kill us."

Tyson grimaced. "Then we do nothing?"

Charlie nodded and crossed to where two chairs stood at the center of the room. "Better make yourself comfortable."

Tyson noticed his head feeling lighter, and each time he breathed in, he smelled something slightly sweet.

He stumbled to the chair, noting a water bottle beside him on the floor, and reached for it.

His hand barely closed around it when the gas took its effect, and he slipped into unconsciousness.

Tyson woke several times, blurrily peering around, always slumped over in his chair. Sometimes people moved around him. One injected him with something. A camera in the corner always tracked his movements, and within moments he would be unconscious again.

The third time it happened, Tyson fought the effects of the gas, struggling to stay alert, and when he realized he would fail again, he slipped his consciousness instead into the astral realm, watching his body slump over next to Charlie's for a long moment.

At least here he could watch over their bodies and think of a plan. They didn't seem injured, though he didn't know what had been injected into them.

Time stretched on, and he grew bored. No one had entered the room, and Charlie hadn't moved. He drifted out of the building to look out on the dulled sky of the physical plane. Demons had taken over even there, all headed for the swirling pit in the sky that would take them to Earth.

*Tyson!* A cry echoed all around him, and he felt a great rush of tension and fear as a ball of pure light energy barreled into him.

He untangled himself from the energy and it took form as a frantic, wide-eyed woman with curly black hair.

"Mandi?" Tyson asked, not believing what his eyes were seeing.

"Tyson! I can't believe I found you. The demon queen will find me any moment. Don't talk, just listen," Mandi said. "I have information you have to get to Anna, or one of the leaders of the T.R.S."

Tyson closed his mouth and listened as Mandi spun one of the wildest stories he'd ever heard. Demon possession. Zeke imprisoned. Consorts and false gods.

By the end, his mind was spinning.

Storm clouds seemed to form on the horizon of the astral realm, and Mandi glanced behind, then back at Tyson, urgency in her eyes.

"Say you believe me," she begged. "Say you can do something."

"I've been taken by some human rebels, but I think we can escape. I just have to—"

"I have to go!" Mandi cried, her astral form bleeding away into pure light. "She can't find you."

Then the streak of energy was gone, zipping into the sky like a shooting star in reverse.

Stunned, Tyson flew back down to his body, still sitting in the dark.

Harper had been right about the Eternal Source. They couldn't trust them because they weren't the true Source. They were a demon. And not just any demon, Ragranoth's consort. He owed Harper a big apology when they were reunited.

Suddenly, the light in the room flickered on, fluorescent bulbs pulsing. Robyn, the dark-haired woman who had been with Terran before, strode in and slapped Tyson full in the face.

*Ow,* Tyson thought, touching his cheek as he felt an echo of the sting from the astral realm. He flew down and reconnected with his body, gasping to life.

He sat up, his arms still bound around a metal chair. Charlie sat beside him, her head still lolling, Robyn grabbed her by the chin and slapped her smartly.

Charlie startled awake, and her yell filled the small room.

"Give them some water," a gruff voice said from the front of the room.

Tyson glanced over and saw Terran.

"How long were we out?" he asked.

Terran scratched his chin. "Almost three days, I reckon. I wasn't overseeing most of it, and the days blur together. Sorry about the time loss. It's a necessary evil."

Tyson reeled. Three days? Three days he'd been held unconscious? How was he alive? Had Harper returned to D.C. yet? Better question, how had their tests not detected the magic in his or Charlie's blood? Were they faulty somehow?

Seeming reluctant, Robyn uncapped a water bottle and held it towards Tyson's mouth. He closed his lips and turned his head away.

"How do we know that's not poisoned after what you did?" he asked.

Robyn shrugged and took a gulp from the water bottle, making a show of swallowing, then handed it back towards him.

Grudgingly, Tyson allowed her to give him some of the water, some of it dribbling down the sides of his chin and onto his shirt. The woman turned to Charlie, who drank eagerly.

Terran spread his arms wide, grinning. "Well, you passed the tests!"

"What tests?" Tyson asked warily. How long had he been unconscious?

"We tested your blood for reactions to three substances that detect shifters and some magic-users. It takes a few days, but it's worth it to guarantee that you're not one of them." The man said bitterly.

Robyn stepped back, tossing the empty plastic bottle to one side, and crossed her arms. "Your tests were wrong this time, dad. I had their bags searched and look what we found." Her eyes gleamed with malice. She bent down towards Charlie's bag and pulled out a troll doll and a bundle of sage.

Terran scoffed. "A toy and a bundle of weeds doesn't mean anything. Your paranoia is getting to you, Robyn."

"Not just a bundle of weeds. What is this, witch?" Robyn asked, waving it under Charlie's nose.

"Sage," Charlie said.

"It's a smudging stick. Witches use them," Robyn said, shoving the bundle towards her father for him to inspect.

"A witch, eh?" Terran smirked, pulling a lighter out of his pocket and flicking it open. "We know what to do with those."

"No!" Tyson shouted, holding out his hands. "She just likes the smell. She uses it for...for..." His mind went blank. What else could a sage bundle be used for?

Charlie rolled her eyes. "I use it as a bug repellent. The mosquitos were awful this summer, traveling through the woods and sleeping outside all the time. Burn that for a bit before bed and the smoke would make them leave us alone. Stinks to high heaven, but it hardly proves I'm a witch." She snorted. "Are you killing everyone who drinks tea?"

Terran paused, frowning. "The trolls are odd, though. How many are in the bag?"

"Like fifty," Robyn said.

"Thirty-six," Charlie argued.

Tyson wanted to slap his forehead. She was making it worse, but she wouldn't look at him and take the hint.

"It'd make sense for you to keep one or two, but that many is a burden. I've heard witches can animate objects, make them into little spies to do their bidding. Maybe they're like familiars." Terran glanced at Robyn, who dropped the sage bundle and nodded.

"I've heard of stuff like that. And we can't afford any mistakes. Looks like your tests were wrong," Robyn said.

"Why does everyone assume I'm a witch?" Charlie muttered.

Tyson shot her a glance. Getting picky about titles wouldn't help their cause.

"You can't burn her," Tyson said again. "Not without any real evidence."

"Oh, we don't have to burn her," Terran said. "I was mostly kidding about that. We're not complete barbarians. But the reason we brought you to this room, closed off from everyone else, is that we can just tie you up and leave you in here. No food, no water, you'll last a few days and then you won't be our problem anymore."

It was so brutal and efficient, Tyson didn't know what to say for a moment. Even magic could only do so much against a coffin room like this. He knew Terran was operating from a place of fear. He didn't know the man's story, or his daughter's. He just knew they would do anything to survive, to protect their people. He couldn't fault them for that.

It was time Terran knew what exactly he was dealing with.

Tyson was tempted to shift into full polar bear mode, but he resisted, instead casting an impression of his polar bear essence into the air above him, a fierce snarl on the bear's face as the translucent image roared silently above him. He crossed his arms, staring Terran down.

"You really don't want to do that," Tyson said.

Confusion crossed Terran's face. "You're a shifter? The tests should have caught that!" He turned and dove for the automatic rifle Robyn had leaned against the wall when they'd first come in, but it was gone, bouncing along on top of the small army of trolls that Charlie had animated to steal it just a second before.

Tyson grinned as the trolls untied his feet and hands and he stood up.

"You're out magicked and outgunned. Back down, Terran, and listen because I'm only going to say this once." Tough words that Tyson didn't really mean, but he had to posture to make himself appear a bigger threat than he was so Terran would take him seriously.

A gun clicked.

Charlie cleared her throat.

Tyson glanced over and froze at the sight of Robyn holding a pistol to Charlie's skull.

"Put the bear away and make the trolls bring my father his gun," Robyn snarled.

"If you'll just listen—" Tyson started.

"Now!" Robyn shouted, shoving the barrel of the gun harder against Charlie's head.

Tyson let the image of his polar bear essence vanish. He put his hands in the air, a show of good faith that he would comply, since his threat didn't work.

Charlie's finger flicked, and the trolls scurried to do her bidding, dropping the rifle at Terran's feet.

Terran picked it up and immediately pointed it at Tyson.

"I don't know what you are, but I know I ought to put you down now," Terran said breathlessly.

"Not if you want to keep our world intact," Tyson said, licking his dry lips. "I know how to stop the demons, and I want to get rid of them just as badly as you do."

Terran laughed, harsh and loud. "I know better than to believe that. They're your dogs. How do I know you haven't brought them down on us while you distracted me with your lies? They could be swarming this place."

Tyson shook his head. "I don't control them. Their leader, their Autarch, isn't on our side. She's not on any side. Look, I know this is hard to believe. Just a few months ago, I was just like you. I was human, I worked in a naturalization camp, forcing paranormals to comply with government mandates before they were allowed to re-enter society. And then my dormant powers surfaced. I'm not a threat; I'm just a guy who has a bit of magic I'm still learning to control."

Terran's eyes nearly bugged out of his head, and then he busted up laughing.

Tyson watched him with some concern that the gun in his hand could go off at any moment.

Fortunately, Terran regained control of his emotions, wiping at his eyes with one hand. "You really expect me to believe all that? You were human, and then you weren't? These things don't just happen. You're born a magic bastard, or one of them changes you. You don't just become one overnight." Terran raised his gun again. "I've killed dozens of you. You're no different than the rest."

"Except I don't want to kill you," Tyson said, crossing his arms and staring Terran straight in his one open eye.

Terran opened his other eye, hesitating.

"Pull the trigger, dad. He's lying to save his own ass," Robyn said.

"I'm not lying," Tyson insisted. "I don't want to kill you or any human. I don't want to control you, either. I understand you better than you know, since up until two months ago I was one of you, working for the government to curb the paranormal population. But right now, my biggest concern is the demons, and I'm willing to wager it's your biggest concern, too. How many of your people have they killed? How long will you survive if they take down the power supply? The water? This world is doomed if we don't get rid of the demons, and I've just come back from a trip to the astral realm asking a literal god how we can do it."

That seemed to finally reach Terran. He actually lowered the rifle, staring wide-eyed at Tyson.

"You're not bluffing, are you?" Terran said in amazement. He glanced at Robyn, who shook her head, but her own expression had changed from pure hatred to a sort of angry curiosity. She pulled her gun away from Charlie's head.

"He's telling the truth," Charlie said. "Not that you'll believe me any more than him, but he's been working with the T.R.S. these past few weeks, and he was there when the demons attacked the Tower."

Confusion crossed Terran's face. "The demons...attacked the paranormal rebels? At your headquarters?" His eyes went wide with alarm. "What about the President?"

Tyson shook his head. "I don't know what happened to her. If our leaders managed to get away, maybe they were able to get her out, too. The goal was never to kill her, only work with her until we convinced the rest of the world to accept that paranormals deserve to be treated with as much respect as humans," Terran snorted at that, but Tyson continued. "Whatever you believe about us, when it comes to the demons, we're on the same side. No one wants to die a brutal death at the claws of those monsters or be possessed. If you just come with us to meet up with our leaders..."

Terran snorted. "You mean the ones that have disappeared? The ones that have stopped attending press conferences? Your precious leaders are probably dead or possessed, if they haven't joined with the demons willingly. I'd put my money on that last one."

Tyson was losing confidence that he'd convince Terran to join his side, but he made one last, desperate attempt.

He spread his arms wide, exposing himself in a show of vulnerability meant to provoke trust. "Give us a chance. I can lead you to whoever is left from the T.R.S., and we can take the demons out together. After that, maybe you will change your mind about shooting us, but at least we'll have a world left to fight over."

He held his breath, watching Terran's eyes shift back and forth as he worked over Tyson's words in his mind.

After a long, terrifying moment, Terran dropped the arm holding his gun and motioned to Robyn to do the same.

"Okay. You can take us to your leaders. But the instant I receive any hint that you or your people intend to double cross us, this bullet goes in your head, the next one in your friend's, and we won't stop until every one of your kind is dead," Terran growled.

Tyson closed his eyes from relief and a wave of exhaustion. "I wouldn't expect anything less," he said at last.

It might have been the worst idea in the world, but it was the only option they had. If he could get Terran to talk to Jack or his brother Dak, or if Anna returned by then, perhaps they could come to a mutual understanding and team up long enough to banish the demons. Maybe in fighting together, the humans might come to see the paranormals as something other than their enemy.

After that, they'd have the impossible task of getting the rest of the world to agree to make some changes, but Tyson would settle for merely postponing the end of the world if it meant he had the chance to see Harper again.

# CHAPTER THIRTY

## HARPER

THE FIRST NOTE REVERBERATED through the cave, coming from the Chief's open mouth.

Quinn came in high with a whistle Harper recognized from the primary bars. He had started with the Song of Persuasion. She admired him for it—he would try to bend their grandfather's will first.

But Chief Aguta had no gentle intentions. Tones bounded off the cave walls, clashing with Quinn's notes and somehow taking the power out of them, turning it into a mere whistle without magic.

Quinn's eyes widened, and he tried the song again, finishing the first bar and moving into the second. The primary songs were the foundation of the more complex tunes that advanced raven born learned. They had plenty of power in themselves, especially combined with strong intention. Quinn had started learning the more complex songs, Harper knew, but she didn't realize how much he knew until now.

The primary tune changed, shifting into the advanced version, and picked up pace. Wind whipped around the cave in answer to his Song. He'd stolen his power back from the chief.

The two raven shifters faced each other, their wings spread in such a way they created a circle in the middle of the room.

Quinn's tune changed, soaring high and dropping low. A wind picked up in the underground cavern, twisting through the doorway behind Harper and reaching for Chief Aguta.

The chief's tone dropped to match, and the wind redirected, pushing against Quinn and forcing him back.

"You have learned to persuade the wind. That is very good. More than I assumed you knew. But you do not know enough to maintain control when another tries to take it from you," Chief Aguta said, dropping his song. The wind died with it.

Quinn didn't bother replying, and Harper watched as his expression shifted in his concentration, choosing the next Song to fight with.

A wild yell echoed across the walls, turning into a kind of song Harper had never heard before. It contained all the untamed wilderness, an impression of sheer cliffs, frigid nights, harsh heat, unrelenting storm. And all of it turned on Quinn.

Harper felt it in that place inside of her that all her Songs came from, the place that felt small and inadequate in the face of the power her grandfather turned on her brother.

"Quinn!" Harper screamed, as if to warn him, but though Quinn managed to slice through the attacking song with his own arrow-like tune, the wild song snapped straight through the paltry defense and struck Quinn full-force.

Quinn's body flung back against the rock wall, sending a cascade of smaller rocks and dust from the ceiling.

Harper ran, ducking under the falling debris, and kneeled at Quinn's side, checking his breathing. Shallow and erratic, but there. His heart beat as well, and as soon as Harper knew he wasn't dead she rocked back on her heels and stood, stalking towards the chief.

"How could you?" she growled, hands clenched into trembling fists at her side. "Do you know what I've gone through to be with him again? I found him and lost him several times over, and I am not going to lose him to you."

"Then Sing, fledgling," Chief Aguta said, voice hoarse. "I will dismantle you and your false beliefs in the same way I have your brother."

He must have expended a lot of effort in that last attack for it to be strong enough to knock Quinn out. The question was, did he have enough stamina for another strike like that? Or did Harper have a chance with her primary bars and the fear of inadequacy beating a broken rhythm in her chest?

Harper turned away, too angry to even look at the chief. She tried to clear her mind and gather every bit of information she'd learned in the past few weeks about the Songs. It wasn't much, and by the time her breath had steadied, the fear had returned in force.

She glanced up, catching Anna's gaze on her.

"Teach me something," Harper said, low enough the chief would have to work to hear her.

"What?" Anna asked, her expression startled.

"You know how he fights. You know I don't stand a chance. But if you could give me something, anything, with which to fight him, what would it be?"

"Focus. Hold your intention in your heart." Anna spoke in a low voice, husky with emotion. "Either the Songs of Raven are in your soul, or they aren't. But I've seen them there, through your gaze. You just have to free them."

Harper found herself fighting the wave that crashed through her soul, wiping away the false beliefs that had lived there for weeks. Her mother didn't see her as a failure; she believed in Harper and accepted her as a daughter. And Anna hadn't told her that she couldn't do it, or that she should have practiced more.

When it really counted, she'd told Harper of the strength and power she saw in her daughter.

Harper squared her shoulders and faced the chief again.

He looked powerful, his muscular body and massive wings straight and proud. But his eyes told the real story. He was tired, and he had spent far too much of his energy on pride and fear. Yes, the chief was afraid.

Just as she was afraid her power would destroy those she loved, the chief must have feared the same as he faced his only granddaughter in the Ilau Toqu.

"Are you sure you're ready?" Chief Aguta asked.

His words pried into Harper's mind, giving the fear more room to grow. Harper clenched her teeth and pushed against the fear, reigning in her thoughts. She was in control. And she would listen to her mother's advice.

*Either the Songs of Raven are in your heart or not. Hold your intention in your heart.*

Harper breathed in and thought of everything she wanted her song to do. She'd done it before, incapacitating an entire group of paranormals intent on killing Tyson in the forest at Camp Silver Lake. And she'd used her power again to subdue hundreds with the aid of other bird shifters at the Washington Monument in D.C. Both times, she'd focused her intention and let the song flow out of her. Getting caught up on the technical points of singing the songs of her people was what had cramped her magic and put it in this box that limited and frustrated her.

Now, she gave herself permission to let it be what it would be.

A Song of Binding. But not manipulating her grandfather's will, forcing him to comply. No, the type of binding that mended wounds in flesh and minds. The kind that knitted torn things together, binding them back into their true form.

It was time someone Sang this family back together.

Once she had that vision in her mind, Harper opened her mouth and let the notes flow out, trilling, eerie, beautiful notes unlike anything she'd practiced in the training rooms. She heard hints of the primary bars, hidden beneath the complex melody she wove with her own heart. Her wings and hands relaxed at her side. She refused to posture and pretend at this fight.

For a drawn out, blissful moment, Harper caught a softening in the chief's expression, the wrinkles on his face slackening, anger dissipating, as if he was caught up in her song. All she had to do was get it to sink into his heart. She sent the song out stronger, penetrating deeper into the hearts of all who listened because she realized that it was the kind of song that all could benefit from.

She'd chosen healing rather than violence. It was so obvious now, Harper wished she'd thought of it before Quinn had gotten hurt. But her song was working on him, too, and she saw him stir from the corners of her eyes.

Three piercing shrieks and the wild song split the room again, the discord between her notes and the chief's rattling Harper's soul. She took a step back, the weight of his attack crushing against her shoulders, reaching into that place inside her as if to rip away her Song.

No. He couldn't have the hope and healing she offered. He would take it and twist it or crush it into something that served him. If she lost this fight, she and Quinn would be forced to sing songs of destruction, to choose hatred like he had.

Chief Aguta's song beat against her, pushing back her Song of Binding and bringing Harper to her knees.

Tears streamed from her eyes as she sang, but eventually, her untrained voice gave way.

Chief Aguta stepped forward, light from the hole in the rocks above streaming down across him, making him look like a destroying angel. His eyes gleamed with the confidence that he would win this fight.

Harper slumped over, supporting herself on all fours, panting and trying to gather the energy for another Song, but she felt as if everything had been taken out of her. She closed her eyes, bracing as the chief's Song wrapped its way around her, stealing her breath, stealing her motivation, her desire to fight, and Harper found her body complying without being told.

The Song forced her to roll over on her back, arms and legs flat, and her eyes opened into the blinding streak of sunlight piercing the cavern.

Harper fought against the binding of her grandfather's song, and managed to push up onto her elbows, straining to open her mouth and let a Song flow out.

The Song shifted, cracking like a whip against Harper's chest. She cried out and fell back, pain blossoming across her body. She'd never known a Song could cause so much pain.

A shadow stepped over her form, and at first, she assumed it was Chief Aguta, come to gloat, but the form was too slim, the wings shorter, and when the face turned down to glance towards her, Harper recognized Anna, fear and anger written plainly across her face.

"You're the same man you were when I came to you with pictures of your grandchildren and pleaded with you to let us raise them in the safety of the village," Anna cried out.

Harper could only lay still, recuperating what strength she had left, preparing her lungs for a final song.

"You were past saving," Chief Aguta replied. "Quinn and Harper will get the education and training they should have received in our lore and our ways. We will purge them of their outward thinking, and they will remain to strengthen our tribe and our numbers, as it should have been from the beginning."

"Did you hear nothing I just said? You had your chance with them. And you refused it." Anna clenched her fists and adjusted her stance over Harper. "I stayed away to protect them—both from you and the government. When you learned the government was on our trail, you killed my husband and tossed me out like I was nothing to you. Not your daughter, not a tribe member. Maybe I made a mistake in not bringing my children for you to meet then, maybe they could have softened your heart in ways I failed to, but if it meant I spared them from seeing their father killed, then I don't regret it for a moment. I only regret not being brave enough to go back for them while I had a chance, for believing they were safer growing up without my presence to endanger them."

Harper gasped as her mother's words sank in. How many times had her mother wished to come for them, only to have agents find her trail? How many times did she try before she joined the T.R.S. and decided that even if her children were lost to her, she would do her best to create a future for them?

Harper turned her head towards the chief.

He showed no sign of understanding, his gaze hardening instead. "If you'd brought them here, at least they would have had a place. You ruined them."

"We still have a chance," Anna said, her hands relaxing at her sides. "We could create a future, a country, where they are free to fly the skies anywhere they like. But you don't see it. Your vision is closed, and because of that, the Tulukaruq are doomed."

Chief Aguta's protesting reply was drowned out by the notes that filled the air, next, and Harper recognized the Song she had tried to sing, the Song of Binding that healed, and this time she felt it in her own soul, reaching past her heart and into her gut, into her womb, light and warmth filling the wounded spaces and making them stronger than before.

Her body still trembled with weakness, having expended her energy in the Song, but her mind was fortified, and when she looked at her mother, she saw a shining strength that washed out her grandfather's anger and revealed him for what he was—a coward who had chosen pride and fear over his family.

A surge of pity overwhelmed Harper. Her vision blurred as she looked at her grandfather, remembering how she'd admired him when they first met, seeing him as a pillar of strength that had somehow held onto a dying community. But now she saw the truth—he was the reason the Tulukaruq tribe had dwindled to almost nothing.

Anna's song reached a crescendo that filled the cavern, and Chief Aguta crumpled to the rock-strewn ground, wings slumped around him.

Harper's grandmother waited until the last notes of the song trailed away, then entered the dimly lit circle, crawling to her husband.

Anna stepped over Harper and reached a hand down to her.

Harper took it, digging deep for the strength to stand. Resting even for a moment had brought back some of her vitality, but she still had to lean against Anna for support as her legs trembled and wobbled.

Quinn crossed the room, blood on his forehead and a grim expression on his face. "We're leaving, I assume."

Anna glanced towards her parents wearily, then nodded. "There's nothing more we can do here."

"I wish there was a way to tell the rest of the tribe, to give them a choice," Harper said.

"Even if we did, none of them would come. You two are strangers, raised among the rest of the world, and I am the prodigal daughter, returned but not welcomed. No one would listen to us."

Ahna glanced up from their grandfather, whose chest rose and fell indicating he was unconscious, not dead.

"Do you have to leave?" Ahna asked, voice trembling.

"You've been talking to him for years. Has he ever shown any sign of changing his mind?" Anna asked.

Ahna bit her lip, then shook her head.

"Tell everyone you can that we'll be in Washington, D.C. if they change their minds," Anna said. "We could use all the help we can get to send the demons back where they came from."

Quinn came up on Harper's other side and looped Harper's arm over his shoulder, taking some of the burden of support from their mother. Together, mother, son, and daughter walked from the cave and left their tribe and the lands of their ancestors behind.

# CHAPTER THIRTY-ONE

## ZEKE

ZEKE LAY STILL, EXPECTING Boris to come after him again but unable to stand. Judging by the pain of each breath, he'd cracked at least one rib. He raised his head to look for Boris and found him kneeling by Sasha, stroking her glossy fur as she lay motionless, murmuring soft words to her.

She whined, her tail thumping on the cement floor, and Boris broke down with a sob, his massive shoulders shaking. His prized fighter had been bested.

His soft spot for the she-wolf was his undoing. Sasha came to life in a blur of gray fur and snapping jaws, going straight for the dog fighter's throat and crushing it with a single, swift bite.

Blood sprayed over her gray fur, and Boris's dying scream ended in a gurgle as his body slumped to the floor.

Sasha licked her reddened muzzle and whined, stepping out of the sticky puddle pooling around Boris. She glanced at Zeke with her yellow eyes, then lowered her head and front legs down in submission.

*Alpha*, she said.

*Come on, let's get out of here,* Zeke said, already exhausted. He stood, wincing at the pain from numerous cuts and the agony of his broken ribs. He tested out a few steps and found he could walk with a limp.

To his shock, Sasha bumped up alongside him, offering her bulk in support as she led him to the stairs.

*You're hurt?* Edgar's voice rumbled through Zeke's mind.

*Of course he's hurt, idiot,* Frank snarked back.

Mike whimpered with concern through the connection.

Zeke had forgotten what it felt like to have others feel his emotions and pain, to have to reassure them. To be a leader. He'd end the connection as soon as he could. They didn't need to remain tied to him, and they deserved their freedom after being imprisoned by the inhuman madman that now lay dead at the bottom of the arena.

Sasha's voice surprised Zeke, and his next step slipped as she spoke.

*Sorry guys. I-I have a lot to apologize for. I'll start by apologizing for hurting our alpha.*

*You'd better,* Shira growled.

Sasha flinched beside Zeke.

Zeke brought their attention back to him. *Guys, let's focus on escaping. Anyone know if there's anybody here other than Drew?*

*Is Boris dead?* Shira asked.

*Yes.* Zeke and Sasha replied together. *Sasha killed him,* Zeke added, finally reaching the top of the stairs.

He had to pause and regain his breath and strength. He felt Mike and Edgar send him some through the bond, sensing his weakness and wanting to lend their aid. He thanked them, wishing he could find some water to drink, but pressed on regardless.

When they reached the first door, Sasha stepped away from him and they considered the hurdle together.

*You need to get this collar off me,* Zeke said at last, exposing his throat to her.

*But...* Sasha started, fear rolling off her.

*How long has it been?* he asked, mentally closing them off from the rest of the pack for a bit of privacy.

*Almost a year,* Sasha said meekly. She shuffled her paws, whining and bobbing her head in distress. *I don't know if I still can. In the beginning, he* made *me. He used me.*

Zeke snarled with a violence he didn't know he had within him. She didn't have to say who *he* was.

*Why didn't you kill him sooner? You don't have a collar,* he said, then regretted how accusatory it sounded. It wasn't always a simple matter to murder an abuser, no matter how much they hurt you.

Sasha confirmed as much when she responded, *He did use the collar at first. Put me through conditioning training, made me wear it as a human and a wolf. And he always had Shira. He'd threaten to use her too, to kill her if I attacked him. I knew I could probably kill him, but it was so damn hard to fight against what he'd trained my body to do. I would tell my body to do one thing, and it would ignore me. The training was too strong. I...I was too weak.*

Zeke limped forward, butting his head under Sasha's and nuzzling her neck. *You're not weak. Boris was a bastard of the worst kind. It'll take time, but your body will become yours again.*

She trembled beneath him, and Zeke took in a deep breath, hating himself for what he was about to do.

*Sasha, I'm going to command you to shift and take off my collar. You can go back to wolf as soon as you do, but I can't get this collar off by myself and we can't get through this door as wolves either.*

*Okay*, she said, her voice barely audible in his mind.

Breathing deep, Zeke barked, hitting Sasha with the force of an alpha command. She jerked as the command struck her, her eyes dilating wide, becoming a beautiful, human blue color. Her back arched and her yelp morphed into a yell as her body wrenched itself back into human form.

She was built solidly, her dirty blonde hair swinging in front of her face. She was also completely naked, and Zeke glimpsed the bruises from Boris's abuse in the moment before he glanced away. He wanted to go back to the arena and kill Boris all over again, but there was no point ravaging a corpse.

Sasha's fingers fumbled at Zeke's neck, taking what felt like ages to unclip the complex buckle that held the shock collar on. When it finally fell away, Zeke shook his head and had to resist the urge to roll.

He failed, flopping onto his back and wriggling in the most satisfying way at the sensation of free movement and nothing constraining him.

Sasha actually giggled, then she shifted again.

Zeke traded his wolf form for his human one, standing to his full height and stretching with a groan. His broken rib made him double over, and he regretted the stretch as he prodded his wounded side. Two broken ribs, if his assessment was correct.

He grimaced, then glanced at the wolf beside him.

*Damn, you're handsome in that form,* Sasha grumbled, sounding displeased.

Zeke laughed. *I'm taken.*

*Yeah, yeah,* Sasha said, sighing in the wheezy way wolves did.

Zeke worried for a moment, but their connection seemed content rather than strained. Sort of the way it had felt to be around Kamri, who had led their last pack with him, and Zeke had hope that things would stay calm between them for the short time he led this strange shifter pack.

He opened the door and led the way down the winding halls, pulling up before the final door, which he assumed was the door leading to the kennels. Indeed, he could hear Mike's whining on the other side, and Frank's cat-like yowl.

"It's locked," Zeke said, turning to Sasha. "Who has the key?"

Sasha whimpered, scratching at the door, then seemed to freeze. She spun around and ran down the hall.

Zeke cursed and followed her, putting pressure on his ribs with one hand. Running felt like hell.

Sasha led him to a room with a window like an office, where Drew sat dutifully typing away on a computer and sipping soda, blissfully unaware of his boss's demise.

Zeke tried the lever-like handle. It turned beneath his hand, and he nudged the door open.

Drew didn't even turn. "I'm almost finished with the flights, boss, just let me—" He did turn, then, and let out the most girlish scream Zeke had ever heard come from a man. Zeke slid his arm around Drew's throat, squeezing just tightly enough to frighten him.

"Keys," Zeke said, not bothering with a full sentence.

Sasha growled threateningly for good measure.

Drew grabbed a set off the desk, handing them towards Zeke.

"Which one?" Zeke asked before taking them.

Drew picked up a silver one that looked like four others on the ring, except for a green dot of permanent marker on one side.

"That's for the room, this is for the kennels," he said, pointing to another one with a blue dot on it.

Zeke took the keys with his free hand, pocketing them, then let Drew go.

"Where's…Boris?" Drew asked, gasping and rubbing his throat.

"The last place you want to be," Zeke said, heading for the door.

"What am I supposed to do now?" Drew asked, voice edging towards total panic.

Zeke glanced back at the scrawny, frightened man, giving him the most wolfish smile he could muster. "If I were you, I'd book a flight on Boris's dime and get the hell out of here before the shifters get out. Rumor has it someone is about to free all of them."

Zeke shook the keys in his hand and left, enjoying the glimpse he got of Drew's scramble back to the computer as he passed the office window.

Sasha trotted impatiently ahead, glancing back as if to make sure Zeke was following.

*Keep up*, she huffed.

"I'm bleeding and have cracked ribs," Zeke replied. The reminder that most of his wounds had been inflicted by her made Sasha cower. "I'm not holding it against you. Just…patience while I limp along."

Sasha slowed her pace slightly, stopping at the door to the kennel room.

Zeke shoved the key into the lock and flung the door wide, stopping at Edgar's cage first. The key with the blue dot slid in and turned easily, releasing the padlock into Zeke's hand. He swung the door wide and immediately went for the thick shock collar around Edgar's furry neck. He unlocked the mechanism holding it shut, and the collar dropped to the ground.

Edgar barreled into the narrow stretch between the kennels and knocked Zeke over.

"Ow," Zeke said, groaning at the strain on his ribs. He shoved at the bear. "Pull yourself together. I have to free everyone else."

Edgar shifted, suddenly standing before Zeke as a man wearing a tight blue biker outfit, far lankier than Tyson expected him to be for how big his grizzly form was. He grinned and rubbed at the grown-out scruff on his face, his eyes the same ones in his human form as his bear form.

"Hey, man! Let me help you up, there. So sorry, I get a little carried away sometimes," Edgar said, giving Zeke a hand up.

"I'll unlock cages, you get the collars off," Zeke said, moving towards Frank a few cages down. He opened the door, and the bobcat slinked out, sitting patiently in front of Edgar.

Shira next. Zeke unlocked the door and watched the gray wolf pad out to meet Sasha, who was nearly her twin in appearance. They had slightly different mottling patterns and mask-like markings around their eyes, plus Shira had blue eyes and Sasha had yellow.

The sister wolves rubbed along each other's lengths, messages passing between them that Zeke had a sense of through his alpha connection. He didn't want to pry, so he deliberately forced the emotions away and turned to the final cage where Mike was bouncing like a terrier.

Zeke laughed. "Do you ever calm down?" He unlocked the cage, then bent to do the collar since Edgar was still working on Shira's. As soon as the shock collar was off, Mike shifted into a naked teenage boy, grinning from ear to ear.

Zeke blinked in shock. "How old are you?"

"Eighteen. Just turned, like a week ago. You know how much it sucks to spend your eighteenth birthday imprisoned by a madman like Boris?" Mike rolled his eyes and glanced down at his lanky body. "So...got any spare clothes?"

Zeke glanced at his own biker shorts and shook his head. "Sorry, man. You're gonna have to be a wolf for a bit longer."

"Seriously?" Mike moaned.

"Public nudity is still illegal, even when the world is ending," Zeke said.

Mike shifted back to his scrawny black wolf form, nosing Zeke's hand, his tail thwapping against him as he passed towards Frank and Edgar.

Frank, it turned out, was a red-headed guy with a decent set of muscles and a French accent, which Zeke found hilarious since it didn't translate in his head at all, but as soon as the guy spoke it was super obvious what his nationality was.

"I am a lynx, actually, not a bobcat," Frank said, every bit as fussy as a human.

Edgar kept clapping him on the back, making the human Frank hiss in a very lynx-like way.

Shira still hadn't shifted, seeming to prefer to remain in her wolf form. Zeke didn't begrudge her, letting his shifter pack choose whatever form they felt most comfortable in, except for the naked teenager who was still grumbling about the forced modesty.

"Gather round everyone," Zeke said out loud, waving one arm to bring everyone in. "We're almost out of here. All that's left is to walk out those doors. I couldn't have done it without you, truly."

*Yeah, right. You've got the body of a god,* Sasha retorted, wolf eyes raking over him.

Zeke wiped a hand down his face. "I took a beating in there, and I never would have gained the knowledge or courage I needed without you. All that to say, I owe you as much as you owe me, and I'm not going to hold you to this pack. You're free to go. I hold no bond or oath over you."

Five sets of eyes stared at him.

*You know that's not how it works, right?* Sasha said. *Once a pack is formed, you have to un-form it by casting out each member individually. Once all members are cast out, you'll feel the alpha power leave.*

Zeke cocked his head. He'd never heard of a pack dissolving like that before. But then, packs didn't usually just...dissolve.

"Okay, then. Who's first?"

Mike whimpered. *I don't want to leave the pack. I don't have anyone else.*

Zeke breathed in. "Okay, Mike stays."

"I've never tried a pack before. I think it might be kind of fun with you. Provided you let me read my books," Edgar said with a grin, crossing his arms over his chest.

"You're a bear. How does that work?" Zeke asked desperately.

Edgar shrugged. "Beats me. Let's give it a go, eh?"

Frank held up a finger. "I, for one, will—"

"Be staying as well," Edgar interrupted, putting the lynx-shifter into a headlock and rubbing his knuckles into his head.

Zeke waited until the bro-torture was done before double-checking with Frank, who despite his surface loathing for the bear shifter and the idea of being in a pack, seemed to have decided to stay.

Throwing his hands in the air, Zeke moved on to face Sasha and Shira, who looked at him simultaneously with wolfish grins and just wagged their tails.

"Don't you have a family pack to return to?"

*It's been just the two of us for a few years now. You're stuck with us,* Sasha said.

*It was her idea,* Shira said. *But I'm not leaving my sister, so yeah, you're stuck with us.*

"You guys realize this is a terrible idea? We're the weirdest pack ever. Plus, you just met me. What if I'm a power-hungry psychopath?"

*Then I'll take you down,* Sasha said, nudging her wolfish body past him and trotting towards the open door, Shira following.

Zeke sighed.

*Where to, boss?* Mike asked, bounding up to Zeke and nipping at his elbow like a puppy.

Zeke shifted, feeling the ease of this form despite his soreness. The moon was waning now, and the shift would get harder and harder as the new moon approached. He hoped all this was over by then so he could relax in his human form with Mandi at his side.

Emotion choked him, and he struggled to get the words out to his pack.

*We're going to find my friends. The leaders of the T.R.S., if they're still alive, are our best chance at getting this messed-up world back in order so we can make a home for ourselves.*

Amidst the joyous howls and roars, Zeke led his pack out of that hellish place and into the sunny, broken streets of D.C.

It took them the better part of the day to run towards the Tower. Fortunately, spending the past several weeks on patrols had allowed Zeke to learn the different areas of D.C. fairly well, and with his nose and the knowledge of Sasha and Shira, who had lived in D.C. their entire lives, they made swift progress towards the epicenter of the capital.

Everything seemed normal, except for the lines of cars headed out of the city, and the strange feeling that overcame Zeke any time he entered a shadowy area for too long. He started avoiding the shadows of buildings, even walking in the street to get out of them.

*What's with the shadows? Superstitious?* Sasha asked, trotting up beside him.

*I don't like how they feel,* Zeke admitted, in his werewolf form for the ease of travel. His mother and father were incredibly superstitious, warding off evil with the sacred eye at any hint. Zeke wasn't like that, but he was paranoid about what might have happened at the T.R.S. since he'd left.

And if the locals were fleeing, it must have been something big. He picked up the pace, his ribs aching each time his paws landed on the cement, but he gritted his teeth and kept going until the Tower was in sight.

Zeke scrambled to a stop, his claws digging into the pavement.

*Woah,* Edgar said, ambling up beside him. *That's a big hole.*

A hole was all that was left of the Tower the T.R.S. had taken up residence in. A giant, gaping, swirling hole that looked like something a hoard of demons would crawl out of.

Maybe one already had, Zeke realized in horror as he glanced around at the nearby buildings, which looked like they'd been through a bombing.

*Where are the demons?* Zeke mused to himself.

*Demons?* Mike squeaked.

Zeke cursed himself out for saying that over the connection. It would take some getting used to, having everyone in his head unless he specifically blocked them out.

*The shadows,* Sasha said.

Zeke looked closer at the shadows around him, which were lengthening with the afternoon sun. The deepest ones had eyes, and the longer he looked the more body parts appeared. Knobbly legs, bat-like wings, scaled tails.

*You're right, Sasha,* Zeke said. *They're in the shadows. As soon as the sun goes down, this place will become a living hell. We have to find cover.*

Zeke bent his head down and started sniffing, looking for a familiar scent, anything that would lead him to where the leaders might have gone, but it was useless. The demons must have arrived days ago, meaning that anyone Zeke had known was long gone.

Question was, had they fled the city altogether or were they hiding in the backups?

*Come on,* Zeke growled, commanding his pack to follow him. Not to force them, just to unite them, as he'd started to feel their panic and uncertainty creep through the bond.

Zeke ran them through the streets, realizing they had less than two hours until the shadows would start to bleed together and strengthen the demons enough that they might consider coming out to attack a small pack of shifters.

Fortunately, the nearest shelter Zeke knew of was only a few blocks down. Long blocks, filled with panicked drivers honking horns and fleeing from the epicenter of the new hell trying to take over earth.

Zeke bolted down the metro station stairs, claws sliding on subway tile as he ran under the abandoned ticket gates. No trains were running, and the station was abandoned, except for the stiff body of a dead homeless busker, still clinging to a broken guitar.

Zeke ran to the end of the metro station and sniffed around for the loose brick in the wall near the third pillar. His panic was rising, in spite of himself, and he had to force his mind to slow down so he didn't miss the brick that would trigger the false wall to give way.

It was one of the most secure hideouts the T.R.S. had, most of the others being apartment buildings, houses, even an office building. But this one had been built for the most discretion, to be used only in the case of the greatest emergencies. It was too close to the swirling hell pit for Zeke's comfort.

Zeke found the brick and pressed it with his nose. The tiles cracked apart in a zig-zag pattern pulling away from each other to reveal a tunnel lit with a flickering line of exposed bulbs.

*Come on. We'll be safe here,* Zeke said, taking in a long draw of air, scenting it until he was certain there was no threat.

No threat, but there was a faint scent of someone familiar, and it made Zeke's heart race. Maybe luck had finally shown up.

His pack followed him silently into the tunnel. Zeke barked instructions at Frank to find the lever that would close the secret door behind them. It got much darker after the door closed, even with the string of bulbs. Every so often, there'd be a stretch without lighting as they wound further and further underground until the tunnel opened into a wide, arched room below the city.

Fires dotted the area, lighting a man-made river of sludge in the middle.

*It reeks!* Mike said, rubbing his nose with his paw.

Zeke grimaced. *Welcome to the sewers, pal.*

A flurry of activity caught Zeke's attention. He turned to face the small group of people that stood from the nearest fire, some holding guns, one holding a glowing ball of magic in their palm.

"Is that my man Z? No way, man!" Jack's voice rang out from behind the group that had stood, and they parted to let the man running up to them through.

Messy-haired and grinning, face full of bruises and soot, Jack met Zeke, who shifted into his human form in time to take Jack's hand.

"How'd you recognize me?" Zeke asked.

"That's how I first met you. I'll never forget it," Jack said, laughing. "I thought you were dead, man. You never came back from that date with Mandi, and then she..." he trailed off, studying Zeke's gaze.

"I know, Jack. Something happened that night to tip me off. I ran back to tell you, but I got captured by some lunatic dog fighter, and it looks like I was too late."

"Sounds like you have a story to tell," Jack said, running a hand through his hair. It was a testament to the lack of cleaning facilities that Jack's hair stood on end after his fingers went through it. "Unfortunately, you're right, and I hate to be the one to tell you—your girlfriend is the Demon Queen."

# CHAPTER THIRTY-TWO

## HARPER

HARPER HAD NEVER FLOWN so far, so fast in all her life. They didn't have to worry about being seen now that the president had formally pardoned all paranormals, so they traveled until the sun went down and then flew until their eyes drooped and their wings couldn't bear them up anymore, roosting in trees like literal birds for a few hours before taking off again.

The next morning, they stopped somewhere in Canada for breakfast. Anna produced a shiny plastic credit card from her pocket and ordered a literal ton of sausage and egg sandwiches and hash brown cakes from a fast food restaurant.

They ate as they flew, which was a first for Harper. Feathers still fell from her wings now and then, but they weren't nearly so quick to dislodge, and Harper didn't notice any difference in her ability to climb through the air.

Every beat of her wings carried her farther from her ancestral home, but Harper found that this time, she didn't feel a pull to return.

They had burned that bridge, possibly forever. The part of her that should have been grieving felt a bit numb, and somewhere over Canada, she asked Anna about it.

"You're in shock, most likely," Anna said, soaring closer.

Quinn came up beside her, listening in.

Anna continued. "But shock aside, that Song you sang…it was unlike anything I've heard before. A true Song from Raven, if I ever heard one." She glanced at Harper, her short hair whipping across her face. She smiled. "I knew you could do it."

Harper looked away, warmth growing inside of her with a feeling that she'd always longed for.

"So, you and dad…you came here, asking to be let back in the clan? Was that the trip you took where you left us with that witch?"

Anna nodded. "Stephen—your dad and I—we disagreed about whether we should bring you kids along. But we truly didn't know what the Chief would say, and we didn't want to endanger your future by traveling if we could help it. It was the biggest mistake of my life." Anna's voice broke, and she ducked her head.

"I thought you'd be safe with our friend, but it was always our plan to return. After Stephen was killed, things were bad for me. I picked up some agents on my way back and they caught me. I escaped the camp they tried to put me in, and I ran from everything." Anna shook her head, tears on her face drying in the frigid wind. "I ran from all the memories of my life with Stephen. I ran from you both. It was a dark period for me. The Songs…I couldn't remember any of them at times, my soul was so disconnected from itself. But that's no excuse. I owe you both an apology."

Harper really could have gone for a hug right then, but they were all flying mid-air a couple thousand feet up from the ground, so landing and having a hug session wasn't an option. She settled for giving Anna one of her rare smiles, her own eyes misting over as she realized everything her mother had gone through to keep her safe.

"Sometimes protecting those you love looks like betrayal, I guess," Quinn said.

"Sometimes it is betrayal," Anna said. "Look, I know I've hurt you. I missed out on so much of your lives. It'll take some time to overcome that. But I want to. Your grandfather couldn't see it, but I can. I choose family over pride, over accomplishment, over my own safety. I'll choose you from now on."

Harper's heart soared higher than the clouds she passed through, water droplets collecting on her wings. She shook them to get the extra water off.

Despite what had happened with the Tulukaruq tribe, she felt more hopeful than she had in a while. She leaned into the warmth of the unfamiliar feeling, knowing it could change at any moment, and appreciated the emotion all the more for its rarity in her life.

"So, what's our plan when we reach D.C.?" Quinn asked sometime later.

Anna answered swiftly, back in commander mode. "Recon. Find out what remains of our army, get in touch with Tyson and see what he's discovered. Hopefully he made headway with the humans in the area. We're going to need all the fighters we can get."

Harper nodded. It was a sound plan. They had a few more hours of fly time before they reached the Tower. By then it would be nightfall. They would need a secure place to stay overnight, and she doubted the Tower was an option.

"Which hideout should we crash in? Grandma Jean?" It was ideal, being close to the Tower.

"How about Cousin Lou?" Quinn said, referring to an apartment complex on the other side of the Tower. "It's farther away, but it's more likely that we'll run into someone who can give us a rundown of what's happened recently there, rather than calling around until we find someone."

"It could also be empty," Harper commented. "The demons might have razed everything."

"We'll know in an hour," Anna said, keeping her gaze straight ahead as they crossed over the Pennsylvania-Maryland border. "Anyone need a pit stop? Because we're not landing until we get there otherwise."

They found a gas station easily enough, so at least they didn't have to find a wooded area.

After nearly three days of flying, Harper was ready to land and put her wings away for a while. Eat an elephant. Maybe sleep for a solid day, if the impending war with the demons didn't get in the way. She somehow doubted luck would be on her side, but she could wish, couldn't she?

The rain stopped and started for a while, and then a swarm of truly dark clouds rolled in seemingly out of nowhere. Harper had enough experience with magic to know that these clouds weren't natural, and she didn't like the look of the bright violet lights flickering deep in the clouds. Lightning? Or magic?

The three raven shifters dropped below the clouds, watching warily. They had to get to shelter before this storm hit.

Harper's heart clenched tighter and tighter at the large areas that were seemingly without power, becoming more frequent the closer they got to D.C.

Her wings beat at the air, each stroke a struggle. Her lungs burned, but she pushed on.

"Okay, little sis?" Quinn asked, flying closer to her. "I could carry you for a bit."

Harper only shook her head, rather than waste breath on words. They only had a few miles to go. She'd made it this far.

"Look at the roads," Quinn said, also sounding breathless now that Harper focused on his voice.

"The people are running from the demons," Anna said, glaring at the crowded highways.

Even as high up as they were, the sound of honking horns and faint shouts of irritated drivers floated up to Harper's ears. The highways were deadlocked, all exits leading out clogged. She even saw a few accidents. She didn't see any flashing lights, and she wondered what had happened to first responders. Had the demons already made their move?

She got her answer a few moments later, as they flew a little higher and entered the city proper. It was far too dark to be D.C., and yet it was.

Near the center of the city where the T.R.S. Headquarters Tower had been, a gaping maw had opened. A mile wide, swallowing the Smithsonian museums and stretching towards the White House, which had several chunks taken out of it and looked like an abandoned mansion out of a horror movie.

"The Tower is gone," Harper said. She licked her lips, the skin there chapped from several days of flying, and blinked rapidly as if she could clear the images below from her eyes and everything would return to normal.

"Is the abyss portal complete? It looks complete," Quinn said, sounding anxious.

"Not only that," Anna said, pointing at the broad fields that surrounded the White house and the nearby memorials. "See the dark figures? There are hundreds of the demons already here. They're spreading out, seeking to destroy, kill, and bring those with strong magic back to their mistress. No doubt she feeds off the magic, and she'll use it to finish building that bridge between realms."

"So...are we demon hunting now? Or finding a place to sleep? Because after all that Singing and flying, I'm sunk if we have to add demon fighting to the list," Harper said, fighting to suppress a surprisingly strong yawn that snuck up on her. She wanted to be alert and badass, but fatigue had crept up on her. Without a nap and some serious food, she'd be useless.

"Same," Quinn admitted, flashing Harper a tired smile. "We need to rest and find our people."

"Agreed," Anna said, scanning the ground below. She pointed towards the east and angled downward.

"There's Cousin Lou. Let's see if anyone is home."

Harper followed Anna, trying to keep her eye on the magically formed storm in the sky and the demons on the ground at the same time. Seeing several of the demons take flight, Harper pushed herself to fly faster, grunting with the strain she felt through her wings and shoulders.

"What's the hurry?" Quinn said, seeming to catch up with her almost effortlessly.

"See those bat-things? Yeah, trying to avoid them," Harper managed between breaths.

"They haven't seen us yet. Keep going," Anna urged.

A moment later, a screech split the air, and Harper's hopes plummeted. They were yards away from the hideout still, and the flying demons must have spotted them. Getting inside wouldn't help them now, it would only lead the demons to them.

Anna dropped back slightly. "I'll distract them and meet up with you when it's safe. You two get to safety."

Harper opened her mouth to object as she wheeled around to meet her mom and fight the demons with her, but Quinn grabbed her shoulder and shoved her back towards the hideout below.

"Come on! She's trying to save your life, idiot."

*But I just got her back*, Harper screamed in her mind. She didn't say the words out loud. Her heart raced with exertion and fear as she flew through the darkening sky.

"Split up and circle around," Quinn said from beside her, his long dark hair flowing behind him like a black streamer.

Harper glanced over her shoulder and saw Anna dipping and weaving away from three bat-like demons. None of them seemed to notice Quinn and Harper, or maybe they didn't care so long as they got to have some fun with Anna first.

Harper wrenched her eyes away and focused on performing the maneuver Quinn had suggested, dipping low enough in the streets that a larger building hid Anna and the demons from view, and then she landed at a run, her legs wobbly as a newborn calf's after several days of nearly non-stop flying.

She jogged around to the front of the apartment complex. "Which number?" she asked as Quinn ran up and joined her in the metal stairwell leading down to the bottom floors.

"Start with the closest one, I guess. Do you remember the code for the locks?" Quinn asked.

Harper did. She typed it in, and the green light flashed. She slammed on the handle and shoved the door open, stumbling into a dark apartment.

"Hey! Anyone here?" Harper called. Behind her, purple lightning flashed, followed by a thunder crash that sounded like the jaws of hell closing.

Quinn shoved her further inside and slammed the door shut, making sure the mechanism locked as he slid the deadbolt above the handle.

"Pumpernickel!" He shouted wildly.

Oh yeah. The spell code. Harper had forgotten.

Quinn shook out his feathers. "Sorry for pushing you. The demons lost mom and remembered there'd been more of us. I didn't want them to spot our movement," Quinn said. "Don't turn on any lights yet."

"Got it," Harper said, rubbing her hip where she'd struck the side table next to the couch. "There's a phone in here somewhere, right? With all the contact info."

She moved further into the dark apartment, occasional flashes of lightning illuminating the interior dimly through the curtains. She found the kitchen doorway and moved around the room, opening drawers and shuffling through papers.

"Whoever stayed here was not neat," Harper said, poking through the piles of junk and papers on the kitchen counter, looking desperately for the unit's cell phone.

Quinn entered, glanced at the counter, and made a face. "Maybe they took it with them."

"You'd better hope not," Harper said, moving a stack of books she couldn't read the titles of. "Ah-ha!" she exclaimed, holding up the device.

She pressed the button on the side, but the screen remained dark. "It's dead."

"Of course it is," Quinn muttered, moving closer to the counter.

Her shoulders slumped, and she felt like she was about to cry. She didn't cry very often—not often enough, by Tyson's standards—but she'd make an exception at the moment. She'd just flown across the United States hoping to reunite with Tyson and anyone left from the T.R.S. after being rejected by her tribe.

A few tears were certainly warranted, but Harper held them down, biting her lip and scanning the counter for the cord, clutching the phone like the lifeline it was. Each flash of lightning pushed Harper closer to the edge of panic, until at last Quinn pulled something dark and dangling from the pile, sending papers cascading to the floor.

"This it?" he asked, holding it out to her.

Harper checked the end to make sure it would insert into the phone's charging port and nearly jumped up and down.

"Yes! We got it. Thank you." She gave Quinn a quick side-hug, startling him with the sudden show of affection, then jammed the plug into the wall, tightening the USB cord in the plug end and inserting the other side into the phone.

The screen blinked to life, showing 0% for a second until it ticked up to 1%. Harper set the phone down and crossed her arms. She'd need a few percentages at least before she could make any calls.

Quinn opened the fridge, blinding Harper with the light that flooded out. She hissed, and he stepped in front of the opening to block as much as he could. He'd brought his wings into his back already, Harper realized, and she took several breaths before doing the same, letting her wings meld into her back so they wouldn't be in the way as she moved around the tiny apartment.

"Anything good?" Harper asked, avoiding asking the question she really wanted to ask—whether their mom was doing all right out there, why she wasn't at the apartment yet, whether they should go look for her. All of which were questions that either couldn't be answered or would get a firm "no" from Quinn.

"It's all bad, except the condiments," Quinn replied, switching to the freezer. He pulled out a few frozen dinners, holding them up in the light of the freezer so she could see them. "Chicken cordon bleu, or..." he squinted at the packaging. "General Tso's?"

Harper made a face. "Ew. Uh, not the Chinese food."

"Got it. At least there's a microwave." He unpackaged the dinners and started one cooking, leaning against the counter as it whirred around in the tiny white box. He glanced at her, arms clasped over his chest, looking as if he wanted to say something but didn't know how to say it.

Harper let him stew for a minute, but when he'd glanced at her for the fifth time and started rubbing his neck, she couldn't stand the suspense any longer.

"What is it?" she snapped, coming off harsher than she'd intended. She forced her expression to soften, although with how dark the apartment was, she wasn't certain Quinn could see her. They had a lot of abilities, but night vision wasn't one of them.

"I wanted to ask you what happened with the orb," Quinn said. "The Eternal Source...when I was alone...with Them, They said you wanted to get rid of your memories of me. That you'd asked the orb to take them away."

Harper blinked. "But I didn't. They demanded my memories as payment. I tried to stop them. I—" she slowed down, eyes darting back and forth as she tried to remember back to a month ago when the whole situation had happened with the beryllium orb. She had never wanted to forget Quinn. Never. She hadn't chosen to have them taken.

The microwave beeped, and Harper startled, then relaxed slightly, rubbing her arm with her hand.

"I can see why you don't trust the Eternal Source," Quinn muttered, handing the black plastic tray of food out to her.

Harper paced in the cramped room, her wet tennis shoes squeaking on the linoleum. "They've lied before. They lied to me and stole my memories. They lied to you about what happened so you wouldn't trust me. Why? To make us hate each other? To distract us? What else did they lie about?" Her steps faltered, and she finally looked up at Quinn. "What if they're not on our side, like they lead us to believe? What if they're not the Eternal Source at all?"

# CHAPTER THIRTY-THREE

## TYSON

"THIS IS A TERRIBLE idea," Charlie hissed the moment Terran and Robyn left to gather their team of people to go with Tyson to the nearest backup hideout for the T.R.S.. "You know he's going to double-cross you, right?"

"Other than throw your trolls at him, I'm not sure what else to try," Tyson said, rubbing his temples. He picked up the brown lunch sack Robyn had thrown at his feet and rummaged through, pulling out a soggy peanut butter and jelly sandwich, a decent-looking apple, and a bite-sized candy bar.

"With your abilities, we could dreamwalk out of here and find the remaining members of the T.R.S., share the location of Terran's group, and approach him with our guns blazing, rather than the other way around."

"And lose any sense of trust we've built up in the process," Tyson said around a mouthful of sandwich. He finished chewing and took a swig from the plastic water bottle Robyn had also given him, then sighed and looked over at Charlie, who had started on her own sandwich.

"I know this isn't ideal. I'll give whoever we're able to find as much warning as possible when I contact them from the hide-out, provided it hasn't been infiltrated by the demons. Working with the human rebels is the only way we can get enough manpower to fight the demons."

"These trolls aren't useless. They could sneak out of here through the ventilation system, go wherever we tell them to, and deliver a message. They could get a key to this place and unlock the door from the outside. Bring us a weapon. Just about anything you can think of, they can do."

"Is that why you brought so many of them?" Tyson asked. He couldn't help not trusting them entirely. Creepy toys shouldn't be able to act of their own free will.

"That's part of it. They can also act as my eyes and ears, so I can plant them in a room and hear what the conversation is about. That's how I know Terran is planning to betray you. I ordered one of these little guys to jump on his back and hide in the room he ended up in."

Tyson froze mid-bite. "You sent a troll to spy on Terran? Charlie, if he finds it, any trust between us will be ruined!"

Charlie grimaced. "There's no trust, Tyson." Her eyes grew unfocused, and Tyson had the sense that she was seeing through a different set of eyes. Her troll's eyes. "Terran is giving the order for his team to open fire as soon as you identify any of our leaders."

She blinked, coming back into the room, then slapped her thighs. "That settles it. We need to bust out of here."

"No, we don't," Tyson said, taking several large chomps out of the apple and chewing furiously. "We know what he's planning to do. We just won't identify any of our leaders, and we'll find a way to convince Terran that working with us will have more benefits than working against us. Maybe there's a resource they're running low on that we have back in the Tower, provided it's still standing..." He trailed off, remembering the vortex he'd seen in the astral realm. How big was that portal on Earth? Was the Tower even still standing?

He sighed again, spreading his arms helplessly. "I don't know what else to do, Charlie. But my gut says leaving isn't an option. We have to ride this out and see where it leads. If there's any chance of an alliance, I want to take it."

"I think you're holding onto hopeful ideals and far too much faith in humanity, but I came here to help you, not argue with you. If that's your decision, I'll do what I can to help. Starting with this insane mission to get the humans on our side." She shoved the last bite of sandwich into her mouth and stood, wiping her hands. "Look sharp, they're coming."

Tyson jammed all his garbage into the paper sack, chugged the last of the water, and stood next to Charlie, looking expectantly at the door.

A moment later, the locks clicked, and the door handle turned.

Robyn entered, startling at the two prisoners waiting for her. "We're ready to move out. Tyson, I need the address of where we're going. I don't think I need to tell you twice that any surprises we encounter will lead to both of your deaths."

"Understood," Tyson said, nodding and ignoring the side-long glance from Charlie. He appreciated that she trusted him enough to go along with this plan, half-baked and hair-brained as it was. He just hoped they all survived.

Robyn waved Tyson and Charlie into the hall after her, and Tyson gave her the approximate location of the hideout he'd been headed for before the humans had nabbed them. His heart rate increased as their group merged with another small group of four people holding guns, hardened expressions on their faces. They didn't look like the kind of people you brought on a diplomatic mission, each one carrying multiple grenade-shaped items along their belts and several guns and knives on their persons.

Terran met them at the entrance to the outside. Tyson wasn't sure if it was convenience or oversight that he and Charlie were being allowed to walk out of the building without being blindfolded as they had on the way in, but he was grateful he could see.

"If we come across any demons, I'm hiding behind you," Tyson said to Terran, joking to break the tension that had settled into his gut like a rock.

Terran gave him a cold, hard stare. "If we see any demons, I'll be throwing you at them as a distraction so my men can get away."

Tyson swallowed his retort, which included a great line about polar bears being too heavy to throw, but he'd decided it would be a bad idea to antagonize the man holding the high-powered automatic rifle.

Terran nodded to the people surrounding Tyson and Charlie. "These two will lead us to those in charge of the T.R.S., and we will see for ourselves if what they say about the demons holds true. You see anything even slightly funny, shoot first, ask questions later."

The speech seemed entirely unnecessary to Tyson, but it was likely a tactic meant to intimidate Tyson into complying more than anything. He was starting to wonder what he would do if any demons attacked them. If he shifted, Terran's men would likely assume Tyson was working with the demons rather than against them. But in his vulnerable human form and outside the astral realm, Tyson didn't have much in the way of fighting ability.

He suddenly missed Harper very, very badly. If she were with him, she'd have put Terran in a headlock and threatened him within an inch of his life. Not very diplomatic, but it was a comforting image that made Tyson smile until Terran caught sight of his face and narrowed his eyes suspiciously.

At this point, Tyson should probably pray Harper and Terran never met.

Terran led the way through what seemed like the utility area of an office building, taking them out a heavy metal door that let out into a parking garage. He nudged Tyson forward, raising his eyebrows.

"Lead the way," Terran said.

Tyson moved to the front of the group.

Charlie tried to follow, but Robyn grabbed her arm. "You stay by me," Robyn growled. "And no tricks."

The September sun had broken through the heavy clouds, reflecting garishly off puddles of rainwater on the cement.

Tyson stepped in one and soaked his tennis shoe straight through, grimacing as the filthy water sloshed between his toes. He carried on, head high, through the oddly silent downtown D.C. street, a street that normally would have been filled with cars containing tourists on their way to see the great sights at the capital's center.

The only cars he saw were abandoned, doors swinging slightly in the wind, seats slashed and windows shattered by what could only be the massive claws and jaws of demons. It looked like the demons that had emerged from Ragranoth's portal had had a heyday the past several nights, wrecking everything they could get their hands on.

Tyson stopped looking too closely when, in one of the cars, he caught sight of a human body sitting upright, swollen with death and held up by a blood-soaked seatbelt, its eye sockets hollowed out.

If his face could turn green, he was certain it would have as the peanut butter sandwich he'd eaten threatened to make a reappearance, but he managed to hold it down until they'd passed the car, and then a cool breeze scented with polluted rainwater alleviated the nausea somewhat.

The closer they wound towards the Tower and the location of the hideout, the more bodies they saw, and not all of them appeared human. Tyson saw the furry bodies of several shifter breeds, their coats matted with blood.

Witches, with ritual markings on their faces, some holding wooden or crystal wands they used to focus their power. Even a bird shifter, its wings bent at unnatural angles that made him want to vomit all over again, but he couldn't look away this time. He forced himself to scan the bodies and faces, looking for those that were familiar to him.

To his immense relief, he found none, and soon they'd passed the streets that had become battlegrounds and walked onto the street where the hideout was located.

Tyson approached cautiously. This hideout was one of the many nondescript townhouses and apartments the T.R.S. had prepared in case they needed to evacuate the tower with little warning. They had built up quite the reservoir of funds and purchased properties nearby wherever possible, for the protection of their members. Tyson had been impressed when he'd heard about the depth of their preparation, and he was even more grateful now that it would provide a way for him to contact whoever remained from the T.R.S..

"There ain't no booby traps in these places?" One of Terran's men asked, a short guy with a buzz cut and short, dark facial hair that he kept rubbing against his shoulder.

"No booby traps," Tyson confirmed. "Just a spell that will trigger when I enter, which I'll disable with the passcode."

"Magic," the woman next to him spat, adjusting her grip on her gun.

Tyson rolled his eyes. "In a year or two, everyone will want a magically secured door. Just you wait." He approached the electronic lock above the door handle, noting the three scratched symbols on the side that indicated this was a T.R.S. hideout location. He punched the six-digit code he'd been taught into the number pad, tension draining from his shoulders as the light turned green.

Tyson ducked his head into the unit. "Hello? Anyone around?"

Silence answered. He glanced back at Terran, who waved his gun in Tyson's direction and nodded, as if giving Tyson permission to proceed.

Tyson entered the apartment. The stale scent of an unoccupied space filled his nostrils as he breathed in, bracing against the tingling magic that searched him upon entry. The password that would disable the magic was "pumpernickel," which had no meaning other than being an unusual word that most people could remember in a pinch.

Tyson muttered the word under his breath, careful not to let Terran hear as he crowded up the townhouse steps behind Tyson.

"Everything good?" Terran asked, eyeing the darkness beyond the doorway where Tyson still stood barely inside the townhouse.

The magic finished scanning him and dissipated harmlessly.

"Enter quickly. The magic will reactivate after a short time," Tyson said, moving out of the way and motioning everyone inside.

Terran, followed by Charlie and Robyn, entered the townhouse.

The man with the short facial hair rubbed his chin on his shoulder and grimaced. "I ain't keen on it, Terran. I'll keep watch outside if you don't mind." Several others nodded and murmured their agreement.

Terran shrugged. "Suit yourselves. Trinity, Mitch, you coming in?"

The two climbed the stairs and entered the townhouse in answer, keeping their hard stares locked on Tyson. The door shut behind them.

"Now what?" Terran asked, glancing around the small living space.

Tyson moved further into the living room, walking backwards so he didn't turn his back on Terran. "I start making calls. A directory to the main hideouts in the area is kept here. Those hideouts are the ones that the bulk of T.R.S. members will flee too, including the leaders if they're able. I'll call around until one of them picks up and hope the phones are still working."

Tyson wound around the worn false-leather couch in the living room and headed for the kitchen, where he opened all the drawers until he found the unit's cell phone. It took a moment to boot up, and a moment longer for Tyson to remember the swipe pattern that was standard on all T.R.S. devices.

Terran entered the kitchen, opening cupboards and checking the fridge and freezer.

"It's all empty. Do they expect you to starve if you have to bugout?" he asked.

"There's food in the pantry. Dry goods, non-perishables. Help yourself," he added, scrolling through the directory saved into the phone's contacts.

Each of the hideouts had a code name that looked like a family member. He started with Aunt Aida, listening to the cheap phone's tinny ring until he gave up and dialed the next one, Uncle Chris. He worked his way down the list, getting dud after dud until, on his sixth call titled "Grandma Jean," the line clicked, and he heard a breathy voice greet him on the other line.

Tyson clutched the phone, shifting his stance and glancing nervously at Terran.

"Hey! Hi. Um, it's Tyson. Tyson Miller calling from—" He glanced at the phone in his hand, checking the name this place was identified as. "Cousin Millie's."

He ran his free hand through his hair, trying to remember the rest of the protocol for making sure the other person knew he was affiliated with the T.R.S. and not some rando who'd found the phone and decided it would be fun to make some prank calls. "Um...I like pumpernickel bread."

"I prefer rye," the other person said, giving the response code phrase. "This is Charity Wheeler, answering for Grandma Jean. It's good to hear more of us got away."

She probably didn't know who he was, Tyson realized. He needed to see if Jack or Dak had made it to this hideout, or if they hadn't, if Charity could connect him to them.

"Listen, Charity, I'm glad I made it too, but I've got a big opportunity I need to discuss with—" Tyson paused. It probably wasn't smart to say his name where Terran could hear. The leaders had numbers assigned to them for instances just like this one. "Number two. Can you get him on the line?"

"Number two is unavailable. Will number one be sufficient?" Charity said in her airy voice.

"Yes. Either is fine," Tyson said, glancing at Terran, who sat at the kitchen table with his gun trained on Tyson, waiting for him to say something that would give Terran an excuse to blow his head off, no doubt.

Tyson turned around swiftly, shoving the image that thought produced out of his mind.

"Hey-o, Tyson," Jack's casual, country accent came over the line with a familiar ease that made Tyson relax an iota. Despite the tense situation, Tyson found he was able to smile.

"Hey there. Listen, I've got something of a situation here, and I figured you were the best person to talk to about it." Tyson scrambled to think of how he could explain this in a way that wouldn't make Jack think he was compromised. Which he wasn't, but if he said the wrong thing Jack would think he was being threatened, and Tyson didn't want that.

"Sure, bud. What can I do you for?" Jack asked.

"I—" Tyson froze as the cold muzzle of a rifle pressed into his back through his shirt.

"Tell him you have a bunch of your people with you. Too many for this place, and you need to relocate," Terran growled.

Tyson closed his eyes. He'd known Terran would betray him, he just hadn't expected it to happen so soon. He figured Terran would wait until he had the address for the T.R.S. hideout, but maybe he didn't like to leave things so far out of his control.

"Tyson, everything all right? Tell me what the weather's like. Say it's started raining again if you're in danger. Is it demons or humans?"

Tyson licked his lips. He appreciated Jack's attempt to help, but Terran was too smart, and talking about the weather was too out of context for him to buy it. Not to mention that Tyson had no way to indicate who was threatening him without Terran catching on immediately, and by then Charlie and Tyson would both be dead.

"Put him on speaker," Terran growled. He motioned for the others in the house to be silent.

"Jack, it's nothing like that. We've just got a lot of guys here and it's feeling a bit crowded," Tyson said.

"Really? There's a lot of you, huh? I heard you're at Cousin Millie's. That's not a big place to share."

While Jack was talking, Tyson shifted the phone into speaker mode, projecting the man's voice into the room.

"Mute it," Terran whispered.

Tyson did. Jack kept talking.

"Sounds like we need to get you guys some more space. A lot of the ones closer to the Tower got blown up or swarmed with demons. We've got loads of space down here. Send as many guys as you need and make sure you're one of them. We could use a dreamwalker onsite right now, especially one with a counseling background like you have. People are freaking out, and we need a plan. Have you heard from Anna?"

While Jack prattled on, Terran had whispered exactly what he wanted Tyson to say, and Robyn had brought Charlie into the room, a gun to her head.

Ideas spun in and out of Tyson's brain as he reeled from emotion to emotion. Anger, frustration, and desperation took equal turns.

He unmuted the phone. "Jack, that all sounds great. Yeah, I'll bring the guys over. It's good to know there's a place for us to go.

I hope you have some dry clothes for everyone, I think it's going to rain again on our way over there." Tyson added the last part, hoping Terran wouldn't think it too strange, but Terran didn't do anything except give Tyson a wicked grin.

"Hang up," Terran said, gesturing to the phone.

"We'll see you within the hour," Tyson said, hating his sluggish thoughts for not giving him some better way to warn Jack.

"We'll be ready for you," Jack said. Anyone who didn't know him wouldn't have heard the hard edge that had suddenly appeared in his voice, but Tyson had been in enough virtual meetings with the man that he caught it, and he knew that by "ready", Jack meant he'd prepare his people for the fight Tyson was bringing to their door.

Hopefully, Jack also understood that Tyson had no other choice.

# CHAPTER THIRTY-FOUR

## HARPER

THE ETERNAL SOURCE MIGHT have lied to them—might not even be who they thought they were. What if the god they'd asked for help was actually working for the other side? Harper's thoughts reeled at the implications.

"I think they made it pretty clear they're on the side that will create balance. They told us to unite humans and paranormals, after all." Quinn dug around in a drawer next to the sink and pulled out a fork, spearing the chicken with it, acting so casually Harper wondered if he'd heard her.

"But what if they're *not*? That could just be a useless task meant to distract us," Harper said, moving forward to take the still-steaming tray from Quinn. She almost dropped it as the hot food burned her through the plastic, but she adjusted her grip and took the food to the table.

"Knife, please," she said, when the food proved too much for her fork.

"We met the Eternal Source in a Higher Plane. How could that be corrupt?" Quinn asked.

"I don't know. Except," Harper spoke through a steaming hot bite of saucy, breaded chicken, sucking in air to try to cool the food down. She waved her fork in the air. "Except remember how Charlemagne said that anyone in the astral realm can make those pocket dimensions, and make them look like anything? Make you see anything, feel anything, if you aren't experienced enough? What if a super powerful demon—maybe even more powerful than Ragranoth, I don't know? What if one of those got out of the lower abyss and made a pocket dimension and somehow re-routed the entrance to the Eternal Source? What if the last thing we want is to do what they said?"

Quinn stared at her, eyes wide. "Harper, you have to talk to Tyson about this. He's the only one I know who might be able to find out if what you're saying is correct. But if it is...we don't want to be doing anything the Eternal Source—or whatever being might possibly be posing as them—said."

"I know!" Harper said, shoveling the hot food into her mouth faster. She stood and crossed the room, checking the phone's charge. Seventeen percent. She powered up the device, chewing the food in her mouth, then went to the sink and got a drink of water.

Her hands trembled, splashing water down her front as she gulped it.

"Start calling," Quinn urged, taking his food from the microwave and blowing on it. He walked towards the living room. "I'm going to check the news, see what else I can find out."

Harper stood by the counter, holding the plugged-in phone up and scrolling through the directory. Where to begin?

She picked a random name on the list. The line to Cousin Millie's rang without picking up, and she dropped the call and picked another one. Aunt Sybil. Uncle George. On and on it went, each call ringing until Harper was forced to give up.

After the 11th call, Harper unplugged the phone, grabbed her now-cool chicken dinner, and headed for the living room to plunk down on the couch next to Quinn, who was alternating between news stations on the television, the volume so low Harper could barely hear what was being said, but he had the captions going.

The call to Cousin Joe dropped and Harper let the phone slide from her ear into her lap.

"No one is picking up."

"They can't all be dead," Quinn insisted, turning towards her.

Harper raised her eyebrows. "Actually, they can. What if Tyson didn't make it to a hideout? What if demons got him? Or humans?" There were so many factors to consider, so many ways this could go wrong. Harper didn't like any of it.

"What if we're all that's left?" Harper asked.

Quinn's gaze softened. "Look, that's not going to happen. There are T.R.S. headquarter locations in other states. We'll just fly to one of them and make our stand there. This isn't the end of the world."

Harper busted up laughing, an unstoppable, hysterical laugh that made Quinn look at her like she was a madwoman.

"What's so funny?"

"It *is* the end of the world!" Harper said, her high-pitched laugh edging towards endless waves of giggles. She breathed through her lips like she was blowing through a straw, trying to calm down, but every time she thought she'd stop another wave of laughter would go through her.

"Harper, shut up! It's the president," Quinn said, turning the volume up on the tv.

Harper's laughter stopped abruptly as President Evans, the President of the United States, stepped to the podium.

She looked stoned. Her hair had been put up in a bun, but it wasn't tidy, as if her hair hadn't been brushed or the person doing her hair hadn't known what they were doing. She didn't wear a suit coat over her stained blue button-up.

President Evans swayed on her feet, clutching the podium as if for dear life. When she looked at the camera, her blue eyes were filled with dark splotches.

Harper gasped. "She's possessed."

"Are you sure?" Quinn asked. "How can you tell?"

"Well, her eyes didn't look like that before. And there's something off about the way she moves, her expression...I'd guess she's been fighting the possession. Do you think it's Ragranoth?"

"I don't know. Shhh," Quinn said as the president began her address.

"Mortals of earth, I know you're listening. My message is for all who inhabit this planet. Your time has come to an end."

And then, the president exploded. The human body split, shredding as the demon emerged.

Her pure, powdery white body stretched to nearly nine-feet tall. Human-female in appearance, too thin, too perfect, except for the mandibles Harper could see in her open mouth.

"I am Ragranoth, Autarch of the final abyss. I have come to rid this plane of humans and all who oppose me. Those who do not oppose me will be allowed to live in my new realm. Present yourselves for reckoning and reuse. Those who do not present themselves will not be given recourse for survival." She grinned, flashing blackened, needle-like teeth.

The curtain behind the demon Autarch moved, and a frightened, familiar face appeared briefly to the left of the podium.

Harper shot out of her seat on the couch, pointing. "That's Mandi! Quinn, she's alive!"

"There's no way," Quinn said, standing and moving closer to the screen.

The curtain had fallen back, and the face was gone, but Harper knew what she'd seen. Goosebumps moved up her arms.

"She managed to escape. Or at least, the demon didn't kill her. She's alive," Harper whispered, then realized the demon queen was still talking. She needed to pay attention.

"Together we will usher in a new existence and remake this world to suit our needs. Come to me and pledge yourselves or die." Leathery, white wings unfolded from Ragranoth's back, and her mouth opened to reveal too many rows of teeth and a set of mandibles.

She shrieked into the camera, and then the video image went sideways as the camera fell to the ground and the connection fuzzed out before going black. Apparently, the camera man had ditched the scene. Or maybe he'd been killed by one of Ragranoth's demons, there was no way to know.

The station put up some "We'll be back shortly" message screen, then cut to commercials.

Quinn turned off the tv. "Well, at least we know what we're up against."

"Why does she need us to come to her?" Harper wondered out loud. "Why not just raze the earth and be done with all mortals? Why does she need them?"

"Magic?" Quinn suggested.

Harper snapped her fingers. "That's it. She must have drained her resources trying to create her bridge to the final abyss.

She has her army, but it's not enough. She wants to create a permanent connection, and maybe there's someone there she still wants to bring through. An ally, perhaps?"

"She's a demon queen. I don't think she needs anything other than her hoard and her own immense power," Quinn said darkly.

He was probably right, but there was still something odd about Ragranoth's request. If she wasn't trying to open the portal wider or deeper, what was she doing?

Harper glanced towards the curtained window. The violet lightning still flashed every few minutes, but no demons had come to tear the apartment to shreds.

"Do you think it's safe to go look for mom?" Harper said, swallowing as the word "mom" left her lips.

He raised his eyebrows. "When did you start calling Anna mom?"

Harper squirmed. "It just feels weird to call her by her name now. I think...I think my mind is finally starting to accept that she is that person in my life. Mother is too formal, and calling her Anna is just weird."

"I don't think I ever expected you to call her that. I fig-ured...well, I'm glad. It gives me hope for our family."

"We have to survive this demon invasion first," Harper said. "And that means finding her. She should have made it back here by now."

"Yeah, she really should have." Quinn pushed himself up off the couch and crossed the room, carefully moving the curtain aside just enough to look out. "Look at them swarming! It's like someone kicked a wasp nest."

Harper twisted in her seat and caught a glimpse of what Quinn saw as lightning streaked the sky, the purple light illuminating dozens of winged creatures, black and white, flying through the air.

Harper pushed off the couch and released her wings. Her sore and stiff flying muscles screamed at her as she extended them, but she ignored the pain, heading for the door.

"We can't afford to wait until morning. She'll be dead by then. I'm not going to sit around here and make useless phone calls."

Quinn moved swiftly, blocking the door as Harper reached for the knob.

"You can't go out there," he said, crossing his arms over his chest. "Those flying demons will be on you in an instant. We need to stick to the plan—try to find Tyson or the other leaders of the T.R.S. and trust that mom is okay out there on her own. She's been taking care of herself and hiding from dangerous monsters for a long time."

"The government was mostly comprised of humans. I wouldn't exactly equate them with soul-hungry demons," Harper retorted.

Quinn grinned. "I could argue against that."

Harper punched his arm. "Don't distract me with humor. Now isn't the time. We have to get out there and find her."

"After you make five more phone calls," Quinn demanded.

Harper threw up her arms. "Fine. But it won't make a difference. I'll make your damn calls, and then I'm going out there."

"I'll come with you," Quinn said. "It's utterly stupid, and we'll probably get killed, but as you so wisely pointed out earlier, it's the end of the world. Dying now or dying later probably won't make that big of a difference in the long run."

Harper leaned over the back of the couch and snatched up the phone. To her surprise, the moment she picked it up, the phone started vibrating in her hand. She nearly dropped it in shock.

The name "Grandma Jean" flashed on the screen.

Harper picked up. "Hey, who is this?"

"Is that any way to speak to your grandmother?" a male voice on the other end of the line said.

Harper gave Quinn a confused look, then remembered there was a whole conversation protocol filled with code phrases that had something to do with bread that she was supposed to remember. Unfortunately, she didn't have the patience for any of it.

"Listen, buddy, you'd better tell me who you are. This is Harper King and Quincey King. We're Anna's kids and if she dies because you're delaying me with nonsense, I will personally fly you into the sky and drop you."

"Harper!" Quinn hissed, probably about to lecture her on treating others with respect.

Harper glared at him as the person on the other end of the line stammered their apologies.

"So sorry. Just doing my job. Listen, Jack asked me to call everyone and tell them to meet at Grandma Jean's. We've been compromised, and we need all the fighting power we can get here."

"Compromised? How?" Harper asked.

"Human rebels discovered the location of the underground hideout. Some yokel named Tyson got scared and spilled the beans," the guy on the other line said, sounding bitter.

"Tyson?" Harper screeched. "As in, Tyson Miller?"

"I don't know the guy. I'm just the messenger. All I know is that he's over at Cousin Millie's and he's in trouble. Jack took a team over to deal with him."

"Deal with him?" Harper growled, clenching the back of the couch so hard her fingers hurt. "What does that mean?"

"I don't exactly know, see? I'm not privy to the inner workings of our leaders' minds. If you're fond of the guy, you might want to get over there. Jack's a nice guy on a good day but cross him, and he's the worst enemy you'll ever have. Anyway, that's the message. If you're in, you're in. If not, I wish you luck."

The line clicked, going dead, and Harper stared at the phone in horror.

Not only had Tyson somehow endangered the surviving members of the T.R.S., but the T.R.S. seemed to have taken it on themselves to take him out. He'd gone from hero to traitor in the matter of a few days, and Harper couldn't for the life of her figure out why Tyson would do such a thing.

"What is it? Why do you look like that?" Quinn asked, eyeing her warily.

"Tyson's in trouble," Harper said, shoving Quinn to the side and undoing the locks on the door. "He needs us."

"We're all in trouble. Let him figure it out. What about mom?" Quinn asked.

"I don't know where she is, but I do know where Tyson is. We have to get to him before the T.R.S. They think he betrayed them, and they're going to kill him."

Harper tucked her wings tight against her back and shoved the door open wide enough for her to slip through. She jogged up the apartment steps, picking up speed as she sprinted down the sidewalks and spread her wings before launching into the sky.

Whatever Tyson had done, Harper doubted he deserved to die at the hands of his friends.

# CHAPTER THIRTY-FIVE

## TYSON

TYSON TURNED ON TERRAN, anger fueling him past his sense of self-preservation. "What the hell, man? I trusted that you'd at least give us a chance. But to turn around and threaten me like that? Manipulating me into taking you into the T.R.S. stronghold to destroy our leaders? It's the worst of humanity. That kind of bigoted prejudice is the reason we're all in this mess."

Tyson's chest was heaving by the time he finished, his breaths coming in rapid gasps that made him light-headed.

"Pretty speech, but it's obvious you're in the minority. Where were your ideals when Mitch's son was out for a run and got violently attacked by a werewolf? Where were you when Trinity was spelled by a warlock and raped by him? And how 'bout my wife? Were you there when my wife was drained by a vamp in a parking lot on her way home from work?" Terran shouted, veins standing out on his head. "Don't stand there and spout your fanciful ideals when real people that we love are out there dying because your kind can't control themselves!"

Spittle flew through the air, landing on Tyson's cheek. He blinked. He had seen this rage before. He'd seen it in the eyes of hundreds of people. Most recently, he'd seen it in the liquid amber eyes of a certain fox-shifter that wanted him dead, all because his ten-year-old self hadn't known any better than to tell the men in suits that his best friend could change into a fox.

But he'd also seen the guilt in the teenagers that came to Camp Silver Lake. He'd seen what the persecution had done to them for crimes they didn't commit. And he'd seen the numbers that showed someone with paranormal abilities was statistically more likely to kill themselves than someone else.

"My heart goes out to every person who has ever been affected by any accident causing the death of a loved one. My parents died in a car crash caused by a werewolf coming into their power in the middle of the freeway, causing a car pile-up involving over a dozen vehicles and five deaths. Including the new werewolf. I didn't dedicate my life to killing every werewolf I encountered just because one happened to be there when my parents died. I dedicated my life to understanding them, and to be honest, I kind of failed at that until I became one."

Tyson dropped the phone on the counter, leaning against it. Unable to look into Terran's face, instead he saw the faces of those he'd talked to during his internship at Camp Silver Lake, especially the ones that had left camp and had never been heard from again, the line of faces ending with Fletcher's beaming smile. He was sick of violence, of death, of fighting.

He pushed himself off the edge of the counter, turning to face Terran, who stood speechless, staring at him with a puzzled look on his face.

"There are murderers and rapists and worse among your kind," Tyson said. "But I don't automatically assume that every human I run into is going to hurt me. Because I believe that there are more of you that are good than bad. Why don't you afford us the same basic courtesy as your fellow men?"

Terran's jaw tightened. "Because you aren't human."

Tyson glanced at Charlie, who had tears streaming down her face. She was smiling at him, though Tyson didn't know why. He'd just said what he wished he'd realized much earlier—that it didn't matter whether someone was human or paranormal. They weren't more likely to kill someone because of it. And if more violent actions were being taken by one side or the other, it was likely in response to something the other side had done.

The answer, then, was for at least one side to decide to stop getting back at the other side, and to realize that there were no sides. The arrival of the demons should have allowed that to happen, but it appeared that humans like Terran, at least, would rather fight a useless war than see the real one that needed to be fought.

Tyson crossed the room and sat at the kitchen table, putting his head in his hands, gathering his thoughts before he spoke again, knowing that they could be his last. He wished he could call Harper on that phone and tell her he loved her, but there wasn't time, and she probably wasn't in a place with a cell location even if he'd had a number for her.

Probably for the best that she didn't hear his blubbering last words, anyway.

He pictured her in his mind, steadying himself, and then he spoke, keeping his eyes fixed on the faux woodgrain of the table surface supporting his elbows.

"I won't take you to Grandma Jean. The hideout, I mean. Not if you're just going to kill more people. If we go, you leave the guns, and you agree to talk with Jack about joining forces and getting the demons back to their hellhole. Because I guarantee that if we don't address that problem first, you'll realize quickly just how wrong you were to lump us in the same group as the demons."

Tyson did glance up then, making eye contact with Terran, who glanced around the room licking his lips, holding his gun up in his trembling grip.

"You-you'll take us there, all right," Terran said, voice cracking and betraying his fear. "Or I'll put a bullet—"

Tyson stood, knocking the chair back into the wall. He channeled Harper's fierce, no-nonsense attitude as he glared at Terran.

"I am so sick of that gun of yours," he said, drawing a symbol in the air with his hands, imagining he held his ulu knife, and its tip was cutting into the air instead of his finger.

A fiery orange light illuminated Terran's face as the symbol formed between them.

Tyson sent it forward, his intent to immobilize, not kill. But, of course, Terran didn't know that.

He scrambled for the trigger, aiming at Tyson's head. Tyson watched calmly, breathing in and sending up a force field as he blew his breath out. The shimmering shield went up as the shot rang out and the bullet pinged off it. The shield fell, having only been intended to prevent a single attack, and Tyson didn't bother to raise it again as he watched the symbol he'd drawn make contact with Terran's chest.

The man screamed.

Tyson laughed. "It doesn't hurt," he said, trying to sound reassuring rather than amused. "You're frozen, not being tortured."

He walked up to Terran, who was, in fact, immobilized but still standing, his eyes wide as they darted around the room.

Robyn made a choking sound. "Stop! Don't get any closer!"

"What will it take to show you that I'm not going to hurt you?" Tyson asked, turning to face her. "And I suggest you don't hurt my friend. If you hurt her, I might decide to avenge her. And then I will get violent." He said it so calmly that somewhere inside a very logical voice from his time in school wondered whether he might be becoming a psychopath, but Tyson shoved it away.

Now was not the time to question his sanity. He needed to calm these people down and convince them to talk to the people at T.R.S. or get himself and Charlie away from them and try to find a less violent-crazed group.

Robyn, to his surprise, stopped. She even lowered her gun.

"What are you going to do?" she asked.

"I'm going to let Terran go after all of you put your guns down," Tyson said, motioning towards the ground with his hands.

Hesitantly, the three humans lowered their weapons, even Mitch, who looked like he'd developed a tic as he rubbed his chin with his shoulder about a dozen times in the time it took him to bend down with his rifle and straighten back up without it.

"Grenades, tasers, bombs, whatever else you've got, put them on the couch," Tyson said, far more calmly than he'd felt. He'd used this training dozens of times as a counselor, calming enraged and terrified paranormals. He'd never had to use it with humans, though, and it amused him for some reason. They really weren't so different from each other.

"Now, Robyn, take the gun from your father. You should be able to pry up his fingers. I'll let you do it, so you know I'm not going to hurt him," Tyson said, moving towards Charlie. He leaned over to her as they watched Robyn comply with his request. "Charlie, I need one troll on each person, prepared to knock them out using nerve points. Can they do that?"

"Sure can," Charlie said, opening the top flap of her bag and letting eight trolls out. She glanced at Tyson. "Two each. For assurance. You want me to send some to the guys outside?"

"Terran will convince them there's no need for violence once we're done here," Tyson said, turning back to the large man, now bereft of his gun.

"Let me tell you how this is going to go. I'm going to unfreeze you, and you're going to promise not to harm me or Charlie, and we're going to go to the T.R.S. headquarters location together, no weapons. Because we're going to talk about how we're going to take out hundreds, if not thousands of demons, so my friends and I can close the massive portal the Autarch has opened in the middle of this city. The sooner we do that, the sooner we can get back to fighting each other, but until the demons are gone, I expect you to conduct yourself as if we're business partners. If you don't, I guarantee that polar bear I let you glimpse earlier is for more than just show. I am capable and willing to destroy you if you try to sabotage me again."

Robyn glanced from Terran to Tyson, her brow furrowing. "You're not waiting for a response, are you? Because I don't think he can talk."

"Of course not," Tyson said hurriedly. He breathed deep, connecting with the magic at his core and letting it flow through him, the symbol to release drawing itself in the air, his intention moving his finger in the right pattern.

Terran gasped as movement suddenly returned. He lunged towards Tyson, a malicious grin on his face.

Tyson didn't hesitate. He shifted so fast into his polar bear form that his clothes shredded. The bear filled the kitchen, and he roared, spittle flying in Terran's face.

"I was kidding, I was kidding!" Terran screamed, jumping behind the kitchen counter and cowering there.

Tyson put his massive paws on the counter and loomed over, staring at Terran on the floor and considering the man.

"I was just psyching you out. In hindsight, it was really, really idiotic," Terran said, both hands in the air.

Tyson shifted back to his human form, head spinning with the fast transitions. Fortunately, he'd taken to keeping a set of biker clothes on beneath his regular clothes, So he wasn't naked. Because that would have significantly cut into his position of authority in this situation.

Tyson crossed his arms. "I don't like threatening you. I'd rather you just respect me as a fellow sentient being and stop these games. If I can't trust you, I'm going to lock you in one of the back rooms and take Robyn with me."

Robyn walked around the kitchen counter and helped her father off the floor. "Will you listen to him, dad? The more he talks, the more sense he makes. We don't stand a chance against the demons on our own. We might actually need their powers and abilities."

Tyson raised his eyebrows. *See? Not so hard.*

Terran reached a tentative hand out to Tyson. "I'm sorry. I'll be better behaved, I promise." He grinned wryly.

Tyson shook his hand firmly. "Be honest and don't kill us. That's all I'm asking. Now, let's get going. Those shadows are getting longer, and I don't want to get held up by the demons."

Charlie headed for the door and Tyson gestured for Terran, Robyn, and the two others to follow her, bringing up the rear.

He eyed his shredded jeans and t-shirt. "Charlie," he called before she opened the door. "I'm going to check in the back for some clothes."

"Nothing wrong with those. You look fine," Charlie said. "They show off all your muscles. Makes you look more intimidating."

Tyson rolled his eyes and headed into the bedroom on the first floor. The first drawer was men's underwear in various sizes, which was encouraging. He moved on to the next drawer, finding shirts. He found a blue t-shirt in a medium and pulled it on, then opened the third drawer and found shoes. Tyson looked at his bare feet, suddenly grateful he was an average size.

The front door opened. Charlie must have decided to have Terran explain things to the rest of the team outside while Tyson got dressed.

Removing a pair of tennis shoes, he moved to the next row of drawers, finding shorts in the top one. He grabbed a pair of black ones in his size.

As he stepped into the shorts, a scream sounded from the front of the apartment. Shouts erupted.

Things hadn't gone well, apparently. Tyson bolted, leaving the shoes, wondering if he should strip the clothes off and shift to his polar bear form or wait.

He tripped on the threshold and nearly fell on his face, windmilling his arms until his feet caught up with him. A hand landed on his neck from behind, shoving him to the ground.

Tyson caught himself on his hands, stopping himself before his head hit the pavement. He turned his head to the side, watching as a pair of booted feet walked past to stand in front of him. He pressed up from the cement, raising his head to come face-to-face with Reya.

Red hair flowing past a black leather jacket over a black shirt, Reya looked every inch a badass. Where she'd gotten the clothes and, apparently, the shower, Tyson could only guess.

Tyson pushed off the ground, coming to his feet.

"Nice of you to join your friends." Reya waved around the circle of demons, each one holding a struggling mortal in their grasp.

A white pincered one held Charlie, whose bag of trolls lay on the ground, its contents scattered. The trolls were inert, and Tyson wondered why they weren't attacking, when he saw the claw over his friend's throat.

"You joined the demons?" he asked. "Do you hate me that much or is your soul just that twisted?"

He turned up his aura sense, scanning the dark, pulsing waves that exuded from Reya.

"I do hate you that much," Reya snarled, her expression warping, her aura darkening further. "I couldn't think of a better way to get my revenge on you than to make sure everything you've worked for is destroyed."

Tyson's gut clenched, and his mind raced. He could shift, but the moment he did Reya would give the demons the order to kill everyone else there. And then there was his other power. The one he'd used to heal numerous others influenced by the darkness. Could he heal her?

He curled his hands into fists and brought all the symbolic runes he knew to mind, trying to feel out which one felt right. None of them did. He had to stall.

"I know you hate me, Reya. But these people have nothing to do with what's between us. Let them go," he said.

"Oh no, they're staying. I have to have some way to make sure you accept your punishment like a good little traitor. Now, kneel," she said, gritting her teeth.

Tyson obliged, slowly getting to his knees, wondering if he faced torture or death, execution-style. He almost expected Reya to pull a glowing sword from the air, but she just stared at him.

"It's not too late to change your mind," Tyson said softly. "I promised to help you find your family, and I will. They might still be out there."

That seemed to snap Reya out of whatever stupor had overcome her, and she snarled at him, the fox showing through briefly as her face furred over and her eyes flashed gold.

"You won't get anywhere near my family ever again." She raised a clawed hand and brought it down on Tyson's face, slashing through the skin on his cheek.

Tyson couldn't prevent the hoarse shout that left his throat at the burning lines of pain etched into his face.

Breathing heavily, he forced his eyes to focus, then raised his hand in the air, extending one finger to draw a symbol.

"I'm sorry you're hurting so badly. I should have been able to do this on day one, but I blamed myself."

Reya's eyes narrowed. "What are you going to do?"

"Heal you," Tyson said, and he drew the first symbol he thought might work swiftly in the air and pushed it at Reya.

It struck Reya's aura and dissipated without seeming to affect her, just as it had when Tyson had tried to heal her before. He gritted his teeth and tried again, sketching a different symbol this time.

Panic entered Reya's rage-filled gaze. "Pin him!" she screamed at the demons as she jumped out of the way of the burning orange symbol Tyson had sent at her. She landed a few feet away on all fours, the symbol vanishing uselessly behind her.

Two demons emerged from behind those holding the others hostage and headed for Tyson.

Tyson pushed to his feet and backed away, frantically drawing another symbol. He tripped over the steps to the apartment and fell, landing hard, but he hardly noticed the pain in his tailbone as he watched the symbol touch Reya and absorb into her skin without effect.

His magic still didn't work on her. He hadn't let go of his guilt.

Reya turned her head, her red hair hanging over her face. She smiled with satisfaction at the despair on Tyson's face as the demons closed in, shoving his shoulders down into the pavement.

Tyson's head hit the hard service behind him with a blinding crack, and spots swam in his vision. He struggled against the demons' grip until their talons pierced his skin, burning pain making his vision worse.

He lifted his head to lock eyes with Reya. It was over. She'd chosen her side, and he'd failed to help her.

"Killing me won't bring them back," he said.

Reya straightened to standing. It looked difficult for her, like something prevented her from moving easily. Maybe that last symbol had done something. But it wasn't enough.

"No," she finally snarled, flexing her hands. "But Ragranoth intends to make the world anew, and I intend to make sure you're not here to ruin it for me."

# CHAPTER THIRTY-SIX

## MANDI

GASPING, CHOKING, SCREAMING, MANDI emerged from the darkness, thrust forward as the other soul, the soul of pure darkness, was sucked out of her. She landed on all fours on the ground, sobs suffocating her.

The first thing she realized, other than the beautiful silence in her thoughts, was the clearing of her vision.

She could see. Truly see.

And the demon queen that had possessed her had taken another form—the President of the United States. She had discarded Mandi's body in favor of another.

Mandi remained frozen and paralyzed on the ground, watching as the demon shredded the human woman's body she had taken on and revealing a body of pure, chalky white, two hooved feet stamping the ground, leathery wings sweeping over Mandi's head, her bloody gash of a mouth speaking something into a microphone on a podium to what looked like a sparse crowd of press.

Screams erupted, gunshots went off, and the demon leapt from her place on the elevated stage and ripped into the innocents below.

Mandi's muscles unlocked, her brain screaming at her to run. She took her chance, crawling on hands and knees behind the blue curtain with the president's crest on it. She crawled, praying, begging any deity that might hear her, that she could get out of the demon's grasp.

"Did you forget your promise to serve me?" The hoarse voice like a thousand voices crawled into Mandi's ears and she tried to stand, to run, but a clawed hand caught her shoulder, and the demon queen turned her around, gazing into her eyes, worming her way back inside.

"I may have no need for your body for myself, but there are others that need to be brought here. You will be the perfect vessel to bring them physically here."

Black demons tied Mandi to a steel table in an empty room. Gagged and bound, Mandi strained against her bonds and screamed as loud as she could until the demons performed their rites and used her body as a portal to let the spirits of greater demons enter the physical realm.

Her body quivered and shook. She vomited once and nearly died, which forced the demons to remove her gag, but then they couldn't muffle her unending cries for help.

The demons that emerged from her grew more twisted, more wicked, their essences tainting her soul until Mandi wasn't certain any part of her was human anymore. They dipped into the well of magic inside of her again and again, using it with her blood to power the rituals that pulled the demons out of the abyss to inhabit her body briefly before they were strong enough to come through fully.

Every moment, Mandi wished she could die. She wished she'd managed to tell Zeke to kill her. She wished Ragranoth would use her sharp claws and teeth to end it all.

Mandi, coven daughter and crystal healer, had become a portal for the fiends of hell.

# CHAPTER THIRTY-SEVEN

## TYSON

REYA EXAMINED HER CLAWS, licking Tyson's blood off of them. "You're probably wondering how I found you. I found a witch to portal me here from that godforsaken garage in the middle of nowhere. After that, following your scent was simple. It was just a matter of biding my time."

"But why? You know the demons will destroy everything. They might even destroy you."

Reya leaned in closer, keeping her eyes locked on his. "If I have to burn the world down to kill you, it would be worth it."

She was mad. Insane. No one in their right mind would betray all of mortality to get revenge on one person. Tyson had failed to heal her. Maybe she couldn't be healed. Maybe she was so far into her delusion, nothing would convince her to change her mind. Even his magic.

"I'd hoped to find you with your delightful girlfriend, so I could kill her first while you watched, but watching you die an agonizing death alone will have to do," Reya said. "Ragranoth even gave me a special gift to do it with."

She grabbed his throat, and Tyson's head bent back as his neck started to burn. He stared into the sky and the unnatural, swirling storm clouds filled with violet lightning that filled it. His vision wavered as Reya adjusted her grip, her flesh somehow burning his.

Through his lidded gaze, he caught a glimpse of feathered wings flying overhead, and he smiled through the pain, turning his head slightly to catch Reya's confused stare.

"Why are you smiling?" she growled.

"Because you got your wish," Tyson said, eyes traveling back up to the sky, where Harper flew through the air towards them, rage contorting her features.

She barreled into Reya from behind before the fox shifter could react, rolling across the pavement with her in a headlock.

"Kill them!" Reya gave the order to the demons in a guttural, choked voice. Harper pulled back, her arms locked around Reya's throat. Harper screamed, and Tyson smelled that acrid burning stench again.

All hell broke loose in the street as humans brandishing weapons and shifters erupted from every side and attacked the demons.

Jack darted past Tyson, grinning as he raised a gun and shot it five times into the closest demon.

The demon barely flinched and swiped at Jack's chest with vicious foot-long claws, but a bear shifter flung itself at the demon.

"What are you doing here, Jack?!" Tyson shouted, ducking as another shot rang out.

"Your call was too weird. I couldn't leave you alone to deal with this. And we could really use a dreamwalker right now," Jack said.

Tyson shook his head. "I'm sure glad you showed up."

"Now we gotta stay alive," Jack said, diving back into the fray.

Harper's scream split the air. Tyson spotted her pinned under Reya, Reya's hands on her bare arms. He took off running, shredding his second set of clothes for the day as he shifted into his polar bear form.

Roaring, he swiped at Reya and knocked her off Harper with a single blow. The fox shifter tumbled heels over head and landed in a crumpled heap a few feet away.

"Thanks," Harper breathed, standing and shaking out her wings. "So, she's with the demons, I'm guessing?"

Tyson nodded, unable to speak as a bear. He wanted to nuzzle his face into Harper and let her scratch behind his ears, but they didn't have time. They had to save their friends and get out of there.

Harper launched into the air as a demon charged at them. Tyson ran forward, jaw opening to catch a mouthful of demon flesh. Claws bit into his side, but Tyson took a chunk out of the demon's stomach, spraying a vile black substance across his white fur and the pavement.

He spat at the nasty bitterness coating his tongue.

The demon stumbled forward again, claws raised, hissing at Tyson. Tyson drew up to his full standing height, coming eye to eye with the demon, and swiped with his massive paw. He struck a solid blow to the demon's head, taking a stinging swipe to his ribcage. The demon burst into a cloud of ash that swept away in the wind.

Landing on all fours and pausing to catch his breath, Tyson surveyed the street-turned-battlefield. He caught snippets of song and realized Harper wasn't alone—Quinn flew near her, aiming their songs at the demons, confusing and distracting them enough that the shifters and humans on the ground were able to kill them. A grenade went off further down the street, and Tyson recognized the short, dark-haired form of Mitch from Terran's team, cackling madly in the middle of a cloud of demon ash.

"Robyn!" Terran's desperate yell broke the air.

Across the street, a demon held Robyn to the ground, grinning madly with a warped human face on a monster's body, its mouth a wide, bloody slash. Robyn kicked at it, but her human strength was no match for the demon, and she had no weapon.

Because Tyson had made her leave them in the house. He started for her, dodging three humans fighting off another bird-like demon. Just a few more steps.

Charlie charged in front of him, conducting a veritable legion of plastic troll dolls. She bellowed something incoherent—Tyson suspected in Latin—and the wave of trolls overtook the demon. It reared back off Robyn and swatted at the dolls as if they were flies.

Charlie turned towards Tyson and grinned. "Not bad for an old hag."

Tyson grinned, if a polar bear could grin, but then he caught sight of the demon covered with trolls surging for Charlie.

He tried to scream for her to watch out, but all that came out was a garble of anxious bear sounds.

Charlie's head turned, but too slow, as three wicked demon claws erupted through her chest and midsection.

Her expression turned shocked as she glanced down at the claws emerging from her body.

"I..." she said, then licked her lips and stumbled forward. "Tyson..." she tried again, and then she crumpled.

Tyson bellowed through the polar bear form, raising his arms and pawing the air in a challenge to the demon. When he landed, fully intending to charge the demon and rip it to shreds, to his shock he collapsed in his human form, hands and knees scraping against the pavement.

He'd been warned about this. His emotions had destabilized his aura, so he wasn't able to maintain his polar bear form. Tyson stood up anyway, curling his fingers over his stinging palms to make fists, and he faced the demon as it shook off the trolls that had become inert and powerless with Charlie's death.

Charlie's death. Tyson blinked, glancing at the body that lay lifeless in front of him, her bright red blood spilling in the street. Suddenly, his vision narrowed and everything sounded far away. He tried to focus. Something about a demon? Someone screamed, but not at him.

No, definitely at him.

Harper flew past, tackling the demon with a knife in her hand. Where had she gotten the knife?

Tyson snapped out of his stunned state a split second later, the sound of battle crashing over him like a wave.

"Harper!" he screamed, watching her go down with the demon. He ran for her, not sure what he'd do human and weaponless, but he couldn't let her do this alone.

Harper's head shot up, and she screamed at him.

"Behind you!"

Tyson whipped his head around in time to see a fox baring its teeth in his face seconds before it slammed into him, sending them both to the ground. Tyson's head slammed into the pavement, and he saw stars as he tried to close his hands around the fox's jaws and keep them away from his throat.

The tiny dagger-like teeth ripped at his hands, and she snarled with a fury Tyson had never seen in an animal. Then again, this was no ordinary animal. This was a shifter, an animal filled with all the volatile rage of a human being who was hurting more than he could comprehend.

He stopped fighting, then. He let his arms drop and focused on his breathing and the intricate motions of his fingers instead.

He must have shocked Reya pretty good with the sudden change, because the fox stopped attacking and stared at him a moment.

Tyson took advantage of her surprise and thrust his hands between them, a symbol for immobilization already formed.

The symbol hit Reya directly in her furry chest, the blast throwing her off Tyson. She landed stiffly on the ground, legs straight out, body frozen.

Tyson stood, grimacing at the scratches on his human body from where his polar bear form had gotten hit. Blood soaked the tight shirt across his chest, a shallow scrape showing through the cut fabric. His face stung where Reya had scratched him, and the burns on his throat ached.

He glanced quickly around at the fight, noticing Jack led an entire squad of about ten individuals against the last demon. It didn't stand a chance, squawking like a cub looking for its mother.

Four people stabbed, shot, or bit at the same time and the horrible thing went silent, vanishing in a puff of ash.

Tyson's shoulders slumped, then he nearly jumped out of his skin when something landed beside him and put a hand on his shoulder.

"Oh shit—Harper, never do that again after we've just battled for our lives, okay?" Tyson said.

Harper blinked at him. "I don't think I've ever heard you cuss like that. I must have scared you pretty bad." And then she grinned ruthlessly.

Tyson rolled his eyes, then froze. He was standing here with this woman that he loved, that he'd been separated from. This woman had saved his life multiple times. Why was he wasting this moment with *banter*?

He flung his arms around Harper, careful enough to avoid her wings. He gripped her to him, not caring if he was crushing her a little bit. He had to feel her heart beat against his, to feel her lungs fill with air.

She gasped and wiggled until he loosened his hold, pulling back just enough to gaze up at him with wondering, wide brown eyes.

"What's gotten into you?" she said.

"I'm an idiot, and I owe you everything forever," Tyson said. He wasn't making much sense, but he didn't care. He released her. "Wait, where's Anna?"

"She distracted some demons that came after us. We haven't seen her since," Harper said, the skin around her eyes tightening. She seemed to be trying to hold off her emotions, but Tyson knew how difficult it had to be to not know where her mom was after all they'd been through.

"I'm sure she's lost those demons and found one of the hideouts to hunker down in. She could already be back at Grandma Jean's, for all we know," Tyson said reassuringly.

"This is cute and all, but there are more demons on their way, and I do not want to repeat that any time before I've had a good meal," Jack said, walking up to them. "Let's get back to Grandma Jean's. Quinn here mentioned that you guys have a plan."

"A plan that needs to change. Drastically," Quinn cut in.

Terran stepped up, covered in a muddy, gory mixture of ash and blood. He walked right up to Tyson, a wooden stake in one hand, a brick in the other. "Someone needs to answer for what happened here today," he said with a growl.

Tyson leaned way back, almost doing a backbend and bumping into Harper, who shoved her way in front of him, getting into Terran's face.

"Anyone who has a problem with Tyson saving our butts will have to answer to me," Harper growled back.

Terran's face morphed into a feral grin, and he looked over Harper's head, raising his eyebrows at Tyson. "This yours?"

"Harper and I…" Tyson trailed off, not sure what to say. They hadn't officially decided anything. He swallowed.

Harper glanced back, giving him an incredulous look, somewhere between affection and anger, a line Tyson still hadn't figured out not to cross.

Fortunately, affection won out, and Harper just rolled her eyes. "You still got a problem?" she asked Terran.

Terran shook his head. "Nah, it's just kinda fun the way his eyes bug out of his head."

Harper grinned and shot Tyson a mischievous look. "Yeah, I get that. He's all yours."

"What are you…? Ah, geez." Tyson said as Terran came closer. The guy had several inches on Tyson and loads more muscle. Intimidating, to say the least. Tyson tried to channel his inner dreamwalker, polar bear, wise-sage, whatever it was that gave him mojo.

Terran slapped him on the back. "Your friend saved my Robyn tonight. I should have given you both more respect, and for that, I'm sorry. You've proven that humans and paranormals can, and probably should, team up for this demon fight. I'm going to reach out to the other human groups in the area, pass the word about a meeting tonight with the T.R.S. With a bit of planning and a lot of luck—"

"And some magic. Don't forget magic," Jack said, cutting in.

Terran shot him a glare. "—and whatever resources and abilities everyone brings to the table, we might actually beat these demons back to their hellhole before they turn earth into one."

"That is…" Tyson began, glancing from Terran to Robyn and around the whole group. "Incredibly open-minded of you. Thank you." He swallowed past the lump of emotion that had come up at the mention of Charlie, then cleared his throat. "So, meeting at your place, Jack? Can I give Terran the details?"

Jack waved his hand. "Sure. Just make sure you tell your human buddies that I might be human, but if any of them show up looking for a fight, I will personally tie them to a roof and let the demons eat them alive. Got it?" He raised his expressive eyebrows.

Terran laughed. "You got it. I know you're probably good for it, too. Maybe whatever disease you caught that made you think it was a good idea to hang out with these monsters and magic-users will infect the rest of us."

"I can only hope," Jack said. He rotated his finger in the air. "The rest of you, pack it up. Meeting's in three hours, and we've got to go clean our rooms. Y'all live like pigs."

There was an air of banter and hope hovering above the ash and body-strewn street. Four people, including Charlie, had died in the ambush.

Tyson's eyes landed on Reya, who was still paralyzed by his magic.

"Jack! Wait!" he called out.

Jack turned.

"Can we bring Reya? She betrayed us to the demons, but I don't think we should kill her for it. She's just...hurting," Tyson said nervously.

Jack eyed the frozen fox. "Will the spell you put on her hold?"

"I think so. Honestly, I don't have much experience with it," Tyson said.

"I think we can handle her if she unfreezes. We should tie her up a bit first. She one of ours or someone you picked up?"

"One of the storage unit recruits," Tyson said. "The ones Violet preserved."

"Ah," Jack said, motioning for the bear shifter, now in human form, and a woman next to him to pick Reya up. "Yeah, we've had some trouble with those. Most have been too weak to be much help with the fighting, but a lot of them are willing. Others...well, let's just say we have a section in our underground bunker specifically for them."

Fortunately for everyone, there was an entrance into a tunnel system leading to the bunker they called Grandma Jean's nearby. Half an hour later, Tyson, Harper, and Quinn left the darkness of the tunnels and entered what was practically an underground metropolis.

Someone had carved out dozens of caves from a cave system that existed underneath D.C., and that had become Grandma Jean's, named after Dak and Jack's grandmother who apparently always had a place to put someone up. The complex underground system had been stocked with non-perishables, medical supplies, weapons, and other equipment years ago.

Tyson was grateful for the foresight of others and the example of Grandma Jean when he joined the line for a bowl of warm, cheesy potato and sausage hash made from dehydrated rations and canned foods. He sat next to Harper, who scooted over on the wooden bench in a wide-open area that had been designated as the mess hall.

"How did it go in Alaska?" Tyson asked.

Harper's fork faltered on the way to her mouth. She shook her head. "Not good. As you might have guessed by the lack of the mighty Tulukaruq battalion we promised, they aren't coming. And not only are they not coming, I almost killed my grandfather." She shoved her next bite in her mouth, chewing with a vengeance.

Tyson put a hand on her leg. "Hey, I'm sorry it didn't work out." He wanted to ask about the circumstances that had led to her "almost" killing her grandfather, but he didn't want to make her relive it now when she was clearly exhausted.

Harper put her fork down, looking out at the small crowd eating their dinner. "You know, it's funny how you don't seem to realize how much you care about someone until you're separated from them, and you don't know if you'll see them again?"

Her hand landed on his, which still rested on her knee. Her thumb rubbed against his. Tyson's stomach heated up, flooding the rest of his body with a tingly warmth that made it hard for him to think. Was it hot in this cave, or was it just him?

"Hordes of demons seem to have a way of putting things into perspective," he said, shooting her a smile.

He wasn't prepared for her sudden move forward, and the kiss she planted solidly on his lips. He fumbled for a moment, placing his bowl in his lap so he could free his hands and cup them around Harper's face, push them into her hair, bringing her as close as possible.

Harper pulled away first, breathless and flushed and, thankfully, grinning. Then her face morphed into one of horror. "You're bleeding through your shirt."

Tyson opened his mouth to say it was fine, it was dry, but then he looked down and realized that some wound must have opened because his shirt front had a long slash of bright red through it, making it stick to his chest. How hadn't he noticed it?

Suddenly, he felt faint. He leaned towards Harper, and she set her bowl down and moved his so she could grab him.

"Let's get you to a med tent," she said, motioning down the corridor that their orientation guide had said led to the medical and supply tents.

Tyson had to admit, having Harper hover around the poor nurse that attended him was far more amusing than it had any right being. First, Harper had insisted on coming into the tent with him, which had put the nurse in a mood right off the bat. Then, she'd helped Tyson remove his shirt, berating him for moving at all since it opened the wide, but shallow gash in his chest further.

Tyson had to bite his lip to keep from laughing as Harper tried to take the antiseptic from the nurse because she "wasn't applying it right."

"Do you want to finish here? Because I know when I'm not wanted," the nurse said, fortunately good-natured enough to figure out what was going on and not get mad.

"Sorry," Tyson said as Harper snatched the tube of ointment and started smearing it across his chest. "She's a bit...overprotective."

The nurse crossed her arms, laughing. "You don't say. Well, she's an excellent nurse, I can give her that. Next time just tell me you plan on taking over."

"Done," Harper said, passing the ointment to the nurse. "Bandages?" She held out her hand expectantly.

Tyson and the nurse exchanged exasperated looks, and the nurse fetched the bandages.

Harper reluctantly let the nurse take over after her own attempts to attach the bandages hadn't gone well. She even admitted the nurse had done a pretty good job, which only made the nurse laugh as she gave Tyson a sucker for being a good patient—and putting up with Harper, she said under her breath—and sent them out the door.

"How much time do we have before the meeting?" Tyson asked, sticking the small round sucker into his mouth. Cherry wasn't his favorite, but he wouldn't complain. It seemed to calm his nerves the moment he tasted it. Maybe he should have pressed the nurse for one for Harper. Since he hadn't, he pulled it out of his mouth and offered it towards her.

Harper made a face, but cocked her head as if considering. Then, she yanked the sucker towards her, watching Tyson the entire time she tasted it, making him flush from his hair to his toes.

He took it back from her, so bothered he almost didn't hear her response to his question.

"Fifteen minutes. We're going to have to book it to the meeting hall."

"I can't go that fast. Don't want to mess up your fine work," he said, gesturing to his chest. He held out his arm, and Harper took it begrudgingly.

"If you would just let me handle the fighting, then you don't have to get injured, and I can stop worrying about you."

"Fussing, you mean. Like a mother hen," Tyson shot back.

Harper punched him in the shoulder.

"Ow! You planning to add to my injuries?" he joked.

Harper smirked. "If you don't behave. Let's go see if the paranormals and humans can get along for five seconds in a room together."

# CHAPTER THIRTY-EIGHT

## HARPER

IN FACT, IT TURNED out humans and paranormals couldn't get along for five seconds together, but despite several scuffles and shouting matches, they managed to make it through an entire multiple hour-long meeting without drawing blood.

The humans would bring explosives and weapons. The paranormals would protect them with shields and fight alongside them. With sheer numbers and a bit of magic, they might stand a chance in closing the bridge to the lower planes of the astral realm.

Harper hadn't had a chance to warn them about the Eternal Source, but in the end, she realized it didn't matter. Only those that had been there and heard the Eternal Source say someone had to sacrifice themselves needed to know. Herself, Tyson, Anna, Quinn, Charlie, and Reya. Well, Reya hardly counted as she was locked up in a holding cell and Charlie had been killed.

Of those people, only Anna and Tyson didn't know what Harper's instincts were screaming at her. She clenched the bottom of her seat until her fingertips hurt, glancing over at Tyson every so often to see if he would mention it, but he remained silent.

At last, Jack and Dak declared the meeting over and sent everybody to complete their assigned tasks.

Harper stood, pulling Tyson to the side once they were through the door.

"Why didn't you tell them about the Eternal Source?" Harper asked.

Tyson rubbed his arm, glancing at the others leaving the room. "Mandi contacted me in the astral realm while I was being held by Terran. She was possessed by the Autarch and overheard her talking to...I guess her consort? Another really powerful demon. Mandi said this demon king pretended to be the Eternal Source and tricked us. The willing sacrifice will open the gate the rest of the way, not close it." Tyson gazed into Harper's eyes and swallowed. "You were right. I'm sorry...I'm sorry I doubted you. I never should have called you crazy. Your instincts are often right, and I'm an idiot for letting my fear override that."

The sore spot in Harper's heart diminished at the apology. It didn't disappear entirely, but hearing Tyson say he should have listened to her definitely felt good.

"Did I hear you say Mandi contacted you?" a familiar voice said from behind.

Zeke walked up to them, looking exhausted, limping on one foot. "It's good to see you two made it. Mandi came to me, too. I told her to find Anna because I couldn't help her at the time."

Harper hadn't heard what had happened to Zeke yet, but she had noticed the odd group of shifters he'd been talking to earlier and guessed there was quite a story behind his injuries and new friends.

"Yeah, she warned me about the demon queen's consort. I didn't bring it up in the meeting because it doesn't really change anything. If he comes through that portal, we're pretty much doomed. From the sound of it, the Autarch can't get the portal all the way open without a willing sacrifice. Fortunately, only a handful of us heard that."

Fear pricked its way into Harper's heart. Tyson knew now that they couldn't trust what the Eternal Source had said, but Anna didn't. If she had survived the demons' attack earlier and showed up at the battle, would she try to sacrifice herself?

Harper wouldn't let that happen. She would keep her eyes out for her mother and the moment she showed up to fight, Harper would do everything in her power to make sure she knew the truth about the Eternal source.

Thinking about how she wished she knew if her mother was alive or dead made Harper remember what she'd seen on TV back at the apartment.

"Mandi is alive, by the way, or she was a few hours ago," Harper said, glancing at Zeke.

Zeke blinked. "How do you know?"

"I saw her on TV. Behind the podium, on stage with the demon when she gave her address as the President. I'm certain it was her," Harper said, spreading her wings slightly. She was swaying somewhat unsteadily. She needed to sit down.

"Thank you," Zeke said, his voice breaking. "Good luck tomorrow. If we all make it out of this, I'll invite you to our wedding." He waved and left the two of them, walking swiftly down the corridor with his hands in his pockets.

*Wedding?* Harper's heart lifted at the thought. If they all made it out, there would be a wedding. If anyone deserved it, it was

Mandi and Zeke. She felt a hand on her shoulder and glanced up into Tyson's face.

He jerked his head towards the door, and she followed him out in a daze. She'd been awake since sunrise that morning, had flown several hours, and had barely sat down at the apartment with Quinn before ending up in a demon battle. She needed sleep desperately, but she had until noon tomorrow to find Quinn and train the other bird shifters in a Song she barely knew. They were going to attempt their original plan to bind the demons through the raven song, despite the fact that they only had a handful of original tribe members among them.

Harper wished suddenly and fiercely for her mother to show up.

Tyson's arm wrapped around her shoulders. "Hey, are you all right?"

Harper blinked away the tears stinging her eyes and forced a smile. "Yeah. Let's get ready to kick some demon butt."

Tyson chuckled. "Okay. But don't think I can't see how tired you are. I'm going to get set up with the other clairvoyants and start bringing people here through portals. Meet me in the mess hall in four hours. I'll find us a place to crash."

Harper nodded, and Tyson leaned down to peck her on the cheek, then split down a different hall.

Harper squared her shoulders. She didn't have the knowledge or skill of her mom, but she had an older brother who had a bit more skill than she had, and some of the other raven shifters, if they'd survived, had been training for longer than she had. She'd ask them to help and hope that when the time came, their combined voices and wills would be enough to bind the demon queen.

"Let's go over it again," Quinn said, tapping out a rhythm with a spoon on a flat rock that he carried as he paced in front of the room.

Harper tried not to groan. They'd been singing the same bars for hours, trying to memorize the notes and complex rhythms of the Song of Persuasion and the Song of Binding.

Quinn had taken over teaching the bird shifters they'd found—about a dozen of varying species but only three others from the Tulukaruq tribe. Quinn drilled them furiously, stopping the moment anyone screeched out of tune or missed a note, attacking the song practice like it was a battle itself. Maybe to make up for failing when he'd tried to bend Chief Aguta's will in the Ilau Toqu before.

Harper took a sip of water from the water bottle in front of her and breathed a lungful of air in, trying not to let the fatigue get to her.

Several sets of footsteps came from the corridor outside the room they practiced in, then several loud voices arguing...in the Inuit tongue of their ancestral tribes.

Harper exchanged a shocked glance with Quinn, who strode for the room's entrance and threw open the curtain covering it, revealing a huddled group of bird shifters, their inky black wings betraying their lineage.

"Silla! Tarkik! What are you doing here?" Quinn asked.

"We've come to help," Silla said in English, patting Quinn on the shoulder. "Grandmother Ahna told us of your need and convinced us of the foolishness of our chief. We are ashamed of his actions, and we come to restore our honor as your tribe."

"As long as you aren't dating that *namigiak* anymore," Tarkik said gruffly.

Quinn bristled slightly, then relaxed his shoulders. "No, she is not here, and we are no longer together. Come in, we need you to help us learn these Songs."

Harper counted them as they filed in. Seven. Seven members of the Tulukaruq tribe. Two women and five men, all with serious but kind faces, lining up among the other bird shifters. There to help them.

Sent by her grandmother.

Harper stood to greet them. "Thank you for coming. We are in desperate need. Most of us weren't raised in the tribe, and Anna has gone missing. We could use your wisdom."

Silla joined Quinn at the front of the room, and the teaching began again in earnest. With the wisdom of an elder from the Tulukaruq tribe, the singers made more progress in the next hour than they had in the previous three.

Finally, voices exhausted, Quinn called it a night. "Everyone, let's break. Rest your voices and meet back here at six a.m. sharp for more practice."

He approached Harper, putting a hand on her shoulder. "Especially you, little sis. Get some rest."

"What time is it?" Harper asked, suppressing a yawn and stretching her arms and wings out to either side.

"After midnight sometime," Quinn said, glancing at the others as they started to leave.

"I wish mom were here," Harper said, rubbing her hand down her face.

"Me too," Quinn said, smiling at her. "Now, get out of here."

Harper stumbled from the room towards the mess hall, wondering if Tyson had waited for her or if he'd given up and gone to bed.

He was the only one in the mess hall when she arrived, his hair tied up out of his face as he sat in a relaxed meditation position.

Harper sat down on the bench next to him, not sure whether she should speak and disturb his focus or not.

His eyes cracked open a second later, and he unfolded his legs and arms, stretching.

"You came," he said, voice hoarse. "I was starting to wonder whether you had found a corner somewhere to sleep in."

Harper adjusted her wing, so it didn't get crushed as she leaned her head on Tyson's shoulder.

"I'll fall asleep right here if I have to," she murmured, eyelids growing heavy.

"Oh, no you don't," Tyson said, shoving her up and standing.

She lost her balance without his support and almost fell over on the bench but caught herself and stood grumbling.

Tyson reached out a hand. "I claimed a spot just for you. Much more comfortable than this bench, I promise."

Harper took his hand, curiosity waking her mind up a bit as she followed him through a maze of corridors. She admired the caves that had been carved out of the underground walls and fortified with a network of iron and steel, each one covered in boards or curtains or anything else people had found to create a semblance of privacy.

"Don't tell me we're all the way at the back," Harper moaned, her feet aching. Actually, everything ached, and even the floor looked like a good alternative to standing at the moment.

"It's worth it, I promise," Tyson said, moving past a stretch of what looked like perfectly good, empty chambers.

Finally, he stopped at what must have been an older section of tunnel. The supports in the ceiling were wood instead of steel, and the electric lights had stopped a hundred feet back.

Tyson pulled back a heavy black covering that served as a door and gestured for Harper to go ahead of him.

Harper eyed him, then tightened her wings against her back and ducked through the blanket doorway.

She gasped at the softly lit chamber. A glowing golden ball hovered against the ceiling, obviously enchanted as it bobbed along.

Tapestries and blankets hung on the wall, making the space feel close and cozy, if a bit claustrophobic.

A mattress rested on the floor against one wall, piled with pillows and what looked like a relatively clean blanket.

Harper turned, taking in the whole room, her eyes landing on Tyson, who looked at her like she was the only thing in the world.

"You put this together for me?" she said, breath catching in her throat. Her fingers rubbed against her palms at her sides.

"For us. If that's okay," Tyson said with a rush. His hand came up to rub through his hair, but it stopped halfway, as if he remembered he'd put his hair up.

Harper cocked her head at him, then glanced at the one bed. "You mean...sleep together?"

Tyson put his palms up in front of him. "It doesn't have to be like...like anything you might be thinking." He rubbed the back of his head, grimacing. "Man, this is more awkward than I expected. I was just hoping that we could spend the night together, alone, like we haven't been since this whole thing really began. I wanted to hold you, if that's okay, and just pretend tomorrow isn't happening, since we don't know..." He trailed off.

Harper swallowed. "Since we don't know if either of us will make it out."

Tyson threw his hands in the air and reeled around, looking at the ceiling. "When you put it like that, I want to run instead of fight."

"You could, you know," Harper said, biting her lip and glancing away from him. "You've done your part. You could stay here. Not everyone needs to fight."

Tyson stared at her. "Yes, they do."

"Someone has to take care of people that get injured," Harper insisted, looking up at him. "That could be you."

"No. Not a chance. Not while you're out there," Tyson said, grabbing Harper's hands in his.

Desperation rose in Harper's chest, hot and demanding. She needed him to stay here. She needed to know that he was safe. She searched his eyes, trying to find the words to tell him what she was feeling.

"What are you trying to prove?" she finally asked.

Tyson's hand caressed her cheek. "I'm trying to prove that you don't have to be scared when I go out there tomorrow. That you don't have to wonder if I'm coming back. Because I am not fragile, Harper. Not near as fragile as your confidence in me."

Harper flinched, closing her eyes. She breathed in deeply, gathering her courage. "You're not fragile. It's just that..." Her shoulders tightened up, creeping towards her ears. She ducked her head, not wanting him to see the way her face was screwing up as she tried not to cry.

"I've realized that I'm overprotective. I try to stop you from going on dangerous missions and using your abilities because whenever you put yourself out there to fight an enemy or heal someone broken by evil, all I can see is that day in the forest at Camp Silver Lake. You in the arms of the vampiress with her teeth on your throat." Harper shivered and finally looked at him. "I see you getting slashed by that demon. I see you hurt, and I want to do everything in my power to keep it from happening again."

Tyson's thumbs stroked both sides of her face, wiping away the tears from the edges of her eyes as they fell. He traced down her round, full cheeks, smoothing over faint scars and the small mole she had just above her mouth. His thumbs hovered there, then eased across her bottom lip, tugging on it slightly.

Harper gasped at the sudden flush of warmth that tingled through her, wishing she didn't feel anything at that moment. She didn't want to feel anything this strongly, and then lose the person she cared about.

When she looked up at Tyson, she realized that he understood. Maybe he even felt the same way. She wanted to step away, to put coldness and distance between them again and stop this coaster they were on, but she couldn't bring herself to do it. Her hands betrayed her, sliding across Tyson's t-shirt and grasping the fabric as if he she were drowning, and he was a lifeline thrown out towards her.

"I couldn't stand it if I'd never woken up to my magic and couldn't hold my own and fight at your side. If I had to sit on the sidelines, be left behind, just hoping you'll return, I'd go insane.

I want to be strong for you." His voice broke, but he held eye contact with her.

Harper searched his eyes, waiting for him to go on.

He drew in a breath. "I want to be strong for you because if I'm weak, if I'm not enough to keep up with you, you're going to leave. You're going to go find some muscled, raven-shifting warrior, and I wouldn't even be mad at you for it because you deserve that, if you want it. You deserve someone who can keep up with your fire and passion. So, I'm going to fight, and I'm going to prove to you that I'm worth keeping around."

Something broke inside Harper. Some barrier she'd been unable to cross before. Some line that had held her back from expressing her true emotions. She crossed it now, crossed it for him so she could show him all that he meant to her.

"Tyson, how did you ever get it in your head that you're not everything I want? My people have rejected me time and time again. I am done seeking their approval. I want you. Everything that you are. The badass dreamwalker, the polar bear, the man."

Her breath trembled as she put her hand on his jaw, stroking his skin through his beard. Tyson closed his eyes, and Harper moved her hand to the back of his head, running her fingers beneath his hair and tugging him gently closer.

"What are we going to do about this?" Tyson murmured, his lips practically touching hers.

"About what?" Harper asked breathlessly.

Tyson pulled back slightly, gazing into her eyes intently. "Our bond. The feelings are still there, but there's an emptiness…" he licked his lips. "Do you feel it, too?"

Harper nodded. "I do." Then laughter bubbled up inside of her, filling the cave room. "We're idiots."

"What?" Tyson asked, looking perplexed.

"You're a healer. And I-I discovered something, a Song, while we fought my grandfather. The Song healed Quinn, it healed something between me and my mother, and it almost healed our relationship with my grandfather, too." Her breath caught as she locked her eyes on Tyson's. "What if I sing it, and it heals our bond?"

"And I could try my magic...do you think we should use them together?" Tyson asked, his eyes lighting up with excitement.

Harper nodded. "That feels right."

Tyson's thumbs rubbed little circles on her arms. "Let's do it."

He released her, concentrating on the air in front of him as he sketched several symbols in the air.

Harper watched, her breath growing shallow with awe at the skill and intuition he possessed.

"How do you know what symbols to choose?" she asked.

"I just...follow my instincts. It usually works," Tyson replied. He finished drawing a third symbol, then nodded. "That's it. Now, your song."

Trembling, Harper sang the Song of Binding, letting it wrap around her and Tyson, binding them together. She focused on that place inside of her that had felt hollowed out ever since her song had broken their bond. She thought of it mending, of it returning stronger than ever.

And just as before, the Song wove its way out of the feelings of her own heart. Not out of control. Not forcing something she didn't feel. She sang a true Song that bound her again to this man she loved.

Tyson moved closer as her Song neared its end, his hands gripping her waist and drawing her in towards him until there was no space between them.

The symbols he'd drawn moved with him until they touched both of them at the same time, flaring with bright orange light.

Harper's chest filled with warmth and light and love so full it almost hurt, but she kept singing until she reached the final crescendo, and the last note hung in the air. Her heart pounded and her head spun. She clung to Tyson's shirt, a giddy feeling swirling through her. She couldn't see for the light that surrounded them, and then Tyson's lips closed against hers and the light flared even brighter, then narrowed, becoming a golden thread that thrummed with life between them.

They had done it. They had healed their bond.

Harper stood entwined with Tyson for a long moment, lips moving, hands caressing and exploring, warmth moving through their bodies. Tyson kissed along Harper's cheeks, her jaw, her lips, her neck, her ear, her hair, until at last, breathless, he'd made his way to her forehead, where he paused, pressing his lips there while her hands reached again for him, asking him to return to her lips and start again.

He obliged, kissing her softly one more time, before pressing his forehead into hers and murmuring, "If you asked me a month ago if I pictured doing this with you, I'd have said you needed to get your head checked."

"I'd have agreed with you," Harper said, laughing.

Tyson rubbed his thumb across her fingers, holding them in his grip. He kissed them, one by one, then slid his hand down her arm to the hem of her shirt, tugging it upward a bit before he leaned back to look at her face with an asking expression.

She'd already crossed the line of emotional vulnerability, and she was ready for this. Ready to dive deep with him to a place she'd never gone with anyone.

With one swift motion she removed her shirt, tugging it over her wings in a gesture that she managed to make graceful.

Tyson's gaze roved over her body, lit up with both hunger and delight.

Harper's hands went to the button at the top of her jeans, and Tyson stopped her, taking her hand in his.

"We don't have to," he said, voice husky. "I don't want you to...you know, regret anything. If we survive."

Harper cupped her wings around them, trapping the heat between their bodies, and looked up into his eyes.

"I want this. I want you. I would want this whether the world was ending or not. You're not talking me out of it now. So long as you want this too, I'm not backing out. Provided you managed to rustle up a condom somewhere," she teased.

Tyson flushed in the glow from the floating orb above and pulled a crackling square package from his pocket. "Med tent had some. I went back and asked."

Harper lunged for him, pushing him towards the bed with a passionate kiss. She felt his lips curve under hers in a smile.

She hadn't told him yet, she realized. What she'd wanted to tell him since before the demons had attacked, something she'd only become more sure of in the time they'd spent together and apart. She yanked out of the kiss that made her blood burn inside her and licked her lips.

"I love you," she said at last. "I love you and I want this. I've wanted this for a long time. All this time I thought I was angry at you, at the world we live in, at everyone around us. I thought they kept us separated, but it was me all along. Me and my stupid fear."

Tyson stopped the flood of words with a long, hard kiss. He ran his hands down her back. His touch made her shiver, then heat rushed through her as he spun her around and walked her backward towards the bed, bending her down onto it. Her wings spread out beneath her, fanning around her head. She tightened them up around his back, enjoying his shiver as her feathers tickled his skin.

"I love you," he said. "I will love you through this and whatever comes next. Even when you're angry." He grinned cheekily and bent to kiss her again.

Harper smiled back, her hand rubbing down his chest to his waistband. She tugged him closer, over her.

"Let's make this a night to take with us, whatever tomorrow brings," she said, grabbing his shirt.

He stripped it off. The sight of his bandaged chest almost stopped her, worry flashing across her mind, but Tyson kissed away her concern, starting at her neck and working his way down.

When all was said and done and the demons were banished back to their abyss, Harper hoped they got more of this. More time together without the stress of running for their lives or the world ending. She didn't even want to consider what would happen if the demons won tomorrow. Tonight, she would pretend that they didn't exist.

# CHAPTER THIRTY-NINE

## ZEKE

ADRENALINE AND FEAR KEPT Zeke working through the night, unpacking weapons from boxes, training others in the use of them, stopping briefly to eat, and then carrying on. All night his mind worried over what he'd been told by Harper—Mandi was alive.

At least twelve hours ago, she had been. Until Ragranoth shed her skin like a husk, and no one had any news of her since.

But she had to be alive. Zeke willed it with every pound of his heart, every intake of breath.

The pack noticed his preoccupation and worked silently alongside him, watching him out of the sides of their eyes. They didn't argue, didn't complain, simply came to him every time a task was completed and asked for a new one.

After midnight, realizing they were flagging, Zeke commanded them to go to bed. One by one, they filed off, until only Sasha was left, tugging at the baggy clothes hanging off her human frame and twirling a strand of hair around her finger.

"What?" Zeke said, when the silence grew so loud it seemed to pulse in his ears. The word came out more harshly than he intended, and Sasha's hackles raised.

"You're not doing yourself, or her, any favors by working yourself to the bone and moping, you know," Sasha said.

Zeke shot her a glare, lifting a box onto the back of a truck being loaded. It would be driven to the surface, its contents distributed as soon as the signal was given.

"I'm fine. You've been through a lot in twenty-four hours. You need sleep."

Sasha snorted, crossing her arms. "And you don't? Alphas aren't gods, Zeke. We all have faces we don't want to confront in our dreams. The ones that appear when our bodies and minds go quiet, the ones we couldn't save, the ones who killed them. We're willing to follow you, but we're not willing to stand by while you make poor decisions, and staying up all night before a major battle against demon hordes is a poor decision."

Zeke paused before the dwindling stack of boxes and rubbed at the stubble on his face. He sighed, pressing his fingers into his eyes. She was right. He knew she was right. Then why did it feel so hard to stop?

"I can't go out there tomorrow and fight without knowing where she is, what happened to her," Zeke said at last, dropping his hands by his side.

Sasha watched him with unblinking, golden eyes. "Then go find her."

"I can't. I'm assigned as a battalion leader. They'll expect me to stay with my group."

"Then ask permission to leave. The leaders here respect you, Zeke. I see their respect, their deference to your ideas. You've established yourself as a pack leader here without even realizing it." She smiled, a sudden, wolfish grin that caught Zeke off guard. "Seems like you were born to be alpha."

The words echoed right into his heart. His father had said as much when Zeke had been there a few weeks ago—that he'd known the moment Zeke was born, that he'd had to explain it to Zeke's mother. That inborn alpha instinct was the reason Zeke had fought with his father almost every day of his life, the reason that Zeke couldn't be with his family pack now. The reason he had to create his own pack.

Looking at Sasha, who had started working again but watched him with frequent side-glances, Zeke realized she was right.

Mandi was his pack. Sasha and the others were his pack. Even some members of the T.R.S., he was starting to see, were his pack. They would respond if he called for aid, without hesitation. They might even share the same bond a werewolf alpha had with his pack members, even though they weren't wolves. It was the oddest thing he'd ever heard of.

"Okay, I'll ask," he said. He paused, then, "Will you come with me?"

Sasha obliged, sliding the last box into the truck, leaving the back open for any others who would need to add supplies, then walked alongside Zeke to where Jack and Dak were giving orders in a hectic circle of people cycling in and out.

Zeke felt a slight sense of recognition, the sensation he felt when a pack member was near.

Jack was one of them. A willing participant in Zeke's widening circle of pack members. Zeke tugged on the bond he felt, and Jack glanced over the heads of the half a dozen people asking him questions, as if the human somehow sensed Zeke.

Zeke smiled, and Jack finished helping the others, excused himself, and squeezed past the crowd.

"Man, you look like trash. Get some sleep, will ya?" Jack said, tone teasing, but his eyes looked worried. He clasped Zeke's hand, bringing him in and slapping him on the back in greeting. "What can I do for you?"

"I need you to find a different leader for battalion G," Zeke said.

Jack looked surprised. "Oh? Why is that? You know you're the man for the job. G has a lot of humans on it, plus you're so level-headed in general..." He trailed off, as if catching some hint of what Zeke's thoughts were. "Mandi."

Zeke nodded, shoving his fists into his pockets. "I can't think straight without knowing where she is, Jack. My mind is frantic. On the outside I look calm, but I promise you my mind is a mess. I have to go and look for her."

"Not alone," Jack said firmly, looking from Zeke to Sasha. He kept his eyes on Sasha. "You make sure he doesn't go alone."

"Yes, sir," Sasha said, giving Zeke a pointed look. "His pack will look out for him."

"You'll need to replace us in G," Zeke said again, wanting to make sure that the humans in that battalion weren't left without the protection of the shifters they were promised simply because of Zeke's broken heart.

Jack put a hand on Zeke's shoulder. "You let me worry about battalion G. Carry on with the plan as usual but consider your-selves your own battalion with a special mission. You'll leave with the others, then split off to search once the signal is given. If Mandi's alive, she's being held prisoner, and it's likely there will be others. I can't see any reason this demon queen would keep prisoners unless she needs bodies for other demons. I'll meet with Dak and the rest of the council and brainstorm where you can hold any possessed people if necessary. You're going to eat something and lie down before you pass out."

Sasha nudged Zeke in the ribs. *Told you so,* she said through their mental connection, smirking at him.

Zeke rolled his eyes at her. "All right. I'll get a few hours in. Thanks, Jack."

Jack grinned. "Any time. You know I mean it."

Zeke smiled back at him and left the rebellion leader to his duties, heading towards the corridors that contained little cave rooms that dotted the massive wall-like pockets. He'd been assigned a room, but he hadn't been inside it since getting here, and now, trudging down the hall beside Sasha, he realized just how exhausted he was.

"Come on," Sasha said, tugging his arm and leading him away from the area he was certain his room was in. "I want to show you something."

Zeke let himself be led down one of several offshoot tunnels, clearly carved out by man rather than the earth herself. These were the larger rooms, where people shared with a significant other or their family or...

Zeke's thoughts froze as Sasha paused in front of a curtained entrance and drew back the black blanket hanging there.

Inside, a light glowed softly over a pile of resting bodies.

Zeke recognized the massive hulk of Edgar, the bear shifter, first, Frank curled under one of the paws bigger than the head of his lynx form. Shira had her back to the bear, her blue eyes open and staring at Zeke and Sasha as they entered.

Mike rolled over next to her, stretching on his back, paws in the air and looking as puppy-like as ever in his sleepy state.

"What's this?" Zeke asked, mind too fatigued and shocked to come up with the answer himself. He knew what it looked like—a pack cave, where the whole pack could sleep together, meet, eat, whatever they needed to do. Together.

What he didn't understand was why.

"We're your pack," Sasha said simply.

*Yeah, boss,* Edgar said, his bear mouth yawning before he settled his head back down.

"Don't call me boss," Zeke said, a smile twitching at the corners of his lips.

*Fine. Alpha,* Edgar huffed.

Shira laughed through the mental connection. *Whether you like it or not, what we said before still stands. We want you to be our alpha. We've taken the bond. You just need to get it in your thick skull that you have a pack standing beside you, and we're not leaving.*

Not trusting his voice, Zeke nodded, glancing into the eyes of each of his new friends. He stripped off his outer layer of clothing, leaving the skin-tight layer underneath, then shifted into his wolf form and nosed and prodded around the pile of dozing shifters until he found his place, right at the center, and curled up.

It felt weird doing this after so long. The last time he'd slept in a pack pile had been Camp Silver Lake, and it had been discouraged by the higher-ups so they hadn't done it often. And not everyone had participated with full trust as they did now, snuggling in closer, their backs pressing into Zeke, a paw nudging him, each one making contact to let him know they were there, they would fight with him, they would fight for him.

Zeke fell into a swift, restful sleep, hope replacing the despair in his mind.

Tomorrow, he would go find Mandi.

Morning in the caves was chaos. Zeke woke to the hum of excitement and terror that permeated the air, passing like a message through the scent of the hormones of those that passed by the pack's cave.

When Zeke stirred, stretching and standing up to step over Sasha and Mike tangled beside him, the rest of the pack woke up.

Mike bounded over to Zeke and licked his face, tail wagging. Zeke barked and nipped at the teenage wolf playfully, before assuming the seriousness of his role.

*Plans have changed for us. We've been given the assignment to seek out and rescue any prisoners Ragranoth might be holding. I suspect they'll be in the White House, if anywhere, now that the Tower is gone. Get some breakfast and line up with the others behind battalion G. We'll go in with them, then split off when the signal is given.*

The others acknowledged the assignment, and most of them shifted into human form and got dressed.

Once breakfast was done, the morning passed in a flurry of activity, each person on a mission of their own as humans arrived in droves and everyone got outfitted with weapons and supplies.

Zeke checked in with his pack. He'd assigned several of them to be in charge of obtaining packs with basic supplies. As a rescue team, he wanted to have food and water and medical supplies to manage anything they ran into.

Before Zeke knew it, he heard Jack's voice over a megaphone connected to a string of loudspeakers set up around the main chamber.

"Listen up, folks! It's time to get this ball rolling. No matter what, stay with your battalion. Protect the person next to you—human or not, we're all in this against the demons, you can solve your petty squabbles if we all survive." He chuckled at that, and some of the crowd responded, laughing or smiling, glancing around at the human strangers now among them. Some of the newly arrived humans had started making friends with the T.R.S. group, but most of them hung back, clinging to their fellow humans and looking at the paranormals with a mixture of hatred, curiosity, and fear on their faces.

"Whatever happens today," Jack continued. "The world will know by our example that it's possible for humans and paranormals to work together, to eat together, to fight together. Remember why we're doing this—to save our world from the demons who would destroy all life and take it for their own."

A cheer went up, even the humans in the back joined in, and Jack started calling out battalion numbers, sending them out of the caves through various exits from the bunker known as Grandma Jean.

When G was called, Zeke called out to his pack and led them out of the darkness of the caves into the storm-ridden streets of a broken D.C.

The battalion didn't march in perfect formation. Instead, they scattered, some in groups or pairs, some walking alone, mimicking what intel-gatherers had brought back to the leaders of the T.R.S.—that there were paranormals responding to Ragranoth's threat from the day before.

They had streamed into the city overnight to present themselves to the demon queen, fearing the demon's threats of death.

Zeke couldn't help staring at the hundreds of paranormals responding to the demon's call. How could this many be willing to pledge themselves into her service? Did they know how likely it was they went to their deaths?

As morbid as it was, Zeke couldn't help but feel grateful for the cover they provided as battalion G blended in with the gathering crowd and marched towards the capital.

Anticipation made him itch to shift into his wolf form and run. It wouldn't have seemed out of place, either, as many of the rogue paranormals around him were in various shifter forms, and some of his own pack had already shifted.

The crowd stopped, compressing and filling the streets between buildings as they moved as a single unit closer to the White House.

A microphone whine echoed through the air. Mike whimpered in anticipation next to Zeke.

*Steady,* Zeke warned through their connection. He checked in with the others scattered nearby through the crowd.

An ethereal voice split the air, singing acapella, the song soaring across the waves of gathered people.

Zeke's face split into a grin as he recognized that voice—Ian, the siren from Camp Silver Lake. He couldn't see the dark-haired man, but his voice had, at times, been a lifeline for Zeke in the naturalization camp. He'd recognize it anywhere.

"It's time, it's time," Ian sang. "It's time to give back what we've been given. It's time to fight for our freedoms."

Magic wove through the lyrics, and any residual fear drained from Zeke's mind and heart, the music invigorating him.

This was the sign. Everyone hoped that when the gathering paranormals heard the siren song, they would join in the fight.

Yells went up around Zeke, and somewhere ahead, the front of the wave agitated. Several explosions punctuated the air.

A terrifying screech broke through the siren song, as if attempting to drown it out. The magical influence lessened, and then Ian increased his volume, the final lyrics ringing out, ending with a single word that the crowd took up as a chant.

"Fight! Fight! Fight!"

The crowd surged forward, and a dozen bird shifters picked up where Ian's song left off, weaving the lingering effects of his siren magic with their own.

Winged demons rose above the throng, diving down and picking people up only to drop them screaming into the writhing crowd.

Spells and guns went off, bright lights and sounds punctuating the air.

*Time to get out of here,* Zeke said to his pack, ducking down a side street with Mike on his tail. Zeke shifted, Mike followed suit, and Sasha and Shira joined in their wolf forms.

Edgar barreled in from another street, Frank at his side hissing, his ears flat.

*What's up?* Zeke asked the lynx.

Edgar laughed. *Oh, Frank doesn't like music much.*

*Music is fine. Just not that punk...rock...whatever that was,* Frank grumbled.

The pack dodged down several streets, wary of demons, but the crowd seemed to have drawn them all to the capitol grounds, where the raven born and her people still sang, attempting to bind the demons' will to their own so they could be killed by the human-paranormal army.

*Head for the White House,* Zeke called to his pack. They ran together, Edgar trailing behind the faster wolves, but Frank stayed with him.

Zeke's paws flew over the 9-ft fence around the White House grounds, coming at the building from its side.

Edgar charged through, crumpling the iron bars like they were toothpicks, his grizzly jaw open wide in a sort of grin.

Zeke barely paused to make sure everyone made it through before taking off at a sprint. He'd expected to find more demons here, but the fighting crowd seemed to have drawn them all off, and the White House stood stark against the dark clouds above, various parts of its facade torn off in chunks and littering the once-lush lawn.

Purple lightning flashed above, giving everything an eerie shadow and for a split second, making Zeke see double.

Sprinting down a hedge-lined path, Zeke came across a utility door. Exactly what he'd hoped for. He shifted into human form and grabbed the handle, but it stopped with a jerk. Locked.

*Allow me,* Edgar said, and everyone backed away to let the grizzly through, including Zeke.

With a roar that nearly burst Zeke's eardrums, Edgar smashed the handle, crumpled the door inward, and wrenched it off its hinges, tossing the metal door across the White House lawn until it landed, its corner embedding it in the lawn like a piece of abstract art.

Edgar grunted and backed up, receiving the howls of celebration that went up around him from the rest of the pack.

Zeke shifted again, using the heightened senses of his wolf form to read the air.

Demons smelled of sulfur and smoke, making Zeke's lips curl up to reveal his teeth.

*Do we go towards the demon smell or away from it?* Zeke asked, looking down the hall ahead and then down the hall to his left.

Sasha joined him at the front of the pack and sniffed. *I say towards. They're probably using the prisoners for something.*

Zeke couldn't withhold his growl at that thought. He hated that she was probably right.

*I say left,* Frank said. *If for no reason other than to be contrary.*

*He probably just wants to say "I told you so" if the rest of us are wrong,* Edgar grumbled. *I say straight.*

*Straight!* Mike barked.

Shira shushed him. *There's no telling who is in here. We don't want to let them on to us. We could split up, you know.*

*All right,* Zeke said. *Edgar, Frank, take Mike with you. Check every door. Call out through the connection when you find something, or if you get into trouble.*

*What are we looking for?* Mike asked, sniffing in circles on the carpeted floor.

*Human smells,* Zeke said. *Emotions, like fear, anger.* He took off down the hall, Mandi's scent drifting into his memory as his nose searched for it at the edge of every door he passed. It was a scent he couldn't have described to anyone else, a scent he knew with every fiber of his being.

The first hall yielded nothing, nor the second. He checked in with the other part of the pack, but they'd found nothing but dust and fading scents and were headed back in their direction.

Zeke's heart pounded the further they explored, and then he found the door to a back stairwell, and it opened with a creak. The lights didn't come on when he stepped down, and he found a light switch on the wall, but when he flipped it nothing happened. Power was out in this part of the building, and not even the glow of a green exit sign could be seen.

Fortunately, his wolf form could see in the dark better than his human one.

*Meet in the east stairwell,* Zeke said, shifting.

*Nearly there,* Edgar said.

For a moment, Zeke wondered if the bear shifter would have trouble with the stairs, but he didn't have time to worry. He bolted down the slippery, vinyl covered stairs, skidding across the linoleum landings one at a time, practically barreling head first down the winding staircase until he reached another door. Sniffing it, it seemed to lead into a parking garage of sorts. Zeke kept going, and as he descended, a singular scent grew sharper.

The scent of her.

Zeke yelped and raced faster, tail wagging like a flag behind him. Sasha and Shira kept pace with him, catching onto his excitement, and knew they were close.

More scents crashed around him, all of them witches or warlocks from what he could tell. Intriguing.

Zeke shifted so fast his bones were still untangling and rearranging when he grabbed the door handle and pulled.

The scents of sulfur, fear, and agony washed over him, plying him with their intensity. His stomach roiled, and he nearly lost his breakfast, but he forced himself to step forward into the empty hall.

The nearly empty hall, that was.

A single demon stood in front of one of the heavy utility doors, each with a small rectangular window. Most of them were dark, including the one the demon guarded.

*Demon,* Zeke warned as Sasha and Shira exited the stairs beside him.

*On it,* Shira growled.

The two gray wolves charged, snarling, and leapt on the demon, ripping at the wings on its back, shredding through the leathery folds of skin, clawing and biting.

Shira took claws in her side, but she barely flinched as she locked her jaws on the demon's neck and bit down.

The demon's thrashing stopped, and it went limp and turned to dust.

*Ugh. Demons taste nasty,* Sasha complained, but her tail wagged as she trotted up to Zeke.

*Good work,* Zeke said, approaching the door. The handle turned, but the door wouldn't open. It was locked by magic, and a thorough search of the floor where the demon had vanished didn't reveal anything that might unlock it. If it had held a key, it was dust along with the demon.

Edgar and the others arrived a few moments later, and even the bear's brute strength didn't make the magic yield.

*Excuse me,* Frank said, sauntering forward and shifting into his human form with a fluid motion. *This is my forte.*

Zeke watched in awe as the lynx shifter cast a spell.

*My mother was a witch,* Frank explained wryly as the glowing teal magic wrapped around the door handle, looking as if it warred with another force at work there. *Step back,* Frank warned.

Everyone complied, and a split second later, the handle exploded, sending metal shrapnel into the wall behind Zeke. Fortunately, he'd ducked at just the right moment.

*Yeesh, a little more warning next time, yeah?* Edgar said, shaking his fur and dropping bits of metal to the floor.

*Sorry,* Frank said, not sounding at all apologetic.

Zeke led the way into the room. The scent of vomit and piss mingled with pure, human terror.

"Hello?" Zeke called.

"Please!" a hoarse voice screamed. "No more! No more! Just kill me!" It was a man, clearly not Mandi.

At Zeke's request, Frank lit a ball of magic in his hand and floated it towards the center of the room, where a balding, middle-aged man lay strapped to an inclined metal table.

He thrashed about at the sight of the glowing ball, but then stopped when his rolling eyes landed on Zeke's human face, and then he started weeping.

"Oh, thank Gawd! You're human!" he cried, straining against his bonds.

In the light of the magic ball, Zeke saw that the man's clothes were crusted with blood and vomit and something else—something silvery and sticky.

"Are there others?" Zeke asked breathlessly as Edgar and Frank worked on the man's bonds.

"There are, yes. I think so. I hear them scream sometimes." The man shuddered, and his eyes went wide and glassy.

Frank helped the man off the table. "We'll get you out of here. Zeke, where do we put the ones we rescue?"

"Someone should stay with him. Try to get his name and give him food and water. The rest, come with me."

Zeke left the room, determination burning in his chest. He shifted and headed down the hall, leaving Edgar to help the man. The others followed Zeke, silently prowling the halls, moving as quickly as they dared.

Eventually, the other demons in the building might catch on to the fact that someone was taking out their fellow guards. They needed to use the element of surprise while they still had it.

The next demon went down as easily as the first, and they freed a woman who only seemed to speak Spanish. Surprisingly,

Mike spoke the language, though a bit haltingly, and was able to translate.

Shira left to escort the woman back to Edgar, and joined them as they moved down the hall, rescuing four more people before their luck ran out.

None of the witches they rescued were Mandi. Zeke began a dialogue with himself, preparing for the possibility that Mandi wasn't here, that she wasn't alive at all. But part of him refused to give up, and he approached the next room with as much hope as the first, Peering around the corner at the squat goblin-like demon with wings three times its height standing sentinel at the door.

*Now!* Zeke barked and shot around the corner, heading for the demon with his killing instinct honed in on the soft areas. This demon had a tortoise-like plating on most of its body, except near the groin and throat.

Zeke leapt up, jaws wide, and the demon reeled around, hissing and gibbering with a beak-like mouth. It jumped so high its head brushed the ceiling, and Zeke sailed beneath it. The demon landed on him, cackling in triumph and clawing at Zeke's hindquarters until Sasha grabbed the demon's head in her jaws and crushed his skull, turning it into ash.

She stood panting and spitting out the vile demon blood. When she looked up, she froze, staring past Zeke at something behind him.

Zeke turned his head slowly, fur on the back of his neck rising before he'd even seen what awaited him.

The sulfur scent in the air had quadrupled, clinging to the inside of Zeke's nose and burning it. He held in a sneeze as his eyes landed on the robed demons filling the hall—six at least. Something was different about these. They were taller, all white as chalk and wearing white robes, crests on their head like crowns. They seemed to be some kind of leaders, their robes reminding Zeke of something a religious priest or priestess might wear.

Zeke bared his teeth. *To me!* he called to his pack, pulling on them with the alpha summons. Frank and Mike, who had stayed behind to help the last room's occupant, responded with a howl and a growl that Zeke heard with his ears and in his mind. They would come as fast as they could, but they might be too late.

He braced himself in an attack position at the front, but Sasha and Shira passed him.

*We'll hold them here,* Shira said.

*Go find your Mandi,* Sasha added.

*I can't leave you two to deal with these demons on your own,* Zeke insisted.

*We won't be alone for long,* Sasha said, and as if in reply a roar shook the hall, making the demons glance away from the wolves in front of them.

Sasha and Shira attacked.

Zeke dodged and squeezed past the demon priests, feeling a set of claws rake at his back. He slipped out of the demon's grasp and bolted down the hall, blind with adrenaline and worry for his pack and Mandi.

To his shock, none of the demons followed him, and then he heard the demons' cries as his pack crashed into them, and he smiled to himself.

*Give 'em hell, guys.*

No one responded, but Zeke felt them in his mind. Knowing his pack would follow once they could, Zeke lifted his nose to the air and, for the first time, caught a whiff of the scent that filled his dreams every night—the scent that to him, meant he was closer to home than ever before.

Mandi.

# CHAPTER FORTY

## TYSON

ON THE ROOF OF a nearby building, Tyson gazed across the capitol grounds in awe and dismay. Demons, humans, and paranormals fought, explosions rocking the ground and making the building beneath Tyson vibrate.

His hand squeezed into a fist, remembering how it had felt to hold Harper's hand. Now, she flew in the air, wielding her Songs like spears, dropping demons like flies as she and her team of bird shifters made their way towards Ragranoth.

Wherever the bird shifters passed, singing their ethereal tones, the demons above and below froze, as if paralyzed. Anyone nearby would attack with renewed vigor, and clouds of demon ash puffed into the air.

As soon as the bird shifters passed, however, the demons unfroze, as if the song could only reach so far.

Tyson's heart clenched tighter the closer Harper drew towards Ragranoth.

The demon stood at the edge of the vortex of darkness where the Tower had once risen. The vortex had grown in size, and lightning shot both into it and out of it, creating a flickering tornado of crackling power that even from this distance, tingled against Tyson's skin—an almost painful prickle accompanied by a sense of death.

The bridge was nearly complete.

Ragranoth stood in a pool of blood, her demons bringing paranormals to her. She drained them of magic, an invisible line connecting her to the portal bridge behind her, all the energy she drew going into the bridge she was creating. After sucking out the magic, Ragranoth slit each person's throat and tossed them in a growing heap of bodies.

Tyson stood on a building almost a mile away, opening portals for those he'd called the night before.

Harper was relieved, no doubt, that Tyson wasn't in the thick of it yet, but as he concentrated on the next set of locations he'd been given to portal people from, he knew that time of relative safety was drawing to an end.

He'd drawn some attention from the demons in the sky and on the ground. Harper had taken out every demon that attempted to fly for him for as long as she could, but she was out of reach now, closer to Ragranoth than before where the demons flew thicker to prevent her passing, and she couldn't circle back to stop the stragglers headed for Tyson.

Tyson breathed deep and took a seat, dropping his chin to his chest and drawing strength from his core. He'd gone so deep into his magic by now that he felt the line of his ancestors, male and female, all the way back to the first dreamwalker blessed by the gods to walk among men. With the strength and intuition of a thousand, Tyson opened three portals at once.

Two figures slithered through the first one, joined on either side by a veritable army of slithering, winding serpent women and men.

"Tyson!" The familiar sound of his cousin's voice made his eyes fly open. He nearly lost control of the left portal, but he held on, not standing to greet the green-scaled serpent woman that approached him with a familiar man at her side.

"Becca. Avaan," Tyson said.

Becca's tail morphed to legs, and she knelt down, embracing him. "I can't believe this is real. I mean, of course it's real, we're here, and you opened those portals and it's amazing, but I can't believe it."

Tyson couldn't believe she was there, either. He hadn't heard from her since they'd gone their separate ways when she left to find a cure for the Lamia curse. Apparently, she'd failed to a degree, since she was still a snake woman. But Avaan...

Tyson turned his attention to the serpentine man, a coiling black tail in place of his legs.

"The tables appear to have turned," Tyson said, looking pointedly at the man's tail.

Avaan laughed, then smiled at Becca. "What can I say? She brings out the best in me."

Becca shifted back into her serpent form, her lithe serpent body curling into Avaan's a moment before she turned her attention to the horde of demons fighting the rebel armies below.

"Where do you need us?" she asked, gesturing to the forty or so lamia gathered on the roof.

Tyson let the portals close when it seemed like all the people had made it through, then stood, dusting off his pants, and pointed towards Ragranoth.

"That's your goal. Get to the demon queen, kill her or distract her so the raven songs can bind her."

Becca nodded, her blonde ponytail swinging behind her. She grabbed Avaan's hand and gazed at him, something unspoken passing between them, and then she turned to her people.

"Attack the white demon and stop the sacrifices. Do not attack any humans or other shifters," Becca said. And then she led the slithering army down the side of the building, their serpent forms somehow finding things to hold on to, until they ran into demons crawling their way up.

Tyson grimaced. His time had run out. He glanced towards where he'd last seen Harper in the sky, and his heart nearly stopped. He couldn't see her through the cloud of flying demons that surrounded her team of bird shifters. Tyson watched as long as he could, straining his eyes, and then he realized if he wanted a chance at seeing Harper again, he had to haul butt off this building.

Breathing deep, he opened a new window in the air and stepped through, walking into the astral realm. In the sea-green tunnel, the walls seemed too thin, almost translucent, and he realized with a start that he could still see the battle happening in D.C.

The realms were blending.

He walked out of the other end of the portal to the right of the swirling vortex at the edge of the fray near Ragranoth where the demons were the thickest.

The bear of the arctic roared out of him, and massive paws instead of feet hit the pavement in front of him as Tyson stormed out onto the battlefield, leaving trails of demon ash in his wake.

Tyson felt the battle cries of his thousand ancestors, their hearts beating as one in his chest. Pressure built inside of him, bursting forth as a roar that sent a stream of light into the sky.

The aurora borealis shot through the dark storm clouds, shredding them with shifting lights of white, blue, green, and even a brilliant reddish pink. The light flowed like rivers, shooting for the swirling vortex.

Tyson's jaw finally closed, aching slightly, and he watched in awe as the power of his ancestors cut through Ragranoth.

The demon screamed and whirled around, searching the crowd for whoever had interrupted her ritual.

Tyson swatted an attacking demon away with one blow of his paw, sending the monster to hell in a cloud of ash. As it cleared, Ragranoth's glowing violet eyes landed on him and gleamed with hunger. Her furious screech rent the air, and then the glowing eyes of a hundred demons turned on Tyson. As one, the demons left their individual fights, sprinting, crawling, flying towards Tyson.

They were on him in an instant, claws digging into his fur. He turned dozens into ash with his claws and jaws, but there were too many, and with their combined strength they dragged him forward.

Towards Ragranoth and her rivers of blood.

# CHAPTER FORTY-ONE

## HARPER

THE AURORA LIGHTS SHOT through the cloud of the demons swarming around Harper and through the gap; she caught a glimpse of something huge and white being dragged towards where Ragranoth stood on her bloody platform.

The demon queen shrieked orders at her hoard in a language Harper didn't understand, clearly agitated. She had stopped all the other sacrifices while she waited for the white form—a bear shifter, Harper realized—to be brought to her.

A polar bear shifter with the light of the aurora reflecting in his coat.

Harper's song cut off as her heart sank. *No, no, no!*

Quinn flew by, catching her by the arm. "We need your voice!"

Harper shook her head, unable to speak, and yanked her arm from his. He looked where she was looking, and his expression tightened. He motioned towards the other bird shifters, making a line with his arm straight for the path that had been cleared through the demon swarm, a straight path to Ragranoth.

"Fly!" Quinn screamed, and the small contingency of bird shifters swooped down and through the now-closing gap.

Harper led the way, Quinn close on her tail. Water streamed from her eyes in the cold wind that blew past her.

The muscles in her abs and shoulders screamed at the abuse, but Harper pushed as fast as she could.

She had to reach Tyson before Ragranoth got her claws on him, before she stole his magic and put it into the portal, and...

A raven shifter swooped in front of Harper, the side of her head matted and bloodied.

Harper pulled up to prevent herself from crashing into the woman, wings jerking back. She flipped end over end, then righted herself. Quinn had already caught up with the raven shifter, and they both glanced back to Harper.

"Harper, watch out!" Quinn yelled as a white, flying demon crashed into her, sending her reeling through the sky.

Harper drew the knife Charlie had given her as soon as she righted herself, slashing the air as the demon lunged for her.

The knife missed, and the demon snapped its beak at her arm, the tip cutting through her skin.

The demon grabbed her wings, and they tumbled through the sky, falling towards the waves of demons and mortals fighting below.

Harper kicked at the demon, desperately trying to free herself. She jerked her head up, eyes scanning the sky for Anna. She had to tell her. Had to get to her before it was too late. Where had she gone?

The demon punched Harper in the face, making her see stars.

Harper adjusted her grip on her dagger and plunged it into the demon's ribcage, pulled it out, and rammed it in again.

The demon screamed, and its grip slackened as it dropped away from Harper, who tumbled closer to the ground, finally snapping her wings open and climbing again.

She still couldn't see Anna through the bird shifters fighting flying demons above. Was she one of them? Fighting with the flock?

A single figure darted across the stormy sky, like an arrow shot towards the portal to the demon realm.

"Anna!" Harper screamed, pumping her wings as hard and fast as they would go. Her lungs and muscles burned, telling her to slow down, but she couldn't. Not when her mother was flying to her death and the destruction of them all.

Anna glanced back one time, at the edge of the vortex of clouds above and the swirling aether below. She gave Harper a sad smile, then shot forward, flying faster than Harper knew possible.

Harper's wings nearly gave out as she strained forward, wishing, hoping that she could go just a little faster, fly a little harder, scream a little louder, but it wasn't enough. She was too late.

She watched in horror as Anna dove into the center of the portal, giving herself up to death to save the world for her children.

A world that was now doomed because of her.

Harper's blood ran cold, and her eyes went to Ragranoth, whose claws were buried in Tyson's side. Ribbon-like streams of aurora magic flowed out of him, past Ragranoth's ecstatic face, flowing into the swirling dark portal behind her.

A thunderclap shook the air, and the darkness of the portal flowed to the sides, opening a hole in the center that looked like a reflection of the night sky, except the stars were red and none of the constellations familiar.

The bridge had opened.

Ragranoth drew her claws from Tyson, cutting off the flow of magic, and let out an exultant scream. The demons all around her let out chittering, growling cheers of their own.

Harper squeezed her eyes shut. They couldn't have failed. This couldn't be happening. Anna was gone, and Tyson...

Harper's eyes shot open. Tyson was still alive, forgotten by Ragranoth in her celebration of the portal's finalization.

Quinn, now slightly ahead of Harper, landed first. He wrapped his arm around Ragranoth's throat, yanking her back from the edge of the bridge to the abyss.

The demon's claws scrabbled at his arm, but Quinn held on, and he opened his mouth and sang.

Harper landed next to Tyson, crawling forward and shoving aside the fur on his neck to feel for his pulse.

She couldn't find it. Oh gods above, why couldn't she find it?

Quinn shouted and Harper's head shot up. Ragranoth held him by the throat, raising him in the air above the bloody ground, her too-wide mouth a viscious slash in her face.

"I've won, you flying rat. Join me or die." Her tongue flicked out and licked Quinn's cheek.

Quinn replied with the first bars of the Song of Persuasion, and Ragranoth shrieked and thrust him away from her. Quinn flew thirty feet across the blood-soaked ground, hitting the pavement with a sickening crunch.

"Quinn!" Harper screamed, and she stood to go to him just as a clawed hand wrapped around her middle, yanking her back. Harper gasped as the claws cut into her, her anguish more for Quinn than her own pain. She thrashed, beating her wings in the demon's face, kicking at its stomach, slamming her head back into its face until it dropped her.

She scrambled to her feet and ran for Ragranoth, no plan in her mind except revenge for those she loved. She jumped, mouth open wide to sing something, anything, but Ragranoth turned at the last moment and swatted Harper away like she was nothing more than a bug.

Harper hit the pavement and skidded across the blood-soaked surface for several feet before stopping, one wing beneath her getting coated in the sticky substance.

She staggered to her feet, her right wing dragging awkwardly alongside her. It hung at the wrong angle, and Harper realized she couldn't feel it. The wing was numb for an instant, and she stared, uncomprehending, until the horrible reality struck her.

Her wing had broken.

Her left wing shivered so violently, Harper reached out and grabbed it, anchoring herself to it.

And then the pain of her broken wing hit, flowing through her with such force it brought her to her knees, a scream on her lips.

"That's more like it," Ragranoth said.

Harper bit off her anguished cry and, panting through the pain, turned to face the demon queen.

Ragranoth grinned too widely with too many teeth. "There's someone I'd like you to meet. After all, you're the one who gave him that first dose of power with that little deal you made. All the memories of your dear brother. Love is such an underestimated power. I have you to thank for waking him up."

She waved her arm towards the portal as a clawed hand larger than a bus reached up from that endless pit of red stars and grasped the cement, cracking it. Another hand emerged, white as Ragranoth's chalky skin but ten times larger.

The whole air trembled, and the ground shook like an earth-quake as a monstrous demon dragged itself from the portal, its moon-like eyes glowing silver.

Harper staggered back in shock. Seventy feet tall, muscled with a bull-like head, lion paws for feet and a viscious scorpion tail, the demon of all demons emerged, stepping on either side of Ragranoth and dwarfing her.

It bent down, sniffing at Ragranoth, who rested her claws across the giant's cheek almost tenderly. It rumbled something in their language, and Ragranoth's laugh pealed across the bat-tlefield like the toll of a death bell.

"Meet Issachar, consort of the Autarch. You might know him better as the form he was trapped in thousands of years ago, the Beryllium Orb. Or as his most recent alter ego posing as the Eternal Source."

Harper's lungs didn't seem able to fill fully as she gasped, staring up at the demon taller than most of the nearby buildings still standing.

"Isn't he magnificent?" Ragranoth said, cackling with plea-sure. "He's here to make the transition go more smoothly. And it's all thanks to you. To your whole family, really. If you hadn't made that first bargain and broken him free of the orb, and your mother hadn't given her life thinking it would close the portal rather than open it enough for him to come through, well, we wouldn't be having this conversation, and he wouldn't be here in all his glory." the demon queen's eyes gleamed with pleasure.

Issachar's bellow shook the ground as he swept his massive hand across the battlefield. Demons took to the air or scrambled for cover, some of them getting caught in the giant's blow, but most of the bodies it swept up were mortal, getting crushed under the huge hand.

Harper sank to the ground, afraid to look at Quinn or Tyson for fear of realizing they were both dead. She couldn't do this alone. She had nothing left. Her chest felt hollowed out, no Songs left to sing. She glanced at the sky, where the ribbons of aurora light had been swallowed up by the dark clouds crackling with violet electricity.

Not a single bird shifter remained in the sky.

"Now we will truly begin to make this world our own," Ragranoth cried as Issachar scooped the demon queen into his hand. He stretched to his full height and walked forward, stepping over Harper, wading into the battle and scattering or crushing fighters wherever the demon walked.

Harper slumped forward, catching herself in a half-kneel before she hit the ground, her head bowed. She had no weapons. She couldn't fly. She was almost certain she couldn't Sing.

Demons streamed past her, ignoring her, not considering her enough of a threat to even bother killing. She might as well be dead.

A flash of red darted at the corner of Harper's vision, and she glanced up warily, prepared for another horror, but to her shock, a fox wove between the demons' legs and trotted up to her, panting.

The fox shifted into a naked, red-haired woman whose amber eyes met Harper's.

"Reya?" Harper said, confused. "But you were in the holding cells...how did you...? Why...?"

Reya shrugged. "I escaped. Came along to see which side might win. Saw you get your asses handed to you."

Harper's jaw tightened. "You betrayed us to the demons. You already picked your side."

"See, that's what I thought too," Reya said, standing and holding a hand out to Harper. "And then I saw the humans that joined your insane fight, and I saw Tyson charge the demon queen and basically give his life to save the world, and I realized I wasn't actually willing to let the world burn to watch him die. It was…worse than I had imagined."

"You couldn't have decided that sooner?" Harper hissed.

There was no hint of malice in Reya's face as she stared at Harper, hand still extended.

Harper stared at it but didn't take it yet. "I don't believe you've forgiven him. Just remember this—you might hate him, but somebody loves him. And if, when this is over, you so much as look at him, I will hunt you for the rest of your days."

"Sounds fair enough," Reya said.

Harper clasped her hand, then pointed at the giant, white form of the Issachar, consort to the demon queen. "Now, what can we do against that?"

"Think outside the box," Reya said, grinning. She held out her other hand and a ten-foot spear made of blue light flashed into it like a bolt of lightning, just as it had in the astral realm.

Harper gaped. "How'd you do that?"

Reya pointed at the gaping hole in the earth that led to the lowest abyss.

"When Ragranoth connected our realms, she really ought to have considered more carefully what would happen. The rules of earth no longer apply—welcome to the new level of the astral realm," Reya said, spinning the double-ended spear in her hand, then throwing it at the nearest demon, which screeched and burst into ash.

The spear recalled into Reya's hand with a snap.

Harper shook her head. "Not only do I not know how to do that, but I'm injured." She gestured at her wing.

Reya sucked in a breath. "Yikes, that looks like it hurts. But we're in the astral realm now, Harper. Imagine yourself a new one."

"How?" Harper asked.

"Will it. Think of what you want, hold it in your mind, and it will appear." Reya glanced to the side, distracted by the demons that charged at her. She grinned wickedly and tossed her spear up, as if weighing it in her hand, then nodded at Harper. "Go on, then. I'll try to hold these guys off. But I expect you to join me. I can't fight the whole hoard by myself."

Harper gritted her teeth as Reya ran off. She sat back on her heels, clenching her fists in her lap, and tried to think of what Tyson would tell her.

Clear your mind. Deepen your breathing. Focus.

She focused on her wing, on the wrongness of it, and willed it to be made right.

Something tingled at the base of her wing. Harper closed her eyes, concentrating on the sensation flowing through her body.

Strong. Unbroken. Fly.

The pain vanished. Shocked, Harper's eyes flew open. A teal glow illuminated the ground in front of her, and as she stretched her wings to either side, she caught sight of her left one, the feathers black as normal, and the right side, the feathers glowing a brilliant aquamarine color.

Harper laughed, flapping the two wings, and ran forward, launching herself into the air. She imagined herself a sword, and it appeared, flickering to life in her hands. Like the wing on her back, it felt like an extension of herself, and she had to hold both in her mind or she knew they would cease to exist. She rose above the hoards, eyes fixed on Issachar's back.

She gave a battle cry, aimed her astral weapon between the demon consort's shoulder blades, and surged through the air on wings made of light and sheer force of will.

# CHAPTER FORTY-TWO

## MANDI

THE STEEL DOOR OPENED with a slam, waking Mandi from her fitful slumber. She'd had a rare moment of rest after the demon priests and priestesses had finished their rituals for the night. They'd remembered to give her water and feed her, not near enough, but enough to keep her alive. They wanted her alive for their rituals, to use her as a living portal, and the door opening meant they had returned.

Mandi found a scrap of will to live and used it to scream at the top of her lungs, begging, pleading that they not gut her magic again, not allow another demon to violate her essence.

"Mandi?" a familiar voice croaked.

Footsteps drew near.

Mandi refused to believe it could be true. He was dead. He wasn't here, wasn't seeing her like this, blood and vomit caked into her skin and hair. She laughed, then convulsed with sobs.

Fingers pressed against the faint pulse in her neck, then a large, soft hand slid beneath her head, cradling it.

"Mandi, can you hear me?"

Zeke. Her precious, beloved Zeke.

Mandi wanted to open her eyes and prove that she was right. She begged her mind to work the mechanisms that would uncover her eyes, but she'd grown so used to squeezing them shut to avoid seeing the atrocities that she had helped bring forth that she couldn't bring herself to do it.

Instead, she wept.

Zeke didn't ask her any more questions. Instead, he got to work. He sawed through the straps on her lower and upper legs and over her stomach and arms. The bonds fell away, and her muscles screamed as he helped her off the table.

Mandi fell into him, unable to hold herself up. She didn't know how long it had been. Maybe only hours, maybe days, maybe weeks. She only knew that hundreds of demons had exited their abyss through her body, and she felt completely drained of all strength.

Zeke scooped his arm under her legs and carried her.

"What happened?" Mandi asked.

"I'm getting you out of here," Zeke said.

Mandi's eyes finally peeled open, blinking blearily under flickering fluorescent lights. She flopped her head against his chest and forced her neck to bend so she could see him.

She saw him.

Her Zeke.

He was real, and he had come for her.

# CHAPTER FORTY-THREE

## TYSON

TYSON LAY STILL ON the pavement, life-force and magic draining out of his body. It wasn't completely gone, but the wounds Ragranoth had left somehow kept pulling more. It would be gone soon, and he would be dead.

He wished he had the energy to open his eyes and see what had happened to Harper. He'd heard Ragranoth declare the rise of her consort and Harper cry out in agony. She was hurt. She needed his help, but he could hardly move, much less fight.

He felt the barrier between the astral realm and the physical plane diminish until the two became one, and energy began to flow into him instead of out.

And then, he left his damaged body and found it easier than ever to connect with his astral form, though it was weak due to the magic Ragranoth had drained out of him.

The Eternal Source—the real one—existed somewhere. Something had created the universe and all the beings in it. If he went the proper way through the astral realm—all nine levels of it, rather than a shortcut—would he get to petition the true Source of all things?

He had so little magic left, he doubted it, but it was the only thing that he could do.

Tyson flew towards the portal in the ground and flew through it, straight into the sea of crimson stars.

The world flipped, disorienting him until he managed to right himself and get his bearings.

The sky of crimson stars was above him, now, and he floated over a vast ocean so dark, he couldn't see where it began and ended. He knew it was an ocean because of the familiar shushing of water, and the gleam of the stars off its choppy surface.

As he hovered far above the black surface of the water, shapes emerged and flew through the portal into the stars and vanished—demons being called from the deep by their queen, many of them larger than the demons there now.

The biggest ones, the ones weighed down by the most darkness, made buoyant by their master's newfound power, were getting through to the physical plane. They would wreak havoc and turn the earth into a new hell.

Tyson drew a sigil in the air, smaller than usual—a symbol that gave him light but also shielded him from view. Demons flew past him faster and faster, until hundreds were in the air around him, flying into the portal above.

He had to act. The longer he remained here, the more the darkness rubbed at what remained of his magic, tainting it in its weakened state.

How did he get out of this place?

Tyson looked up, knowing that the sea of stars above wouldn't help him do anything except return to the physical plane being ravaged by demons.

The astral planes were places of intention and will. Tyson reached out a hand, focusing his intention to open a portal to the only place he knew there was someone who might know what happened to the real Eternal Source.

A glowing orange line followed his fingertips, and a section of the abyss fell away, revealing a different sea in a space between planes, where craggy cliffs were slashed by vicious waves and even more vicious bird-women resided.

Tyson plunged through, zipping the entrance to the abyss behind him. On the other side, his spirit form immediately plummeted to the ground, forced to abide by the laws that existed in this plane, of which gravity was one.

He slammed into the ground much harder than he would have before, unable to catch himself with his magic. The reservoir that burned inside him was strangely empty. He could hardly feel his ancestors. How far could he go before it emptied completely?

He pushed himself to standing and forced one foot to follow the other along the narrow cliff. He got nearly to the other side before the harpies appeared, screeching their displeasure at his presence.

"Lyvaphe!" Tyson called out, addressing the tallest harpy with the smoky gray wings.

"You!" The harpy replied, yellow eyes flashing. "We warned you what would happen if you returned to this place. We are no longer bound to ferry souls on to the Eternal Source. They find their own way."

"You tricked us," Tyson shouted, not bothering to choose his words carefully. The harpy's beaks and claws could shred a soul, he knew, but he was doomed regardless if this failed, so he didn't have much motivation to be political.

The dark-feathered harpy with the strange markings on her feathered face narrowed her eyes. "He has no respect for our bargain. I say we dash him against the rocks now."

The third harpy, with brown in her wings, jumped up and down, flapping and squealing. "Oooh! Yes! Red, I want to see red!" She cackled and leapt at Tyson, but Lyvaphe held her back.

"No, Mynera. Xynis. We are still bound by our honor. No Song can free us from that. If he accuses us, let him defend his accusation. Then we may pass judgment." She hissed at the end, the feathers on the back of her head standing on end in a crest.

"When we came before, we bargained that you would allow us to pass into the presence of the Eternal Source. But the portal beyond your nest took us into the den of a demon posing as the most high, and that demon now walks freely on Earth, ravaging the mortals there, seeking the death and destruction of all."

Xynis was the first to start laughing, her high-pitched laughter like the call of a deranged bird. Mynera joined her, and even Lyvaphe seemed amused.

"Little mortal. You think we can control what goes on beyond?" Lyvaphe said, her beaked mouth smirking.

"Some keeper of the entrance you were. You didn't even know that which you guarded. How long have you been sending souls to the demon Issachar? I'd wager that you knew what you were doing, hoping the demon would free you once he was freed. In fact, I'd wager you had a bargain." Tyson glared at the harpies, who each became very interested in a different part of the sky, sea, and ground. "It is you who broke our bargain, and I call upon your honor, the honor you claim to be bound by, to make recompense."

"And how would you have us do that?" Xynis snapped. "We are no longer the keepers of the entrance to the True Source."

Tyson crossed the arms of his astral form. "No, you're not. But you still know how to get there."

The three harpies glanced anxiously at each other until Lyvaphe snapped.

"Oh, very well! I will take him. Hold tight, mortal, or you'll be dashed on the rocks." The gray-feathered harpy woman ran towards Tyson, and he ducked, assuming her talons would dig into his astral form and that would be the end of him. But instead, they closed around his arms and lifted him from the ground, pulling him into the sky.

Lyvaphe flew across the ocean for miles until the rocky cliffs where her kind nested disappeared, and an island shaped like a spiral came into view.

If Tyson stared too long, the spiral started to move, the surface shifting and changing so no two parts were the same, except for the center, which always remained the same.

Lyvaphe flew over that center stone and dropped Tyson.

Screaming, Tyson fell for an eternity, passing through the image of a flat stone outcropping that had been the center of the island, spiraling down through miles of rock, water, pockets of gas, magma, into water again, then through a mist that coated his skin and burned like fire.

Something caught him. He had the sensation of being held, but not by arms or any substance he could recognize. As far as he could tell, he hung suspended in a nothing that stretched in all directions. He had no sense of form, and he could not see. It wasn't darkness, just as it wasn't light. He no longer seemed to have eyes.

"Mortals are not allowed here before their time," a single, clear voice said.

It sounded familiar and strange at the same time, and the sound of it made Tyson want to cry, but he didn't have a voice, or tear ducts for that matter. He'd been reduced to just his soul, hovering in this strange sphere between time and all physical and mental planes.

"I will unform and reshape you. You will forget this place, you will forget me," the voice said, as if to itself.

With every ounce of will he possessed, Tyson shouted at the being. No sound came out, but there was a sense of pause from whatever entity this was.

"No? Intriguing. You know, whatever your distress, I assure you someone has gone through worse. You are meant to go to the physical plane, build upon your essence, and return to become formless once more, mixed into the aether of all kind and shaped again into something new, thus having everlasting life," the being said, sounding pleased, as if it had come up with this itself. Perhaps it had.

Tyson tried to form words with his will again, this time finding it easier, though it made the center of him ache, and he realized he had to have some sense of himself if he could feel that, even if he couldn't use any of his physical senses.

*Are you the one they call the Eternal Source?* Tyson's voice had no volume, it sounded like a thought that he projected.

The important thing was the being seemed to hear him.

"I am the True Source. The Eternal Source died. I took his place, forming the formless and unforming them again, always adding to the Source well at the center of all existence. It grows, and we grow, and life continues. These demons you think of, even they are forms that become formless, and those that die at their hand simply return to the void of the formed, to be made new."

*No one will have anything to be born to if the physical plane becomes a new abyss,* Tyson argued. *That's what is happening right now. The demons will claim the realm of earth for their own. We have to stop them.*

The sensation of amusement drifted over Tyson. "We must stop them? We? I do not intervene. I am not a god like the gods you mortals invent to assuage your fears and place your blame, invest your pride and grant power over you. I am part of the Source. All emerge from the Source, and all return in their time. Even those that claim immortality eventually make the journey here to be reformed. Reformation is nothing to be afraid of."

Tyson's entire being trembled. It sounded so much like a naturalization campaign the government had launched years ago to get the paranormals to turn themselves in. *Reformation is everything to be afraid of,* Tyson shouted. *Reformation is death!*

"So melodramatic. That is how you were created. Sometimes I forget how amusing you mortals are with your limited sense of self. Something you say does trouble me, however. And it has to do with balance. If all things are reformed at once, we will have to start over. I do not wish to start over. What we have created is good."

*Yes, it's good,* Tyson said, eagerly latching onto anything positive. *Can you help us?*

"The balance has to be restored somehow. What would you have me do?" the True Source said.

Tyson wished he could palm his face. How could a being as powerful as a god not know what to do in a situation like this? Or was this a test?

"Test. Yes, I like that word. Quest is even better, but we don't have time for a quest. So, a test it will be. Are you ready?"

Tyson hadn't even answered the True Source's question about what he would have them do.

"I formed you. I know you. I know what you would say. Asking was merely a matter of formality," the True Source explained.

"And listening to my answer wasn't?" Tyson said out loud. He issued a string of weird sounds, testing out his vocals. They existed again. He existed again! In fact, he stood fully formed on the flat stone at the center of the spiral island, alone.

"Hello?" he shouted, seeking the True Source. They did not respond, and Tyson stood perplexed for a moment, wondering what he was meant to do.

*Think it, and it shall be done, champion,* the True Source said into his mind.

Tyson glanced at his hands for some reason. They just looked like his regular hands, or rather, the hands of his astral form, but there was a sense of power surging through his system, foreign and endless.

He was channeling the True Source.

# CHAPTER FORTY-FOUR

## Harper

HARPER DROVE HER GLOWING astral sword into Issachar's spine back all the way to the hilt. Steam hissed from the wound, scalding Harper's hands and face. She reeled back in the air, screaming, and dropped her sword, and with it, the will that had created her new wing.

She spiraled towards the ground, her injured wing flapping uselessly, the wind jerking at it.

Closing her eyes as the ground approached, Harper reached out to Tyson, wishing she could see him one last time before she died, hoping that somewhere in the great beyond, their souls might meet again.

Harper's fall slowed, then stopped. She opened her eyes one at a time; she'd stopped only twenty feet from the ground. Her breath came from her in gasps, and she looked up at what had caught her, and nearly passed out.

A polar bear the size of a mountain in the same colors as the aurora borealis shone in the now-clear night sky. The bear grunted, its warm breath cascading down on her.

the wing to knit itself together momentarily with the magic swimming in the air.

Once she had a wing, she formed a sword. It stopped halfway through, and she had to drop it, chest heaving with the strain. When she tried again, she formed a smaller weapon, a glowing knife that fit nicely in her hand. She'd have to go close range, but it would do.

Harper drew in a deep breath and gathered as much energy as she could, riding Reya's flaming back as the fire fox worked with the aurora bear to drive Issachar closer and closer to the gaping sea of crimson stars at the center of the capital.

Bracing herself, Harper flared her wings and sprinted up the fox's head, launching into the air with the knife outstretched.

Gouts of steam erupted at random from the demon consort's massive body where Tyson's claws and Reya's jaws cut through demon skin as if it was made of water and air wrapped in skin. Harper dodged a geyser of steam as she flew, straining for the demon's shoulder.

Her wing flickered, and she dipped dangerously to one side. Reeling awkwardly, Harper grabbed Issachar's arm as it flew past her. She clung to the swinging limb until her astral wing stabilized, then leapt off and flew the twenty yards to the demon's shoulder, landing in a crouch.

Ragranoth's eyes opened, and she hissed, baring her multiple rows of teeth.

"Accept, mortal, that you've lost!" Ragranoth said, beginning to peel herself from the place where she'd attached to her consort's neck.

"Not while I still have breath in my body," Harper said, standing, swaying as the demon giant stumbled.

She sprinted across the broad shoulder, jumping around the bumps and small spikes dotting the demon's skin. She yelled and jumped for Ragranoth, trying to reach the demon queen before she had fully separated.

Reya circled the demon, darting behind him and blocking his path as he stepped backward.

Issachar tripped, falling over the giant fox.

Harper glimpsed the red stars in the portal below, and her wings snapped out, catching her. She flapped twice, driving herself forward with enough momentum that her astral knife caught Ragranoth in the throat and sliced down through her chest to her sternum.

Then, Harper twisted, flapping hard to escape the pull of the bridge to the abyss. A clawed hand caught her injured wing, and Harper screamed, wrenching against the demon hand threatening to pull her down.

With a horrifying snap and blinding white pain that lanced down Harper's back, she was freed, but her vision wavered between light and darkness, staring at an aurora sky as her astral wing vanished and she went limp.

A mighty paw caught her before she fell into the abyss, dragging her away from the crimson stars and back to the physical realm. She sobbed with relief and the pain in her wing.

Then she felt herself rocked, and her blurry, darkening vision caught sight of two dark eyes that held the universe inside, and then the night closed in, and she lost all sense of self and time.

# CHAPTER FORTY-FIVE

## TYSON

TYSON KEPT HIS EYES closed as long as he could after he woke up. Everything hurt, and he was still processing the fact that he had woken up after channeling the power of an omnipotent being and getting turned into a god-bear.

When he finally did crack his eyes, it was in a dark, silent room, where he lay on a couch with his entire torso bandaged, an IV drip attached to his arm, and two people curled up in an armchair beside him.

"Becca?" Tyson murmured groggily.

The woman stirred, pulling her blonde hair out of her face. She had a bandage on her head and one of her arms, and her t-shirt was covered with blood, but otherwise she seemed fine.

"You're awake!" Becca said, sitting straight upright so Avaan, still dozing on her shoulder, fell off and woke with a start.

"*Amira*, must you always move with such force?" he moaned, tugging the blanket further up his body.

Becca stood, tossing the blanket off her own legs and crossing to Tyson, ignoring her love's protests.

"How are you feeling? You've been out longer than I thought."

"How long? What day is it? Are the demons gone?" Tyson asked, moving to sit up. The motion pulled at his wounds beneath the bandages, and he winced, settling back in a semi-upright position against the arm of the couch.

He jerked again. "Harper!"

Becca pressed firmly against his shoulders. "Lay down and I'll tell you everything. Well, everything I know, anyway. I'm sure there are others that want to know what you know, because you seem to know more than anyone else about what happened."

"I have no idea what you're talking about," Tyson said, relaxing slightly as Becca propped a pillow behind him.

She raised her eyebrows. "Really? So that massive aurora polar bear spirit thing wasn't you? Oh, must have been another dreamwalker I know," she joked.

Tyson rolled his eyes and fidgeted with the blanket in his lap. "Okay, I might know something about that. But you first."

"Harper is fine. Well, fine in the best sense of the word, which is that she's alive. She's in a different room, receiving similar treatment. She lost a lot more blood than you." Becca's smile faltered, and she glanced away from Tyson.

"I have to see her," Tyson said, tossing the blanket off and earning himself another wince.

"Not so fast, Romeo," Becca said. "You're not strong enough, and she's not awake yet. I have strict orders to get some food in you, water, meds, and then the doctor in residence will clear you for movement. Those aren't paper cuts on your chest, and your magic also took a hit, which apparently can make your healing much slower than normal. So, settle down and be a good patient, and I will tell you the minute Harper wakes up. Okay?"

Tyson reluctantly nodded and settled back into the couch, letting Becca fuss over him, checking his bandages, changing them out, and waking Avaan to fetch Tyson some food.

Tyson mowed through the canned chicken gravy over rice with canned vegetables on the side, along with a Jell-O cup that almost made him feel like he was in a real hospital. The building being used as a sort of emergency first-aid center clearly wasn't a hospital, but they must have picked the least damaged building in the vicinity, some sort of office.

Once he finished, he plied Becca with his questions all over again, and she finally told him what had happened after the god-bear disappeared and he re-entered his body. The last thing Tyson remembered was catching Harper in his too-large paw over that yawning abyss filled with red stars, and then the sensation of falling.

The conversation and banter between Becca and Avaan was a good distraction from the grief that hovered in Tyson's awareness. Charlie and Anna were dead, and thousands more innocents from both the human and paranormal sides. It would take a lot of time to sort through the rubble and rebuild, and some things couldn't be fixed so easily.

He fell again in his dreams that night while he slept, fell in a waterfall of red glowing stars and aurora lights until he landed on the scratchy carpet in his pitch-dark room, sweating and breathing hard as if he'd run a mile.

His chest ached, but he seemed to be in one piece, so Tyson rolled over slowly to get back into the bed, but he couldn't see it because of the golden line blocking his vision. It followed wherever he moved, pulsing brightly every few seconds, leading through the door of his room.

He checked his arm where the IV line had been earlier, then remembered it had been removed before he fell asleep. Relieved, he stumbled through the door and down the hall, holding onto the walls for support, continuing around the next corner, and another, until the golden line went through another door.

Tyson stood outside, breathing fast. His chest ached, but he didn't seem to be falling apart, so he breathed out slowly, collecting himself, and opened the door.

Harper lay on her stomach on a wide, flat bed, her head on her arms, one wing bandaged and tucked against her body, and the other...gone.

Her wing was gone.

The golden line, which ended at Harper, pulsed a few more times, then faded away. Tyson followed the path it had shown him and knelt on the floor beside Harper's bed.

She turned her head. Tears glistened in the dim moonlight filtering through the blinds on her window.

Tyson reached up and wiped at the tears on one side of her face, cupping her cheek in his hand.

As bad of a counselor as he had been, he knew there were times when no words could help, so he sat in silence with her, stroking her cheek, her hair, just being with her until she fell asleep. Finally, he curled up in the cushioned chair beside her bed and drifted off, his hand still on her arm.

This time, he didn't fall. He didn't even dream.

# EPILOGUE

## HARPER

HARPER ADJUSTED THE STRAPS on her sleeveless navy blue dress, then turned and swayed to one side, losing her balance. Her right arm flailed out but failed to counter the imbalance, and she yelped, knowing she was about to fall.

Tyson's hand shot out and grasped her, gently tugging her upright and into his arms.

"Still figuring that out, huh? Guess I better keep you here," he murmured into her hair, swaying back and forth with his hands rubbing down her back in small circles, managing to ease some of the knots that tightened up on her right side with how much she overcompensated for her missing wing.

Harper's throat had closed up, so she made a small sound of agreement and buried her face in his chest, grabbing the lapels of his fancy suit coat for a moment until she felt brave enough to face the world again.

"It's all right to cry, you know. Grieving isn't a linear process," Tyson said.

Harper laughed at his counselor voice and stepped back from him, fanning at her face. "Becca spent ages on this makeup. I am not crying." She sniffed loudly, breathed out, and tightened her remaining wing against her back.

The doctor that had tended her had suggested getting it amputated. There was a mass of scar tissue from the broken wing that Issachar had wrenched from her body, followed by the intensive surgery to remove the exposed bone still attached to her wing joint in her back, and it prevented Harper from withdrawing her remaining wing into her back as she'd always been able to do.

Harper wasn't ready to part with her last remaining wing. In the weeks since the demons had ravaged D.C., she'd spent time in recovery with Tyson spending almost every waking moment at her side. Except when she got too angry and made him leave because she didn't want to hurt him when it was herself she was angry at.

She couldn't really explain why, either. She hadn't done anything wrong. In fact, she'd done everything right. And she still had her Songs, the magic of the Tulukaruq people.

But she couldn't fly. When the portal to the lowest abyss had closed after Ragranoth was killed and her consort fell, everything on the physical plane had returned to normal. Or at least, as normal as it got after demons devastated the Capitol and killed the President of the United States.

Reformation would take years. A decade or more. But thanks to the leaders of the human rebels and their new relationship with the leaders of the T.R.S., peace talks were moving forward, and compromises were being made.

Harper had turned down every offer to be part of them. At least for now. She was healing, both body and mind, and she was in no place to try to become the next co-president of anything.

She looped her right arm through Tyson's using his body weight to help her balance out the lilt in her step she had with the weight of the wing on her left side.

"We don't have to do this," Tyson said for the fifth or sixth time that night, his blue eyes gazing seriously down at her.

Harper took a shaky breath in. "Yes, we do. You're Zeke's best man, and I'm not going to ruin that for either of you. Besides, we have to emerge sometime, and I'm sick of this room."

That got a chuckle, and Tyson patted her arm, heading for the door. "Okay. But we can leave any time, so just say the word. And I'll punch everyone who mentions your wing or looks at you pityingly."

"That's why I keep you around," Harper said, putting on a far braver face than she felt. Inside, she felt small, like a child, and she definitely wanted to do nothing but put on pajamas and curl up in bed with Tyson, but she wouldn't be the one to ruin Zeke and Mandi's wedding.

Everyone had been looking forward to the event since the couple announced it several weeks prior. Harper thought they might wait a bit, especially since the city was still trashed, but Zeke and Mandi had insisted it be soon. The last time they'd waited, the world had literally gone to hell, so this time they weren't taking any chances.

Their announcement had set a sort of trend. That and the end of the world made everyone make rash decisions Harper was almost certain they would regret. She had specifically avoided the subject with Tyson, so much so that he'd asked her why and she had totally lost her cool, ranting about how she wasn't even a whole person yet and she couldn't give him three-fourths of herself, and she needed time.

He'd apologized profusely and hadn't brought it up again, which Harper was extremely grateful for.

She made it down the elevator and through the front doors to the waiting car, a walk she'd practiced every day the past week.

Fortunately, the burns on her arms and face from the demon Issachar were healing nicely, and other than the wound in her back still healing, she felt almost normal.

Almost.

Harper gasped when the car rounded the bend and arrived at the wedding site. Zeke and Mandi had chosen the pillared D.C. war memorial. Even on the chilly autumn day, the sun shone bright, and the trees' leaves had just changed from green to orange, brilliant against the blue sky.

Everyone had given all they could in the effort to make the wedding beautiful, somehow finding wide swaths of pale pink cloth to decorate the chairs and aisles with. The flowers were all fake, but the food wasn't, and as Tyson escorted Harper from the car past the refreshment table, her mouth watered.

Becca waved Tyson over to where she sat next to Avaan.

"I saved you seats!" she said, chipper as always.

Tyson thanked her and helped Harper sit down, but he remained standing. He was a member of the wedding party.

A van pulled up, causing every head in the crowd to turn, but it wasn't Zeke yet. Instead, a whole line of people piled out, looking enough like the bridegroom that Harper assumed they were his family. The dark-haired werewolves found the chairs blocked off for them and sat, looking around uneasily, except for the triplet sisters who beamed and chatted to each other with excitement.

Moments later, a sleek white limousine pulled up, gleaming in the noonday sun. Zeke stepped out dressed in a gray suit with a pink vest and tie to match the decor, the smile on his face so infectious, it even made Harper smile.

From the other doors in the car, several men and women stepped out. Jack and Dak came first, identical in their navy suits that matched the one Tyson wore, followed by the motley members of Zeke's new pack that Harper wasn't totally familiar with yet, and then the final best man, who looked across the crowd and instantly locked eyes with Harper and pulled a ridiculous face that made her snort through the tears that prickled at the corners of her eyes.

Quinn.

He'd had bandages on his head up until a week ago, and yet the thing he mourned most was that the doctor had been forced to shave his long hair to stitch the wound in his scalp.

Harper was just grateful he was alive. After everything that had happened, she wasn't certain she could have survived these past weeks if she'd lost everything she held dear, her wings and the only family she had left.

Losing her mother had been hard enough.

Quinn approached them in the moments before the ceremony started, nudging Harper's elbow.

"Good thing that's not you two up there. How smart is it to get married at the end of the world? I mean, the divorce rate will be insane."

"Quinn! We're at a wedding!" Harper hissed, elbowing him in the side as he laughed.

"He's just jealous he doesn't have a plus one," Tyson said, leaning in towards Harper.

"I asked Reya, but she had other plans," Quinn said stiffly, straightening the lapels on his suit.

Harper raised her eyebrows. "Oh? Hopefully not completing her revenge." She'd warned the fox shifter, and she'd meant it. Missing wing or not, Harper wouldn't let Reya near Tyson.

"Nothing like that," Quinn said, rolling his eyes. "She's over that. Well, mostly. She got assigned to looking for other storage units like the one she was placed in under Violet's spell. Rumor has it there were other witches and warlocks doing the same thing to save paranormals. Maybe more of us made it out of the camps alive than we first thought."

"And she might find her family," Tyson said. "That's good for her."

Harper agreed, and she couldn't help but feel relieved the fox shifter wouldn't be around for a while. Harper needed more time to heal before she could properly intimidate anyone.

Tyson squeezed her hand and took his place on the gazebo next to Quinn. Ian took up the microphone on the side, winking at Kamri sitting in the seat closest to him. Harper hadn't had time to hear how the she-wolf and the siren had come to be in D.C. after everything, but there would be time for more stories while the city was being rebuilt.

"If you'll please take your seats, Zeke and Mandi would like to get married now," Ian announced.

The words brought chuckles as the rest of the guests found their seats and settled down, and then Ian began to sing.

Harper closed her eyes, scrunching her nose. *Screw the makeup,* she thought as the tears flowed.

She forced herself to open her bleary eyes so she could watch Mandi walk down the aisle, resplendent in a form-fitting wedding dress that totally suited her, as did the not being possessed.

Harper held it together until she saw the way Mandi looked at Zeke, like he was her family, her whole world, her everything, and then she cried shamelessly into Becca's shoulder, ignoring Becca's protests of the mascara and foundation job she was ruining.

After the vows, Tyson took Harper around, claiming he had to show her off or some nonsense. Eventually, they made their way to congratulate the bride and groom in person.

Mandi looked into Harper's eyes and clasped her hand in her own dry, soft ones. Then she reached into the pocket of her wedding dress with one hand and pulled out a stone.

"Rose quartz. For clarity and love," Mandi said.

"Is everyone getting rocks?" Harper asked, pocketing the smooth stone, remembering how Mandi had helped her decide to go out into the forest and save Tyson what seemed like a lifetime ago.

Zeke leaned forward, grinning. "Just about. She made me fill my pockets with her favorites. Even the wedding favors are crystals."

"If I'd known the theme, I would have picked up a few rocks off the side of the road and wrapped them for your gift," Quinn said from behind Harper, having snuck into the line. He finished off his glass and stepped forward.

Harper swatted him. "Hey, this is our chance to talk to the happy couple."

"Just doing what brothers do best—Interrupting," Quinn said with a grin.

Harper laughed. It felt good to laugh. She twined her fingers into Tyson's and leaned in to whisper in his ear.

He nodded at her suggestion, and they said their goodbyes, then wandered off across the grass away from the wedding towards a particularly inviting tree.

Tyson shed his jacket and laid it on the grass for Harper to sit on. She dropped with a sigh, stretching out her wing as Tyson sat beside her. He twisted around and put his head in her lap, grinning up at her.

She picked up a leaf and twirled it in his face.

"You know," Tyson said, blue eyes reflecting the tree branches and bright sky. "I think this is the happiest I've ever seen you, the most carefree. I like it."

"Me too," Harper said. "I think you'll get to see a lot more of it. Of course, I'm still complaining during physical therapy. And every meeting I have to sit through with Terran."

Tyson laughed at that and kissed her hand. "I'll try to limit the number of meetings. You have no political finesse."

"No, but I can break up the political bull and get to the point. Have you ever noticed how short the meetings are when I'm in them?" Harper grinned wickedly, and Tyson laughed, and it was the most incredible sound.

They sat in silence for a moment, Harper twirling a leaf in her hand, Tyson closing his eyes to rest.

"Do you think they're proud of us?" Harper asked suddenly.

"Who?" Tyson cracked an eye open, squinting.

"Fletcher. Violet and James. My mom. Are we doing this right?"

Tyson sat up, wrapping his arms around his knees. "I think that if we keep moving forward and let our hearts lead us, then yeah, they're going to be proud."

"What was it like, meeting a god?" Harper asked.

Tyson laughed nervously. "Well, the True Source was…odd. Had some strange ideas about life. I think it's been alone too long. Someone should get them a friend."

"You *would* think that," Harper said, leaning her head on his shoulder.

He carefully looped an arm around her, avoiding the area of her back that was still sore, and folded himself around to kiss her deeply. Harper kissed him back, finally allowing herself to enjoy what was coming next.

She was done waiting for life to get better. From now on, with Tyson by her side, she would make it what she wanted it to be. No more waiting, only freedom. Freedom, and the infinite possibilities of what could come next.

**Ready for more books by Bree Moore? Read "Thief of Magic: Shadowed Minds book one" next!**

# Find out how Harper's Journey began, with this prequel novella!

## A runaway with secrets. A vampire with answers.

Harper has spent years running—from foster homes, the system, and the truth about who she is. But when a ruthless vampire informant offers a lead on her missing brother, she's forced to take a dangerous risk. To gain his help, she must navigate the deadly supernatural underground, where trust is a luxury and betrayal lurks in the dark. How far will she go to find Quinn, and what will it cost her in the end?

**Want to read Harper's story for free? Visit authorbreemoor e.com/ravenblood for a free ebook!**

# SPECIAL THANKS

Writing any book is a huge undertaking, but writing the last book in a series belongs in another category altogether!
I have so many people to thank. Starting with you, dear reader. If you read Raven Born soon after it was published, you've been on this journey with me for over three years. Thank you for your reviews, your encouragement, and for supporting me in my publishing journey. I have the best readers in the world.

My writing group – Rachel W., Karma C., Rachel H., for all of your advice in early drafts and your emotional support when I decided to give the manuscript a year's worth of space and struggled with feeling like I had failed. Especially Rachel W., who stuck with me through the entire thing and read it when it was at its worst. I can't believe it's been 10 years of writing together!

To my beta readers – Beth K., Amy W., and Rachel W. (Dragon Rachel), and Rachel W. (Other Rachel), you read through this beast of a manuscript and helped me whip it into shape. I think I owe Amy a formal apology for emotional book trauma (otherwise known as PTBD – Post-Traumatic Bree Disorder, which she's patent-pending recovery kits for, I believe, lol). I couldn't have done this without any of you.

Some of you may be wondering if there's any story left to be told in this shifter world of mine. The answer, for now, is no. I do not plan to write anymore full-length novels in this series. But be sure to look up Forest Torn, Serpent Turned, and Siren Called if you haven't read them already. These are bonus novellas that explore Harper's early teen years, Becca and Avaan's story, and Kamri and Ian's story. If they're not published by the time this book is done, they will be soon, and I hope you enjoy following up with some of your favorite characters.

If you want to read more of my urban fantasy books, your next stop will be the Shadowed Minds series, where you'll get to know Lee and her gang and hopefully love them as much as you've loved Harper, Tyson, and the others in the Lost Souls series.

Until next time!

Bree Moore lives in Iowa with her husband, seven children, and two cats. When she's not busy homeschooling or folding laundry, she sneaks off to write more fantasy.

Bree writes urban and epic fantasy to explore different worlds with amazing creatures and magic systems. She enjoys giving her readers a story that is both entertaining and emotional, with a healthy dose of romance. When she's not writing, Bree can be found foraging for edible plants, watching fantasy shows and movies, or hanging out with her husband and kids.

Published works include: *The Shadowed Minds* series, the *Lost Souls* series, and *Shadows of Camelot* series. She's currently working on *The Plague King Chronicles*.

Visit www.authorbreemoore.com for a FREE fantasy book!

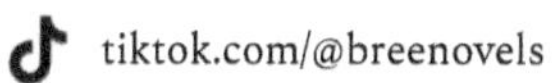 tiktok.com/@breenovels

instagram.com/breenovels

<u>**Shadows of Camelot**</u>
The Lady's Last Song
The Queen's Quiet End

<u>**Shadowed Minds Series**</u>
Prequel: Thief of Lies
Thief of Magic
Thief of Aether
Thief of Bones

<u>**Wings of Rebellion Series**</u>
Prequel: Raven Blood
Raven Born
Serpent Cursed
Coven Bound
Serpent Turned
Siren Called
Rebel Sworn

<u>**The Plague King Chronicles**</u>
The Keeper of the Well
The Quill and the Vial
The Arrow and the Ivy

<u>**Of Dusk and Dawn Collection**</u>
Sacrifice for the Standing Stones
Vows Beneath the Frozen Stars